MARY BALOGH, who won the *Romantic Times* Award for Best New Regency Writer in 1985, has since become one of the genre's most popular and bestselling authors. She has since won four Waldenbooks Awards and a B. Dalton Award for bestselling Regencies, and a *Romantic Times* Lifetime Achievement Award in 1989. *A Counterfeit Betrothal* is her most recent Signet Regency Romance.

CHARLOTTE LOUISE DOLAN has lived throughout the United States and in Montreal, Taiwan, Germany, and the Soviet Union. She is the mother of three children and lives in Idaho Falls, Idaho. Her most recent Signet Regency Romance is *The Resolute Runaway*.

SANDRA HEATH, the daughter of an officer in the Royal Air Force, spent most of her life traveling to various European posts. Her latest Signet Regency Romance is *Lord Kane's Keepsake*. She now resides in Gloucester, England, together with her husband and young daughter.

MELINDA MCCRAE, who holds a master's degree in European history and takes great delight in researching obscure details of the Regency period, lives in Seattle, Washington, with her husband and daughter. Her most recent Signet Regency Romance is *A Highly Respectable Widow*.

SHEILA WALSH lives with her husband in Southport, Lancashire, England, and is the mother of two daughters. Her first Signet Regency Romance, *The Golden Songbird*, won her an award presented by the Romantic Novelists' Association. Her most recent Signet Regency Romance is *The Arrogant Lord Alastair*.

A REGENCY SUMMER

Five Stories by

Mary Balogh

Charlotte Louise Dolan

Sandra Heath

Melinda McRae

Sheila Walsh

A SIGNET BOOK

SIGNET
Published by the Penguin Group
Penguin Books USA Inc., 375 Hudson Street,
New York, New York 10014, U.S.A.
Penguin Books Ltd, 27 Wrights Lane,
London W8 5TZ, England
Penguin Books Australia Ltd, Ringwood,
Victoria, Australia
Penguin Books Canada Ltd, 10 Alcorn Avenue,
Toronto, Ontario, Canada M4V 3B2
Penguin Books (N.Z.) Ltd, 182–190 Wairau Road,
Auckland 10, New Zealand

Penguin Books Ltd, Registered Offices:
Harmondsworth, Middlesex, England

First published by Signet, an imprint of New American Library,
a division of Penguin Books USA Inc.

First Printing, June, 1992
10 9 8 7 6 5 4 3 2 1

 REGISTERED TRADEMARK—MARCA REGISTRADA

Contents

Summer Escapade

by Charlotte Louise Dolan

July 1816

MARIGOLD KINDERLEY sat in the window of her room at Mrs. Wychombe's Select Seminary for Young Ladies in Bath and tried very hard to hold back her tears. It would not at all do for her best friend, Lady Sybil Dunmire, to see her behaving in such an infantile way merely because her heart was breaking.

"Algernon is nineteen, and Bartholomew is sixteen, and Cedric is thirteen, and they are the 'bigs,' " Clara Perkins recited, "and the 'littles' are Desmond, who is nine, and . . . and . . .oh, blast, I can never remember what the cousin's name is that starts with 'E'." She thought for a long moment. "Eugene?"

"Eustace," Marigold said automatically, wishing with every fiber of her being that some miracle would occur that would allow her—instead of Clara—to spend the first month of the summer holidays visiting with Sybil's family near Bath.

"Oh, yes, Eustace. He is seven, and after him comes Ferdinand, who is five, and Giles, who is three, and Horatio, who is the baby. I must say, Sybil, you are indeed fortunate that your father's cousin named his sons by the alphabet. Otherwise, there would be no way to keep them properly sorted out."

"It is not all that difficult once you meet them. Even though they are all towheads, they do not otherwise resemble each other closely," Sybil replied.

Marigold had heard so many stories about the adventures of the 'bigs' and the 'littles,' as Sybil called them, that she felt she could have picked them each out of a crowd without ever having met them in person.

"I can scarcely wait," Clara said with a sigh. "I vow, I shall not be able to sleep a wink tonight."

Marigold sat up a little straighter on the window seat and strained to see down the street. Was it? Yes, it was. "Mickey is back with the post," she said.

Without even a by-your-leave, Clara shot out of the room to intercept him. At sixteen, a full two years older than Marigold and Sybil, Clara already had a beau: Wilcox Ratherton, age twenty, currently studying at Oxford.

Neither Mrs. Wychombe nor Clara's parents had any idea, of course, that she was carrying on a clandestine correspondence with a young man of only marginal expectations, and Clara fully intended them to remain in ignorance as long as possible. She had therefore bribed Mickey O'Banion, the young lad who assisted Mr. Peabody with the heavier work around the school, to deliver her mail to her personally before Mrs. Wychombe ever saw it.

Marigold did not envy Clara her beau, rather she was jealous of the fact that Clara could dash down the stairs without anyone reprimanding her. She, on the other hand, was so sickly, her uncle had given strict orders, which Mrs. Wychombe carried out to the letter, about the activities she was to be allowed to participate in—nothing which could not be done sitting down—and the foods she was and was not to eat. She was even excused from the first hour of lessons after lunch so that she could lie down and rest.

It was all terribly embarrassing, and Marigold knew the other girls in the school had assorted nicknames for her, which she always pretended not to hear. Only Sybil was kind to her and had made the other girls stop their more obvious teasing.

"I am sorry you cannot come home with me also," Sybil said, coming over and sitting down beside Marigold. "Do you not think your uncle would allow you to visit for a few days at least?"

"Anything is possible, as Miss Medleycote would say," Marigold said, "although in this case it is unlikely, since he has never so far allowed me to visit anyone. And I am afraid before he would consent to such a scheme—if indeed he could be persuaded—he would more than likely insist upon visiting your mother first and personally checking the dower house for drafts, and he would make her promise not to let me out of her sight or let any animal come near me or let me go out if the weather is the least bit inclement or be exposed to the sun long enough to get sunstroke." She sighed. "Before she even laid eyes on me, I am sure that your mother would be quite put off, and your cook would likewise be disgruntled with the extra work involved in preparing separate meals for me, for really it would be a great deal of bother for her."

"Do you never get tired of eating porridge for breakfast? And a coddled egg for lunch? And milk toast for supper? Do you never wish you could have a cup of hot chocolate or a bowl of peaches and cream or—"

Marigold could no longer hold back her tears, and in an instant Sybil was hugging her and patting her on the back.

"Of course I get tired of the same old thing every day," Marigold said passionately. "Everything else smells so much better—the roast beef and York-shire pudding and the fresh scones with honey and . . . and all of the things you get to eat. Some times I feel getting sick would be worth it, just to know what some of those things taste like."

Sybil pulled away and looked at her in astonish-ment. "You've never even *tasted* them?"

Marigold shook her head.

"But then, how do you know they will make you sick?"

Marigold thought it over. "Actually, I cannot re-member ever being sick, but more than likely that is because Uncle Terence has taken such good care of me. I have been told that my mother became extremely ill whenever she ate something that did not agree with her, and since I take after her in looks, it is quite logical to assume that I take after her in other things, is it not? My uncle has con-sulted with a great many doctors, including a Lon-don physician of great renown, and they have all been in agreement on that."

"But *my* question is, have you ever eaten them and gotten sick?" Sybil repeated insistently.

"I cannot remember ever being allowed to eat anything except my special diet."

Sybil stood up and began striding energetically back and forth. "Well, Algernon would say that this is all rubbish. He is not at all impressed with what even the most learned authorities claim is true. After all, at one time everyone was convinced the earth was flat. No, Algernon is a proponent of the scientific method. 'We cannot know something is true until we test it,' is his motto. Sometimes what everybody *thinks* is true *does* turn out to be true. For example, last summer we experimented and found out that eating too many green apples really does give you a horrible stomachache." Sybil clutched her stomach and staggered around the room, the most hideous expression of agony on her face.

"But on the other hand," she continued, her features once again composed, "sometimes what everyone accepts as true is nothing but pure nonsense. Among the things Algernon has disproved is the supposed *fact* that touching toads gives a person warts. Last year he caught two fat beauties in the woods, and we kept them in the summer house, and all of us 'bigs' played with them every day, and not a one of us got a single wart. We named them Jump and Hop, by the way, and I was quite sorry that we had to turn them loose, but no matter how I pleaded with him, Algernon would not let me bring them back to school with me."

Marigold suppressed a shudder at the thought of sharing her room with two toads, much less touching them.

"So no matter what anyone says, it seems quite obvious to me that if you have not eaten a particular food, you really don't know if it will make you sick or not. Therefore, I think you should try experimenting and see. And as Algernon would say, what is the worst thing that could happen if you ate something that was forbidden? True, you might get sick, but on the other hand, it is doubtful that you would actually *die* from eating a French pastry or a muffin."

"No, you are wrong," Marigold pointed out glumly. "The worst thing that could happen is that Uncle Terence would discover what I had done, and he would instantly remove me from this school. And then he would hire a governess for me instead, and I would spend the rest of my days shut up at Kinderwood Manor."

"And years from now," Sybil said, making her voice low and spooky, "the villagers will see a ghostly apparition wandering through the moonlit gardens, and they would know it was the ghost of Marigold Kinderley, who died from eating a spoonful of . . ." She paused, and looked furtively around the room, as if expecting someone to be lurking in the shadows. Then, with her eyes darting frantically from side to side, she crept forward and whispered the fatal words, "of *currant jelly*."

Marigold dissolved into giggles, and Sybil collapsed laughing beside her. "Some day," she said, "I am going to be a famous actress and appear on stage at Covent Garden. Algernon says that after we are married, I may—"

They were interrupted by Clara's return. Although she was clutching two letters in her hand, one look at her face was enough to inform Marigold that neither of the missives was from Wilcox. "He has forgotten me," Clara wailed, throwing herself down on Marigold's bed. "He has thrown me over for another woman, undoubtedly some scarlet hussy who lurks around the University, hoping to ensnare some innocent young man and trap him into marriage."

"You received a letter only last week," Sybil pointed out most prosaically, "and doubtless tomorrow you will get one for this week."

"Tomorrow is too late—we shall be gone to Dunmire Abbey."

"Then console yourself that you did get two letters, even if they are not from your precious Wilcox," Sybil pointed out.

"They are both from my mother," Clara said crossly, "and one of them is not even for me. It is for Mrs. Wychombe. I do not know why Mickey gave it to me in the first place. Now I shall have to sneak it back into the pile of mail and hope no one notices me."

Listlessly she broke the seal on one of the letters and unfolded it. Scanning the lines, her face turned an alarming shade of red. "Well, of all the nerve! Ooooh, it is just like Aunt Maude! I vow, she delights in spoiling every bit of pleasure I might have."

"What has she done?"

"She has quite ruined my holidays, that is what she has done. With only the flimsiest of excuses she has foisted my repellent cousin Drucilla off onto us for the entire summer. As a result, my mother has withdrawn her permission for me to visit you. Of course, Aunt Maude waited until the last minute and then just *deposited* my cousin so that my mother had no time to think up a good excuse to put her off."

Standing up, Clara picked up the letter for Mrs. Wychombe and started for the door, but Sybil darted in front of her and blocked her path. "No, wait! I have just thought of the most clever plan!"

Clara's face brightened. "You know how I can permanently dispose of Drucilla? She is the most revolting slug, you know, and I doubt even Aunt Maude would miss her if she were gone forever."

"No, of course I am not going to do such a thing. But what I think is that it would be an absolutely marvelous idea if Marigold could come to Dunmire Abbey in your place."

At her friend's words, Marigold's heart began to race. She knew how ingenious Sybil could be—what absolutely fantastic ideas Sybil could come up with. Usually her plans were quite impractical and impossible to implement, but they were still enormously delightful to contemplate.

"In my place? You would take *her* instead of *me*?" Clara shot Marigold a look of disgust, and Marigold shrank back on her window seat. "Well, you can just forget about it. I would not lift a finger to help that pathetic malingerer."

"Fine," Sybil said, opening the door and standing

aside. "And you need have no worry about Mrs. Wychombe catching you in the act of slipping the letter from your mother in with the rest of the mail." Folding her hands together under her chin, Sybil gazed piously up at the ceiling. "I fear my conscience is troubling me so greatly, I must unburden myself to Mrs. Wychombe. She will be most distressed to hear that you have been carrying on a clandestine correspondence with a most unsuitable young man."

Scowling, Clara pushed the door shut again. "Very well, I shall listen to your plan, but I cannot believe that you actually *wish* to have that—that wretched little pudding-heart spend the summer with you."

"Oh," Sybil said with a wink for Marigold, "we have been rubbing along tolerably well this term."

The plan was simplicity in itself. Marigold would simply pretend to be Clara, who thought of very many objections to the plan. "But I am blonde, and Marigold has black hair, and someone is bound to notice her entering your cousin's coach."

But for every objection, Sybil was able to propose a way to deal with the problem. "You shall loan her your blue cloak, and she can pull the hood over her head, and no one will be able to see either her face or the color of her hair."

"My blue cloak? But it is new! I don't wish to let—"

Rolling her eyes, Sybil turned and marched resolutely toward the door, but Clara caught up with her and blocked her way. "All right, she may borrow my cloak. But there is still the problem of her luggage." She pointed to Marigold's trunk, which was packed and ready for her departure the next day. "How are you going to persuade Peabody to put Marigold's trunk in your cousin's coach instead of in her uncle's coach? Hmmm? Answer me that!"

"I still have a half crown left over from Christmas. For that much money, Mickey will contrive to get the right trunk into the wrong coach with no one the wiser."

Finally, after several more objections, Clara acknowledged that the plan might possibly succeed, and by the time she retired to her own room to change for the farewell dinner, she was almost persuaded that she had been wholeheartedly in favor of the scheme from the beginning.

"Are you sure you want me to come with you?" Marigold asked, once she and Sybil were alone. "Will it not spoil your fun to have to limit your activities to what I am allowed to do? And your cousins may be upset to have me there, also."

Casting her a challenging look, Sybil said, "Who says we are going to pay any attention to that silly list of things you may and may not do? As for Algernon—and he is the only one of my cousins whose opinion matters—he will most likely thank me for providing him with a subject for his scientific experimentation."

For a moment Marigold was tempted to refuse to participate in Sybil's scheme. Being experimented upon did not sound at all appealing. But remembering how Sybil had been her champion and defender all term, Marigold mentally vowed to cooperate with Algernon, no matter what the cost to herself.

"You are still looking worried," Sybil said, eyeing her skeptically. "Please, do not feel you have to put yourself out on my account. I thought you *wanted* to visit my family, but if you prefer to return to Kent and stay with your uncle all summer, that is entirely up to you."

"The problem is my uncle," Marigold said. "It has just occurred to me that he will be terribly worried when he gets here and does not find me waiting for him."

"Oh, pooh," Sybil replied, "do not let that stop you from coming with me. From all that you have told me, he worries constantly even when you are under his own roof. So if he is going to worry about you if you go with me, and worry about you if you do not go with me, then you might as well do what is most enjoyable for you."

Sybil's logic was unassailable.

Peering out the window the next morning, Marigold saw their marvelous plan coming all unraveled. "Oh, we are undone! My uncle has arrived before your cousin's coachman."

Hurrying over to join her, Sybil remained undaunted. "No, all is not yet lost. Already I can see my cousin's coach coming down the street. We must be very brave and also pray for a miracle. As Algernon would say, what is the worst that could happen? We could get caught, that is what, and then we would each get a thundering scold. On the other hand, if we do win free, we shall have a grand summer. Are you game?"

"Yes," Marigold said, trying to display as much resolution as Sybil, "I am ready. Nothing ventured, nothing gained."

"That is precisely what Algernon would say," Sybil said approvingly.

Terence Kinderley alighted from his coach in front of Mrs. Wychombe's Select Seminary, wishing that on such a beautiful day he could be driving his phaeton. But his niece could never tolerate the long journey back to Kent in an open carriage. As it was, her indifferent health required them to travel at such a moderate pace, it would take them four days to accomplish what would normally have been a two-day affair.

Standing aside for a boy who emerged from the school carrying a heavy trunk on his back, Terence was surprised to be hailed from a passing phaeton.

He turned to see Captain Darius St. John—no, he corrected himself, no longer captain, his friend was now the Duke of Colthurst. Walking over to the carriage, he reached up and shook the proffered hand. "Colthurst, well met."

"Kinderley, why did you not let me know you were coming to Bath? Are you staying long? Do you have time to make us a visit while you are in the area? Elizabeth will be more than pleased to see you. We are expecting an addition to our family in about three weeks, and consequently Elizabeth is finding life intolerably tedious. She has sent me into town to exchange books for her, and she is feeling most frustrated that she cannot simply come and choose them for herself."

"That is indeed good news, and I congratulate you most sincerely. I would be delighted to pay you a visit," Terence said, feeling an honest regret, "but unfortunately, I am here to pick up my niece—my brother's child—and we shall need to start for home directly."

"Could you not delay your trip even for one night? It has been so long since we have seen each other, and even longer since we had an opportunity of any real conversation. And you need not worry that your niece would be bored, for Elizabeth would be most happy to have her company."

It all sounded so pleasant—and exactly like the kind of informal visit Terence preferred over a large house party—but it was totally out of the question. "I am sorry, and I hope you can convey my deepest apologies to your lovely wife, but my niece is a very sickly child, and I have had to make advance arrangements for lodging and special meals for the trip home. I am afraid at this late date it would be impossible to change all the preparations."

"I am indeed sorry to hear that she is unwell."

"Unfortunately, she takes after my sister-in-law, who was always sickly from the time she was an infant. Delia died when Marigold was only a few weeks old, and my brother followed her to the grave less than a year later. Being in charge of a child who has such delicate health has been a great responsibility, but I have had the loyal support of my staff, who have been unstinting in their efforts to provide my niece with the most judicious care."

He looked up at the stone edifice behind him, through whose portals chattering, laughing girls were streaming out to climb into the waiting carriages and coaches, and his face darkened.

"Perhaps when you bring her back in the autumn, you can plan to stay with us a few days," Colthurst suggested.

Turning back to his friend, Terence continued to frown. "As to that, I am not entirely convinced it was a good idea to allow her to come here. But this was her mother's school, and it seemed only fitting that Marigold be allowed to attend for at least one term."

"I am sure no harm will have come to her here," Colthurst assured him. "Our nearest neighbor, Alicia, Viscountess Dunmire, sends her daughter here, and both of them have nothing but praise for Mrs. Wychombe's entire staff."

They talked for a few minutes more, catching up on the events of the last several years, and then Terence excused himself. Entering the school, he sought out the aforementioned Mrs. Wychombe, who gave him a very glowing report of his niece's academic progress.

"To be sure, Miss Marigold is still quite pale and

not at all as robust as we might wish, but at least she has come through the term without catching any infectious disease—not that my young ladies are prone to such things," Mrs. Wychombe hastened to assure him.

He was not at all reassured. His greatest fear had always been that Marigold would be carried off by some childish complaint, such as measles or chicken pox. He pulled his watch out and rather pointedly looked down at it.

Taking his hint, Mrs. Wychombe rang for one of the maids. When the girl appeared, the headmistress instructed her to fetch down Miss Kinderley. Then Mrs. Wychombe offered Terence a cup of tea, which he declined.

The clock on the mantel ticked away while the conversation languished and died, for the maid took an extraordinary amount of time before she reappeared looking quite flustered.

"Oh, ma'am, Miss Kinderley is not in her room, and her trunk is not there neither. I asked Peabody, and he says he don't remember carrying it out so it should be there but it ain't, and I checked out front, too, thinking one of the other young ladies might have taken it by mistake, but they is all up and gone, ma'am, and there is only the one coach left, and when I asked the coachman, he said it was Mr. Kinderley's coach, ma'am, and I do believe Miss Kinderley has run off is what it looks like to me, ma'am."

"Nonsense," Mrs. Wychombe said flatly. "You are talking absolute rubbish."

For the first time since he had entered the room, Terence was in complete agreement with the headmistress. His niece run away? The very idea was ludicrous—totally preposterous.

"Her trunk may have been mislaid, but I am sure that if we check the schoolrooms and parlors thoroughly, we shall find Miss Kinderley curled up somewhere with a book, totally oblivious to everything going on around her," Mrs. Wychombe said sensibly.

"You see how pointless it is to worry?" Sybil asked as soon as the coach had left Bath behind. "You were afraid we could not succeed, and yet we walked right past your uncle while he was engaged in conversation with his grace, and neither of them paid us the slightest attention. Not that it would have mattered if your uncle had stared right at us, since that cloak is most concealing."

"His grace?" Marigold asked, trying to hide her melancholy. There was no way to pretend she had not heard her uncle say she would not be coming back for the fall term at Mrs. Wychombe's.

"The Duke of Colthurst. They live quite close to Dunmire Abbey, and he and his wife have the most engaging pair of twins. We shall have to ride over and see them quite soon." She stared at Marigold. "And why are you looking as if you have just eaten a pickle? Don't you like babies?"

"I cannot rightly say," Marigold replied honestly. "I have never been around babies, or indeed had anything to do with children younger than I am."

"Never been around babies? But that is—that is unbelievable!"

"Believe it," Marigold said rather crossly. "In case it has slipped your mind, I am an only child, and since I am not allowed to play with any of the children in the village, and since I have no cousins, I think it is quite easy to understand."

"I admit you have told me that before, but somehow I did not fully comprehend until just now what it signified. So you have truly never held a baby?"

A single tear slid down Marigold's cheek, and she surreptitiously wiped it away with the back of her hand. "No, I have never held a baby or played tag or ridden on a pony or gone wading in a brook or touched a toad or—or done much of anything at all." A second tear followed the first, and then a third and a fourth in quick succession.

"Well, you need not cry about it now. After all, that is precisely why you are coming home with me—so that you can do all the things you have never been allowed to do."

"That is not why I am crying," Marigold said with a sniffle. "I am crying because—" She retrieved a handkerchief from her reticule and blew her nose. "Because my uncle said he is not going to send me back to school next term. Did you not hear him?"

"I heard him say something about not being sure you would be coming back, but—"

"But nothing. He does not need to be sure. If it *might* rain, we stay home from church. If there *might* be measles in the neighborhood, our household is entirely quarantined. If it *might* not be a good idea for me to continue at Mrs. Wychombe's, then I suspect that a governess has already been arranged for."

"Well then," Sybil said with a grin, "you must look on the bright side. You told me the worst that could happen if we got caught is that your uncle would keep you home next term. Since he is apparently planning to do that anyway, we might as well enjoy ourselves."

Marigold thought it over and had to agree. She had nothing to lose and everything to gain, so she would stop worrying and enjoy a truly grand holiday.

Never had Terence felt such a rage. He was closer to physical violence than he had ever been before, and the object of his ire was a woman! A totally incompetent, ineffectual female, who had the gall to pass herself off as a qualified headmistress of a reputable seminary for young ladies!

Mrs. Wychombe had had the entire school checked, and Marigold was nowhere to be found, with or without a book in her hand. Nor had the missing trunk turned up.

"I am sure," Mrs. Wychombe now said, casting him a look of utter despair, "that Miss Medleycote will be able to tell us something. She is in charge of the younger girls and is a most competent, reliable, efficient . . ." She withered under his gaze.

Terence did not bother to issue threats. Mrs. Wychombe was not such a fool that she did not realize the future of her school was in dire jeopardy.

Before she could offer up any more excuses, the door was thrust open, and a tall, sensibly dressed young woman hurried into the room. Spotting Terence, she checked her headlong dash and at a more decorous pace moved to stand shoulder to shoulder beside her employer.

"We have asked you to come in—" Mrs. Wychombe began, but Terence interrupted her.

"Mrs. Wychombe seems to have mislaid my niece, Marigold Kinderley," he snapped out, "and if one of you does not produce her for me immediately, I shall not hesitate to tell everyone of the lax conditions prevalent here."

Looking not the least bit intimidated, the younger teacher said, "That is, of course, your privilege, but why you would wish to have your niece's name bandied about in a vulgar manner, I am sure I cannot fathom."

There was dead silence while Terence considered how delighted the high sticklers in Bath would be to spread scurrilous gossip about his niece. They would not worry unduly about destroying the reputation of an innocent young girl or blighting her future forever.

"You are quite right," he said finally, anxiety driving all anger out of him. "Assigning blame is futile at this point. The only thing that matters now is recovering my niece before she comes to any harm."

"Despite your low opinion of my school, I have never before 'mislaid' a pupil. Please believe me when I say that all of us here share your concern for Miss Kinderley's well-being," Mrs. Wychombe pointed out. "We shall certainly make discreet inquiries and do all in our power to find her, short of causing a scandal, of course."

Terence thought for a minute, then asked in quite a reasonable tone of voice, "Can you provide me with a list of my niece's special friends? Perhaps one of them may know something about this matter."

Miss Medleycote got a strange look on her face, and with a shock, Terence realized it was pity. "Your niece has only the one friend," she said quietly, "and that is Lady Sybil, the daughter of the dowager Viscountess of Dunmire. Fortunately, they live quite close to Bath, so it will not take long for a message to be sent there."

The name rang a bell, and additional questioning elicited the answer that yes, Dunmire Abbey was but two miles distant from Colthurst Hall.

"There is no need for a messenger," Terence stated. "It will be quicker for me to go there in person and inquire after my niece."

"Are you feeling at all queasy?" Sybil asked, concern in her voice.

"Queasy?"

"Do not look so baffled. You yourself once told me that your uncle's coachman always drives at a most moderate speed so that the jouncing about will not make you ill."

Marigold considered her stomach, which seemed perfectly calm, and her head, which was not in the least bit aching. Looking out the window, she saw the landscape rushing by at remarkable speed. Surely they were going at least ten miles per hour!

"Well," Sybil asked impatiently, "do I need to tell the coachman to slow down? He will stop at once if we ask him, since he is not at all fond of having people be sick in his carriage."

Marigold began to smile. "Uncle Terence has always told me that I am prone to motion sickness, but it would appear that after scientific experimentation—for we can consider this an experiment, can we not?"

Sybil nodded her agreement.

"It would appear that in this case Uncle Terence is dead wrong," Marigold concluded.

Sybil gave a crow of delight and to Marigold's astonishment, promptly crawled up on the forward seat, slid open a little wooden panel, and told the coachman to "spring 'em."

Marigold heard the crack of the man's whip, and the coach surged forward at an even more dizzying speed.

"How do you feel now?" Sybil asked, settling herself back on her seat. "Are you beginning to feel at all ill yet?"

"I am feeling quite exhilarated," Marigold replied. "Do you suppose we can go any faster?"

Sybil shook her head. "But if you wish to be even more daring—" She rummaged around in her bandbox and produced two French pastries which were crusted over with sugar and finely chopped almonds, and which were only slightly squashed. Handing one to Marigold, Sybil crammed a good half of her own into her mouth.

With great trepidation, Marigold took a much smaller bite, but even so, some of the red raspberry filling oozed out and tried to run down her chin. She managed to catch it with her finger and then closed her eyes in rapture as the most glorious flavors blended and mingled in her mouth.

"I think," she said after she finally swallowed, "that I have surely died and gone to heaven." Without further hesitation, she took a second, much larger bite.

Unable to think what else to do, Terence sought out his only friend in Bath and found the duke in the lending library in Milsom Street, perusing the latest offerings from the Minerva Press.

"Colthurst, the most dreadful thing," Terence began, his voice unsteady with emotion. Then he broke off, realizing to his added dismay that several pairs of ears in the vicinity were now straining to hear what he was going to say, even while their owners strove to look as though gossip were the last thing on their minds.

With a glance around and a knowing smile, Colthurst laid down the slender volume he had been considering, took Terence by the arm, and led him out of the shop. Walking back down the street in the direction of Mrs. Wychombe's school, the duke waited only until they were out of earshot of any passersby, before inquiring, "Is it your niece? You know my invitation to come for a visit was not a mere formality. If she is not well enough to travel, I insist you must stay with us until she is fully recovered."

"She is lost," Terence blurted out.

"Lost?"

"Lost, misplaced, kidnapped—I do not know what has happened to her. It is the most astonishing thing—she has simply vanished along with her trunk. Mrs. Wychombe has had the gall to suggest that Marigold might have run away, but that is too absurd an idea to take seriously."

Colthurst thought for a moment. "How old did you say your niece is?"

"Fourteen, but what has that to do with the case?"

"Neither fourteen-year-old girls nor fourteen-year-old boys are noted for their common sense, and although I do not think any of Mrs. Wychombe's pupils have ever tried it before, I believe we average about one runaway school girl in Bath per year. But there is no cause to panic since, in all but a few cases, the girls have been successfully retrieved before they were thoroughly compromised."

"Compromised? But I tell you this is all patently ridiculous. What with the regulations Mrs. Wychombe imposes—or rather, that she *claims* are in force—plus the strict requirements I have laid down for Marigold's care, I cannot believe that my niece has had an opportunity to meet any males of whatever age since I left her here at the beginning of the term."

Ignoring his objections, Colthurst asked bluntly, "Is she an heiress?"

As much as he wanted to deny what his friend was implying, Terence could not. While not rich enough to stagger the imagination, when she reached the age of one-and-twenty his niece did stand to inherit enough to make her a tempting target for a fortune hunter.

"It is amazing how some men can sniff out money," Colthurst said, "and once they have found a tempting target, they are incredibly ingenious about arranging a casual meeting. In general, charm is their stock in trade, and convincing a young girl that she is in love with them is a relatively easy matter. And the more innocent and inexperienced the child is, the easier they can persuade her."

"I cannot believe that Marigold could be so taken in," Terence said, but his protest sounded hollow even to his own ears.

"The only other alternative is that she has run away to avoid going home. You mentioned rules you have imposed for her own good. Perhaps there have been too many restrictions?"

Terence stiffened at the implication that he was a harsh guardian. "All of the rules have been for her own good, and she has never even hinted that she felt them oppressive. I love my niece dearly, and I am sure she returns that affection in full measure."

"Then we must discover who may have persuaded her to elope."

Elope. The word Terence had been avoiding was now said. *Run away* had sounded so much less damaging—less permanent. "What do you suggest?"

"Young girls generally confide in someone. In her letters did she mention any particular friends?"

For some reason Terence did not want to reveal his niece's lack of popularity. "Her best friend is apparently the daughter of your neighbor."

"Lady Sybil? But that is indeed fortunate. She is quite a sensible girl, and I shall be most happy to accompany you to Dunmire Abbey and introduce you to the family."

Such was his relief that at last there was something he could *do*, that Terence made only a token protest. "But the books for your wife?"

"There is no need to delay on that account. Tomorrow I can send her dresser, Miss Hepden, into town to make a selection. She is better versed than I am on which authors my wife is fond of, and she shall undoubtedly do a better job than I would have done."

* * *

"Clara, my dear, I am so pleased that you could come for this visit," Lady Dunmire said with a welcoming smile.

Marigold did not respond until she felt a sharp pinch on her arm. Then she remembered that *she* was supposed to be Clara. "Thank you." There was another nudge. "I am so glad to be here." Without waiting for another prompting, she added, "Sybil has told me so much about all of you, Lady Dunmire."

"You must consider yourself one of the family while you are here," Sybil's mother said. "And now, if you are anything like my daughter, I imagine you are feeling quite peckish. Tea will not be served for another three hours, however—"

"Thank you, Mama," Sybil said, grabbing Marigold's hand and dragging her out of the room. "You must remember that you are supposed to be Clara," she hissed as they hurried along the corridor. "You almost betrayed us both in there."

"I am sorry. I shall try to do better."

At the end of the hallway, Sybil opened a door and they descended a short flight of stairs. Marigold was astonished to find herself in the servants' hall. And even more amazed when no one protested.

On the contrary, the housekeeper hugged Sybil, the butler pulled out chairs for them to be seated, and the cook immediately began filling the table with platters and bowls and tureens from which came the most tantalizing aromas. Apparently the servants were used to Sybil's appetite.

In all that abundance, there was not a single item of food that Marigold was normally allowed to eat. But after her experience with the French pastry, she had no hesitation about sampling each and every dish. She did not realize how much she was eating until the cook smilingly reminded her to save a little room for tea, which would be in two and a half hours, and would feature cherry tarts.

"Tomorrow we shall start teaching you to ride," Sybil said, giving the swing another giant push.

Soaring up into the air, Marigold was inclined to think that riding could not be nearly as exhilarating as swinging. She did not know which she enjoyed more, the swooping up higher and higher, or the sudden falling away, which tickled her stomach in the most delightful way.

She was giddy with laughter until looking out over the countryside, she saw something that destroyed all her happiness in an instant. Immediately lowering her feet, she dragged them on the ground and quickly brought the swing to a standstill.

"Sybil—" was all she could say, but that one word held a world of desperation.

"Are you feeling queasy? Perhaps we should not have tried the swing so soon after eating?"

Wordlessly, Marigold indicated the carriage coming at a brisk trot down the lane, and tears began to collect in the corners of her eyes.

"Is that your uncle's coach?"

Marigold nodded, causing the tears to spill over and run down her cheeks.

"What fun!" Sybil said, hurrying over to crouch down and peek through the garden hedge, so that she could see without being seen.

"Fun? How can you say such a thing? There will not be any fun for me now that my uncle has found me." Marigold joined her friend on the grass, ignoring the possibility of stains on her skirt. Together they watched the carriage turn in at the drive and pass out of sight.

"What makes you think he knows you are here?"

"Why else would he have come?"

"Well, of course he is trying to find you, but

there is no reason to think he is expecting you to be *here*." Standing up, she began to tug Marigold away from the house. "Undoubtedly my mother will be sending for me in a few minutes, so we must be sure that 'Clara'—that is you, don't forget—is *not* conveniently accessible." Relentlessly she began pushing at Marigold. "Go down that path, and you will find the summer house. Wait there until I come for you. And do not waste any time worrying. You know what a splendid actress I am."

"You are going to lie to your own mother?" After knowing Sybil for an entire term, Marigold was quite accustomed to Sybil's little fibs, but somehow evading one of the silly rules at school did not seem as heinous a crime as telling one's own mother a falsehood.

"I promise you I shall not say one single thing that is not absolutely true," Sybil replied with a wicked smile. "And if your uncle makes unwarranted assumptions based upon what I say, I am sure that is not my concern."

Terence's first thought was that Alicia Lady Dunmire was much too young to be a widow. Even assuming that she had married right out of the schoolroom, to have a daughter the same age as his niece would make her at least thirty-three, four years younger than he was.

Her complexion was flawless and her eyes, which were a lovely shade of blue, were unlined. With her slender figure, she did not look a day over *twenty*-three, and yet for all the youthfulness of her person, her manner displayed a maturity beyond her years.

"I am sure that you will be able to recover your niece," she said calmly after he explained the events of the day. Her composure somehow made him feel more hopeful than he had felt since his niece had turned up missing.

Abruptly and without warning, the door to the sitting room was thrown open with so much force that it crashed against the wall. Startled, Terence swung around, expecting to see a schoolgirl. What he saw was two grubby little boys, one with a bleeding nose and the other with the beginnings of a black eye.

"It was all his fault," the smaller boy cried out, pointing to his companion. "I won his marbles fair and square, and he refused to give them to me."

Producing a man's handkerchief from some hidden pocket, Lady Dunmire folded it into a pad, tilted the child's head back, and pressed the cloth to his nose.

"But we are forbidden to gamble, and I say that was gambling, so I *don't* have to give him my marbles," the older boy said, his fists still tightly clenched.

"We shall discuss this later after our company has departed," Lady Dunmire said. "For now, Desmond, I need you to find Sybil for me and ask her to come in here. And after you have spoken to her, you will see cook about a beefsteak to put on your eye."

Terence was astonished—no, he was appalled by her callous attitude. Did she not intend to summon the doctor? Here she was sending that poor injured child on an errand when he should have been put to bed! As shocking as that was, it was even less easy to understand why the boys had been allowed to fight in the first place. Surely if they had been adequately supervised, their quarrel would never have come to physical blows.

He had to bite his tongue to hold back certain pithy comments, but Colthurst, who knew this family well enough to step in and take charge, was merely smiling patiently.

"There now," Lady Dunmire said a few minutes later, "I believe the bleeding has stopped, Eustace. Run along to the kitchen and get your face washed."

"I confess to curiosity," Colthurst said after the boys had departed. "How do you intend to adjudicate the problem with the marbles?"

Lady Dunmire smiled. "Why, I do not intend to interfere at all—or at least not much. All the marbles will simply be put away, and the boys may not have them back until they themselves come to an agreement about the proper ownership."

"I shall have to remember that trick when Louisa and the twins are older," Colthurst said. "Right now the three of them do not understand the concept of 'mine' and 'yours,' so they are quite happy to share."

Terence felt quite left out of the subsequent conversation, which was mostly concerned with ways to manage conflicts between siblings. On the other hand, the stories they were relating made him thankful that he had only the one niece to raise.

In due course, Lady Sybil appeared, looking only slightly less bedraggled than the two boys. When the situation was explained to her, her eyes got big and round, and her expression was most serious. "Well, all I can tell you is that Marigold did not go down to breakfast with me. And on my way back to my room, where I *thought* she would be waiting to say good-bye to me, one of the older girls stopped me in the hall and said—But perhaps I should not repeat what she said? For it is, after all, only hearsay, and I did not actually see Marigold with my own eyes climbing into a chaise with the dancing master quite, quite early this morning."

"The dancing master?" Terence asked in astonishment.

The girl turned her soulful eyes on him. "Mr. Lucaster is considered quite handsome by some of the girls, although I have always felt he was a bit undersized and a little too pretty for my tastes. I should not wish to run off to Scotland with him, for I have always considered him to be rather weak and shallow. Still and all, I can see how he would appeal to a timid girl like Marigold."

"Scotland? Surely you are not saying she has eloped with the dancing master," Terence said, but his protest carried no conviction.

"Indeed not! I could never believe that Marigold would be so lost to propriety that she would do such a shocking thing as elope," Lady Sybil was quick to assert, but her expression made it quite clear that she did believe precisely that.

"Perhaps," Lady Dunmire said, "your friend Clara might know something more?"

"Oh, I am sure Clara has not the slightest idea where Marigold is at this moment. Disliking Marigold as she does, Clara would probably tell an outlandish story about some ridiculous scheme Marigold had for running away. But I shall let Clara know that you wish to speak to her, although it will take me a considerable time to convey the message, since she is presently quite distant from this house."

A considerable time? When he heard those appalling words, all of Terence's newly acquired calmness deserted him. Merciful heavens, what was he doing sitting around here wasting even more time while his niece was being abducted to Scotland? For an abduction it had to have been, no matter if that silver-tongued rogue, Mr. Lucaster, may have persuaded her to come away with him.

Every minute Terence wasted put him that much farther behind the eloping pair, so he declined Lady Sybil's offer to find her visiting school friend—who was not, or so he had twice been told, a particular friend of his niece—and as quickly as good manners allowed, he took leave of his hostess.

"You may borrow my phaeton if you wish," Colthurst offered magnanimously when they were on their way back to Colthurst Hall. "Your coach is a bit heavy for speed. And you may certainly have any of the nags out of my stables for the first stage. I only wish there were more I could do to assist you. But with Elizabeth's confinement so close, I cannot accompany you."

Terence sat sunk in misery. To think it had come to this. After all the pitfalls he had avoided—after all the illnesses and injuries he had managed to prevent—his niece's entire future was now foundering. She was coming to grief because of a wretched dancing master. It did not bear thinking about.

In an attempt to distract himself, Terence inquired how many children Lady Dunmire had.

"Eight sons," Colthurst replied. "The eldest, Algernon, is already up at Oxford, and the youngest is only three months old."

"At Oxford? But—" Terence could not believe that Lady Dunmire was old enough to have a son at university.

"But what?" Colthurst asked, looking at him strangely.

"Either her son is a child prodigy, or Lady Dunmire has discovered the secret of eternal youth," Terence said.

Colthurst looked puzzled, then his face cleared. "Oh, you were asking about the *dowager* viscountess. She has just the one daughter, whom you have met. Alicia's husband, the fourth viscount, died in a hunting accident shortly after Sybil was born—he was a neck-or-nothing rider. The eight boys I was referring to belong to his cousin, who is now the fifth viscount."

Terence thought for a moment, but Colthurst's

answer had only raised more questions in his own mind. "But if the boys are not her sons, why did they come to the dowager viscountess to settle their dispute? Surely they would have gone to their own father or mother."

With a smile, Colthurst explained, "The present viscount is a good man and a fine neighbor, but I am afraid he is totally preoccupied with new farming methods. He is so fanatic about such things as mangelwurzels and methods of sowing corn that I almost could believe that he is not aware of precisely how many sons he has."

"And the boys' mother?"

"She is too indolent to exert herself in the slightest, and if her sons approached her with a request, she would doubtless turn them over to one of the servants."

Terence found it disgraceful that the widow should have been imposed upon to such a degree. Some of his disapproval must have shown on his face, for Colthurst continued, "Before you condemn the boys' parents entirely, keep in mind that Alicia has chosen of her own free will to mother the boys."

Terence wanted to ask more questions about the dowager viscountess, but he held his tongue lest his friend begin to wonder at his curiosity. When he thought about it rationally, he had to wonder himself why he had such a strong desire to know more about the young widow.

Granted, she was quite beautiful, but Terence had met many a beautiful young lady before. In fact, before he had retired from society to assume the care of his niece, he had been considered quite a catch.

But although his life had changed forever when he had taken on the duties of a surrogate father, he had never regretted his decision. Oblique hints had been dropped at the time by various young ladies, who had each indicated her willingness to become Marigold's step-mama, but in truth, Terence had never felt any particular affinity for any of the applicants for that position.

So why did he, after all these years, find Alicia Lady Dunmire so intriguing? Why was he feeling so much curiosity about her when his mind should be fully occupied with his niece? He felt mildly guilty, as if he had been disloyal to his deceased brother, and so he bit back the questions he longed to ask—such as whether or not anyone special was courting the beautiful widow.

Really, Alicia Lady Dunmire thought while taking tea, it was astonishing how much her daughter's friend Clara was able to eat. One would almost think the poor child had been starved for years, the way she was stuffing food into her mouth.

Although Mr. Kinderley had not requested Alicia to do so, now that the opportunity was at hand, it seemed appropriate to question her daughter's friend about the missing schoolgirl. "Clara, we had a visitor today—a Mr. Kinderley. He is the uncle of one of your classmates, and he is most distressed that his niece is missing. Did you happen to see Marigold climbing into a coach with the dancing master?"

Clara's mouth was—as it always seemed to be— too full for her to speak, but she shook her head quite vigorously, even while helping herself to another portion of syllabub.

"Then did you perhaps notice her speaking to a stranger?"

Again the shake of the head, before Clara reached for the plate of cherry tarts. The child's abominable manners were not a very good advertisement for Mrs. Wychombe's Select Seminary, but Alicia did not bother to reproach her.

Having been an active child herself, she knew firsthand what a relief it was to escape the restrictions of boarding school, so she did not make even a token protest when the two girls finished gulping down their food and with only a quick "may we please be excused?" darted back out into the sunshine.

As was her custom after taking tea, Alicia went up to the big house to visit with the present Lady Dunmire. Strolling along, Alicia absently let her mind return to her earlier visitor.

Even thinking about him caused the blood to tingle in her veins in a way she had not felt since . . . since her husband had died so many years ago. It was not merely that Mr. Kinderley was handsome, although no woman would have been able to find fault with his dark hair, clear gray eyes, and athletic build.

Nor was it merely the admiration in his eyes when he looked at her—admiration she was so used to seeing in men's eyes that she scarcely even noticed it any more.

This time she had felt such a strong attraction that she wanted to go to him and touch him. It was almost as if there were some mysterious bond between them—as if they somehow belonged together—that had caused her to be more aware of him than she had been of any of the dozens of men who had wished to court her.

It was too bad he had been so stiffly disapproving of her.

Disapproving? For a moment Alicia wondered why that word had popped into her head, but then she recalled the fleeting look of censure that had crossed his face when the boys had interrupted their conversation.

Remembering the way Mr. Kinderley's lips had pursed up—quite like the fussiest old maid—Alicia began to believe that his niece might very well have preferred eloping with a charming dancing master in lieu of returning to her uncle, who was doubtless one of those nagging types who did not understand about giving children permission to behave childishly. For a moment she was of half a mind to believe that he deserved the worry he was now feeling.

But then she recollected that Bartholomew had run off to join the army when he was thirteen, and his parents had certainly not been to blame for that. No, as adult as they might seem at times, young people below the age of seventeen or eighteen—and even some of that age—frequently did things that they considered perfectly reasonable, but that adults found totally illogical.

"I hear you had visitors today," Cousin Edith said without preamble when Alicia joined her in her sitting room.

The image of Mr. Kinderley's face, which had been hovering around the edges of Alicia's mind, now sprang to the forefront, but she found herself strangely reluctant to share the memory with another. "Yes, Colthurst dropped by for a short visit. He tells me Elizabeth is quite down in the dumps. The baby is due in three weeks. I believe I shall drive over in the next day or so and visit with her. Do you wish to come with me?"

Cousin Edith, whose indolence was well known in the neighborhood, was quick to drag out her usual excuses—the weather was too warm, her digestion had been a trifle off, and she felt as if she might be coming down with something. "But in any event, it is not his grace that I am interested in," she said in conclusion. "Did he not have another gentleman with him? A Mr. Kinderley?"

Her heart racing but her voice amazingly calm, Alicia explained about the missing niece.

"A niece, you say? How fortunate he is not her father. I assume he is a bachelor then?" Cousin Edith asked with a coyness that indicated quite clearly that Alicia should not be letting any golden opportunities slip by her.

Hoping she was not betraying herself with a blush, Alicia looked down at her teacup and said, "I am sure I could not say. Being an uncle does not preclude being a father, you know. Doubtless he has a wife and a dozen children of his own at home."

Cousin Edith was easily deflected, since matchmaking required more energy than she was used to exerting. The conversation moved on to more trivial subjects than runaway nieces and uncles who might or might not be bachelors.

But the question nagged at Alicia all the way back to the dower house. Was Mr. Kinderley a bachelor?

At the third hostelry they visited in Bath, Terence picked up the trail of his niece and her abductor. Although the head hostler had no knowledge of the dancing master, one of the grooms was better informed.

"Sure, I knows Lucaster by sight—quite the coxcomb, he is. I rented him a green chaise with yellow wheels," the lad reported. "He picked it up at seven this morning."

"Which means the scoundrel's got a good ten hours headstart on us," Sweeney, Terence's coachman, grumbled irritably.

"Aye," the groom agreed, "but you'll be pleased to know the paltry fellow didn't even have the wherewithal to hire a team. He's got naught but a pair pullin' his chaise, and seein' as it's heavier than this phaeton, I reckon the blackguard can go only 'bout half as fast as you can. I can give you full directions as to the probable route they have taken, and with the full moon tonight, you two can take turns drivin'. Doubtless you can catch up with that fortune hunter by mid-mornin' tomorrow, at which time you can take turns thrashin' our Mr. High-and-Mighty Lucaster, who's allus puttin' on airs."

Sweeney and the groom exchanged opinions as to the proper treatment for the unfortunate Mr. Lucaster, but Terence did not really care what punishment was meted out. So long as Marigold was recovered safe and sound, the dancing master could simply remove himself from the picture.

And if he was reluctant to depart, Terence would be happy to assist him.

"Oh, thank goodness," Sybil said, "there is Algernon at long last. Quick, Marigold, if we want to have a private word with him, we must stop him before he turns in at the drive." Jumping down from the low wall they had been standing on, she set off at a run down the lane that ran past Dunmire Abbey.

Even though the wall was only three feet off the ground, Marigold could not quite bring herself to leap down as recklessly as her friend. Sitting down first so that her feet were only a foot or so off the ground seemed a much more sensible way to descend.

Not quite sure how she should then proceed, she finally took a deep breath and used her arms to push herself off the wall. To her amazement, she did not break her leg or her head, nor did she even so much as turn her ankle. Feeling flushed with triumph, she dashed after Sybil, who by this time was standing beside the phaeton, talking to the driver.

Running was every bit as exhilarating as swinging, Marigold discovered, but unfortunately it required a great deal more energy—energy she found she did not have in any abundance. By the time she reached the other two people, she was panting and her heart was pounding in her chest.

Then she looked up at Sybil's oldest cousin, and her heart began to race even faster. She could well understand why Sybil intended to marry him—and why, doubtless, every young lady who met him would sigh over him.

Towhead was not the word to describe a young man with guinea-gold locks and a classical profile. In fact, no words were adequate to describe the heir apparent to Dunmire Abbey—who was now looking down at her with mild distaste.

Instinctively, Marigold took a step backward.

"I cannot think what you had in mind, cousin, bringing home such a puny creature," he said. Yet, despite his hurtful words, his voice was melodious and most pleasing to Marigold's ears.

"I thought you would be happy," Sybil retorted with an impish grin.

"Happy? To be saddled with a visitor who cannot run even a few steps without wheezing like a broken-winded nag?" He looked down his nose at Marigold, and since he was sitting above her in the phaeton, his look of haughty superiority was doubly effective. "I suppose she can amuse herself with the 'littles,' but I decline to allow her to tag along after us."

He picked up the reins to signal the horses to continue, but Sybil leaped up and clung to his arm. "Wait," she said, "or you will be very, very sorry. We have a grand and glorious secret, but I cannot tell you what it is unless you promise not to reveal it to anyone."

For a moment Marigold thought Algernon was

going to shrug Sybil off his arm, but apparently he could not completely restrain his curiosity. "Very well, brat, I promise. But your secret had better be good, because you have wrinkled my sleeve."

"Oh, pooh," Sybil said, "as if that mattered when I have such a treat in store for you. This," she said, stepping back down to the ground and waving her arm dramatically in Marigold's direction, "is not Clara Perkins. Allow me to make known to you my particular friend, Marigold Kinderley."

It was such a strange introduction, Marigold was not sure if she should curtsey or not.

"Not the invalid! Ecod, it wanted only this to make the summer complete," Algernon said, rolling his eyes heavenward. "I should have accepted Throckmorton's invitation to go home to Yorkshire with him. Really, Sybil, it is one thing to let you follow me around, but I absolutely draw the line at doing the pretty with an invalidish chit who is not even out of the schoolroom."

"Actually," Sybil said, and now she was grinning broadly, "that is precisely the problem, or should I say, that is the best part of it? You see, we are not at all sure Marigold's health actually *is* delicate. I have discovered that all her life everyone has simply *assumed* that she has a weak constitution."

"Assumed?" Algernon asked, immediately dropping his affectation of bored young man of the world.

"Exactly," Sybil said smugly. "She has not been allowed to exert herself in the slightest, and she has had to eat the most restricted—and the most tedious—diet imaginable."

Scrambling down from his carriage, Algernon handed the reins to Sybil, then walked around Marigold, considering her from all angles. "Tell me, Miss Kinderley, have you ever heard of the scientific method?"

For one desperate moment, Marigold was afraid her voice would not work, but then she managed to croak out, "Sybil explained to me that we cannot blindly accept something as true if we do not conduct experiments to test its validity."

"Very good, Miss Kinderley. Now tell me, do you have any objections to being experimented upon?"

Whereas earlier Marigold had not been at all sure in her own mind that she was in favor of such things, she was now ready—nay, eager—to do whatever was required to win this young man's approval. "I have no objections. Indeed, I am quite looking forward to discovering the truth. And you may call me Marigold." She was quite astonished by her own boldness, but Algernon and Sybil appeared to find nothing amiss.

"Well then, Marigold," Algernon said with a smile that changed his face from handsome to breathtakingly beautiful, "I bid you welcome to Dunmire Abbey. It is a shame that it is so close to the dinner hour, else we could begin our scientific studies at once."

"I thought first we could teach her to ride," Sybil said, quite as if she were Algernon's equal.

"She doesn't ride?" he inquired, cocking an eyebrow.

"She has never been allowed even to touch a horse," Sybil explained. "Nor pet a cat or a dog, or be around any kind of animal."

Tired of being discussed as if she were nothing more than a piece of furniture, Marigold spoke up. "My uncle has always said exposure to animals will give me sneezing fits." He had also warned her that she would doubtless break out in a rash if she so much as touched fur or feathers, but that information she kept to herself.

"Well then," Algernon said, "we shall meet in

the stables tomorrow morning at dawn and see whether horses make you sneeze."

Sneezing would not be so bad, Marigold decided when she and Sybil were walking back to the dower house, but if she broke out in spots, she would be totally mortified.

"Oh," she said, stopping abruptly as another thought struck her. "Oh, dear."

"What's wrong?" Sybil asked.

"I am afraid I cannot, after all, try riding," Marigold said, feeling totally miserable and cast down.

Hands on her hips, Sybil glared at her. "I had not thought you such a pudding-heart. Perhaps Algernon was right—perhaps I should not have brought you home with me."

Pudding-heart? Marigold felt her own temper flare up. "You are entirely too quick to jump to conclusions, *Lady* Sybil," she said in an icy voice. "I am not the least bit afraid of horses." That was a barefaced lie, but Marigold would have died before she would have admitted to the least anxiety. "It has obviously slipped your mind that I do not have a riding habit." Then she childishly stuck out her tongue at her friend.

Sybil only laughed and threw her arm around Marigold's shoulders. "Pooh, that is nothing. I have clothes you can borrow."

"You have two riding habits?"

"Something even better," Sybil said. "I have two pair of breeches I wheedled out of Algernon when he outgrew them. You will find it is ever so much more fun to ride astride—and easier and safer than sitting all twisted around crooked in a sidesaddle, too."

"But . . . but . . ." Marigold felt called upon to object, but she was torn by an intense longing to try every new experience that presented itself. To actually wear breeches instead of skirts—never in her wildest dreams, when she had longed so to escape the restrictions that hemmed in her every waking moment, had she imagined such delightful freedom.

"And you need not fret about what people will say," Sybil said airily. "We shall put our hair up under caps, and since I have so many cousins running wild around the countryside, even if one of the old tabbies in the neighborhood spots us, she will merely assume we are two of Algernon's brothers. I have worn my breeches many a time, and no one has ever suspected, not even my mother. Nor should you worry that any of the stable lads will peach on us. Algernon would bust their heads if they betrayed us."

Marigold was silent, contemplating the treat that was in store for her.

"Well, are you game?" Sybil asked impatiently.

"Do you think I could try on the breeches before dinner?" Marigold asked. "Just to be sure they will fit me?"

The sky had been growing ominously dark, and there was still an hour before sunset. "It's coming on rain," the coachman commented unnecessarily.

The first flash of lightning illuminated the roadway, followed a moment later by the sharp crack of thunder. The job horses they had hired at the last posting house were too apathetic even to bolt, and Terence began to curse under his breath.

"How far to the next town?" he asked.

"We'd be there already if we'd been able to hire proper horses instead of these slugs. The way they're moving, I'd say we're no more than halfway there," Sweeney replied. "We've prob'ly got a good five or six miles to go."

As much as Terence wanted to push on, he knew it was dangerous to be out in the open during such a storm. Positively seething with frustration, he instructed the coachman to see if there were any accommodations to be had in the little village they were approaching.

"Leastways that cursed dancing master won't be able to travel in this weather neither," Sweeney pointed out.

His words immediately conjured up in Terence's mind a vision of his niece being struck by lightning. Suppose that wretched dancing master did *not* have enough sense to come in out of the storm?

The possibilities for disasters were too numerous to count. Suppose Mr. Lucaster determined to push on regardless of the weather? Suppose he lost his way in the dark? Suppose a bridge was out or the roadway flooded? Suppose the chaise overturned? Suppose, suppose, suppose—

When he and Sweeney were safely ensconced in a small village tavern with mugs of hot mulled cider in their hands, Terence found he could not stop worrying. Even if Marigold was safely out of the rain, who knew what miserable accommodations she might be forced to accept?

The sheets might be damp, the beds full of fleas or other vermin, and the food—he shuddered as new worries plagued him. Some wayside inns, he knew, served ale and mutton to every guest as a matter of course. If the dancing master had such limited funds that he could only afford to hire a paltry pair of horses rather than a team, it was doubtful that he would be able to demand of the landlord that he be provided with food that was not a part of the regular menu.

Ale and mutton—ecod, it did not bear thinking about. But Terence thought about it, of course. And about the brigands that might be lurking about waiting to murder the eloping couple in their beds—or in their *bed*? A fresh new worry now overset him completely, and he raged inwardly at the storm and the job horses and the poor roads and Mrs. Wychombe for not being more particular in the teachers she hired and most of all, he cursed Mr. Lucaster for being such a blackguard.

Terence lay awake in his bed long after the noise from the public room below had abated. Unable to stop his thoughts from going over and over the same worries, he was much too tense to fall asleep.

Then unexpectedly, a different vision filled his mind—that of the beautiful and imperturbable Alicia Lady Dunmire, a most unusual female. Remembering the casualness with which she had treated the two injured boys, he could well imagine that she would find his present state of anxiety a source of amusement.

If she were there beside his bed, she would probably gaze serenely down at him with her calm blue eyes and say, "What is the point of worrying?"

He could almost feel her hand reaching out to soothe his forehead, almost hear her say reassuringly, "You can do nothing until tomorrow, so why not sleep? . . . Rest? . . . Dream? . . ."

The stable was dark and warm and quite the most fascinating place Marigold had ever been in. Redolent of hay and grain and horses, the long building was also home to innumerable cats, including two litters of kittens. One set was so tiny their eyes were not even open; but the other batch was five weeks old and their antics had Marigold laughing so hard her sides ached.

Petting the kittens was something Marigold could have done all day, but that was not, of course, the reason for their early morning visit to the stable.

There still remained the matter of the great beasts that stood placidly in their stalls, occasionally shuffling their giant hooves or making funny whiffling noises.

"You shall ride Pattycake," Algernon said, opening the door to the furthermost stall. "She is so old and so placid, even Ferdinand has no trouble riding her."

Placid the mare might be, but she also seemed monstrous big when Marigold was standing beside her. Perhaps learning to ride was not such a good idea after all?

The mare turned her massive head and shoved it up against Marigold's chest, forcing her to take a step backward. In fact, she came very close to sitting down in the straw.

"Pattycake wants the sugar you brought her," Sybil explained. "All you have to do is hold it on your palm and keep your hand flat."

If Algernon had not been there, Marigold would have dropped the sugar and removed herself from the vicinity of the mare's wicked-looking teeth, but she knew as sure as anything that if she displayed the least bit of cowardice, he would banish her to play with the "littles."

As it turned out, feeding the sugar to the horse was the worst ordeal she had to face during her first riding lesson. She had a natural aptitude, or so Algernon told her when he finished instructing her, and she was quite willing to believe he knew what he was talking about.

After all, he was a proponent of the scientific method, so he would not go around making rash statements that could be easily disproved.

On the other hand, she was discovering that Uncle Terence had been totally wrong about a great many things—about almost everything, in fact. No matter how many forbidden things she had done in the last twenty-four hours, she had not once sneezed or wheezed or broken out in spots or gotten queasy or had a fever or a stomachache or anything at all.

Standing now at the base of an enormous oak tree, she realized she had never felt better in her life. To be sure, when she looked up at the platform someone had constructed high in the branches of said tree, she did feel a little nervous at the thought of climbing up there among the leaves, even though it did look to be quite solidly built.

"Uncle Terence would doubtless say that I must avoid heights because they might make me dizzy and I might fall," she said to no one in particular.

With a hoot of laughter, Bartholomew and Cedric and Sybil pushed past her and swarmed up the tree, using the boards that were nailed crossways on the trunk.

"If you wish," Algernon offered magnanimously, "I can go right behind you and catch you if you fall."

"No," Marigold said, resolutely pushing aside all thoughts of falling, "that will not be necessary. But perhaps you could help me get up to the first board. It is rather far off the ground, and I fear I am not strong enough to pull myself up just using my arms."

Willingly, Algernon boosted her up, and slowly she began to make her way, rung by rung, up the tree. She was most thankful that she was still wearing breeches, because a skirt and petticoats would really have been quite impractical for climbing trees.

"Did you know," Algernon said below her, "that horses must be exercised every day if they are to stay strong? I have long been of the opinion that people are much the same. It is quite likely that resting, rather than conserving our strength, only makes us weaker."

Finally reaching the hole in the platform, Marigold climbed through it and then crawled across it on her hands and knees and with great trepidation peered over the edge. She was at least twelve feet off the ground, which made her tingle with excitement. But to her relief, she did not feel the slightest nervousness or fear or dizziness.

"So," Algernon called up to her, "it is quite possible that the more you exercise, the stronger you will become. Are you game to try it?"

"Of course," she called down to him, "I am ready to try anything and everything." So saying, she bravely rose to her feet and stood waiting while Algernon climbed up to join them.

Terence was inclined to believe the dowager viscountess had the right attitude. Worrying about his niece all through the better part of the night had accomplished nothing except to give him a pounding headache.

From now on, he resolved, paying off the innkeeper and climbing back into the phaeton, he would concentrate his energies on retrieving his niece and put all pointless worries completely out of his mind.

His new resolution was put to the test a mere hour later when a cowhanded provincial, who apparently thought himself a notable whip, attempted to pass him on a narrow curve, with the result that Terence was forced off the road. Which would in itself not have been disastrous, had not one of his wheels struck a large rock hidden in the tall grass, resulting in two broken spokes.

Instead of ranting and raving and working himself up into a frenzy at this additional delay, Terence was quite calm when he accepted the dolt's apologies. "You did not also happen to smash a wheel on a green chaise, did you?" he asked in the mildest of voices. "A yellow wheel, it would have been."

The squire's son—or so he introduced himself—hastened to assure Terence that he had been responsible for only one broken wheel that day. Terence forbore asking how many wheels the lad might have destroyed on previous days.

As luck would have it, they were only a half mile from the next village, which amazingly enough boasted a wheelwright. Taking up the boy on his offer of assistance, Terence sent Sweeney along with the broken wheel while he himself stayed with the horses and the phaeton.

The sky was a cloudless blue and showed no sign of the previous night's storm. While he rested on the grassy verge, Terence was not interested in the beauties of nature that surrounded him, nor did he allow himself to fret about his niece's safety.

Instead, he contemplated the wisdom of such maxims as "Spare the rod and spoil the child." Even though he knew full well that he could never in his life actually strike his niece, still he could not keep his eyes from straying to the nearby shrubbery, and he found himself mentally selecting the branches that would make the best switches.

Did the beautiful dowager viscountess approve of whipping recalcitrant children? He had a feeling she did not. Smiling to himself, he wondered what it would take to disturb her calm. Black eyes and bloody noses did not faze her, to be sure. But if someone were to whip one of the children on the Dunmire estate, would she rise up like an avenging angel and smite the offender? He rather thought she might—although he could not picture her as a raging fury. It was more likely that she would remain calm and dispassionate while meting out suitable punishment.

But if someone—such as himself—were audacious enough to kiss her on her soft, sweet lips, how would she react? Would she then remain cool and collected? Was her serenity an indication that she was cold-blooded? Did her tranquility denote a lack of passion?

He had not answered that question to his own satisfaction when Sweeney returned with the mended wheel and the news that the runaways were once again a good ten hours ahead of them.

Alicia smoothed the bedcovers over her young visitor, who looked tired but thoroughly happy.

"I have had the most wonderful day in my life," Clara said, and from the stars in her eyes, Alicia was inclined to think she was not exaggerating. "I almost wish I were a boy so that I could always wear breeches." A look of dismay crept over the girl's face. "Oh, dear, I was supposed to keep that a secret."

"Well, then," Alicia said gently, "we shall simply not tell Sybil that you—'peached' I believe is the term—on her. Besides, I have known about the breeches from the first day Sybil wore them."

"And you did not take them away from her?"

"I suppose I should have, but I remember all too well how bad I felt when my mother discovered I had been wearing a pair belonging to my brother. After she burned them and forbade me even to think of wearing breeches again, I made a firm resolution to give my daughter more freedom than I was allowed."

"Freedom—yes, I agree that is indeed wonderful. But do you know, I have quite changed my mind about wanting to be a boy, because boys cannot have babies, and the very best part of the day was when we went up to the nursery in the big house, and I got to hold Horatio. I have never before been around a little baby, you see, and I had no idea how truly sweet they are."

She continued to rattle on about dear little fingers and adorable little noses, but Alicia did not really pay attention to what the girl was saying. Clara had never been around a baby before? But according to Sybil's letters, Clara was the eldest of a large family.

Alicia could think of only one interpretation for the remark "Clara" had just made—and that explanation was too terrible to contemplate, Alicia could only pray she had been mistaken: That her memory was playing her false. That it was not Clara, but another of Sybil's friends who had so many siblings.

As soon as she finished tucking in both girls, Alicia hurried to her own room, where she opened the drawer of her dressing table and took out the bundle of letters her daughter had sent her from school. Quickly she began skimming them, looking for information about Clara's siblings.

Alicia did not need to read far. In her very first letter, Sybil had described all her new friends—including Clara, who had blonde hair, and Marigold, who had black hair.

With a sinking heart, Alicia acknowledged that her daughter's guest was undoubtedly the runaway, Marigold Kinderley, whose uncle was even at this moment engaged in a wild goose chase to Gretna Green, and that because Sybil had lied and told him Marigold had eloped with the dancing master.

But had Sybil lied? With startling clarity Alicia heard her daughter's exact words—"I did not actually see Marigold with my own eyes climbing into the chaise with the dancing master."

The implication was there, of course, that *someone* had seen Marigold do precisely that, but Sybil had not actually said that either. In fact, when Mr. Kinderley had asked her directly if she were telling him that Marigold had eloped to Scotland, Sybil had said no, she would never believe Marigold would do such a thing.

Alicia could not hold back a smile at her daughter's clever manipulation of the truth. To be sure, Mr. Kinderley would have been saved a long and fatiguing trip to Scotland if only Alicia had remembered her daughter's natural aptitude as an actress and had questioned her more thoroughly.

But on the other hand, Alicia could not completely put out of her mind the look on Marigold's face this evening when she said today had been the best day of her life.

Picking up her daughter's letters, Alicia began to read them again, wanting to learn more about the girl who had come to visit. Upon arrival, Clara— or rather, Marigold—had been as pale and wan as a ghost, but already she was beginning to have some color in her cheeks. So much improvement after only a day and a half was truly remarkable.

By the time Alicia finished reading all the letters, she had discovered that Mr. Kinderley was indeed a bachelor, but she was no longer interested in such things. She was so angry, she wished Mr. Kinderley were there with her: Not so that she could explore the intense attraction between them, but so she could give *him* a black eye. Of all the dismal excuses for a parent—or guardian, she amended—he was the worst she had ever encountered. It was no wonder Marigold was stuffing food into her mouth as if she were starving—that wretched man had kept her on a diet that would make anyone weak and invalidish!

How would he like to eat nothing but that pap he was forcing his niece to eat? And not allowing her to participate in any of the activities at school, not even a leisurely walk in the park—bah, the man was a complete and total idiot.

Alicia hoped the elegantly groomed Mr. Kinderley, who doubtless had ice water in his veins, was having a perfectly miserable journey, fraught with every possible delay, so that Marigold could enjoy a few more days of freedom before she was once more imprisoned by him.

Wretched, wretched man! Alicia was so angry with him, she began to pace the room, wishing there were something she could do to *force* him to leave his niece in her care for the rest of the summer—wishing she had some *right* to dictate to *him* how *he* should act and what *he* should do and . . . and . . . oh, she was in such a rage that she wanted to scream loud enough for him to hear her in Scotland!

Sweeney lowered the horse's hoof to the ground. "I got the stone out, but I'm afraid he's bruised the frog right and proper."

"How many miles to the next posting house?" Terence inquired, knowing that with the way his luck had been running, the coachman would *not* say it was only over the next hill.

"About four miles, I calculate."

Four miles at a slow, limping walk. Undoubtedly a divine punishment for having rejoiced that they had gained a good two hours on the runaways.

But there was nothing to be done. Sweeney climbed back into the phaeton, Terence flicked the reins, and they started off.

At the rate things were going wrong, he would run out of things to worry about before ever they arrived at Gretna Green, he thought with a wry grin.

Elizabeth, the Duchess of Colthurst, looked at her visitor in dismay. "But surely you intend to tell Mr. Kinderley the truth the moment he returns from Scotland," she said.

"No, I most certainly do not," Alicia replied. "I shall concoct some lie—send him off on another wild goose chase. I have to." Standing up, she began pacing back and forth. "I know it is wrong to tell a deliberate falsehood, but it would be even more wicked to allow that wretched man to . . . to imprison that poor girl once again."

With a look of entreaty, Alicia dropped down onto the settee beside Elizabeth and took her hand. "Please, you must agree to help me. If you could only see how much the child has improved in just two days, you would do everything in your power to assist me."

"You are talking as if Terence is the veriest villain, but my husband has been friends with him for years, and I trust Darius's judgment completely."

Standing up, Alicia once more began to pace back and forth, more distraught than Elizabeth had ever before seen her. In fact, now that she thought on it, Elizabeth realized she had never seen Alicia behave in any way other than completely calm and collected.

How odd . . . or rather, how intriguing. Could it be?

"You know my views on child raising," Alicia said, "and I know you adhere to the same philosophy I do, namely that children should not be hampered by unnecessary rules and restrictions."

"But my dear, you must admit that Marigold is a special case since she has a weak constitution."

"Balderdash! You would not say that if you could have seen her climbing up a tree yesterday or trotting around the estate today on Pattycake's back. And as for her delicate stomach, she has been eating more than any one of the boys—positively stuffing herself with every one of the foods that have always been forbidden to her, and she has displayed not the slightest bit of discomfort or distress. Do you wish to know what I think?"

Elizabeth was under the impression that Alicia

had made it very clear what she thought, but she nodded her head.

"I think that people can make themselves sick by quacking themselves. By paying attention to every gurgle in their tummies or every twinge in a joint, they can convince themselves that they are in imminent danger of dying if they so much as set foot out of bed. And precisely because they believe themselves to be sick, they actually become so. Lady Arbuthnot is a case in point, and Squire Henley's father is another example of that kind of idiocy."

"So you think Marigold has been playing the invalid so long she has made herself sick?" Elizabeth asked.

"No, I do not think she has done any such thing. It is all the fault of that wretched man." There was a fire and a fury in Alicia's eyes that Elizabeth had never seen before. "I think every bit of this is her uncle's fault—he is the one who insists upon treating her as an invalid. I would have more sympathy for Mr. Kinderley if he himself were a hypochondriac, but no, he has forced his niece to play that role. It is no wonder the poor child felt compelled to run away. She told me herself she is happier with us than she has ever been before in her life, and I am totally opposed to helping that wretched man find her again."

Looking up into her friend's blazing eyes, Elizabeth had the strongest feeling that Alicia was more interested in "that wretched man" than she was admitting to herself. In all the years Elizabeth had known her, Alicia had never shown the slightest degree of interest in any other eligible bachelor.

Perhaps it would not be so very bad to delay telling Terence where his niece was? Marigold was, after all, perfectly safe under Alicia's watchful eye.

But to send him off on another wild goose chase? No, that would definitely be a blunder. After all, one did not send a prospective bridegroom away from the prospective bride, not if one wished to foster a match between them.

The only stumbling block, Elizabeth realized, was her husband. She could never, under any circumstances, bring herself to deliberately deceive Darius. But if she explained the whole situation to him, might she not convince him that it was in Terence's best interests to be kept in ignorance of his niece's whereabouts?

The coach overturned in the roadway ahead of them was not, unfortunately, a green chaise with yellow wheels. It was also unfortunate that common decency and compassion demanded that Terence stop and render what assistance he could.

"We're but six hours behind the runaways," Sweeney commented gloomily.

"Even if we were to ignore these poor people and continue without stopping," Terence said, tugging back on the reins, "there is no way we can catch up with Mr. Lucaster before he reaches the border." Terence was amazed at his own calm acceptance of the inevitable. "That will not, however, prevent me from putting a bullet through that cursed dancing master's black heart as soon as we catch up with him, whether he has married my niece or not. Well, perhaps I shall restrain myself a bit if, by some quirk, they have not said their vows. Yes, I rather think that if we discover that they are not yet married, I shall merely thrash him soundly."

That evening when they were preparing for bed, Elizabeth threw herself wholeheartedly into the attempt to persuade her husband to go along with her plans. She dragged out every argument she could think of to justify concealing the truth from

Terence, ending with, "Do you not agree that Alicia would make your friend an absolutely splendid wife?"

"If Terence were looking around for a wife, I am sure Alicia would catch his eye," Darius replied, brushing Elizabeth's hair. "But he has always seemed content to remain a bachelor, and I am not in favor of meddling in other people's lives."

"Poppycock. You are presupposing that men are invariably able to recognize their own good fortune when it is staring them in the face. They are far more likely to whistle a lifetime of happiness down the wind than to behave sensibly and court the proper woman."

Given that Darius himself had never intended to marry, and yet he was now most happy and content to be a husband and father, Elizabeth doubted that he could now come up with a convincing argument in support of bachelorhood.

"Very well," Darius said, wrapping his arms around her and nuzzling her neck, "since one must always humor pregnant ladies, who are known to have the most absurd whims, I shall agree not to interfere in your scheme. Under one condition: When Terence returns from Scotland, if he does not appear to be suffering acute mental anguish, I shall remain silent for one week and one week only."

"Two weeks," Elizabeth said promptly, turning in his arms so that she could kiss him.

"One week," her husband said firmly when he could again speak. Then he smiled and added, "But perhaps after one week I might be persuaded to reevaluate the situation before I peach on you two conniving, conspiring females."

It was almost noon of the third day when Terence finally crossed the River Sark and entered the vil-

lage of Gretna Green. The only worry that he had
been unable to push out of his mind for the last
twenty-four hours was the fear that his pursuit of
the runaway couple might not end here in this
peaceful place—that having by now, no doubt, successfully married Marigold, Mr. Lucaster might
have already carried her away, leaving Terence with
all of Scotland and England to search.

After inquiring in vain at several of the inns, Terence discovered his luck, which had been uniformly
bad throughout the entire journey, had finally
taken a turn for the better at the King's Head. Not
only had Mr. Lucaster chosen this most renowned
inn for his wedding, but also for his nuptial night.

"Your niece, you say? Came in a green chaise
with yellow wheels? I'm sorry to have to inform
you that you are too late. I married them myself
yesterday evening, and there is naught you can do
to unhitch them. They're upstairs in my second-best
parlor right at this very moment, enjoying a light
repast," the host, a Mr. Robert Elliot, explained in
a most congenial manner.

Without deigning to answer the man, Terence
took the stairs two at a time. Behind him, Mr. Elliot, who evidently had much experience with furious fathers, wrathful brothers, and enraged uncles,
called out, "Third door on the left."

Throwing open the door so hard it crashed
against the wall, Terence entered the second-best
parlor. And immediately stopped dead in his tracks.

The man who leaped to his feet and who now
stood ashen-faced and trembling was obviously Mr.
Lucaster, since he exactly matched the description
Terence had been given.

The woman who scurried around to hide behind
his narrow shoulders was not, however, a fourteen-
year-old schoolgirl. She appeared to be in her late
twenties, and she bore not the slightest resemblance

to Marigold other than that they both had black hair.

"W-what do you mean by barging in like this?" Mr. Lucaster said bravely. "This is a p-private parlor, and I have rented it for the entire day. Whoever you are, I m-must ask you to leave."

Terence had never before suffered from such mortification. For the first time in his life, he could feel his face grow hot and knew he was undoubtedly blushing bright red. If only there were some way to erase the last few minutes! But there was no way to undo what had been done.

"Forgive me for the intrusion," he said coolly, "but I was informed that you had run off with my niece."

"Do not listen to him, Philbert. He is not my uncle—indeed, I have never seen him before in my life," the bride managed to squeak out.

"My name is Kinderley," Terence said, "and I am seeking my niece, Marigold, who is a student at Mrs. Wychombe's Seminary. She has completely vanished, and one of her friends said she was seen climbing into a chaise in the company of the dancing master, Mr. Lucaster."

"I am Mr. Lucaster," the little man said stiffly, "and I am employed by Mrs. Wychombe to instruct her pupils in the art of dancing and elocution, but I do not believe I have ever met your niece."

"I know the young lady," his wife said, coming out from behind him and approaching Terence, "and I can well believe that Miss Kinderley has run away, rather than returning to her home."

Terence looked down at her in astonishment, which became even more pronounced as she continued to speak.

"A more miserably unhappy child I have never seen in all my years of teaching."

"Unhappy?" Terence said, taking an involuntary step backward.

Glaring up at him as ferociously as a little fox terrier, Mrs. Lucaster continued, "Yes, unhappy. That poor child is so hemmed in by rules and restrictions that she has no joy in her life at all."

"My niece is a sickly child," Terence began in self defense, but the woman in front of him was not ready to listen to reason.

"Well, in my opinion, she would find more pleasure in the grave than she finds under your care."

Terence stared at her in astonishment, and even Mr. Lucaster was clearly flabbergasted at his bride's statement, which went far beyond what was acceptable.

Obviously realizing she had been much too coming, Mrs. Lucaster retreated to stand next to her husband. "I am sorry if that is speaking too plainly for you, Mr. Kinderley, but I have felt such pity for the child. It has fair made my heart ache to see her miss out on so many activities that the other girls take great pleasure in."

"Since you appear to have such an interest in my niece," Terence said stiffly, "perhaps you might have some idea where she has gone—or with whom she might be staying at the present time?"

But unfortunately, Mrs. Lucaster, who as it turned out was the singing teacher at Mrs. Wychombe's Seminary, could give him no more information than her employer had done, no matter how long and how thoroughly he questioned her.

"And now, I suppose, we shall both lose our jobs," Mrs. Lucaster said when Terence was taking leave of them.

"I am sure Mrs. Wychombe will not hold you responsible for my niece's disappearance," Terence said.

The bridal couple glanced at each other. Then

Mr. Lucaster said simply, "Mrs. Wychombe has a very firm rule against employing married couples to teach in her school."

After a moment's consideration, Terence said, "I see. Well, I am afraid I cannot countenance lying to Mrs. Wychombe. If she should ever have occasion to ask me if the two of you are married, I would feel honor bound to tell her the truth."

With dawning hope, Mr. Lucaster said, "If she asks you?"

"In that event, certainly," Terence assured him, and both Mr. and Mrs. Lucaster were profuse in expressing their gratitude.

It was with mixed emotions that Terence sought out his coachman and instructed him to have fresh horses hitched up for the return journey.

On the one hand, Terence was feeling decidedly aggravated that so many people were telling him he had failed to take proper care of his niece. On the other hand, he realized by the time he tooled his team down the long hill into Penrith, no matter how worried he was about his niece, he could not completely suppress his feeling of excitement at the thought of seeing the lovely widow again.

Which in itself was enough to make him question his own sanity. He had, after all, been in her presence less than an hour, and nothing of a personal nature had passed between them. But he could not quite convince himself that the only reason he wanted to visit her again was because it would be discourteous to leave her to wonder about the results of his journey to Scotland.

It should be obvious to the meanest intellect that he could accomplish the same result merely by sending her a brief note.

No matter how he tried to come up with a logical reason for his happiness, the only honest way to describe the emotion he was feeling was to say that he felt as if he were returning home.

Home to Alicia Lady Dunmire, who calmly settled little boys' quarrels, who had lovely blue eyes and kissable lips . . .

Terence was appalled at where his own fancies were leading him. Surely he could not be thinking about kissing the beautiful widow when he should be worrying about his niece?

Should be worrying? How preposterous! Perhaps there was some truth in what everyone seemed to be telling him? Perhaps he did worry about his niece more than was absolutely necessary?

Even if it were true, which he was not yet ready to admit, that still did not give him a legitimate excuse to dream about kissing the delightful Alicia.

The rain was still coming down steadily, giving no indication that it would ever stop. Marigold stared gloomily out the window of her bedroom. She and Sybil had been trapped in the dower house all morning, and it was boring, boring, boring, despite the fact that Sybil's mother had spent several hours playing games with them.

"You cannot make the rain stop by scowling at it," Sybil commented behind her, "so you might as well come away from the window and help me think of something fun to do. I am positive that if we begged her, Cook would teach us to make cherry tarts."

Even this proposed treat could not raise Marigold's mood. "It is not really the rain that is depressing my spirits," she said. "But rather, today has reminded me of what my life was like in my uncle's house. And what it will again be like when I go home again. 'Twill not be just a morning of sitting around the house, but day after day after day with nothing fun to do—no riding, no climbing trees, no playing tag, no fishing in the brook, no wading in the pond. I shall be allowed to embroider and then read a book, or if I prefer, I may read a book and *then* embroider, and that will be the extent of my choices.''

Sybil thought about this for a long time. "Do you know," she said finally, "the best person in the whole world to ask for advice is my mother."

"But if we tell your mother who I am, she will send word to my uncle, and then all will be lost."

"I know that," Sybil said. "I was just thinking out loud, trying to come up with a plan, but I am sorely afraid that there is no solution to your dilemma."

"Do you think Algernon might have any ideas?" Marigold asked tentatively.

"No," Sybil said bluntly. "As intelligent as he is, he is not at all devious. But," she added, grinning broadly, "now that I think on it, you have nothing to worry about, because *I*, on the other hand, am always inventing the most marvelous schemes. Even you must admit that. I am sure that if I just put my mind to it, I can concoct a way to rescue you. Since that is the case, you must trust me and cheer up."

Marigold managed to force a smile, but in her heart she was not at all convinced that Sybil could come up with the solution to the problem, at least not one that was at all practical.

"I have it!" Sybil cried out, leaping to her feet.

"You have thought of a way that I can stay here forever and ever?"

"No, no," Sybil said, waving her hand dismissively. "I have thought of something we can do to keep from being bored right now. We shall cut each other's hair."

Marigold quite failed to see that this was a wonderful idea, and some of her doubts must have shown on her face, for Sybil caught her hand and resolutely pulled her away from the window.

"I am not talking about cropping your hair as short as a boy's, silly. But think how much easier it will be to brush it if it is short. Curly hair gets so tangled when it is long—and short hair is quite stylish, you know. Doubtless it will make us look seventeen or eighteen years old."

That was the deciding argument for Marigold, and she willingly sat down in a chair and allowed Sybil to drape a sheet around her shoulders.

"Perhaps it might be better if we asked one of the maids to do the actual cutting," Marigold suggested tentatively when she felt Sybil take the first snip.

"Nonsense," Sybil replied confidently. "I have watched Betty numerous times when she cut my mother's hair, and there is really nothing to it."

A half hour later, she was willing to admit that it might be a trifle more complicated than she had imagined. "The only problem is getting it to come out even," Sybil explained, snipping a bit more off the right side and then comparing it to the left side. "If your hair did not curl so much, it would be easier to tell how much to cut off. Maybe we should just leave it a trifle uneven—what do you think?"

With a feeling of dread, Marigold stood up from the chair, and leaving a veritable mountain of shorn locks on the floor behind her, she approached the cheval glass that stood in the corner.

The image that she saw in the mirror was not one she recognized. A strange boy stood there looking back at her—a very pretty boy, to be sure, with short black curls hugging his head. "Oh, dear," was all she could think of to say. "Oh, dear, oh dear, oh dear."

"I did not intend to take off quite so much," Sybil explained unnecessarily. "But you must keep in mind that it will grow back. Eventually."

Pulling the sheet loose from her neck, Marigold turned to face her friend. Without voicing the slightest reproof, she began to wrap the white cloth around Sybil. "And now it is your turn to get your hair cut."

"Perhaps," Sybil said as Marigold picked up the pair of scissors, "we might ask Betty to give us a little instruction."

"Nonsense," Marigold said, ruthlessly chopping off a long, dangling curl. "I have it on the best authority that there is nothing at all complicated about cutting hair."

Fortunately, the trip back from Scotland was unmarred by the disasters that had plagued their journey north. That was little enough consolation to Terence when he pulled up in front of Colthurst Hall. Six days wasted, and he was right back where he had started from, both literally and figuratively.

Instructing Sweeney to stable the team and saddle a riding horse, Terence knocked on the door and was soon admitted. A few minutes later, the butler ushered him into the drawing room, where both the duke and the duchess were taking tea.

"From the expression on your face, I would say that you have not yet found your niece," Colthurst said.

"No," Terence replied, "she did not elope to Gretna Green. At least, not with that ridiculous dancing master."

"Would you like some tea?" Elizabeth asked politely, and he accepted the cup she held out to him.

"So, what are your plans now," she asked, once he had taken a sip of the brew.

"Well, I thought perhaps I might visit Lady Dunmire," he said. "The *dowager* viscountess is who I mean, of course."

At his words, the duke and duchess exchanged

meaningful glances, and Terence felt his face grow warm. For the second time in his life, he could not keep from blushing. "Her daughter may have thought of something else that might give me a clue as to my niece's whereabouts," he said. But his rather lame explanation only brought smiles to his friends' faces.

"Sybil might be of help," Darius said. "And her mother is quite renowned in the neighborhood for her common sense and good judgment."

"Yes, that is it exactly," Terence said with relief. From the smiles on the others' faces, he could see he was not fooling them in the slightest. "And she is also quite beautiful," he admitted sheepishly.

"Well, I wish you luck in your endeavor," Colthurst said, and Terence was not so foolish as to enquire whether his friend was referring to his efforts to find his niece or his courtship of the beautiful widow.

For he was intending to court the lovely Alicia, Terence admitted to himself. Indeed, he found himself quite impatient to begin. If only he did not have to set that undertaking aside until after he located his exasperating niece.

Although Alicia Lady Dunmire appeared outwardly calm, Terence was not so inexperienced with women that he failed to notice the subtle signs that indicated the lovely young widow was not as indifferent to him as she was pretending to be.

He could not be sure, but he thought he had seen a flash of pleasure in her eyes when he had first entered the drawing room. On the other hand, that might have been wishful thinking on his part.

"So Mr. Lucaster eloped with the singing teacher and not with your niece?" The widow handed him a cup of tea, and he noticed that her hand was trembling ever so slightly, and her eyes slid away without quite meeting his.

"A Miss Quirin," he replied, wishing he could catch that fine-boned hand and press a kiss on it. "She was quite outspoken and gave me to understand that my niece has been a most unhappy child, and that I have erred grievously in the manner I have raised her."

"From what my daughter has written in her letters, I am sure Mrs. Lucaster is correct," Lady Dunmire said, and now her eyes met his boldly, as if daring him to deny the allegations.

Instead of contradicting her, he smiled at her, and to his delight, she lost her composure, and her cheeks took on a delicate rosy tint.

"Before you also lecture me," he said, "let me tell you that I have already been raked over the coals by a Miss Medleycote, one of the teachers at the school, and by the aforementioned Miss Quirin— now Mrs. Lucaster. Even Sweeney, my coachman, has had the impertinence to point out to me my errors in child raising, albeit in a rather oblique way. He informed me rather pointedly that one cannot keep a foal shut up in the stables day after day merely because it might break its leg if allowed to run loose in the pasture."

"I was going to use the analogy of a young bird needing to test its wings," the widow said with a smile, and Terence noticed that she had a delightful dimple in her right cheek.

The sight of it was so enchanting, he did not immediately reply, and the longer the silence stretched between them, the more pronounced became the tension in the room.

At first the widow glanced nervously away, but when he continued to keep his gaze steady, her eyes were pulled back to his. He smiled encouragingly and finally, to his great delight, she relaxed visibly, and her answering smile was tacit acknowledgment of the attraction between them.

How long he might have basked in the warmth of her smile he was not to discover, for just as he was about to tell her how beautiful she was, the door was thrown open and two young boys barged into the room. Ignoring him, they made straight for Lady Dunmire.

Somewhat older than the two who had interrupted during his previous visit, they were even more disheveled. The one with curly black hair was covered with mud, and the towheaded one had a ripped shirt and a smear of blood on his face, although his nose was no longer actively bleeding.

"He deliberately tripped me and made me fall in a mud puddle," the black-haired one shouted in an enraged voice. "He is a miserable sneak, and I am not at all sorry that I drew his cork."

"I did not do it on purpose—it was an accident!" the towheaded one shouted back, then he socked the black-haired one on the shoulder and got a kick in the shin for his reward.

For a moment Terence thought he was going to be treated to the sight of a mill right there in the drawing room, but Lady Dunmire intervened.

"That is quite enough," she said sharply, and the two combatants merely clenched their fists and scowled at each other. "Both of you are old enough to know that violence does not settle anything."

"He started it," the black-haired one said fiercely, wiping his face with his sleeve. Since his jacket was as muddy as his face, little improvement could be seen. "So *he* needs to be *punished*."

"But I am afraid you are not blameless, either," Lady Dunmire pointed out. "At this point it does not matter who started it or who ended it. Two wrongs do not make a right, so you must share the punishment. But for the present, since I am entertaining company—"

Heads swiveled, and two pairs of eyes stared at Terence. The junior pugilists were clearly astounded to discover they had an audience. The black-haired one immediately gave a squeak of dismay and darted from the room without a backward glance, but the blond one was made of sterner stuff and was still determined to continue arguing his case.

"No more of this, Cedric," the widow cut off his protestations quite firmly. "You will clean yourselves up and then wait in the morning room until I am free to deal with you."

Obviously not satisfied, the boy left the room muttering dire things under his breath that augered no good for his opponent.

"What sort of punishment do you hand out for such offenses?" Terence could not resist asking.

"Well, I do not plan to beat them," Lady Dunmire said, not quite meeting his eye. "No matter how I am sometimes tempted, I cannot very well lecture them on the futility of physical violence and then resort to it myself. No, I shall have to think of a task for them to do, such as weeding the vegetable garden or scouring out pots or something like that. Whether they like it or not, they will have to spend several hours working together, and that is the best cure for childish disagreements like this."

"You are exceedingly wise," Terence said, only just in time stopping himself from adding *for a woman*. Lady Dunmire had more common sense than most of the men he knew, and to qualify the compliment would be insulting. "Knowing children the way you do, perhaps you can advise me about my niece. I confess, I have not the slightest idea where I should begin looking for her."

For a moment, Terence thought he saw laughter

in the widow's eyes, but it must have been a trick of the lighting, for she answered quite seriously. "I cannot think of anything to suggest other than questioning Mrs. Wychombe again. Even if she has failed to discover any additional information, she can give you a list of the other pupils' names and their directions. I am sure if you seek them out, one or the other of them must know something."

Her suggestion had merit, but he felt a surprising reluctance to follow through on it. After the futile dash to Scotland, he had no desire to set out on a journey that could easily involve the rest of the summer.

On the other hand, it was not merely the thought of lame horses and broken wheels that was causing him to want to reject Lady Dunmire's suggestion. It was, in fact, Lady Dunmire herself. She met his gaze quite calmly, but her expression was now shuttered, and he could no longer tell what she was feeling.

He knew exactly what he wanted her to feel— the same attraction that he was feeling. No, he wanted more than that. He wanted her in his life permanently. He wanted to be able to come to her with his troubles, the same way the boys did.

Well, perhaps not exactly the same way as the children.

"Do you know," he said finally, "I rather think that would be a waste of my time."

"You are not going to search for your niece? You are going to abandon her—an innocent young girl?" The widow no longer was displaying her accustomed composure. In fact, despite her avowed renunciation of physical violence, she looked as if she were ready to throw the contents of her teacup in his face.

"Driving all over half of England would be rather inefficient," Terence said calmly. "Instead I shall send letters to each of the girls' parents, asking them to question their daughters. I shall be much more comfortable awaiting their replies at Colthurst Hall, than I would be racketing around the countryside, and I am more likely to find my niece this way."

Alicia looked at Mr. Kinderley in dismay. Colthurst Hall? He was planning to stay in the neighborhood? The success of her plan to conceal his niece from him depended entirely on his rapid removal from the scene—on her persuading him to set off on another wild goose chase.

But he was clearly determined to remain close at hand. Staring back at her just as openly as she was staring at him, he smiled. Not only in the neighborhood. She was willing to wager that he had decided to come calling every day—indeed, she would be surprised if he did not intend to live in her pocket.

How on earth could she keep him from discovering Marigold was right there under his nose?

"Do you not agree that it will be more efficient this way?" he now asked.

"To be sure," she answered faintly, unable to deny that she quite liked the idea of seeing him frequently. Unfortunately, sooner or later he would see his niece when she was not covered with mud, and then she, Alicia, would have a great deal of explaining to do.

Why had she not remembered that deceitfulness invariably led to disaster? When he discovered the truth—and he was bound to sooner or later—how on earth could she explain that she had deliberately lied to him? She had had the best of motives, to be sure, but that was a rather feeble excuse, and not one she would accept from any child under her care.

"I must be going now," he said, rising to his feet.

"I shall obtain that list of names from Mrs. Wychombe, and send out the letters immediately."

After a few polite formalities on her part, he was gone. Like a young schoolgirl, she found herself going to the window to watch him until he was out of sight. She had the lowering feeling that when he discovered her treachery, he would ride out of her life forever.

Ever since her first husband had died, she had politely but firmly sent away all the gentlemen who had come courting her. If someone had told her even eight days ago that she would someday meet a man she wished to encourage, she would have thought that that person had windmills in his head. Moreover, a few short days ago she would likewise not have believed that she herself could engage in deliberate deceit.

She did not feel entirely comfortable with her new self—with the woman who longed to be with one particular man—and standing there at the window, gazing down the now empty road, she almost wished time could be reversed, and that somehow the real Clara had come instead of the pretend Clara.

Which was indeed a totally pointless wish, since if Marigold had not run away, Alicia would never have met Mr. Kinderley, and as unfortunate as the ending would be, she could never regret having him come into her life.

Sighing, she finally turned away from the window. Might-have-beens were unimportant. Marigold was here, under her protection and, willy-nilly, Alicia was going to do her best to make the girl's visit a happy one.

Even if that selfless and noble goal could be achieved only at the cost of Alicia's own happiness.

* * *

Tucking her young visitor into bed that evening, Alicia could tell something was bothering the child.

"The gentleman who was visiting you today—has he gone away again for a long time?" Marigold alias "Clara" asked.

"You are referring to Mr. Kinderley? No, I believe he is planning to stay in the neighborhood for the present," Alicia replied.

"He is not going away to look for his niece? Does he not wish to find her?"

"Oh, indeed he does. But he has decided it will be more efficient if, rather than going in person, he sends letters to the parents of each of your classmates, asking them to question their daughters about Marigold."

The child slid down further under the covers and looked so guilt stricken, Alicia expected to hear a confession, which would, of course, solve Alicia's present dilemma very nicely, since she could tell Mr. Kinderley tomorrow without revealing her own complicity in the deception. Unfortunately, if Marigold admitted her true identity, she would be thrust right back into the miserable situation she had only just escaped from a week before.

But the moment for truth passed without any words of disclosure. Instead, Marigold's features relaxed and she said in a confident voice, "Algernon says that there is no point worrying about what might happen in the future, because if it doesn't happen, then we have wasted all the time we spent worrying. And if things do go wrong, then worrying about them ahead of time doesn't make them better either. That sounds reasonable, don't you agree?"

Marigold looked up at her expectantly, and Alicia had to admit that Algernon's logic was impeccable. Granted, sooner or later Mr. Kinderley would be very angry that she had known, almost from the beginning, where his niece was and had deliberately not told him.

On the other hand, Alicia realized, since the final outcome would inevitably be the same whether she worried or not, there was little point in fretting about the future. It would be far better to enjoy Mr. Kinderley's companionship for as long as she could. At least that way, when it was all over and he had stormed out of her life forever, she would have pleasant memories to look back on.

"Yes," she said finally, "I agree with Algernon. There is no point worrying about things one cannot change."

For someone who had just received assurance that worrying was pointless, Marigold still looked remarkably worried. Finally she asked timidly, "Would it be all right if I wore breeches every day? All the time? They are much more . . . much more *convenient* than skirts and petticoats, and it is such a bother to change back and forth all the time."

With a smile, Alicia gave permission, and she was rewarded when Marigold smiled back. The marked improvement in her young visitor, Alicia decided, made this whole game of deceit worthwhile, even though she doubted Mr. Kinderley would agree.

A week later, Alicia adjusted her riding hat at a jaunty angle, picked up her gloves, and descended to the foyer, where Mr. Kinderley was waiting to ride out with her. To her surprise, she found him quite distraught.

"Did I mistake your invitation yesterday?" she asked with a smile, which faded when he did not respond with a smile of his own.

"Please forgive me," he said, "and believe me when I say I have been looking forward to our excursion today. Unfortunately, this morning I received the last answer to the letters I sent out, and none of the girls was able to provide me with any information about my niece."

"What do you plan to do?" Alicia managed to ask, her calm voice not revealing her inner turmoil. Desperately, she cast about in her mind for some way to postpone the too rapidly approaching confrontation, but she could think of nothing.

"It appears I have made a serious error in judgment. With everyone telling me how unhappy my niece has been, I acted on the assumption that she left Mrs. Wychombe's Seminary of her own free will. Now it appears more likely that she was kidnapped."

"Kidnapped?" Alicia squeaked out. "But surely you would have received a ransom note?" Even as she said it, she remembered hearing from the vicar's wife that young girls who were spirited away by wicked people usually were sold into white slavery on the Continent. No wonder Mr. Kinderley looked as if he were reeling from a terrible blow.

"At this point," he continued, "I can see nothing else to do but go to London, where I intend to secure the services of a Bow Street runner. I can only pray it is not already too late."

"It will not be necessary for you to go that far," Alicia said, unable to look him in the face. "If you will follow me?" Feeling wretched, she led the way out into the garden, then on through the gate. Pointing at the children playing tag on the lawn, she said, "All of the present viscount's sons have blond hair."

It took a moment for Terence to grasp the meaning of what she was saying. Then the picture of his niece drugged and in a brothel on the Continent faded away, to be replaced by the memory of a young "boy" with short black curls and mud on his face.

A white-hot rage ran through his veins, and he

turned toward his hostess, ready to rake her over the coals. It only increased his anger to find that she was already retreating to the dower house—not that she would find safety there.

Approaching the children, who were all shrieking and laughing as they dashed about, Terence began to formulate in his mind the scathing things he would say to the scheming widow. But first he had to deal with his niece, who was as yet unaware of his presence since her back was to him.

One of the littler boys charged at her, and in an attempt to get away, she turned and crashed right into Terence. Catching her by the elbows, he looked down at her. Almost, he could have believed it was all a hoax.

The young girl who lifted her head to look up at him was too vital and alive to be his niece. Her cheeks were too rosy, her eyes sparkled too merrily, her smile . . .

On recognizing him, her smile faded, and a dejected look replaced the happiness into her eyes. "I am not at all sorry I did it," she said, but her attempt at defiance was not very successful, and tears filled her eyes.

Was he such a brute then, that his own niece, whom he loved like a daughter, had felt it necessary to run away from him?

At a word from the biggest boy, the younger children scampered away, leaving only Sybil and the young man, who introduced himself and then explained, "We have been conducting scientific experiments for the last fortnight, and we have determined that your niece's constitution is not at all weak."

"That's right," Marigold said, speaking with unaccustomed forcefulness. "We have discovered that despite what you have always told me, I am not allergic to animals, and I am becoming quite a good rider, and I don't get sick in a carriage even when the driver springs 'em, and I can eat whatever I want without getting sick, and exercise is what makes you strong, not resting in bed, and—and—and I am *not* sorry I ran away!"

With those words, the tears she had been blinking back spilled over, and Terence pulled her unresisting into his arms and began rubbing her back in an attempt to soothe her. Sybil, however, continued to glare at him so pugnaciously, he had a momentary wish that he had a friend to lend him support . . . or to guard his back.

But this was ridiculous—why should he feel defensive? He had done nothing wrong—from the beginning, when Marigold had been a wee thing in his arms, he had had only the best of intentions regarding his niece.

Marigold was upstairs packing her trunk with the help of Sybil and two of the maids, which meant that whether he wished it or not—and he most certainly did *not*—Terence was trapped for a short time in the company of the lovely, albeit treacherous, widow.

He could only hope that the maids, at least, would be efficient, because he did not wish to spend a minute longer than necessary in the company of Alicia Lady Dunmire. Or so he tried to convince himself.

Although there was guilt in her eyes, she looked at him quite boldly. "Not all of your accusations are well-founded," she said with a trace of belligerence in her voice. "To begin with, I did not suspect that I was housing an imposter until several hours after you had departed for Scotland."

"Ah, yes, the wild goose chase that I was sent on by your daughter, who doubtless learned her deceptive ways at her mother's knee," Terence said sarcastically.

"If my memory serves me right," the widow said, her voice icy, "my daughter stated quite plainly that she did *not* believe that Marigold had eloped to Scotland."

"You know and I know that your daughter deliberately tricked me, so let us not quibble about the way she accomplished it. We have more important things to discuss."

"We certainly do." Crossing the room to where a little writing table stood before the window, Lady Dunmire picked up a piece of foolscap and returned to thrust it in his face. "I have prepared for you a list of things that young girls need. I can only hope that your anger at me does not prevent you from following my advice."

Unwillingly taking the paper from her hands, Terence did no more than glance at it. The list was rather long, and the handwriting was not neat and precise—it looked, in fact, as if someone had written it while in a state of high passion.

And that someone was still glaring at him, obviously not the least bit repentant at the unnecessary worry he had been put through. Her eyes, in fact, were flashing at him, as if he were the one in the wrong, and her breast was heaving . . .

Blast the woman, why had she done the one thing guaranteed to destroy their chance for happiness together? The one, unforgivable thing, which made a mockery of all they had shared for the last week?

As much as he wanted to pull her into his arms and kiss her, there was now a wall between them that he could not surmount.

"Why?" he asked, his voice surprisingly hoarse. "Why did you not tell me that first day after I returned?"

He expected her to admit that she had deliberately kept him there to entrap him, but again her answer surprised him.

"Your niece was so happy—she told me she had never been happier in her life. Long before you returned from Scotland, I decided to do whatever necessary to give her a few more days of freedom, or, if you could have been persuaded to go in person to talk to the other girls, even an entire summer of freedom. Seeing how Marigold had improved in just one week, I thought myself justified in taking such measures."

"The end justifies the means?" he asked, not troubling to keep the disdain out of his voice.

"My intentions were good," she replied, her voice every bit as cold as his.

His own intentions had likewise been the best, but no one seemed ready to give him credit for that. "Did you never hear that the road to Hell is paved with good intentions?"

She blanched, as if he had struck her, and the subsequent pain in her eyes was too much for him to bear. Turning away, he said tiredly, "I shall wait in the carriage. Please send my niece out as soon as possible."

During the drive back to Colthurst Hall, his niece was sunk in gloom, but her spirits were no lower than Terence's. Every clip-clop of the horses' hooves was taking him farther and farther away from the deceitful widow—who, he was forced to admit, was the only woman he might have loved.

No, he corrected himself, there was no *might* about it; he had indeed fallen deeply in love with the lovely widow.

Now that his initial anger had faded somewhat, he realized he could eventually have forgiven her for having tricked him. After all, his niece had not been in any way endangered by the deception, and there was no way he could deny that Marigold's health had improved immeasurably during her stay in the dower house.

But what he would never be able to forget was that Alicia Lady Dunmire, the woman he had hoped would become Mrs. Kinderley, had made a complete and utter fool out of him. How many times had he seen the "boy" with the short black curls without recognizing his own niece?

Doubtless the widow—and Sybil and Algernon and even Marigold herself—had derived a great deal of amusement from the fact that he had been blind to what was going on right under his nose.

How could a man be expected to court a woman who had cast him in the role of buffoon? Who had deliberately and effortlessly turned him into a comical fellow who would be right at home in a farce?

He had no way of even knowing how bad the situation actually was. Had the younger children known "Clara's" real identity? Had the servants been in on the secret? Had the present Lord and Lady Dunmire been kept in ignorance, or had they known with whom their sons were playing?

"I suppose now you will never let me ride on a horse again," his niece said, interrupting his thoughts. She sounded even more miserable than he was feeling, although that seemed scarcely possible.

"Lady Dunmire gave me a list of things that young girls need," he replied. "I rather suspect that a riding horse will have a high priority." He was rewarded with a tremulous smile.

"And may I go back to Mrs. Wychombe's Seminary next term?"

"We shall see," he said, and she looked so downcast that he began to wonder if there might not be some way he could allow her to attend the school. If, for example, Sweeney took her there, then he himself would not be in danger of accidentally running into any of the Dunmires.

The rest of the drive was spent making desultory plans with his niece, and when they arrived back at Colthurst Hall, Terence gave Sweeney orders to unstrap Marigold's trunk from the back of the phaeton and load it into his own coach. Then he went to take his leave of his host and hostess.

Entering the house, he found so much hustle and bustle and scurrying about that he might have been forgiven for thinking the Prince Regent himself had come to call.

"It's a boy, sir," one of the footmen explained, a broad grin splitting his face. "Her grace has been delivered of a second son."

With a pang, Terence realized he had clearly extended his visit too long. Although his friends would doubtless say all that was polite, on such a joyous family occasion they must surely be wishing him in Jericho. But still, common courtesy demanded that he say his good-byes properly.

"Would you please tell his grace that I wish to speak with him at his convenience?" Terence said rather stiffly. "I shall wait in the library."

The footman returned so quickly, he must have taken the stairs three at a time, and he was still grinning. "Begging your pardon, sir, but his grace wishes you to join him. Said as how he wants to introduce you to the newest member of his family."

Feeling very much out of place, Terence followed the footman upstairs to the master bedroom, where Colthurst was waiting by the open door. "I understand my congratulations are in order," Terence said.

"Don't congratulate me," Colthurst said, slapping him on the back, "Elizabeth did all the work."

Stepping into the room, Terence saw a tableau that was almost painful in its beauty—not a duchess and a second son, but simply a mother holding her baby in her arms, and when Colthurst moved to join his wife and new son, it only made Terence more aware of how much he himself had lost.

Lost? Or deliberately thrown away?

Watching the new parents cooing to the baby that was a part of each of them, Terence realized that hurt feelings and wounded pride were really quite trivial matters.

So he had made a fool of himself—did that mean he had to compound his stupidity by renouncing the love of his life?

After expressing suitable admiration for the baby, Terence excused himself and returned to the stable, where he was delayed by second thoughts. What made him think that the widow would ever forgive him for the hateful things he had said to her? Maybe it would be better just to return to Kent, where he could, after a suitable interval had passed, write her a letter?

Abruptly realizing that he was falling back into his habit of worrying, something he had resolved not to indulge in any longer, he ordered a horse to be saddled for him before he could have second thoughts about the matter.

Leaving his coachman clearly bewildered and his niece gazing at him mournfully, he set out on the road that had become so familiar to him in the last week.

Just as the dower house came into view, however, his resolution failed him, and he reined in the horse. If only he had some inkling of the widow's feelings! Did she return his sentiments? Did she have any real interest in him, or had it merely been concern for his niece that had motivated her to act as if she enjoyed his company? If only she had given him some sign, some hint, some token of her affection.

But all she had given him was a list of rules for raising his niece. Disconsolately, he retrieved the crumpled paper from his pocket and stared at it gloomily. *Marigold needs her own riding horse,* the widow had written. *She needs friends her own age and she needs to be allowed to*—and here followed a long list of activities most girls were allowed to do and some that usually only boys were permitted—*and she needs freedom to make her own decisions, and*—

With great delight Terence read the last thing the lovely widow had written: *Marigold needs a mother.*

"But I *hate* darning stockings," Sybil blurted out, eyeing the basket of mending sitting between them on the settee.

"Which is exactly why I have chosen this as a suitable punishment for being deceitful," Alicia replied, handing her daughter a darning egg and taking one for herself.

"But there are so many to do," Sybil said indignantly, "and besides, I only wanted to help Marigold." She looked at her mother hopefully, but Alicia did not relent.

Doing her best to hide her own feeling of deep sadness at the thought of having alienated Mr. Kinderley forever, Alicia explained about the dangers of doing bad things for good reasons.

"Well," Sybil said, picking up a stocking and staring in disgust at the hole in it, "despite how angry Marigold's uncle was, if I had it to do over again, I would do the very same thing."

"Perhaps you will change your mind by the time we are done," Alicia said. In her own heart, she echoed her daughter's sentiments only up to a certain point. Yes, she would still want the girls to have concocted their scheme. But on the other hand, she could not help wishing that she had told

Mr. Kinderley the truth the minute he returned from Scotland. Given the strong attraction he obviously felt for her, surely he would have been agreeable to staying on in the neighborhood?

Suddenly her attention was caught by sounds of a commotion in the hallway outside the drawing room, and then the door was thrust open abruptly and Mr. Kinderley entered the room quite unannounced, a maid trailing behind him.

"I asked him to wait, m'lady," the girl said indignantly, but Mr. Kinderley cut her off before she could finish her explanation.

"I need to speak to you in private," he said, giving Alicia such an intense look, her heart began to race.

Eagerly dropping the darning, Sybil jumped to her feet, but Alicia caught her arm before she could escape from her assigned task.

"About this list you gave me," he said, pulling a crumpled piece of foolscap from his pocket, and seeing it, Alicia immediately released her daughter's arm.

Giggling and grinning, Sybil scurried from the room, pushing the maid out ahead of her and firmly shutting the door behind the two of them. Too late Alicia realized she should have kept her daughter beside her for protection.

Without any by-your-leave, Mr. Kinderley sat down on the seat Sybil had vacated. "So you think that young girls should be allowed to climb trees and go fishing and do other such activities," he began innocuously enough.

Alicia eyed him warily, then nodded her head, for the moment unable to speak without revealing her total loss of composure. Could he possibly have returned so that . . . ? But she refused to allow such wishful thinking to lodge itself in her mind. He had come for advice, that was all. There was no more significance to be read into his return visit than there was in Mrs. Pennywell's asking which kind of asters would look best in her garden.

"And you think I should buy Marigold her own horse," he continued, staring down at the paper in his hand.

Wishing very much that she had never given him that wretched list—or at least that she had never added the last four words—Alicia said in a voice that trembled despite her efforts to control it, "Yes, I do think your niece should have her own mount."

"I suspect you are right," he said, picking up the basket and setting it aside. Then before she would object, he moved so close that their knees were touching. "She tells me that Algernon says she has a great deal of natural ability as a rider."

Surreptitiously, Alicia eased away from Mr. Kinderley's knee. Just as casually, he shifted his weight slightly, and somehow managed to be even closer, although his leg was no longer quite touching hers.

"The only problem that I foresee with following your advice concerns the last item on the list. I have been racking my brain, but I cannot figure out any way to give Marigold a mother."

At his words, Alicia's last hopes were dashed, but before she could regain her composure and say something polite, Mr. Kinderley's arm was around her waist, and he was kissing her in a most determined way.

Breathless, she emerged from the kiss to hear him say, "Do you not suppose an aunt with strong mothering proclivities would do just as well?"

His question was clearly rhetorical, because without waiting for an answer, he kissed her again. This time her arms went around his neck, and she was not hesitant about kissing him back.

"Do you know," he said a long time later, "I

have given much thought to Sybil's cousins. They will doubtless feel much deprived if I steal you away from them."

"Do you plan to do that, Mr. Kinderley? Steal me away, I mean?" Alicia asked, looking up into smiling eyes.

"Oh, yes, but not to Gretna Green. I definitely prefer a more proper marriage, although I am not at all sure I can wait three weeks for banns to be called. Perhaps a special license would not be considered too shocking? And you must call me Terence."

What was scandalous was their present behavior. Without giving her a chance to answer his question about the boys, Mr. Kinderley—that is to say, Terence—once again cuddled her close and began kissing her.

But there was no problem, really. With plenty of visiting back and forth, everyone could be happy— perhaps not as happy as she was at this moment, but then few mortals achieved such earthly bliss.

Marigold sat in the hay in the stable loft and tried her best to keep all five kittens in her lap at the same time, clearly an impossible task. But even their antics could not cheer her up. After her uncle had left her with Sweeney, she had climbed up here to be private and had cried until she had no tears left. But all that had accomplished was to give her red, itchy eyes.

When her uncle returned, she would have to go with him, and if she had had any hopes of returning to Mrs. Wychombe's Seminary for the next term, she was enough of a realist to know that she had destroyed her chances forever. Just thinking about it made a few last tears well up in her eyes, but resolutely, she brushed them away.

"So here is where you are hiding," a familiar

voice called out, and Marigold turned to see Sybil's face peering at her from the top of the ladder. Then her friend scrambled up the rest of the way, threw herself down on the hay, and appropriated two of the kittens.

"Why are you so happy?" Marigold asked, "And what are you doing over here at Colthurst Hall? Have you run away from home?"

Sybil, who was grinning from ear to ear and looking quite like the cat who lapped up the cream, replied, "I am not sure I am going to tell a crosspatch like you. Such a long face when we are going to be sisters."

"Sisters?" Marigold asked, removing a kitten who was climbing up her sleeve. "Whatever are you talking about?"

"I should not tell you, for I was eavesdropping when I heard, although on the other hand, it is not my fault that my mother did not notice the connecting door was open to the blue room. It is not as bad as if I had deliberately opened it myself, just so I could listen and see what they were doing."

"So what were they doing? Sybil, if you do not tell me at once what you are talking about, I shall . . . I shall . . . I don't know what I shall do, but it will be truly dreadful."

"Well, actually we are not going to be sisters. When your uncle marries my mother, then we will be cousins, will we not?"

"When they marry? Oh, how wonderful!" But then Marigold's heart sank. "This is one of your little acting games, isn't it? Without quite telling a lie, you are trying to make me believe that my uncle has asked your mother to marry him."

"I shall swear on a Bible if you wish," Sybil said with a grin. "Although now that I think on it, your uncle did not actually make my mother an offer in form."

"I thought as much," Marigold said glumly.

"They just sat there kissing each other for the longest time, and then they began talking about special licenses and your uncle said he did not wish to wait for banns to be called."

"And your mother agreed?"

Sybil thought for a minute. "Do you know, I don't think she did, at least not while I was watching in. They started kissing again, and it was so boring, I came away to tell you. Really, I cannot fathom why grown-ups seem to delight in such things. If Algernon ever tries to kiss me, I shall draw his cork."

Marigold agreed that it was indeed beyond understanding.

The Treasure Hunt

by Mary Balogh

"I THINK I'LL GO DOWN to Brighton for the summer," the Honorable Sidney Hayes said with studied casualness. He was standing at the window in the library of his brother's house on Hanover Square, staring idly out. He swirled the remaining contents of his glass of brandy. "London grows dull—and empty of good society."

Jonathan Hayes, Viscount Whitley, looked up from his task of sorting through the mail on his desk. "To Brighton, Sid?" he said. "I thought you were coming to Esdale."

Sidney shrugged. "Everyone is going to Brighton," he said. "It is the fashionable thing to do."

"I suppose so." The viscount returned his attention to the papers strewn on his desk. "Well, if that is what you want to do. You are one-and-twenty years old and no longer in leading strings. I will be disappointed not to have you with me, though, Sid, it being the first time I will have been home in four years. What the deuce is Weston about, sending me a bill when I settled my account with him just last week?" He frowned down at the paper in his hand.

Sidney cleared his throat. "You might let Connie know that I'll not be home this year," he said. "You could tell her that I have had a personal invitation from Prinny or something like that."

The viscount looked up, the frown still on his face. "Constance Manning?" he said. "Why should I lie, Sid? Why not just tell her you are not coming home? And who has given you leave to call the Regent *Prinny*?"

Sidney did not reply. He found the contents of his glass suddenly more interesting than the activities going on beyond the window.

"She is expecting you?" his brother asked quietly.

"You know women." Sidney laughed lightly. "Always getting romantical notions. Connie is nineteen—twenty this summer—and her thoughts have turned toward matrimony."

"With you?" the viscount asked. "The two of you have always been close friends. You were inseparable until you went away to school. I understood that she was one of the main reasons why you have always gone to Esdale for the summer."

"Yes. Well." Sidney tipped his head back to drain his glass and turned to face the room in order to set it down. "Things changed last year, Jon. She has grown devilish pretty, I would have you know, and all last summer there was scarce a drop of rain or a cloud in the sky and her father was not too strict about chaperones and all that, Connie and I having been friends all our lives. And, well . . ."

"You did not touch her?" Lord Whitley's tone was sharp and he got to his feet.

"You mean bedded?" Sidney looked at his brother in some surprise. "Good Lord, no. What do you take me for? Just some kisses, Jon, and a whole lot of other foolishness."

"Like a declaration of undying love and a proposal of marriage, I suppose." One of the viscount's hands was playing with a paperweight on his desk while he looked keenly at his younger brother.

Sidney scratched the back of his neck. "The thing was," he said, "that it seemed a good idea at the time, Jon. And we have been writing to each other all winter and spring—we always have done so, you know, and I don't suppose it has occurred to Sir Howard that it is not quite proper now that Connie has passed girlhood. And. Well."

"You are not particularly articulate this morning, are you, Sid?" the viscount said dryly. "So she is expecting you to go home and make the proposal official and enter into a formal betrothal."

"On her birthday," Sidney said, wincing.

Viscount Whitley picked up the paperweight and slammed it back down on the desk top. "And so you are doing the cowardly thing and staying away altogether," he said. "And sending me as messenger boy. It is shabby behavior, Sid. Are you sure you are not honor bound to marry her?"

His brother smiled weakly. "I would make the devil of a husband," he said. "Connie deserves better. But I can't for the life of me break the news to her myself, Jon. The pen freezes in my hand when I try. And I know what will happen if I go home and try to tell her. It will be parson's mousetrap, that's what. But no one knows of our promises except Connie. We agreed to keep it a secret between the two of us."

"I should smash your nose—and your teeth for good measure," his brother said, his tone showing quite clearly that he was in no way joking.

Sidney flashed his nervous smile again. "She deserves better, Jon," he said. "You used to be fond of her yourself. She does deserve better, does she not? I don't know anyone I like better than Connie." He paused and looked imploringly at his brother. "You will tell her about Prinny and his invitation?"

The viscount swore with satisfying vehemence.

"You'll tell her," Sidney said, relief in his voice. "Let her down gently, Jon, will you? Connie is the last person on this earth I would want to hurt. I mean it. I'm deuced fond of her. Let her feel that somehow it is best for her to find someone else."

"It should not be difficult at least to convince myself that that is true," the viscount said.

"Yes. Well." Sidney's smile was a little broader. "You're a brick, Jon. I always could count on you. I was supposed to meet the fellows five minutes ago. We are going to watch the mill. Are you going? Should be a good one. I have a wager on that it will go twelve rounds at the very least. I leave for Brighton on Thursday. Will I see you before then?"

"Probably not," Lord Whitley said. "You will doubtless be too busy."

His brother flashed his grin again and was gone.

The viscount stood where he was, staring at the closed door. *A brick! You used to be fond of her yourself.* He swore with marvelous fluency and at far greater length than he had in his brother's hearing.

Constance Manning was sitting on the window seat in the parlor, her legs drawn up before her, her arms clasping them. It was raining outside. It had seemed to do nothing but rain all summer. It was July already.

Lady Manning, her mother, was seated beside the low fire, busy mending some household linen. Constance had laid her own embroidery aside several minutes before.

"Papa should be back soon," Lady Manning said. "I do hope Lord Whitley has accepted our invitation to dinner. It is dull always to see just the same faces, though I should not complain. We have amiable neighbors. But it will be good to see someone new. His lordship has not been home for several years."

Four, Constance thought. "And Sidney," she said. "I can hardly wait to see him, Mama. It seems like forever since he was home."

Lady Manning looked at her daughter over the tops of her eyeglasses before returning her attention to her sewing. "And Sidney," she said. "He always was the most amiable of young men once he grew past a mischievous boyhood. But it would be as well to remember, my love, that he is now a man grown and come of age and that you are no longer children, the two of you. It would be unwise to expect too much of his company. I don't want to see you disappointed or hurt."

Constance watched the rain slanting against the darker background of a tree and smiled to herself. She had kept the secret all over the winter and spring. No one knew but her—and Sidney. But soon everyone would know. Her birthday was three weeks and one day in the future. On her birthday Sidney would be talking with Papa and at the dance in the evening the announcement would be made. She was to be betrothed. And sometime soon— perhaps next summer—she was to be Mrs. Sidney Hayes. She would be married to her dearest friend and would be comfortable and happy for the rest of her life.

"He is to help me organize the treasure hunt for my party," she said. "And he has already reserved the opening set at the dance with me. And two sets at the assembly the week after next. Oh, Mama, I am so glad summer has come at last."

Lady Manning glanced at the window and at the fire and sighed. "If it can be called summer," she said. "Sometimes I wish we lived in Italy or the south of France. Anywhere but England."

"But it *is* summer," Constance said. "Everyone is coming home again."

Georgina Parkinson, her particular friend, had

come home from her second Season in London, and Marjorie Churchill from her first. And Rodney Churchill, Marjorie's brother, was down from Oxford, and Hadley Fleming was home from London. And now Sidney was home.

Constance hated every other season of the year except summer. Oh, that was not strictly true. Of course it was not, she thought guiltily, visualizing spring flowers and autumn leaves and winter frost on the trees. But every other season was lonely and filled with longings that made her feel ungrateful. For Papa, though he was a baronet, was not a wealthy man, and the little wealth he had, had been spent on physicians and medicines for Mama and on journeys for the two of them to sunnier climes. There was no money for a Season in London, for a come-out for his only daughter.

Only during the summer did the longings subside. Then everyone came home. Especially Sidney. Constance sometimes wondered how she would bear her life with patience if it were not for her enduring friendship with Sidney—and the deeper feelings that had developed between them the summer before.

"If the weather would just clear and warm up," Lady Manning said, "perhaps Papa would be able to move my chair outside some afternoons. I long to feel the sun on my face. But it begins to look as if there just will be no summer this year."

Constance turned her head and smiled affectionately at her mother. "It will come," she said. "The sun always shines for my birthday, Mama. And this year it must, because I have the treasure hunt all planned and only the outdoors will do for that."

"I hope so, my love," her mother said.

Constance turned her head back sharply to the window. "Papa is back," she said, watching the carriage proceed to the stable block without stopping first at the front doors for its passenger to alight. "He is going to be soaked. He has gone to the stables. I wonder if Sidney is with him."

But he was alone, she saw as he came striding in some haste toward the house a few minutes later, head bent against the wind and rain.

"Ah," he said, coming into the parlor a short while later and rubbing his hands together as he bent to kiss his wife's forehead, "my two ladies are wise enough to stay indoors and close to a fire. It is a miserable day."

"You are wet, my love," Lady Manning said, brushing at the sleeve of her husband's coat. "You should go and change before you catch your death."

"I thought you would want to know that you will be having your dinner guest," he said, smiling broadly. "You can step up the preparations, Doris. I was the first to call and therefore the first to issue an invitation."

"Oh, splendid," his wife said. "It will be so good to see a different face again."

"What?" Sir Howard Manning said. "The old faces are no longer good enough for you? Do you hear that, Connie, heh? We are no longer good enough for your mama but she must be entertaining viscounts."

"Oh, my love," Lady Manning said, laughing. "What nonsense!"

"And Sidney is coming too, Papa?" Constance asked eagerly.

"Eh?" he said. "Young Sidney? Oh, I daresay. There was no sign of him this morning. He was probably wise enough to keep his distance from all the callers." He chuckled.

"But you did invite him too, Papa?" There was a note of anxiety in Constance's voice.

"Young Sidney needs no invitation to come here,

girl," her father said. "The problem would be keeping him away, now, would it not, if we decided we did not want him here. Where are you off to now, Doris, eh? Can't you ask me to fetch you something but must be so independent? And Connie here too, just waiting to run and fetch for you."

Lady Manning was getting slowly to her feet with the aid of two canes. "I am going to consult Cook about dinner," she said. "And I am not a total invalid, my love, though you would breathe for me too if you could, I do believe."

"Well at least," he said, "let me take one of your arms. Let me be one of your canes, eh, Doris? Watch that rain, Connie." He chuckled as he left the room with his wife. "It might forget to fall if you do not keep an eye on it."

Constance smiled. She did a quick mental calculation. Five hours. He would be here in five hours and then all boredom would be at an end. Never a day passed when Sidney was at home—rain or shine—without his calling at the house on some pretext. Not that he ever needed a pretext.

She wished the Viscount Whitley was not coming too, but there was nothing she could do to prevent that. Anyway, four years had passed since he was last at home. She had been only fifteen then. A very young girl. She was a woman now. And he must be close to thirty. He was seven years older than Sidney. Eight-and-twenty.

She had always hero-worshiped him as a child, as had Sidney. And he had always treated them as an elder brother might—with careless indifference most of the time, sometimes with indulgence, sometimes with open irritation.

And then she had been fourteen and budding into womanhood long before Sidney was anything but a boy, and hero worship had begun to take on a different nature. And the following year, when she had been fifteen. It had been painful that year, her feelings for the handsome and fashionable and twenty-four-year-old Jonathan. She had not been able to sleep at night or look at him without aches in unfamiliar places or talk to him without stammering and feeling her mind turn totally blank—or think of him without taking flight into wild and soaring fantasies.

He had talked with her more than usual that summer and she had longed for his attention and found herself terrified by it whenever it came and quite unable to take advantage of it. She had always turned in noisy relief to Sidney, always her dearest friend and still a boy and quite unthreatening to her fragile and budding femininity.

Not that that summer pain had lasted long. Jonathan had left soon after the traditional Esdale picnic in July. He had left before her sixteenth birthday—and after trying to kiss her at the picnic.

It had been entirely her own fault. It was evening and growing dusk and she had wanted to be among the trees with him, where several other couples—all considerably older than she—strolled. Somehow it had happened—she must have maneuvered it so—and he had clasped her hand that was resting on his arm and dipped his head and kissed her. But his lips had only grazed her cheek because she had turned her head in panic, and had torn her hand from his arm and made a sound that was not quite squeak, not quite scream, but an approximation of both.

"Don't be frightened," he had said, grasping her arm, and smiling at her—as he would have smiled at a very young child. "You are too young, aren't you, Constance? Just a child still. You had better run along and play with Sidney."

She had run. And felt dreadful humiliation for days afterward. And enormous relief when Sidney had brought the news less than a week after the picnic that Jonathan had taken himself off to a friend's house, bored with life in the country. And then anger at his dallying with her and hatred at the fact that he had witnessed her humiliation. And shame that she had behaved in such a way as to make him see her as a child—as he always had.

She hated the thought of seeing him again now, Constance thought, grasping her knees more tightly and resting her chin on them. What if he remembered? But it was foolish to dread meeting him. It had all happened four years ago. Doubtless he had forgotten about it long before. Besides, everything had changed since then. She had grown up and Sidney had grown up. And this summer she was to be Sidney's betrothed.

She was going to be Lord Whitley's sister-in-law.

He would have forgotten, she persuaded herself, feeling her cheeks grow hot. Of course he would. But there was still discomfort in the knowledge that she must face him in less than five hours' time.

She must concentrate her mind on the positive, she thought. In less than five hours' time she would be seeing Sidney.

He was feeling nervous, the Viscount Whitley realized with some annoyance as he handed his hat and gloves to Sir Howard Manning's manservant that evening and waited to be announced. He had not felt nervous during any of the afternoon calls he had made earlier. And he had always been on friendly terms with the Mannings, as had his parents before him. Sir Howard could not have been more hearty with his welcomes that morning.

Perhaps if he had not had a particular message to deliver, he thought, he would be feeling quite in command of himself. Damn Sid! But no, he would be feeling apprehensive anyway, in all probability.

Somehow four years seemed to have rolled away in the familiar surroundings of home and it could all have happened yesterday. He just wished that at least he had not run away as he had. He wished he had stayed and had some sort of talk with her, made some sort of explanation or apology. An apology, certainly. She had been only fifteen years old.

She would have forgotten, he thought, running his hands over the sleeves of his blue coat and touching his neckcloth with light hands to make sure that the folds were still as they should be. Of course she would. As he had forgotten until he had made the decision to come home again this year. Though if he had forgotten, why he would have stayed away so long from a home he had always loved, he did not try to explain to himself.

The viscount followed the servant to the small, square drawing room, smiled, and walked through the doorway. Lady Manning, who had been a semi-invalid for as far back as he could remember, was on her feet, leaning heavily on Sir Howard's arm. Lord Whitley did not immediately look beyond them, but proceeded with his greetings.

"And Connie," Sir Howard said at last, the greetings over. "She has grown up since you saw her last, my lord, eh?"

She certainly had. She had been lovely and coltish when he had seen her last and fallen quite unexpectedly in love with the girl he had always thought of as a mischievous child, inseparable from his brother. She had been developing interesting curves, and her dark auburn hair, piled in curls instead of being worn in braids, had drawn attention to her large hazel eyes. She had been a lovely girl—a girl he had felt guilty for finding attractive.

She was beautiful now, those curves fully developed, though she was still slender, her hair cut into short soft curls that made her eyes appear even more enormous than they had seemed the time before. She was nineteen, he thought, soon to have her twentieth birthday. Definitely a woman.

Her eyes were looking beyond his shoulder when he first turned his own on her. Then she curtsied and looked at him. "My lord?" she said.

A curtsy? *My lord?* Things had certainly changed.

"Miss Manning?" he said and immediately felt uncharacteristically tongue-tied. He could not remember ever calling Constance *Miss Manning*.

"Where is Sidney?" she asked quickly. Her face was flushed, eager, a little anxious.

There had been kisses and promises, Sid had said, and letters exchanged all winter and spring. And she was expecting to be betrothed on her birthday. A thousand damnations to Sidney. How could he say the words and watch their effect on her face?

"Held back, I am afraid," he said, "by friends who insisted that he accompany them to Brighton for a few weeks."

He knew that he should not have mentioned a time limit. He should have given the message just as it was and allowed her to deal with it in her own way.

"For a few weeks?" she asked, and the disappointment in her eyes was quite unveiled. Had she spent time in London and acquired some town bronze, she would have learned how to make a mask of her face. "But he will be here for my birthday?"

"It is soon?" he asked.

"In three weeks' time," she said. "Oh, he promised to be here then."

"Then I am sure he will make every effort to do so," he said, mentally kicking himself for raising hope where there could be none. "How could he not? I am sure he would far prefer to be here now than in Brighton, but some invitations are not to be denied."

"Oh." She looked relieved. "Yes. And Sidney is so goodnatured that he never could put people off, even when he knew he ought. But he will come for my birthday. He will tell them that it is a former commitment." She smiled dazzlingly. "How glad he will be for the excuse. He hates to be away from Esdale during the summer."

And from me, her tone and expression said, though there was no apparent conceit in the girl. It was just that she had not learned to dissemble.

But Sir Howard was offering him a drink at that moment, and Lady Manning was asking him how he found Esdale after an absence of several years, and he withdrew his mind thankfully from a message that had been bungled.

There were to be no other dinner guests, the viscount was half relieved and half sorry to find. The relief came from the tiredness following his journey the day before, several visits both made and paid that day, and a lengthy interview with his bailiff. But he was sorry that he had to lead Constance in to dinner and address all his conversation to her and her parents. And yet, all the time he could not stop himself from remembering that she was the very girl who had kept him so long away, and from wondering if she remembered as clearly as he.

He grew cold at the thought. All that summer, while he had grown more and more besotted with her, he had been aware of her extreme youth and of her discomfort with him and of her obvious preference—though quite unromantic at that time—for Sid. And yet during the picnic, after having fought a battle with himself all afternoon, he had finally given in to temptation during the evening and lured her away among the trees and tried to steal a kiss from her there. The memory of her terror and revulsion made him almost squirm now, and he laughed more heartily at something Sir Howard said than the joke really called for.

And he could not stop himself from glancing at her frequently and wondering at the very powerful attraction that he still felt toward her. He had thought himself immune to the charms of young ladies, though many had been pitted against him during the past several years in London and elsewhere. Perhaps it was the very fact that Constance's charms seemed to be unconscious and were not in any way being directed at him. Or the fact that he knew her to be in love with Sidney. Forbidden fruit—and yet not forbidden. Sidney did not want her.

He did not stay long after dinner. He felt Constance's discomfort when Sir Howard had her seat herself at the harpsichord in the drawing room and sing a song for him. And he remembered that country hours were considerably earlier than town hours. But there was something he had prepared for during the afternoon without consciously knowing that he was preparing for it at all.

"I have invited two gentlemen and two ladies to come walking at Esdale with me tomorrow afternoon," he said. "Weather permitting, of course. I thought a walk up over the hill to the lake would be pleasant, especially since I have not made it myself for four years. Would you care to come too, Miss Manning, and make up numbers? The others are Miss Parkinson, Rodney and Miss Churchill, and Dennis Pernforce."

"Georgina and Marjorie?" she said. She hesitated for just a moment. "That would be pleasant, my lord. Thank you. Mama? Will you need me?"

"Gracious, no, my love," Lady Manning said. "I

shall be only too pleased for you to have an outing with some other young people. It has been lonely here all spring for Constance, my lord."

The girl flushed, he saw as he got to his feet to take his leave. She had been quiet all evening and apparently not quite at her ease. Because he was a near stranger and her parents' only guest? Because she was naturally shy? But he could recall her laughing and shrieking with Sidney at play and chattering away to him when she had not known herself overheard. Because she felt an aversion to him? Because she remembered?

It was impossible to say, he thought, making his bow to her, and allowing Sir Howard to accompany him to the door and watch him into his carriage. But tomorrow he would walk with her and see if he could find some answers. And he must see if there would be some way to break the news that he had not broken that evening.

Her face had been quite naked when she spoke of Sidney. Quite naked with love.

The next day was miraculously dry, though low clouds scudded across the sky and it was chilly for July.

"I am very happy for you, my love," Lady Manning said, "having an outing to look forward to."

But Constance was not at all sure that she looked forward to it. She liked Georgina and Marjorie and had always been comfortable with Rodney. Dennis Pernforce liked to prose on about new farming methods and about his livestock, though he was good at heart. But Lord Whitley himself? She was not particularly happy at the prospect of an afternoon spent in his presence. Her only hope was that he would choose to walk with Georgina or Marjorie.

She had not found the evening of his visit at all reassuring. He was every bit as darkly handsome as he had been four years before and quite as fashionable. The only difference—if there were a difference—was that he seemed more self-assured now, more distant from her world than he had ever been.

She had spent the evening thinking in embarrassment of the hero worship that had pained her not so many years before and of the utter cake she had made of herself at his picnic. And she had hoped and hoped that he did not remember. She had been quiet all evening—Papa had even remarked on the fact after the viscount had left—trying to impress upon him the fact that she was now quite adult, no longer that foolish girl.

If only Sidney had come, she thought with a sigh as she stood in the window of the front parlor, waiting for the Parkinson carriage to come for her, as had been arranged by note that morning. How she would be looking forward to going to Esdale if he were there! And she felt again the dreariness of knowing that she could not expect him for a few more endless weeks—when the summers seemed so very short anyway.

She tied the ribbons of her bonnet when she saw the carriage approach and hurried outside in order to save the coachman from having to get down from his perch to knock on the door. And she rode beside Georgina and agreed that yes, it was wonderful to have his lordship at home again. And yes, he was excessively handsome, or at least, she thought he was—she had not particularly noticed. The lie sounded so false that Georgina burst into merry laughter and Constance was forced to join in.

"Yes," she said. "He is indeed handsome, Georgie. But I like Sidney better for all that." Sidney was shorter than the viscount and had sandy hair and a round, good-natured face. He would probably be stocky by the time he reached middle years, while Jonathan would always be slim.

She spent the next several minutes lamenting to her friend the fact that thoughtless acquaintances had kept Sidney from home by insisting that he accompany them to Brighton.

"But he will be home for my birthday," she said. "That is all that really matters."

"I hope so, for your sake," Georgina said. "And you have talked so much about your birthday, Connie, that I have wondered if you have any secret plan. Some plan concerning Sidney, perhaps?" She looked archly at her friend.

But Constance only blushed and changed the subject. And then the carriage was approaching the large house at Esdale and they could see that the others were there before them.

Please God, Constance thought as Rodney Churchill handed her down to the cobbled terrace before the main doors. But then he turned to perform the like task for Georgina and tucked her arm through his.

"You were going to tell me about that evening at Vauxhall, Georgie," he said.

Marjorie was already smiling politely at some story Dennis Pernforce was telling her. Constance's heart sank.

"We might as well set off without delay," Lord Whitley said. "There will be tea at the house afterward." He smiled at Constance and offered her his arm.

It was a pretty walk, up over a wooded hill past several follies and down the other side again beside a rushing cascade that emptied itself at the bottom into the lake, the bubbling water passing beneath an arched wooden bridge. It was a walk Constance had made a hundred times before, though more often than not she had passed along there at a pace less sedate than a walk. The hill and the woods had been a favorite play area for her and Sidney.

"The weather has cooperated," the viscount said. He looked up at the heavy clouds. "Well, almost."

"Yes," Constance said.

"We will hope that this is the herald of good things to come," he said. "Warm sunshine for the next two months at least."

"Yes."

"We have earned it," he said. "We have scarce had a fine day since May."

"Yes."

"Have we now exhausted the weather as a topic?" he asked, his voice sounding faintly amused.

Constance looked up at him in some mortification. She could not even carry on a polite conversation with him. He would think her rustic indeed.

"But it is good for the crops," she said. "The rain I mean. But then, of course, the warmth of the sun is needed now too, my lord, to make them grow." Her voice sounded stilted to her own ears. Why was it that normally she did not have to think of what she was going to say, whereas now she could think of nothing that might be of interest to the Viscount Whitley?

"*My lord*," he said. "*Miss Manning*. We never used to be so formal. Can we go back to being Jonathan and Constance, do you suppose, without shocking sensibilities?"

The other two couples must be running a race, Constance thought. They were already well ahead, out of earshot.

"I suppose so," she said. "It does not seem quite right, though, calling you—Jonathan."

"But you did it," he said, "without tying your tongue quite in knots. Tell me, have you been remembering yesterday and today what I have been remembering? Has the same memory been embarrassing both of us?"

Oh, dear. "Yes," she said.

"I have been thinking about it this morning," he said, "and it seemed to me that the best possible policy was to bring it out into the open. I did not apologize at the time. I apologize now, Constance. I was an impudent puppy although I was old enough to know better. And you were a child. Will you forgive me?"

"Yes," she said. But she looked up at him in some surprise. "But I always thought the fault was mine."

"Yours?" He looked down at her and frowned. "How on earth could it have been your fault? You have forgiven me. Shall we now forget it and be comfortable together?"

"Yes," she said. But she could feel herself flush and was not at all sure she felt even one little bit more comfortable. She had been a child, he had just said. That was all she had been—someone to be teased. And now the whole thing had been dismissed just as if it had not caused worlds of pain.

"Well, then," he said, "that is a relief."

"Yes," she said.

"And it is wonderful to be home again," he said, looking at the trees, which had closed in about and above them. "I did not realize how much I had missed it."

"There must be so many reasons to stay away," she said wistfully. "It must be marvelously exciting to be in London, especially during the Season."

"Yes and no," he said. "It palls on one after a while, Constance, all the social activity. Sometimes one pauses to wonder if that is life—if it has nothing more meaningful to offer. But there is excitement in it, yes."

"Balls," she said, "and the theater and the opera. Sidney says there is never a dull moment."

"I believe Sidney enjoys the whirl of the Season," he said. "But then he is young. I enjoyed it all myself at his age. Not that I feel quite in my dotage." He chuckled. "But there comes a time when one needs more of life."

The idea of Jonathan's being in his dotage was amusing. Constance smiled.

"You would like to experience it all?" he asked, looking down into her eyes. "Do you feel that you have missed something, Constance?"

She shook her head. "I am well content here," she said. "I have far more to be thankful for than thousands of other poor souls. And Sidney tells me all about it in his letters. And Georgina in hers."

He held her eyes for a long moment. "It is not quite the same as being there for yourself, though, is it?" he said. "Perhaps one day you will be able to dance at Almack's."

"Sidney is going to—" she began, but she stopped abruptly. It was a secret.

"Is he?" he asked. "Are you missing him, Constance?"

But she was saved from having to answer. They had reached the top of the hill and could look out over the tops of the trees to the lake below and the country beyond. The other two couples were standing there gazing about them and agreeing that it was all very magnificent.

"I can remember all the picnics down there," Marjorie said, indicating the lake. "There was no more exciting event during the summers, was there? Of course, we were children in those days and not allowed to attend any assemblies or evening parties."

"I remember your standing up in one of the boats, Rodney," Georgina said, "and falling into the water. It was a blessing you could swim. As it was, all our mamas screamed."

Rodney chuckled. "Trust you to remember such an ignominious incident, Georgie," he said. "I was showing off for that little cousin of Hancock's. The one with the blond ringlets. As it happens, I believe she was impressed by my swimming skills and the fact that I stood on the bank afterward with suitable nonchalance although I felt as if I had icicles hanging from me."

They all laughed.

"My lord?" Marjorie looked brightly at the viscount. "Is there any chance that you are planning to revive the tradition this summer? There really was nothing to match the Esdale picnics."

"I had better not whisper to Mama that you asked that, Marjie," her brother said. "She would scold for a week."

"Then we will all agree that it was my idea," Lord Whitley said. "And I cannot think of anything I would enjoy more. Shall we say next week? That should give me enough time to send out the invitations and dust off the boats, and it should give my cook time to plan the feast."

"Oh, wonderful!" Marjorie said, clapping her hands like the child she tried not to be. "What a splendid idea, my lord. What put it into your mind?"

"The sight of the lake," he said, "and the knowledge that it is July, though it does not quite feel like it. And present company."

They set off down the hill toward the lake in the same order as before. Much as she tried not to, Constance was remembering that last picnic again and its disastrous ending. She wished Marjorie had not suggested its revival. And yet it had always been the pinnacle of summer fun.

"I wish Sidney was coming sooner than he is," she said with a sigh. "I wish he could be here for the picnic. He will be disappointed to know that he has missed it."

"Yes, I daresay," he said. "You are missing him,

mers, has he not?"

"I will have to be patient," she said. "Three weeks will pass soon enough. I have already waited through a whole winter and spring." She should not have added those final words, she thought. No one knew of the ties that bound her and Sidney.
knew of the ties that bound her and Sidney.

"You live up to your name," he said with a smile. "But what if he does not come? What if his friends persuade him to stay in Brighton all summer? That is where the Regent spends his summers, you know. There is a great deal of social life there."

"Oh," she said, raising her voice above the increasing roar of the cascades as they gathered momentum beside the path, "he will be here. Nothing would keep him away on my birthday. We have all sorts of plans. You do not know."

He merely looked at her, his gray eyes steady on hers, and she could feel herself flushing.

"You do know, don't you?" she asked.

"Yes," he said.

She bit her lip and felt annoyance with Sidney. There had been so many occasions when she had been bursting to tell someone—sometimes Mama, sometimes Georgina. But she had kept the promise of secrecy.

"Well, then," she said, "you know that he will come."

"And what are your plans?" he asked. "Apart from the one I already know of?"

The other two couples had walked across the bridge without stopping and were strolling along the bank of the lake. But the viscount and Constance came to a halt at the high center of the bridge and gazed back up at the cascades and down to the water foaming under the bridge. There was a weeping willow just beside the waterfall, trailing its branches down into the water, that Constance had always considered especially picturesque.

"There is to be a treasure hunt," she said. "A long one. It will take at least an hour and perhaps two. I have spent weeks thinking up clues. It will take a long time to set up, but Sidney is going to help me. It will be great fun. And there is to be dancing in the evening. The drawing room is small but we will all squeeze in there. Mama is to play the harpsichord. Sidney has already reserved the opening set with me. At a country dance!" She laughed.

"And what is the treasure to be?" he asked.

She flushed and laughed. "That is the part I have not decided upon yet," she said. "Nothing of any great value, I suppose. The pleasure of the hunt is to be its own reward. At least, I hope so. If it rains, everything will be ruined."

"What will you do if it rains?" he asked.

She pulled a face. "Play charades and cards, I suppose," she said. "The usual things. I want my birthday to be special."

"It will be," he said. "It will not rain, I promise."

She looked up at him and smiled.

"Am I invited?" he asked.

"Of course." She felt herself flush anew. "I should have sent you an invitation yesterday or today. I thought perhaps you would consider the whole thing childish or tedious."

"Neither," he said. "I shall hunt with energy and determination and find your treasure, whatever it turns out to be."

He was standing with his arms draped over the rail of the bridge, one foot resting on the lowest rail. He was looking back over his shoulder at her and smiling. For some reason Constance felt breathless. But no, she would not give in to such nonsense. She was a grown woman now, not a girl in need of a hero. Besides, she loved Sidney. Jonathan was to be her brother-in-law.

"Constance?" he said. "If by some chance Sidney is delayed, will you allow me to help you set up the treasure hunt? And to dance the opening set with you?"

"But he will be here," she said. And yet the look in his eyes gave her the first twinge of uncertainty she had felt. "Of course he will. We are to be—"

"Yes, I know," he said, pushing himself away from the rail and offering her his arm again. "We had better catch up to the others before they disappear entirely over the horizon."

She had not noticed how almost alone they were. She had been alone so many times with Sidney that she never gave much thought to chaperones. But there was a great difference between Sidney and Jonathan. She had never been particularly aware of Sidney's physical presence, which was perhaps a strange admission when he had kissed her several times the summer before and they were planning to marry. But it was true. She was just enormously comfortable with him. She was very aware of Jonathan, of his tall, slim body—with muscles in all the right places—of his dark hair beneath his hat and of his handsome features. Of the musky smell of his cologne.

She felt very much alone with him. As alone as she had felt among the trees during the evening of the last Esdale picnic. And almost as panic-stricken. Almost. But she was a lady now, not a frightened girl.

"Yes," she said, and she slipped an arm through his and hoped fervently that he would not notice that it was trembling. She must think of Sidney, she told herself firmly. "Sidney is not going to be here for the village assembly either," she said. "It is most provoking. I would like to have a word with those friends of his and tell them just how inconsiderate they have been."

She set her mind to making conversation.

Summer came the day of the picnic. There had been almost no rain for the week before, but the weather had been generally dull with only tantalyzing moments of sunshine before the clouds moved over again. On the day of the picnic it would have been difficult to find one cloud in the sky. It was sunny and hot.

It had been the custom of his parents—and Lord Whitley had kept it after them—to invite the whole neighborhood to the Esdale picnic, children and all. Hence its popularity, he had always thought. It was no quiet, sedate affair. And no short affair, either. Although the meal provided was always called tea, it was in reality a veritable feast, and no one ever felt inclined to go home in search of dinner when evening came. Usually it was only dusk and the prospect of a totally dark walk back to the house that finally persuaded people to leave.

The picnickers were always spread over a wide area about the lake. There were cricketers on one large open space and croquet players on a smoother stretch of lawn. There were children beside the bank of the lake, engaged in organized races. Later there would be children everywhere. Their mothers and the elderly sat on the bank and basked in the sunshine and admired the scenery. The three boats were always much in demand on the lake.

Constance was helping Mrs. Sherman with the races, but the viscount strolled over to her.

"As soon as I can wrestle one of the boats free," he said, "I will take it out for a row—if you will come with me."

Constance had a child hanging from each arm and two or three more calling to her. She smiled at him. "Thank you," she said. "That would be heavenly."

But he would not set too much store by the enthusiasm of her answer, he thought as he strolled away to see to it that Lady Manning's chair was in full sunshine—though Sir Howard could always be relied upon to see to his wife's comfort. Constance would clearly be thankful to anyone who would take her away from the children for a few quiet minutes.

He had put anger behind him in order to enjoy the picnic. But all week he had been angry—against both Sid and himself. Constance clearly trusted implicitly that Sid would come, and she was just as clearly deeply in love with him. And yet, he had not had the courage or the decency to come in person to explain to her. He had thought it good enough to send a messenger instead. And the viscount was angry with himself. He should have dragged Sid home by the shirt collar if necessary, instead of taking on such a distasteful and impossible task.

How was he to tell her? Or was he not going to tell her? Was he just going to allow her to be crushed on her birthday, waiting for the arrival of a faithless lover, and realizing by gradual degrees that he was not coming?

Damn Sid, he thought for surely the thousandth time, feeling anger well up in him again and putting it determinedly aside while he squatted in the midst of a group of elderly women and proceeded to charm them into laughter.

A whole hour passed before he finally managed to secure an empty boat. By that time, the formal races had ended and the informal ones had begun to the accompaniment of a great deal of shrieking. He handed Constance into the boat and rowed out onto the lake, into peace and tranquillity.

"The children did not tear you limb from limb?" he asked.

"No." She laughed. "I often help at the school, you know. I like children, even though they can be dreadfully noisy little fiends."

"I did not know that," he said. "About your helping, I mean."

She should have been dancing all winter and spring, he thought, looking into her bright and pretty face and at her auburn hair, which was catching the sunlight beneath the brim of her straw bonnet. And shopping on Bond Street. And gazing about her from a box at Covent Garden. Instead of which, she had been teaching other people's children.

"I do not sit at home all day long embroidering," she said with a laugh. "Everyone is having such a marvelous time, Jonathan. I am so glad you decided to resurrect the Esdale picnic."

"Are you?" he asked. He had thought of it long before Marjorie Churchill had mentioned it, but had not been sure that he wanted to revive the memory of what had happened at the last one. "And are you having a marvelous time?"

"Sidney has brought me out on the lake several times," she said. "But he does not row as well as you. He tends to go in circles." She laughed. "He claims that his right arm is stronger than his left."

Sidney again. He should tell her now, he thought.

"I wonder what he is doing at this moment," he said. "Bathing in the ocean? Out strolling? Getting ready to attend some party at the Pavilion this evening? I suppose he will wangle an invitation there sooner or later. Everyone does. He will find it difficult to drag himself away."

"Well," she said, "if he must be there, he might as well enjoy himself. Though if he were given the choice, I am sure he would a million times rather be here. I hope he comes a few days before my birthday instead of just the day before. I have some clues I wish to discuss with him." She smiled. "You must think it strange that I am so absorbed with plans for a mere birthday party. But it is the first I have had in years. And it is to be a very special one—as you know."

Lord Whitley turned craven and changed the subject. And knew beyond a shadow of a doubt that he would throttle his brother if only fate would set them within arm's reach of each other at that very moment.

He was in love with her again, he realized before he took her back to shore, when their conversation had come to an end and she had turned her face up to the sun and closed her eyes. She was utterly beautiful and enchanting and—sweet. It was a weak word and if anyone had asked him a few weeks before if he would look for sweetness in a woman, he would have laughed. But Constance was sweet and innocent and adorable. And he knew why he had stayed away for four years and why he should have stayed away for four more.

She was in love with Sid, and he—poor fool— was in love with her.

He joined no particular group for the rest of the afternoon and evening, but moved about making sure that everyone was comfortable and had enough to eat, making sure that everyone was happy. And he stood against a tree as the sun fell lower in the western sky, listening to the singing that one group had begun—a strange and happy mixture of folk songs and hymns—and watching a group of young people talking and laughing down by the boats. A few couples strolled along the lake front or among the trees—that old haunt of lovers—intent on a few moments to themselves. Constance was strolling at the water's edge with Hadley Fleming.

He smiled at a small group of ladies, who nodded and raised their hands in greeting to him, and felt longing wash over him. If only he had not frightened her out of her wits when she was a mere child at this very place and on this very occasion, and if only she had not fallen in love with Sid and Sid had not made promises to her—then perhaps he could be strolling off among the trees with her now and kissing her. Perhaps he could have been the one to make her twentieth birthday in two weeks' time a very special occasion. But wishes were pointless.

No one ever gave a definite signal to end the Esdale picnics. Always it seemed that everyone decided at the same moment that it was time to head back to the house and the carriages. This year was no exception. The singers were on their feet, brushing at skirts and breeches to rid them of clinging grass; mothers were rounding up tired and noisy children; couples were linking arms, and the slow trek back to the house was beginning. The sunset was a glorious orange, the lake a shimmering gold.

Constance was bending over her mother, tucking a shawl about her legs before Sir Howard began to push her wheeled chair along the worn path. Constance straightened up and watched them go— and Lord Whitley gave in to impulse.

"Constance?" he called. "May I escort you back to the house?"

"Yes." She turned toward him, her face shadowed in the dusk. Her voice sounded a little breathless. "Thank you."

But he could not go immediately. It would have been unmannerly not to be the last to leave the lake, and one youngster was displaying a scraped knee to his mother, and it had to be washed off with lake water before they set out in pursuit of everyone else. And then the viscount noticed that one of the boats had not been securely tied and would probably float away if he did not retie it himself.

The sky was turning a dark pink by the time he and Constance finally followed the trail of distant voices and laughter.

"I think," he said, "it was a success."

"Oh, yes," she assured him. "It was. Everyone will hope and hope that you will be home next year and every year so that it can be repeated. It has been much missed."

"And will you hope and hope that I will be home next year?" he asked, and then wished he had not.

"Yes," she said very quietly after a moment's hesitation. "It was a wonderful day." She shivered.

"You are cold," he said, looking down at her flimsy sprigged muslin dress.

"No," she said hastily.

But he withdrew his arm from hers and removed his coat. He wrapped it about her shoulders and held it there until she lifted her hands to clasp it at her bosom.

"Thank you," she said, looking up at him. "But there was no need."

The dying light of the sun caught at her face. His arm was still about her shoulders. Her lips were parted and her eyes dark and huge. He closed his hand about her shoulder and lowered his head toward hers until his forehead touched the brim of her bonnet. He kept it there and swallowed before lifting his head again and removing his hand.

"No," he said, "we do not want any such memories of this picnic, do we, Constance? Forgive me?"

"Yes," she said, her voice a whisper. "There is nothing to forgive."

And they walked on side by side, not touching and not talking, the sky above them black and star-studded, the sky ahead of them a deep purple and red.

But there would be memories anyway, he knew. Bitter memories of what might have been. And despite himself he was sorry that he had not drawn her right into his arms and held her slender, shapely body against his, and kissed her mouth. And told her that Sid was not coming home but that he would love her in his brother's place and make her a thousand times happier than Sid would ever have done. He would take her to London and Bond Street and Almack's. And he would give her children of her own to teach and enjoy.

He was engaging in midsummer madness, he thought, walking silently at Constance's side and noticing thankfully that around the bend just ahead of them they would be in sight of the house. He could already hear all the bustle of people finding their own carriages on the terrace and calling out good-night greetings to one another.

Constance had always enjoyed the dances at the assembly rooms in the village inn. Probably, she thought, it was for much the same reason as she had always loved the Esdale picnics. Everyone came to the assemblies, regardless of social status, and so there were not just the same few families to mingle with as there were at all the parties in private homes. Of course, most private homes were far too small to accommodate such numbers.

Constance helped her father hand her mother down from the carriage outside the inn and then hurried inside alone to find Georgina. Papa was going to carry Mama up the stairs, despite Mama's protests.

She should not have been looking forward to this particular assembly, Constance thought. When she had originally heard about it, she had written to Sidney and he had asked in his reply to reserve the opening set and the supper set with her. Not that there was any need to reserve sets ahead of time at a country assembly, but even so, it felt good to know that one was assured of certain dances.

But now Sidney would not be there. There had been no letter from Brighton and she could only assume that he would come within the next few days—certainly well before her birthday, she hoped. She spotted Georgina in the ladies' withdrawing room and was glad after all that she had decided to wear her new lemon-colored silk. She had worried that perhaps she would be overdressed for a village assembly, but Georgina was wearing a gown that must surely have been purchased in London. Constance put determinedly from her mind her disappointment that Sidney was not there and the strange, quite unfounded fears that had begun to nudge at her.

"You look beautiful, Georgie," she said. "A London gown?"

She looked eagerly about her when she entered the long assembly room on the upper floor of the inn a short while later, arm-in-arm with her friend. But he was not there yet. And she felt guilty when she realized that she was feeling eager after all and that she had looked specifically for him when there were any number of other friends and acquaintances to be nodded and smiled at.

He was Sidney's brother. That was all. And it was pure courtesy that had prompted him outside church on Sunday to remark that he had heard there were to be waltzes at the assembly and to ask her if she would reserve the first and the last for him—just as if it were any London ball. She adored waltzing. Sidney had taught her the steps, though he often said that he had two left feet and occasionally she had to agree with him. Jonathan would surely dance well. She could scarcely wait. If only he did not arrive too late to dance the first waltz.

Georgina had told her that most gentlemen did not deign to arrive at London balls until late.

Hadley Fleming rushed to her side to ask for the first set of country dances, while Rodney Churchill was asking Georgina.

And then she saw him. He was not late after all. The dancing had not even begun. He was smiling and talking with Mr. Sherman and Papa. And looking so very handsome in pale-blue knee breeches and a darker blue coat with silver waistcoat and very white linen that Constance's eyes widened.

"All the ladies in London ogled him at all the balls," Georgina murmured into her ear. "I used to enjoy remarking carelessly that he was our neighbor. And I used to positively preen myself when he led me into a set, as he occasionally did." She chuckled. "I wonder who will eventually net him."

"I don't know," Constance said, and she felt that curious fluttering in the pit of her stomach that she had felt on the evening of the picnic when he had been walking home with her and had stopped to wrap his coat about her shoulders—though it had not been the cold that had made her shiver—and had kept his arm about her and almost kissed her.

She had been very thankful at the time that he had not. She was, after all, Sidney's betrothed, even if no one but the two of them—no, three of them—knew of it. And yet, she had dreamed that night, before she went to sleep, that he had not held back but had allowed his lips to touch hers. And the dream had been so pleasant that she had dreamt it many times since. And had felt distressed and bewildered and ashamed of herself. She was to be twenty years old the following week but she could still indulge in the fantasy of hero worship—while she loved and planned marriage with another.

No, she should not be looking forward to this assembly, she decided.

But she was. And she danced with Hadley and Rodney and Dennis and felt happy and exhilarated. She scarcely stopped smiling, she knew, and was dazzling Dennis, if not her other two partners. And yet she could not stop herself, for the fourth set was to be a waltz. And he had danced the first three sets with older, married ladies. She was to be the first young lady he had danced with.

She could feel all eyes on them when he bowed over her hand and led her onto the floor. And she knew that it was neither imagination nor conceit that made her think so, for he was the focus of almost every eye. Constance had heard some ladies behind her remark earlier that it was very condescending of the viscount to put in an appearance at all. He was wearing the same cologne as he had worn before, she thought irrelevantly, when he turned to face her and took her hand in his. Something musky and wonderfully masculine.

"You dance well," he said. "I have been watching you. Do you waltz well too?"

"Sidney taught me," she said, but her words for some reason set him to laughing and her to joining in.

"So what is the answer to my question?" he said at last. "*Do* you waltz well?"

She found herself laughing again, but then the music began and she discovered that *he* certainly did, better than any of the other partners she had ever waltzed with. Her slippers felt as if they scarcely touched the floor.

"Your answer is yes," he said. "You do not need to say it."

She found herself smiling and blushing, and enjoying herself so very much that when he twirled her about a corner, she closed her eyes and felt that she could keep on turning and twirling for the rest of the night.

He was laughing at her, she saw when she opened her eyes. "Constance," he said, "you are wonderfully refreshing. If you had spent time in London ballrooms, you would have learned that the fashion is to look bored, as if you had been to so many entertainments that none had any further surprises or delights to offer."

She sobered instantly. Oh, what a child he must think her. And she had tried so hard when he first came home to show him that she was now a sophisticated lady, quite a different person from that foolish girl who had taken fright one evening at a mere kiss.

"Ah," he said, "I said the wrong thing, did I not? Come, smile again. You looked so very pretty."

Pretty. Girls looked pretty. *Young* girls.

"Have you heard from Sidney?" she asked.

He shook his head.

She looked into his eyes, eyes that had made her doubt on other occasions. And she wanted to ask the question but could not do so. *He is not coming, is he?* she wanted to ask him. But she was afraid of his answer. For if Sidney was not coming and had not written to her either, she could not dare to look into the future and all its bleakness. Only the knowledge of her secret betrothal and the prospect of the future lived in comfort with her dearest friend had helped her to be content with her lot. And she tried so hard to be contented, not to long for what she could not have. She had tried so hard during this spring and the last not to envy Georgina too much.

"Sometimes," she said, "he forgets to write. And I suppose there is little point in doing so when he is to be here shortly."

"The weather has held," he said, "for a whole week. And it will hold for at least another one. I have put in a special order for your birthday."

"Oh, have you?" she said. "That is very obliging of you, I am sure. I did not know that God was your particular friend."

"You did not?" he said, raising his eyebrows while his eyes laughed down into hers. "Did you not see me at church on Sunday? Did I not speak to you afterward?"

She smiled again, and even laughed when he twirled her about a corner once more, and they talked nonsense for the rest of the set. Glorious, delicious nonsense that had Constance thinking that a London ball could not have been more exciting.

It really was good to be home, Lord Whitley was finding. It was true that the assembly rooms at the village inn were plainer than even the shabbiest ballroom in London, and true that the music provided by the pianoforte was far less rich than that of an orchestra, which he was more accustomed to. And the dancers were less elegant and fashionable.

And yet there was a warmth and a friendliness about the village assembly that went far beyond anything he had experienced elsewhere. His neighbors were genuinely pleased to see one another—and him, he felt. And of course, Constance had never been at a London ball.

If he had not known better, he would have believed that she was thoroughly enjoying the evening. She danced every set and smiled and glowed at her partners. He had been delighted to discover earlier that the last waltz was also the last dance of the evening. He looked forward to that last dance with eager anticipation.

But he did know better, of course, about Constance's true state of mind. He knew that she loved Sid and that she awaited his arrival within the next few days with eagerness and impatience. Perhaps the fact that she thought there were only a few days left accounted for her **high** spirits this evening. Would there were another **cause**!

"At last," he said when they came together again and the final waltz began. But the words sounded too fervent. "I danced the waltz after supper with Miss Ferguson and had to concentrate very hard on avoiding her feet with each step."

She laughed. "Unkind!" she said.

"Yes. I admit it." He laughed too. "But it is true, nevertheless."

She laughed again. Her cheeks were flushed and her eyes shone. "I wish this night could go on forever and ever," she said.

"Do you?" There was something about her eyes. His own locked on them and he was suddenly intensely aware of her. All else about them receded from sight and mind.

The fading of her smile brought him back to reality. "Until Sidney comes, at least," she said, and her smile this time was brighter, less dreamy. "I shall tease him about all he has missed in the past two weeks and assure him that nothing he can tell me about Brighton will make me envious."

The moment was gone. They danced in silence for most of the set, talking only occasionally. She was light on her feet and slender and warm to the touch. She smelled faintly of soap rather than any of the heavy perfumes he was more accustomed to with fashionable ladies. Her auburn curls were shining.

He wondered what might have happened if he had not tried to steal a kiss from her too early— when she was only fifteen years old—but had had the patience to wait for her to grow up. What might have happened if he had come home each summer to court her slowly? But nothing would be different, he knew. For always there had been Sid. The two of them had shared an extraordinary friendship ever since early childhood. It was inevitable that she fall in love with him eventually. He himself, on the other hand, had always been too old for her.

"Oh," she said suddenly, looking up into his face with those large hazel eyes, which could always jolt him into heightened awareness. "The music is at an end? Already?" And then she flushed rosily and he smiled. At least she seemed to have lost her aversion to him.

"I am afraid so," he said. "May I escort you down to your carriage? And does it take people as long to get into their carriages and drive away as it used to take?"

She laughed. "But of course," she said.

Everyone always stayed to the very end of local assemblies, and so everyone's carriage or gig was jostling for position at the same time outside the inn. But there was never the chaos and display of bad temper that one might expect of such a situation. Large numbers of people always remembered precious tidbits of gossip or important messages that they had found no time to confide in a whole evening of gossip and dancing.

And so the assembly rooms always became the domain of the ladies and the street outside of the men. The young people always crowded the stairway connecting the two. There was inevitably a lapse of at least half an hour between the ending of the last set and the drawing away of the carriages.

"Shall we join the crush on the stairs?" the viscount asked. "Or shall we push through to the street and take a stroll until everyone decides that it really is time to go home?" He was powerfully reminded of an occasion four years before when he had suggested that she stroll with him. He expected her to choose the crush on the stairs.

"A stroll sounds lovely," she said. "Do you suppose it is cool outside?"

It was. And crowded and noisy. But he took Constance's arm through his and they strolled away from the crowd of men filling the pavement between the inn wall and the carriages. They strolled past shops and houses all the way to the church at the end of the village street. But there was still no sign, the viscount saw when he glanced back, that the crowd was dispersing.

He drew her to sit beside him on the low churchyard wall, her arm still through his. They had not moved out of sight of the inn or the men on the pavement outside it. And yet, the sound of voices was muted. They seemed alone. He covered her hand with his own and caressed her fingers. And he wished he could think of something to talk about so that he would resist temptation.

And yet, was it temptation? Temptation to do something he ought not to do? Sid was not coming back. Soon she would know that—she would know it already if only he had more courage, or Sid more sense of decency. In reality, she was neither promised nor betrothed to any man. Was it not more fear of rejection than reluctance to give in to temptation that held him back?

He lifted her hand and held it to his lips for a long moment. She was looking down at her lap, he saw.

"I have enjoyed this evening more than any other event I can remember," he said. "Especially the first and the last waltz."

He did not think she was going to answer him. Or look at him. Or snatch her hand away from him.

"So have I," she said at last, her voice little more than a whisper.

He returned her hand to his lips and turned it over and kissed her palm.

But the voices outside the inn had become louder and more boisterous, a sure sign that the young people and the ladies were coming outside and the carriages beginning to fill.

"We had better go back," he said, "before your father calls out the militia."

"Yes," she said. He drew her to her feet, gave her his arm again, and walked with her back toward the inn.

They did not speak at all, though the silence between them was not an uncomfortable thing. And she did not once raise her eyes to his until he was handing her into her father's carriage, where her mother was already seated.

"Good night, Jonathan," she said softly, finally looking into his eyes, her own wide and unsmiling.

"Good night, Constance," he said, and he turned away to bid farewell to Sir Howard and Lady Manning.

She was twenty years old, Constance thought, curled into the window seat of the parlor, her hands clasped tightly about her knees, and she felt like a child deprived of a treat, ready to howl with anguish and despair. Everything had gone wrong. Everything. And she was sorry in her heart that the whole of her party could not be canceled so that she could wallow in her misery for the rest of the day. How was she to gather herself together and appear cheerful for a houseful of guests within the next few hours?

She gazed out at the rain, which lashed the windows and sometimes obliterated the sight of the wind bowing the trees. It was quite early in the morning, but she knew that it was the type of rain that would go on all day and into the night. And even if it did stop by some miracle, the ground would be too wet and the wind too chill to allow for a treasure hunt. Besides, there would be no time to set it up before the guests came.

They would have to play charades in the drawing room, and other games that everyone played wherever they went. There would be nothing special about her party at all.

But it was not just the rain. Constance laid the side of her head against the windowpane and closed her eyes. Sidney had not come and neither had any explanation of his absence. She had known somehow that he was not going to come—and Jonathan had known, though he had not told her, only hinted at it a few times. But she could not understand it. Why had he not come? Sidney always came for the summer.

But she knew why. He had changed his mind about marrying her. Now that the time for speaking with Papa had come, he had panicked and just not come at all. Neither had he written to her. It was just like Sidney to behave so. She knew him well enough to know that he sometimes found it impossible to face up to unpleasant circumstances, especially when he knew he was going to hurt someone.

Oh, and she was hurt. Dreadfully hurt. There was a great frightening emptiness where Sidney had always been. She had not even begun to explore that emptiness yet, but it was there and it was already wrapping her in despair. Today was to have been so very special. The rest of her life was to have been special. And now there was nothing. And nobody. No Sidney.

And no Jonathan. Constance pushed to her feet suddenly and pressed one hand to her mouth as she began to pace about the room. She was so confused. Her feelings had churned about inside her all week since the assembly—or perhaps for longer than that. He had waltzed with her and she had felt as if she were in heaven. And he had kissed her hand—even her palm—and she had wanted more. Very much more. Everything there was to be had.

And she had waited for him to call on some pretext the following day, and the day after that.

Apart from a brief nod he had given her at church on Sunday, there had been nothing at all. And that was as it should be. She was to be betrothed to Sidney and Jonathan knew it. But she stopped her pacing suddenly. No, Jonathan knew the truth. He knew that Sidney no longer wanted her. And so he had waltzed with her and kissed her hand.

Because he felt sorry for her. Because he somehow wanted to make up for the disappointment she would feel when she discovered the truth. Because he did not want her to feel utterly rejected. All the time, since his return to Esdale, he had been being kind to her.

The sound of an approaching carriage had Constance whirling toward the window again and setting one knee on the window seat so that she could see who it was. It was the viscount's carriage, she saw, and she felt a great welling of excitement. It would be Sidney. He had come after all. He would have arrived late last night and was coming early this morning to make up for lost time with her. Oh, how she would scold him for not coming sooner.

But it was the viscount who stepped out of the carriage and rushed toward the door, his head bowed against the rain. And her heart somersaulted and sank within her all at the same time. For if he was coming so early, it could only be to inform her that some other commitment was going to keep him from her party after all. She swallowed against the lump in her throat and waited.

It was a long wait. She sat on the window seat, her back to the window, her hands folded quietly in her lap, and waited for all of half an hour before he came into the room with her father, and her mother leaning on his arm. They were both smiling.

"Constance." Lord Whitley strode across the room to her, his hand outstretched. "Happy birthday."

She tried to keep the bleakness of her feelings out of her smile. "Thank you," she said, setting her hand in his and remembering how he had raised it to his lips and turned it palm up just the week before.

"I promised to come help you set up your treasure hunt," he said. "Since the rain will make some changes inevitable, I came early. I hoped you would not still be abed."

"There can be no treasure hunt now," she said. "The house is too small."

"But Esdale is not," he said. "I think we can keep thirty guests rushing about the hallways and up into the attics there for an hour or two without any fear of squeezes in doorways or other disasters. I have spoken with Lady Manning and she agrees that with just a little extra planning the whole party—including the dancing this evening—can be held at Esdale. With your approval, of course. It is your party."

"At Esdale?" she said, her eyes widening. "My party at Esdale?" At Jonathan's vast and magnificent mansion?

"I know you must be disappointed at having to give up your plans for the outdoors," he said. "And it seems that I do not have a great deal of control over the weather after all, does it not?"

"We can have the food taken over to Esdale with no trouble at all," Lady Manning said. "And Cook, too. And the guests can be redirected and will not mind the extra couple of miles of travel when they know what their destination is to be. Oh, I am so happy for you, my love. I have not known what to do all morning to lift your spirits."

But Constance was looking at Lord Whitley. Her party was to be salvaged after all and to be more exciting than it would have been if the sun had shone? And he had come? Jonathan had come with her birthday and her happiness in mind? He had come early in order to help her prepare. He had not come after all to announce some other pressing engagement. She smiled.

"That would be wonderful," she said. "Oh, it would be wonderful!"

"Good," he said. "Then there is not a moment to be lost. I imagine that some of your clues can be used almost as they are. But others will doubtless have to be changed drastically. And we have to find perfect hiding places for them all."

"Mama?" Constance looked at her mother with shining eyes.

"I will send Tessa with you, my love," Lady Manning said. "She is always glad of an excuse to see her sister. And she can help Cook when she finally arrives with all the food."

And so, ten minutes later, Constance found herself seated in the viscount's carriage beside him, her notes for the treasure hunt stuffed into her reticule. Tessa, her mother's maid, sat opposite her, clearly pleased at the prospect of a holiday from her usual duties.

Somehow the rain lashing against the carriage windows did not appear nearly as gloomy as it had earlier.

It had taken them three hours, Lord Whitley realized later when they were in the conservatory and Constance had pushed the final clue down beneath the large leaves of a potted plant.

"There," she said, rubbing her hands together with a flourish and looking up at him with a flushed face and a satisfied smile.

They had sat side by side at the desk in the library for two hours, reading through her notes, puzzling over the rewording of some clues and the complete rewriting of others. She had a vivid imagination and a ready wit, he had discovered. They seemed to have done a great deal of laughing.

And then they had spent an additional hour rushing all over the house—her mood had seemed to preclude a more leisurely pace—planting clues, making sure they were not too readily visible.

"Tell me," he said now, when they were finally finished. "What is the treasure to be? I have spent a great deal of time and energy making sure that no one finds it too quickly, but you have never told me what it is."

"Oh," she said, and she laughed. "Nothing of any great value. Merely an embroidered watch case for the gentleman and a lace-edged handkerchief for the lady. Do you think they will be disappointed?"

"Made by you?" he asked.

"Of course," she said and laughed again. "Treasures indeed, would you not agree?"

"Very definitely," he said. "I am sorry now that I cannot be one of the hunters. I would be able to wear the watch case next to my heart."

Steady, he thought as she bit her lower lip and flushed. *Take it slowly.* She had not mentioned Sid at all, though she must have realized the truth by now. He had stayed away from her all week rather than witness her growing unease. She must be feeling heartache today, however well she was concealing it.

But he was not going to wait forever. He would take it as slowly as seemed necessary, despite the preparations he had made earlier that morning for moving with speed. But move he would. Forever forward until she stopped him. *If* she stopped him. Perhaps she would not. She had seemed quite happy in his company that morning.

"So," he said, clasping his hands behind his back, "are you happier now? All the plans for your treasure hunt have not gone quite awry."

"Much happier," she said. "Very happy." And then she laughed. "You will think me quite childish for being so excited about a mere party when I am twenty years old."

"When you should be behaving as if you are slipping gracefully into your dotage?" he said. His hands seemed to lift of their own volition to frame her face. "There is nothing childish about enjoyment and enthusiasm, Constance. And nothing childish about you."

"Oh," she said, though no sound emerged.

But her lips kept the shape of the word and offered an unconscious invitation that he found quite irresistible despite his recent thoughts on moving slowly. He lowered his head and kissed her. His lips merely brushed hers. But he felt all the warmth and softness and femininity of her.

"Happy birthday," he murmured, lifting his head away from hers, but keeping his hands where they were.

She was looking up at him with parted lips and eyes that were huge and dazed. Her hands, he could feel, were resting at either side of his waist. And it struck him suddenly that despite what Sid had said, perhaps this had been her first kiss. He gazed back into her eyes and lowered his head again.

His arms went about her and drew her against him, and she was as warm and as slender and as shapely as his eyes had told him she would be. And her lips responded to the movement of his. One of her hands, he could feel, was in his hair.

But his temperature was rising, and this was neither the time nor the place. It was far, far too soon.

"Mm," he said, lifting his head and loosening his

hold on her and keeping his voice as light in tone as he could. "Birthday kisses can sometimes be almost too delightful, can't they? We had better find Tessa and get you on your way back home to dress for your party."

"Yes," she said, biting her lip again and flushing again and not quite meeting his eye. "It would be dreadful if I were late for my own party. I hope you will not find it too great a trial, Jonathan, to have your home invaded by thirty guests this afternoon—not to mention Mama and Papa and our cook. It was so very kind of you to make the offer and to give up your morning to help me."

Kind! He smiled at her and clasped his hands behind his back. He would not trust himself to offer her his arm as they made their way back through the long gallery to the main hall, where he would have his carriage called out again and summon Tessa from belowstairs.

But there were voices coming from the hall—one the quiet, refined tones of his butler, the other louder and more boisterous. And Constance heard them too, and her head shot up one moment before she gathered up her skirts and went hurtling along what remained of the gallery and out through the open door into the hallway.

"Sidney!" she shrieked one moment before the viscount reached the doorway himself.

And he stood there and watched as she rushed across the tiles of the hall and threw herself into the outstretched arms of his brother.

"Sidney!" He looked so dearly familiar, standing in the middle of the great hall, surrounded by boxes. His fair hair was disheveled and slightly damp.

"Sidney," she said, wrapping her arms about his neck as his came about her waist and he lifted her off her feet and spun her once around. "Oh, I knew you would come. And you are late, you horrid man. You were to be here to help me set up for the treasure hunt, but you were still trotting down the road as if there was all the time in the world."

"Trotting down the road?" he said indignantly, setting her back on her feet. "We lost a wheel yesterday afternoon, I would have you know, Con. I might have been killed. And all you can do is scold."

"Oh, did you really?" she said, immediately contrite. "You weren't hurt, Sidney? Was anyone hurt?"

"No," he said. "There was just a dratted delay, that's all, Con. I would have been here last night. Jon, how are you?"

He turned to stretch out a hand, and Constance turned too and felt a jolt of guilt. She had not spared one thought for Jonathan in the minute or so since she had heard Sidney's voice. And yet all morning, while they had got ready for the treasure hunt, she had not once thought of Sidney.

And she had allowed Jonathan to kiss her in the conservatory just a few minutes before and had kissed him back. And had felt a deeper emotion than she had ever felt for anyone in her whole life. She looked at him now as the two brothers shook hands and exchanged greetings, and knew that she still felt that emotion. She—

But no. Sidney was home and it was not his fault that he was late for her birthday.

"Happy birthday, Con," he said, turning back to her. "I did not forget, you see, and I could not bring myself to stay away after all. I told Prinny so. I have to go to someone's birthday party, I told him, and so he excused me. He was most gracious about it."

"The Prince Regent gave you permission to

come home for my birthday?" she asked, her eyes widening.

"I have been wondering all morning what you were going to do in the rain," he said. "I thought I would trot over to see you as soon as I had changed and see if I could help you drum up some ideas. What *are* you going to do, Con? And what are you doing here?"

"Oh," she said. "Jonathan has very kindly offered Esdale for my party, Sidney. We are to have the treasure hunt here—it is all set up, and tea and dinner and the dancing in the drawing room. It is very kind of him, is it not? I think he believed you were not coming home and has been trying to take my mind off my disappointment."

She smiled at Lord Whitley. That was all it had been, she told herself—kindness. But now he would realize that he need no longer dance attendance on her. But his kiss? Had that too been kindness?

And what about those feelings she had had when he kissed her and the realization that had been dawning on her gradually over the past three weeks? And the feelings she still had, looking at him now while her arm was linked through Sidney's?

But Sidney had come home, and everything could still proceed according to plan for the rest of her birthday. It could still be a very special day.

She was, Constance realized, feeling utterly confused.

"I was about to send Constance home," Lord Whitley said, smiling and looking quite in command of the situation—surely he would not be looking so if that kiss had meant anything beyond what he had said it meant. It had been a birthday kiss. "She has to dress for the party and be back here in time to greet the first of her guests."

"And I need a bath," Sidney said, wrinkling his nose and looking down at himself. "You can't imagine the inn where I was forced to put up last night, Jon. I'll come over and fetch you in an hour's time or so, Con, shall I? I can pay my respects to your mother and father at the same time."

Oh, yes, there was that too, Constance thought. Oh, goodness, she had waited for it and longed for it all over an endless winter and spring, and now the day had come upon her before she felt at all ready for it.

"You go on up, then, Sid," the viscount said, "and I'll see to getting Constance on her way. I have sent for the carriage already."

Constance stood in the doorway a few minutes later, the viscount at her side, watching the carriage draw up, ready to take her home. And she felt a disturbing chill of depression. They had said nothing to each other since Sidney had gone upstairs. And the gaiety of the morning and the comfort she had felt in Jonathan's presence had gone.

"Thank you," she said, her voice stilted, "for your kindness and time." And she looked up at him anxiously, waiting for him to say something to indicate that there had been more than kindness in his actions, more than a birthday greeting in his kiss. And hoping that there was no more. And reminding herself that Sidney was at Esdale at last and that they were to be betrothed that day. And that she was happy about it. And feeling utterly confused again.

He smiled at her, and she could see nothing but kindness in his smile. "Now," he said, "you can have the birthday you dreamed of after all, Constance. You will have your treasure hunt and Sidney at home too. I am happy for you."

"Thank you," she said. "I knew he would come. I almost doubted—in fact this morning I did. But he has come and my day is complete."

He lifted one hand and touched two knuckles to

her cheek. "Happy birthday, Constance," he said. "I shall hand you into the carriage. If you run down the steps, you will not get too wet. And here comes Tessa."

Constance ran and took his firm, strong hand, and ducked inside the carriage. Tessa came rushing after her. And they were on their way home to get ready for the party, Tessa talking excitedly about the strange phenomenon of two cooks in the same kitchen—Sir Howard's and his lordship's—eyeing each other suspiciously, just like two duelists.

Constance sat back against the comfortable cushions and told herself how delighted she was that Sidney was at home. She *was* delighted. He was her dearest friend and she had a million things she wanted to tell him. And she was excited too. He was going to talk to Papa, and that evening they were going to announce their betrothal.

She tried to tell herself that that other feeling—the one she was trying to ignore—was not mortal depression. He had been kindness itself. He had made possible a wonderful birthday party for her despite the rain, even to the extent of opening his own home to her. It was not his fault that she was still a child at heart and still gave in far too easily to hero-worship.

It was not his fault that she had thought that perhaps that kiss had been a different kind of kiss.

He was going to be her brother-in-law, she told herself firmly.

"So you came after all." Lord Whitley was leaning back against the door of his brother's dressing room. "Brighton was dull?"

Sidney, sitting waist-deep in soapy water, was rubbing more soap into his hair. "Quite the opposite," he said. "But I kept feeling guilty, Jon. I kept thinking of Connie alone and dull in the country here and disappointed about her birthday.''

"Did you?" the viscount said. "So guilt drove you home?"

"Did you tell her that story about Prinny?" Sidney asked. "I did go to the Pavilion, Jon—twice. But it is kept like a hothouse. I was glad to get outside again both times. Did you tell her?"

"Something similar," his brother said. "So you are going to do the honorable thing, Sid, and marry her?"

Sidney, with soap in his eyes, felt for the jug beside the bathtub and poured a jugful of water over his head. "She is expecting it," he said. "We talked about it all last summer and wrote about it all last winter. I suppose it is the honorable thing to do, is it not?"

"Honor but not inclination," the viscount said. "Is that it? Is it fair to her, Sid?"

Sidney sputtered as another jugful of water cascaded over his face. "To Connie?" he said. "I'm devilish fond of her, Jon. Devilish. And you were the one to mention honor when we were still in town. I have not been able to dislodge the thought. And if a fellow must marry, he could do a great deal worse than marry Connie, you know."

"Does she not deserve to be married for love as well as for honor and devilish fondness?" Lord Whitley asked as his brother reached for a towel and stood up.

"And who says I don't love Connie?" Sidney asked. "I could have eaten her all up when I saw her downstairs. I've always loved her, Jon. Look, I've come home in time for her birthday, have I not? I would have been here yesterday if it had not been for that damned wheel. And this evening I'll talk with Sir Howard and the announcement will be made and all will be settled once and for all. I'll be a happy man."

"You love her, then," the viscount said, his tone flat. "You really love her, Sid."

It was not a question. But his brother looked up at him anyway, a little startled, his hands falling still on the towel.

"I love her," he said after a silent pause, during which the two brothers eyed each other intently.

"Well, then," Lord Whitley said, "Constance will have her very special day after all. She has had thoughts for no one but you all summer, Sid. This morning I found her in the deepest dejection, though she put a brave face on it."

"I'll soon cheer her up," Sidney said, tossing the towel from him and reaching for the clean clothes his valet had laid out for him. "I have a mint of stories to tell her about Brighton."

"I think she has already cheered up," Lord Whitley said, "just seeing you. You will be with her during the treasure hunt, then, Sid? And you will be opening the dance with her this evening? I'll fade into the background, then, and let you youngsters enjoy yourselves."

"Youngsters." Sidney chuckled. "But it was jolly decent of you to suggest Esdale for the party, Jon, and to give up a morning to help Connie. I appreciate it."

His brother made a sound that might have been a laugh before letting himself out of the room.

Sidney vaulted into the carriage after Constance. He looked very fashionable in his green superfine coat and pantaloons and shining Hessians, she thought. He even looked handsome to her biased eyes. She reached out her hands to him, and he took them and squeezed them and kissed her briefly and smackingly on the lips.

"You look as pretty as a picture, Con," he said. "Green suits you."

She smiled at him. She had felt pretty when she had twirled before her looking glass earlier. Pretty and happy, and unhappy and bewildered.

"I have so much to tell you," he said. "You would not believe all I saw and did in Brighton, Con."

"And I have so much to tell you," she said, her eyes shining. She let him draw her arm through his and rested her shoulder against his and was thoroughly comfortable. "Jonathan revived the Esdale picnic, Sidney, and it was wonderful. He took me out in one of the boats and managed to row in a straight line." She turned her head to laugh up at him. "And we walked home at sunset and the sky and the water were indescribable colors. And there was a dance in the assembly rooms last week, and it was wonderful. Jonathan waltzed with me twice, and he did not once tread on my toes. You see?" She laughed again. "I am not the clumsy one after all. And we walked along the street when it was all over while everyone gossiped, as they always do, and the air was wonderfully cool."

"Well," he said, "it sounds as if you have been having as good a time as I had in Brighton, Con."

"And today," she said, "when I saw the rain, I thought we were going to be doomed to playing charades all afternoon. But then Jonathan came and suggested that Esdale be used for the treasure hunt. We sat for two hours in the library, thinking up clues and laughing at all the silly ideas we had. But it is going to take all the guests at least an hour to solve all the clues, Jonathan says."

He patted her hand. "I am glad he has been looking after you," he said.

"He has been very kind." There was a short pause in their conversation, and she set her cheek briefly against his shoulder. "I am so happy you have come home, Sidney. This morning I really believed you were not coming. And I think Jonathan did too. He has kept saying to me, 'Well, if he does not come . . .' He offered to help with the treasure hunt if you did not come. He was going to lead me into the opening set tonight if you did not come. He has been very kind." She set her cheek back against his shoulder.

"Well, I came," he said. "I couldn't stay away, Con. I kept thinking of you and missing you." She heard him draw breath. "I'll talk with your papa this evening, then, and have him make the announcement if he approves my suit?"

"Oh," she said. "Yes. I suppose. If you are sure, Sidney."

"It is what we have been planning for a year," he said.

"Yes."

"We will do it, then," he said. "I'll wait until the dancing has started, and then I'll ask for a private word with him. I don't think he will have any objection, will he, Con?"

"Oh, no," she said. "I am quite sure he will not."

"Well, then," he said, "it will all be settled."

"Yes."

They drove the rest of the distance to Esdale in silence, both determinedly happy, both determinedly smiling whenever they turned their heads to look at each other.

He stayed in the background, as he had promised Sid he would. But as the owner of Esdale he felt that he must at least be visible. So he was there in the great hall to greet Constance and his brother when they arrived and to welcome each of her guests when they came a little later.

He remained in the hall when Constance divided

her guests by lot into fifteen couples and provided each couple with the first clue that would set them off on the treasure hunt. Everyone stood in the hall puzzling over the clue before darting off in various directions.

Lord Whitley smiled at Constance and she smiled triumphantly back. But he was standing outside the library door, his hands clasped behind his back, and she was in the very middle of the great hall, Sidney beside her. She looked very happy, the viscount thought, and prettier than he had ever seen her, in her spring green muslin dress, with a matching ribbon threaded through her curls.

He went into the library, leaving the door open behind him, and sat down at the desk where they had sat that morning, their heads together, feeding off each other's ideas, often giving in to absurdity and hilarity. It had been a foolish fancy, he thought. She loved Sid, whether Sid was there for her birthday or not. His continued absence would have made no real difference to anything. It was a good thing Sid had come home when he had. For the idea of patience and taking things slowly seemed to have been tossed aside in the past week. He was only sorry that he had made something of an idiot of himself that morning.

Well, he thought, picking up a paper knife and balancing it on one finger, he was going to have to accustom himself to thinking of her as a sister. A sister-in-law. The thought made him grimace.

The first couple to complete the treasure hunt—Hadley Fleming and Marjorie Churchill—took an hour and a half in which to do so. But everyone agreed, even the losers, that the hunt had been enormous fun and a great improvement on charades or any of the other usual entertainments at parties.

They had tea in the blue salon as soon as everyone had finally come back to the hall and then entertained themselves for the few hours before dinner: strolling in the gallery, sitting in the conservatory, playing the pianoforte and the harp in the music room, playing billiards, or merely remaining in the salon. Everyone seemed thoroughly delighted just to be at Esdale, which had been closed to entertainment for four years.

The party was a success, Lord Whitley decided as he took his place at the head of the table at dinner and smiled across its length at Constance, who as hostess was sitting at the foot. It was clear that all her guests were enjoying themselves and that she was happy. And the best part for her was still to come. He had already had the carpet in the large drawing room rolled up and music placed on the pianoforte for Lady Manning's use. The dancing would begin as soon as dinner was finished—he would persuade the gentlemen not to linger over the port—and she would be with Sidney.

And at some time during the evening her betrothal would be announced. He would see her flushed and quite radiantly happy. And he would walk up to her and to Sid, and wish them happy and kiss her hand. And force himself to remain in the drawing room for the rest of the evening.

He turned his attention and his conversation to Lady Manning, seated to his right. She seemed embarrassed, he thought, and was looking at him a little warily. Yes, he was feeling embarrassed, too. But he talked anyway and saw her begin to relax.

"Well, upon my soul," Sir Howard said, running a hand over the back of his neck. He looked at Sidney, standing stiffly before the empty fireplace in the library. "I don't know what to say, my boy. You have taken me quite by surprise. And I don't know what Lady Manning would say."

"I have been of age these six months, sir," Sidney

said earnestly. "And I have a comfortable fortune. I will look after her, sir, if that is what you are concerned about. I have always been excessively fond of Con—of Constance—of Miss Manning."

"Oh, I know, boy, I know," Sir Howard said. He blew out air from puffed cheeks. "Does Connie know about this?"

"Oh, yes, sir," Sidney said eagerly. "We have planned it since last summer, sir. That is, we have planned to ask for your approval. We have planned to become betrothed if you will agree—and Lady Manning, of course."

"I always thought it was just a childhood friendship," Sir Howard said. "Her mother and I have not realized that it had turned to something else already, though we have thought that perhaps it would in time."

Sidney swallowed. "I love her, sir," he said. "We do not have to marry soon if you think I am too young or she is too young. We can wait, sir. Perhaps two or three years or whatever you think proper. But I know it means a great deal to Connie to have our betrothal announced this evening."

Sir Howard rubbed at his neck again and turned his head from side to side as if his cravat were too tight. "It is just that yours is the second offer I have had today, my boy," he said, "though the other gentleman talked to both me and Lady Manning. We gave our consent for him to ask—we would never try to force Connie's hand, you know. I don't know if I ought to consent to your asking too. Though I cannot for the life of me think of any reason for refusing you. And the final decision is Connie's, of course."

"Someone else wants to marry Con?" Sidney looked intently at Sir Howard. "Who?"

"Oh," Sir Howard said, "I don't think I am at liberty to say that, my boy."

But Sidney did not press the point. He merely turned a shade paler. "Jon," he said.

The baronet looked uncomfortable. "I don't want there to be a family fight over my daughter," he said.

"There won't be, sir," Sidney said. "There won't be."

"Well," Sir Howard said, "you have my permission to talk to her, my boy." He scratched his head. "I had better go and find Lady Manning."

Sidney stood where he was for a long time after Sir Howard had left the room, though he had promised to join Constance in the conservatory as soon as the interview was at an end. He stared unseeingly at the carpet before him.

Constance paced restlessly about the conservatory. Would he never come? Surely Papa could not be keeping him this long. Surely Papa would not have said no.

She should be getting back to the drawing room. She had been there only for the opening set with Sidney and then had left. Everyone would be wondering where she was. Yet she did not want to go back to the drawing room. She wished in her heart that she had contented herself with just an afternoon party for her birthday. It would be over now.

He had danced the opening set with Georgina and had smiled and looked quite at his ease. He had looked the perfect host. And he had been perfect all day, the genial host and yet not in any way pushing himself forward since it was in essence her party, which just happened to be taking place in his home.

He would dance with her later in the evening, she was sure. Possibly a waltz. *Probably* a waltz. And she felt suffocated at the thought. And sick. And just as if she was about to dissolve into tears. Would Sidney never come?

And then there he was, walking quietly toward her, looking rather like a ghost. She stood very still and fingered the pearls at her neck.

"What is it?" she asked. And when he did not immediately reply, "Did Papa say no?"

"No," he said. "No, I mean he said yes." He smiled and looked rather as if he were being strangled. "So I suppose I had better go down on one knee, Con, and do this thing properly. Hadn't I?"

She swallowed. "I don't think there is any need to do anything so formal," she said. "Sidney?"

"Yes?" he said.

"Are you sure?" she asked. "Do you want to do this?"

"Do you?" he asked.

She laughed rather shakily. "I asked first," she said.

"Con," he said, "has anyone else spoken to you this afternoon or evening? Jon?"

"Jonathan?" she said, frowning. "Of course he has spoken to me. He said happy birthday to me for the fourth or fifth time when we arrived this afternoon, and . . ."

"No," he said. "It does not matter. Well, I think I'll just pop down on one knee, Con. It will be something to tell our grandchildren."

She turned away sharply suddenly and found herself biting her lip until she tasted blood. "Sidney," she said, and she could hear that her voice was almost a wail.

"What is it?" he asked.

"I love you so dearly," she said. "I could not love you more if you were my brother. I—. Oh, Sidney."

"Oh, Lord, Con," he said, and there were the beginnings of relief in his voice. "You too? I am fonder of you than I have been of anyone in my life. You know that, don't you?"

"Yes," she said.

"And I promised," he said. "I would not hurt you or let you down for the world, Con."

"Or I you," she said.

There was a silence. "Oh, Lord," he said at last, "what are we saying here, Con? Are we saying the same thing?"

She turned to look at him. "I think so," she said. "You would not be dreadfully hurt, Sidney, if I did not marry you? It does not mean that I do not love you. I will always love you. You will always be my dear friend."

"And you will not be heartbroken if I do not marry you?" he asked. "Truth to tell, Con, I think I am too young to marry anyone at the moment."

She laughed shakily and then sobbed inelegantly. "Oh, Sidney," she said, "may I use your shoulder? Please?"

"Come here, you goose," he said, and he hugged her tightly to him while she laughed and hiccuped and hugged him back. "What idiots we have been. Are we friends again?"

"I don't think we were ever *not* friends, were we?" she said. "You did not intend to come home at all, did you?"

"But I came," he said. "I came because I care for you and could not just abandon you. There. Don't go getting your eyes all red, and they do get dreadfully red when you cry. You can feel free to love someone else now, Con, now that you no longer feel bound to me. There *is* someone else, isn't there?"

She felt her cheeks grow warm. "What a ridiculous idea," she said. "What on earth makes you think such a foolish thing?"

"A little bit of listening and a little bit of observing," he said. "We had better get back to the drawing room, Con, before your papa thinks we have been away too long and forces us to the altar." He drew her arm through his and patted her hand. "And if you should feel like making an announcement tonight—but not quite the one you and I planned—then go ahead and don't worry about my feelings. I will be happy for you, I swear."

"Oh, Sidney," she said a little crossly, "what nonsense are you talking now?"

It was a waltz. She had known that he would ask for a waltz. She smiled at him and felt a great welling of relief again. And of happiness. And there was a little sadness in her too.

"Well," he said, "you are looking very happy, Constance. Has it been as enjoyable a birthday party as you hoped for?"

"Yes," she said. "It has been wonderful. And Esdale has been that extra-special ingredient. Thank you for offering it."

He twirled her about a corner of the room. "I could not help but notice you and Sid and your father disappearing," he said, "and your father reappearing a short while later. Share the secret with me, Constance. When is the announcement to be made?"

She looked up into his eyes. They smiled back at her and were entirely kindly. There was nothing else in them at all. She shook her head and fixed her eyes on his cravat.

"Ah," he said, "I am sorry. I should not have begged a brother's privilege. I must agree to be kept waiting along with everyone else."

"There will be no announcement," she told his cravat so quietly that he had to bend his head forward to hear her. "There is no betrothal."

There was a short silence. "I'll kill him," he said, and she could tell even without looking up that he spoke through his teeth.

"It was mutual," she said hastily. "We were both

agreed. We love each other and always will. But it is not *that* kind of love."

Another silence. "He has not hurt you, then?" he asked.

"No." She could feel her heart thumping. She could feel his hand warm against the back of her waist. She could smell his cologne. The whole world contracted and encompassed just the two of them. And then breathing became a conscious thing and a difficult thing. She looked up at him, unsmiling, and her eyes held on his.

"I think we had better find somewhere more private, hadn't we?" he said when they had stared at each other for what might have been minutes or merely seconds.

"Yes," she said.

The library was lit by a single branch of candles and looked far cozier and more intimate than it had looked that morning.

He took his hand from the small of her back when he had closed the door behind them, and cupped her face in his palms. His thumbs drew circles on her cheeks.

"Did you know that I spoke to your mother and father this morning before coming to see you?" he asked.

"No." Her voice was a whisper, her eyes wide.

"I asked if I might offer you marriage," he said. She swallowed awkwardly.

"They both said yes." He smiled suddenly. "Your father must have wondered whether he was on his head or his feet when Sid spoke to him on the same subject a short while ago."

Constance licked her lips and watched the smile fade from his face.

"You do not love Sid in that way, Constance?" he asked. "Are you sure?"

"Yes." She could seem to speak only in monosyllables.

He looked down at her mouth and back up into her eyes. "Could you ever love me in that way?" he asked.

"Yes." No sound came out. "Yes."

His thumbs touched her lips. "And I you," he said. "I loved you four years ago when I frightened you with my clumsy advances, and I have loved you too much to come home ever since. I have loved you again this summer. I love you now. Have you known it?"

"You were being kind," she said. "I thought you were being kind."

"I do not kiss ladies I feel mere kindness toward," he said.

"They were not clumsy," she said. "I was just too young and—foolish. I worshiped you then. I don't think it is worship now. I think it is love. I *know* it is love."

He set his forehead to hers and closed his eyes. "Will you marry me?" he asked her. "I know I am eight-and-twenty years old and almost in my dotage. But perhaps a young thing like you can rejuvenate me, Constance. Will you?"

She laughed, though the sound was suspiciously like a giggle. "Yes," she said, and suddenly she could not stop laughing. "What an absurd thing to say." She slid her arms up beneath his and circled his neck with them. And she bit her lip and the laughter was gone.

"Mm," he said, "I have won the treasure after all. And it is far more precious than an embroidered watch case, is it not?"

But she could only look up at him with parted lips. His arms came about her waist and drew her tightly against him, and he rocked her wordlessly until he found her mouth with his own and worked it open and teased her lips with his tongue.

"All day," he whispered to her, "I have been

training myself to be a good and affectionate brother-in-law."

"All summer," she whispered back, "I have been training myself to be a good and affectionate sister-in-law."

"Will Sid be hurt or embarrassed?" he asked. "Would it be kinder to wait with our announcement?"

"No," she said. "He has given us his blessing. He knew, though he did not mention you by name. Oh, yes, he did too, though I did not understand at the time. He said he would be happy for me. For us."

"Then what is keeping us?" he asked. "Let's go back to the drawing room and have your father make the announcement, shall we?"

"Yes." She smiled radiantly at him.

"Ah," he said, drawing her against him again as she was about to move away, "I have forgotten one thing."

"What?" she asked.

"I don't believe I have wished you a happy birthday, have I?" he said. "Or given you a happy birthday kiss."

She laughed. "Is a short memory a symptom of being in your dotage?" she asked. "You have wished me happy birthday about five times. And have you forgotten the conservatory this morning?"

He grinned and rubbed his nose against hers. "Absolutely," he said. "You had better remind me, Constance."

"Oh," she said, laughing again and feeling that there could not possibly be one more ounce of happiness in life. "Very well, then."

But it took him a long time to remember. All of thirty minutes had passed before Sir Howard Manning announced their betrothal in the drawing room.

A Country Wedding

by Melinda McRae

1

"CECILY! CECILY!" Delia Montford burst into the morning room, her beribboned braids bouncing about her shoulders. "Robert's here!"

Cecily Montford jumped from her chair, nearly upsetting the ink bottle on the table in her enthusiasm. "It is about time. Did he bring Harry with him?"

Delia nodded. Grabbing her elder sister by the hand, she drew her to the door. "I hope Robert brought me a present!"

Cecily smiled at the thirteen-year-old's exuberance. "Did you think to tell Susannah that Harry is here?"

Delia clapped a hand over her mouth. "I forgot."

Cecily shook her head. "The only thing on everyone's mind is the wedding, yet when the groom arrives you 'forgot' to tell the bride?" Her blue eyes glimmered with amusement.

"I will get her now," Delia said, dropping her sister's hand and racing toward the stairs.

Cecily followed at a slightly more sedate pace, but even her steps were hurried. Her brother, Robert, had remained in town when the family came home to prepare for the upcoming nuptials. Cecily thought six weeks had been quite long enough for him to stay away—particularly when he had promised to be home the previous week. But now he and her future brother-in-law were here at last—only days before the wedding.

She was practically running herself by the time she reached the bottom of the stairs and, indeed, would have launched herself across the entry hall at her brother if the sight of the tall, blond man standing between Robert and Harry had not brought her up short with a gasp of shock.

Ainsley Powell. The physical manifestation of the most embarrassing moment of her entire eighteen years stood before her. She knew—hoped—that she would see him again one day. But not on the eve of her sister's wedding. His presence would spoil everything.

Cecily wished she could turn around and race up the stairs as fast as she had come down. She was acutely conscious of the unfashionable day dress she wore, the large ink stain on her finger, and the fact that her short red curls were intolerably mussed. In truth, she looked her worst. In front of the one man she most wanted to see her at her best.

"Cece!" Robert greeted, holding out his arms.

Cecily gladly turned to her brother, stepping into his embrace with affected calm. "About time you arrived," she said with mock irritation. "We had nearly given up hope."

Robert released her, ruffling her curls with his hand. "You knew I'd get here eventually." He turned to the other man beside him. "Harry here seemed to think there was something important going on at the house this week." He guffawed loudly.

Cecily turned to her brother-in-law-to-be with a smile of welcome. "Susannah will be pleased at your arrival," she said.

"And you are not?" he teased.

She adopted a considering look. "With all the

turmoil caused by the wedding plans?" Cecily laughed at Harry's chagrined look. "I own I am looking forward to having Susannah's room after you take her away. So your arrival is a relief."

"Trust Cece to be so mercenary about it," Robert said in a loud aside. He smiled widely. "Cece, you remember Ainsley Powell, don't you? Wicked fellow was dashing all over the continent, and missed your debut this spring."

"To my great regret," Ainsley replied, bowing slightly. "I am sorry to have missed your come-out."

Cecily dared a glance at his cool gray eyes, and wished more than ever that she could flee. That mocking gaze forcibly brought back the memory of that terrible day six years ago. She could picture it in her mind, in all its embarrassing clarity, as if it had been yesterday. Trailing him about the estate. Skulking in the hall, waiting to waylay him when he left his room. And the most humiliating scene of all, when she had poured out all the longings of her twelve-year-old heart and he'd squashed her aspirations like a bug beneath his foot.

Now, six years later, here he was again. And what was worse, he looked even more handsome than she remembered. His thick, blond hair swept back from his noble forehead, and the tiny cleft in his chin was just as she remembered it. Even the casually tied scarf about his neck did not make him less imposing. He appeared every inch the perfect Corinthian. Her heart gave a painful lurch.

And she could tell by the way he looked at her that he had not forgotten their last meeting.

"It is a pleasure to see you again, Mr. Powell," she replied with calm courtesy. She would not allow him to think his presence disconcerted her in any way. Thank goodness he had not taken her hand or he would have noticed her sweaty palms.

Robert hooted. "Sounds like a polished lady of the *ton*, rather than the hoyden she really is, doesn't she?" He grinned fondly at his sister.

Cecily fought the overwhelming urge to strangle her brother. She was *not* a hoyden. She was a grown woman of eighteen.

He dropped a companionable arm about her shoulder. "And how is the rest of the brood?"

"Delia is beside herself with excitement, and Susannah is . . . managing." Cecily darted a rueful glance at Harry, whose attention, she saw, was now focused on the stairs behind her. Cecily turned, and watched Susannah's decorous descent. No headlong rush down the stairs for her elder sister. Cecily gave an imperceptible sigh. No matter how hard she tried, she would never be able to match Susannah's elegant poise.

"Hello, Harry," Susannah said breathlessly.

"Hello," he replied in a near whisper.

Robert rolled his eyes skyward and took Cecily's arm. "Let's leave the two lovebirds alone. Follow along, Powell." Robert started up the stairs.

"How is Mama?" he asked.

"In a total dither," Cecily replied absently, acutely conscious of the man who trailed behind her.

Why, of all people, had he arrived now, days early for the wedding? When things were in a muddle and she looked like a maid-of-all-work? What could Robert have been thinking, to bring a *stranger* into their midst at such a time? It was as if fate and Ainsley Powell conspired to ruin what was supposed to be a perfect event.

For it was painfully clear that Ainsley Powell held as much attraction for her now as he had six years ago. And her foolish behavior at their last encounter had probably sunk her beyond reproach in his eyes.

Then a determined expression crossed her face. That was the past. She was no longer the idiotic, gawky girl who had entertained a childish infatuation for her brother's friend, and she would make certain Ainsley Powell knew it. During this visit, he would find her to be an elegant, accomplished young lady. One who had successfully navigated the torturous waters of a London Season with nary a misstep. She would erase any lingering memories and redeem herself in his eyes—if it killed her.

Ainsley stared at the wrinkled ruin of his last starched cravat and sighed. He hated the blasted things, and only wore one when it was mandatory. But normally, he could tie a creditable knot when pressed. Tonight, however, he seemed all fumbling fingers. He gave the bellpull an impatient jerk. He'd have to borrow one from Robert—and get his valet to tie it in the bargain. Not an auspicious beginning.

He ran his hand through his hair in growing frustration. He had thought he could handle the situation here with calm equanimity. After all, it had been six years since his last visit. Cecily Montford was no longer a child. She probably looked back on the whole incident with amusement. Pray, she had not noticed the discomfort in his face when he first spied her. He hoped he had covered it well with his mien of calm indifference.

He winced at the memory of their last meeting, still remembering it vividly. Normally, a chit her age would not have even been let loose in company, but for some reason she was that summer. To his everlasting regret. Her unceasing attentions had filled him with mortification. Yet, despite his increasingly cool rebuffs, she would not leave him alone. The chit had pursued him with a determination that bordered on the fanatical.

But his own reaction has been as childish as hers. She had lured him into the summer house with the pretense of a message from another lady—one he was not averse to meeting in that location. Expecting his flirt, he instead encountered a lovesick Cecily, who pressed upon him the most abominably stitched handkerchief he had ever seen. Horrified, he lashed out at her without mercy.

He could have been more gentle, more tactful. But puffed up with his own consequence at one-and-twenty, he had no thought for her sensibilities, calling her a foolish and stupid creature for even thinking one such as he would be interested in a freckle-faced chit of twelve. Wrenching her hands from his shirt, he had fled the summer house in total mortification. It was only later, when he had been able to reflect more rationally on his own behavior, that deep shame crept over him.

He could have managed the whole thing better. He could have taken the wretched piece of cloth as a sop to her affections, knowing she would abandon her infatuation as soon as he was gone. But no, he had to thoroughly crush her without a care for her feelings.

In fact, the whole incident so disconcerted him that he had avoided this household like the plague ever since. Though it had been merely coincidence, Ainsley had sighed with relief when he discovered that his travel plans last spring coincided with Miss Montford's London debut.

He had not wished to come at all for the wedding. Only the knowledge of the disappointment that action would have engendered in both Harry and Robert forced him to agree. So here he was—face-to-face with the living embodiment of the most embarrassing moment of his life. He thought he would be able to handle the situation with his usual aplomb, but now he was no longer certain. Just the sight of Cecily Montford made him feel like the callow youth of his past, and reminded him that he had some atoning to do.

Although, he admitted warily, that first encounter had not gone badly. She had obviously been surprised to see him. The look on her face made that clear. Was she now reliving that horrible encounter in her mind as well? He prayed the years had washed away her remembrance.

Yet she looked so much as he remembered that it did not seem possible six whole years had passed. The red braids had been replaced by a cap of short red curls that made her look little older. And even if she had grown some in the intervening time, he doubted she yet reached his shoulder. In fact, if it weren't for the fact her freckles had disappeared, he would be hard-pressed to agree she had changed at all. Could she really be eighteen?

He wondered now how he was going to apologize for his own shameful behavior. It would help to know what she felt about the incident. Did she hate him? Had she forgiven him? Or worse, did she feel no emotion at all? Lord knew, he still deserved her contempt. Somehow, he would have to find a way to make amends.

It was very difficult for Cecily to quell her conflicting feelings of anticipation and apprehension during dinner. This was the perfect opportunity to show Ainsley Powell that she had outgrown her childish ways. But she was not certain how, exactly, she was to go about showing him that she was now a woman grown.

She silently berated herself for allowing one man to so disrupt her peace. This was a family gathering; a time to enjoy all the aunts and uncles and cousins she saw at only rare times throughout the year. It was a festive celebration.

Yes, she thought, surveying the faces around the table, it would be an entertaining occasion if only Ainsley Powell was not here to watch her every action. It was much, much worse than being on display in London. There, it was an accepted part of one's debut. But here, in her family home, she wished to feel comfortable. Instead she was more nervous than she had been on presentation day.

Fortunately, she was seated at the opposite end of the table from Ainsley, so she did not have to converse with him. Cecily concentrated on being a lively and interesting dining partner for her uncle on one side and her cousin on another, in order to show Ainsley that he was of no concern to her. As a result, she had no recollection of finishing her mulligatawny, even though it was her favorite, and she barely tasted the fish. Even the grilled sweetbreads and curried rabbit provoked no enthusiasm. Not until the ginger cream appeared, did she truly enjoy anything that she ate.

Following dinner, the ladies retired to the drawing room, leaving the gentlemen to their port. Cecily sat down at the pianoforte, aimlessly running her fingers up and down the keys. How best to show Ainsley Powell her hard-won maturity? Should she entertain him with her musical skill? Impress him with her dainty watercolors? Flaunt her horsemanship? Dazzle him with clever conversation? What would work best?

"Cecily, do stop that noise," her mother commanded. "My nerves are on edge as it is without your jangling. Either play a tune or leave it be."

Cecily stood up and crossed the room. She bent down and kissed her mama's cheek. "I am sorry," she said. "Would you like me to bring your sewing basket?"

"No, I would only hopelessly tangle the threads." Lady Lawton directed a glare at her eldest daughter. "Stop fidgeting, Susannah. It makes you look as childish as Delia. Married ladies do not fidget."

"She cannot bear the thought of being parted from Harry for even a moment," Cecily teased. "A minute seems like an hour, and hour like a—"

"Stop it," Susannah cried.

"Now, Cecily, do not tease your sister so," Lady Lawton cautioned. "We do not wish her to become overset with the wedding so near."

"Overcoddled is more likely," Cecily muttered under her breath. She, for one, was certainly grateful that she did not have an excess of sensibilities, as did her sister. She could only imagine that in the not too distant future, Susannah would develop the vaporish airs that characterized their mother's conduct when life became too trying. Although, Cecily had difficulty imagining Harry tolerating such a thing.

That very thought brought a smile to her face, which elicited the same reaction from her father when the gentlemen rejoined them.

"Bored to flinders, poppet?" Viscount Lawton asked his favorite daughter softly. "Shall I get up a game of whist?"

"You shall do no such thing, Edward," Lady Lawton said with an imperious glance. "It is not often that we have the family gathered around us. We should take advantage of that fact."

"Shall I bring Delia down?" Cecily asked sweetly. "I am certain she would enjoy a 'family' gathering."

Her mother squelched her with a quelling look. "Perhaps you would be willing to play for us, Cecily, now that the gentlemen are here. Your uncle was particularly desirous of hearing you play."

Cecily doubted that claim, but nodded in acceptance. Mama had made the decision for her. It would have to be at the pianoforte, then, that her campaign to impress Ainsley Powell would begin.

She looked pointedly at her brother. "Robert, you can turn the pages for me."

"Sorry, sis, but that's a privilege I reserve only for *special* ladies." He turned to Ainsley. "You do it, Powell."

Cecily felt an instantaneous horror at the untimely suggestion. She stole a glance at Ainsley and noted he looked equally discomfited.

"I can manage the music on my own," she said quickly, making her way to the piano. She plopped down on the bench and fumbled with her music, her nervous fingers rattling the sheets.

The papers were suddenly lifted from her hands.

"Allow me," said Ainsley. He sorted through the sheets, organizing them in the proper order, before replacing them on the music stand. "Are you ready to begin, Miss Montford?"

Cecily nodded wordlessly. He stood right behind her, so close that if she leaned back, she would make contact with his body. His very nearness sent a shiver up her spine. It was most important that she do well.

After a few fumbling chords, Cecily's stiffened fingers loosened and she wove her way through first one tune, and then another. She knew she did not have an exceptional talent, but she played well enough for a family gathering such as this. Through it all, she never lost the sense of Ainsley's nearness; she was acutely aware that this was a *performance* on her part, to show him that she had acquired the accomplishments of a lady.

Polite applause greeted her final effort. Cecily slumped slightly with relief, then instantly grew erect. Ladies did not slump.

"That was an enjoyable performance, Miss Montford," Ainsley said as he meticulously stacked the music sheets atop the pianoforte.

Cecily darted him a glance, sensing a note of superciliousness in his tone.

"With diligent practice, anyone may achieve a modest degree of skill," she said, ducking her head in a deliberately coy manner, in imitation of the London ladies.

"I admire your diligence, then."

"Is the pianoforte your favorite instrument?" Cecily asked. Perhaps if she drew him into a lengthy conversation, she could demonstrate how grown-up she now was.

"I rather prefer the harp," he said curtly.

"Perhaps we should encourage Delia to take it up." Cecily did not miss the irritation in his voice and replied in her coolest manner. "In order to make your next visit more pleasant."

"I will very much look forward to that," he replied.

"Thank you for your assistance with the music," Cecily said with a polite smile. He might be deliberately rude, but she was not going to show him that it affected her. In truth, she was half-relieved that he evinced no interest in further conversation. Particularly now, when she had the uneasy impression that he still eyed her with wary apprehension.

"Your servant," Ainsley replied.

Cecily eyed him coolly as he sidled away, acting as if another instant in her presence would somehow be poisonous. Odious man!

Watching Ainsley with cautious glances for the remainder of the evening, Cecily attempted to convince herself that things had not gone too badly. She had put on a creditable performance at the piano, and her conversation for the rest of the evening had been as insipid as any drawing-room talk could be. Her behavior had been totally unexceptionable.

He, on the other hand, had quite deliberately

snubbed her. Undoubtedly, he thought she was still a silly child. He treated her as if he anticipated a repeat performance of that disastrous encounter in the summer house. Could he not see how she had grown into a lady?

She consoled herself with the thought that there were still a few more days until the wedding. Ample time to demonstrate what a lady she had become. Tomorrow, she would continue her campaign to jolt him into awareness.

In the morning, Cecily raced through her toilette, donned her riding habit, and hastened to the stable. A good, bruising ride would be an auspicious start to a day that she knew would be filled with frustrations. With all the preparations for the wedding, there would be a thousand minor *matters of importance* that would demand her attention during the day. And what was worse, she must be on her best behavior at all times, in case Ainsley was in the vicinity. She needed these few moments of freedom to gather her strength for the battles to come.

She held her horse to a sedate pace until they were out of sight of the house, then gave the animal his head. Urging him into a gallop, she reveled at the wind streaming past her ears, its sharp sting bringing tears to her eyes. Here, for a short while, she was free from restraint and care and mannerly behavior.

The headlong pace carried her nearly to the end of the near field when she spotted another lone rider approaching. Cecily tried to check her animal, but it was far too late. Of course she would encounter the very last person she wanted to see. Her hair was a windblown mop, her cheeks were bright red, and no doubt he had seen her riding like a wild hoyden. For an instant, she was tempted to race past, ignoring him, but common sense won her over and she reined in her horse.

"Good morning," she called with forced cheeriness.

"Good morning, Miss Montford," Ainsley said warily, groaning inwardly. He had thought to avoid her by riding so early in the morning. The last thing he wanted was a face-to-face confrontation with her now, when he was still trying to formulate the words of his long-overdue apology.

Cecily eyed him critically, wondering if he had ridden his horse at any pace faster than a walk. He looked immaculate; not one blond hair was out of place. His clothes fit to tailored perfection; his polished boots gleamed in the early morning light. He looked almost too perfect to be real. And it suddenly seemed quite impossible that he would ever look upon her as anything more than Robert's pesty little sister.

"It is an unusual hour to find a lady out riding," he said, attempting to hide his discomfort.

Cecily heard the veiled reproach in his voice. What did he think—that she had come chasing after him? What insufferable arrogance! "I often ride in the morning, Mr. Powell. I find it is a refreshing start to the day."

"Particularly at such an invigorating pace," he said.

"Precisely," she replied with a snap to her voice. "This is not Hyde Park, you know. A good gallop is part of country riding."

"I see," he said. "Then I imagine you found the sedate trots through the Park a great trial this spring."

"Even a sedate trot is not an unpleasant pastime if the company is amiable," Cecily retorted. His nonplussed expression pleased her.

"And was the company in London often amiable?"

"Quite so," she replied archly.

"I can only regret that I was not there to take a firsthand view of the scene."

"That is quite all right," she said. "Your absence was not particularly noted."

He looked taken aback at her set-down. Good, Cecily thought. It repaid him justly for his rudeness.

"You have properly set me in my place, Miss Montford," he said with a tight smile. "Robert said you were quite a success in town."

"Some reckoned it so," she said demurely. "But then, since you were not there, you shall have to form your own judgment."

He smiled weakly, praising the heavens for the fact he *had* been absent from town during that critical time. It was all he could do to endure a few moment's conversation with the girl; he was so wretchedly uncomfortable in her presence. Yet he could not form the apologetic words that would bring him some form of comfort. "I must not detain you longer, Miss Montford," he said coolly. "I am certain you still have some galloping to do."

"How considerate of you," she said with sweet sarcasm, then immediately chastened herself. She could not allow him to goad her into a temper; she preferred him to think she was supremely indifferent toward him. The man had far too high an opinion of himself. It would give her great satisfaction to bring him down a peg or two. With a curt nod of farewell, she urged her horse onward.

Watching her ride away, Ainsley berated himself at the thought of the wasted opportunity. It would have been the perfect time to extend his apologies; they were alone, with no possible witnesses to his shameful confession. By delaying, he had only made his own discomfort worse. Now he would have to deliberately seek her out, and arrange a private meeting. Why was he such a fool?

Ainsley felt the cowardly impulse to flee. Would Russia be far enough away? He could return in another six years. By then, certainly even she would have forgotten that long-ago incident.

But he knew he never would until he had properly apologized for his abominable behavior. With a regretful sigh, he turned his horse toward the stables. Perhaps if he wrote out the words on paper, and practiced them over and over, he would be better prepared when the next opportunity to speak with Miss Montford arose.

The arrival later that afternoon of her cousin Penelope was the brightest spot in Cecily's day, which, after that awkward encounter with Ainsley, had been filled with a number of potential crises. Not to mention her own growing anger at that insufferable, toplofty creature. She ached for another chance to show him how little she cared. How could she ever have made such a fool of herself over someone like him? A man still as full of conceit as he had been six years ago. And to think she had actually *wanted* to see him again.

With Pen's mother to distract Mama, Cecily successfully dispatched Susannah to stroll with Harry in the garden, and drew her cousin into the dining room—the one room in the house that was not crammed with guests—for a comfortable coze.

"I am so glad you are here," Cecily said as she poured tea for her cousin. "I fear I will be ripe for Bedlam before this wedding takes place."

"And, as usual, you are trying to do all of it yourself," Pen chided.

"Well, if I did not, it would not get done," Cecily replied with a disgusted shake of her head. "Susannah is worse than useless. She only comes alive when Harry is present; the remainder of the time she walks about in a daze. And you *know* how Mama is."

"At least let me help now that I'm here," Pen said.

Cecily nodded gratefully. "Although I think things are well in train. There is only the wedding-eve dinner, the wedding, and the reception after to get through."

"Who do you suppose will get the ring this year?" Pen asked wistfully.

Weddings in the Montford family were a great occasion, with the celebration the evening before the wedding nearly as lively as the party afterwards. The traditional pre-wedding dinner was followed with the cutting of the cake. It was almost as exciting as the plum pudding at Christmas to see who received what prize. The penny, to indicate future wealth; the miniature horseshoe, for luck; and the gold wedding band, to the one who would marry next.

And by some strange twist of fate, the cake's predictions had an unerring manner of coming true—at least for the person who captured the ring.

Cecily grinned. "You might like it. Mayhaps it will be all that is needed to make Aldershot come up to the mark," she said. Pen's latest escort had been assiduous in his attentions, but no offer of marriage had yet been uttered.

"Perhaps it will be you," her cousin shot back.

"Robert," Cecily retorted and they both burst into laughter. "I fear if Robert won the ring, it would be the end of the family tradition," she said ruefully. "Wherever would we find a lady who enjoyed mills, hunting, and carriage racing enough to put up with Robert?" That sent them off into another gale of laughter.

"Who else has arrived?" Pen asked when they

had wiped their eyes and recovered some semblance of decorum.

"Uncle Thomas and the boys, of course," Cecily began, ticking off the names on her fingers. "The Howards and Aunt Willis—Uncle Mann's gout flared up, so he stayed at home. And Henrietta arrived with all those giggling girls, who fortunately were dispatched to the schoolroom with Delia."

"No friends of Robert?" Pen asked with marked disappointment. "No one with whom to flirt?"

"Harry's family arrives tomorrow, but I do not know who accompanies them. I think Harry had a few friends coming, but they are staying at the inn." Cecily adopted an attitude of nonchalance. "And Ainsley Powell came with Robert."

"Powell!" Pen squealed. "Whyever did you not say so before?"

"I did not think his presence here was so notable," Cecily replied coolly.

Pen eyed her cousin with a questioning glance. "Ainsley Powell not notable? I daresay he could take his pick of the best households in the country to visit. He is always on the top of everyone's guest list."

Cecily scowled. "I do not see why. He is just another of Robert's rackety friends."

"And one of the most eligible gentlemen of the *ton*," Pen added. "Quite a coup to have him at your disposal."

"Ainsley Powell could vanish into a very dark hole without me missing him in the slightest," she said emphatically. "He is an insufferably arrogant prig, far too puffed up with his own importance."

"Too bad he missed the Season this year," Pen mused. "He would have livened up that dreary time. Perhaps I shall set him up as my flirt for this visit. That is, if you do not object."

"You are more than welcome to him," Cecily

replied hastily. "I only question why you would want to do such a foolish thing."

"Who else am I to turn to for amusement? Robert?"

They laughed at the very thought.

Ainsley, his attention caught by the sounds of feminine glee, quickly glanced into the dining room, wondering if some new beauty had arrived. After one glance, he hastened away. Cecily. Gossiping with her cousin. Damn! He had spent the entire morning composing the most abject apology he could devise, practicing it innumerable times until he thought he could say the words without hesitation. He had hoped to find Miss Montford alone.

But with the arrival of her cousin, his chances would be sorely diminished. He knew they were as thick as inkle-weavers. It would be deucedly difficult to get the girl alone without drawing attention to his actions. And that was the last thing he wished to do. It would only cause untold speculation. He would have to hope and pray that some providential opportunity would arise in the next few days. Surely, with all the fuss and confusion preceding the wedding, he would be able to draw Miss Montford aside long enough to speak his part. Then he could relax and enjoy himself at last.

That thought cheered him immensely, so he was quite willing, when he found Robert, to join in a game of billiards. He did not even mind when he lost. His torment would soon to be over.

Even Cecily could not force herself to wake early enough for her customary morning ride the following day. The exhaustive wedding preparations had taken their toll. She luxuriated in the sinful pleasure of remaining in bed until she knew the rest of the house would be awake. It would be a sedate ride in company today, she realized. Pen was no out-and-outer. But the disappointment at the pace of her ride would be outweighed by her cousin's cheerful chatter—and Cecily's brand new riding habit. In dark blue, with silver braid *a la Hussar*, it made Cecily feel all the kick. Even Ainsley Powell would be impressed with it. She would show him she knew how to cut a dash on horseback.

Robert and Harry were still at the breakfast table when Cecily entered the morning room.

" 'Bout time," Robert said. "Thought you were going to sleep the day away."

"*Some* of us prefer to rest before the festivities commence," she retorted, spreading a heaping spoonful of marmalade on her buttered toast. "Is Pen up yet?"

"We sent her after you," Robert said. He eyed his sister critically. "Cece, have you gone and done something I should know about?"

Cecily eyed him quizzically. "Such as?"

Robert tipped his chair back, inspecting her appearance carefully. "If I did not know better, I would be willing to wager you had joined the hussars." He turned to his friend. "What do you think, Harry?"

"I am not certain," he replied with a careful air. "Do hussar uniforms have quite that much braiding?"

Cecily gave both of them a dampening stare. "I will have you know that this is in the height of fashion," she said.

"Does Papa know you've gone and joined the military?" Robert teased. "He might not like it."

"Wretch," responded Cecily. "Perhaps Pen and I shall ride without you today."

"Oh no, please do not say such a thing." Robert clapped a hand over his heart and adopted a wounded air. "I will expire at the very thought."

"Promise?" Cecily asked eagerly.

"Anything to please you, dear sister." Robert rose and Harry joined him. "When Pen returns, come to the stables. We *might* wait for you."

Cecily felt much better after the return of her cousin, who totally agreed that the new habit was exquisite. She was much cheered by this until they entered the stable yard and found Ainsley waiting with her brother and Harry.

"Ah, here are the laggards at last," said Robert. "Allow me to help you on your horse, Lieutenant Montford. Or was that captain?"

"General," she retorted, snatching the reins from him and leading her horse to the mounting block. "I should have you flogged for your insolence, ensign."

"Yes, General Montford, sir," said Robert, flashing her a mocking salute before he mounted. "Better watch your step, men." He laughed. "Her every command must be obeyed."

Cecily fought against the flaming in her cheeks as the party rode out of the yard. She could cheerfully have throttled her brother on the spot. Once again, she was made to look a fool in front of Ainsley Powell. She had seen his amused smirk. Cecily almost wished she had never purchased the dratted habit. Someday, she would find a way to repay Robert for this.

Ainsley willingly allowed his horse to lag behind the others as they rode out into the sunny July morning. The goodnatured bantering between the siblings amused him. Cecily had put Robert firmly in his place. But all the attention drawn to her riding habit had apprised him of one thing—she might still be small as a child, but she did not have the shape of one. All that silver braid was very cleverly applied to give just the right emphasis to—well—to what he had to admit was a finely developed bosom. He had been so busy worrying about his own discomfort these last days that he had not stopped to take a very close look at the chit.

And it was partly her fault, he thought sourly. That short-cropped, curly hair of hers was most childlike in appearance. No wonder he had not looked beyond the immediate first impression to discover there were some very unchildlike aspects to Miss Montford's features. How could one girl look like a veritable waif one minute, and a highly attractive woman the next? And what was worse, she seemed totally unaware of the dichotomy she represented.

Was that why her presence invariably reduce him to a stammering idiot? My God, he was eight-and-twenty. No one, not even the worst schoolmaster at Eton, had sent his knees to quaking in such a manner. The occasional birchings he had endured as a child seemed as nothing compared to the strain of uttering a few words to her. Let alone apologizing for that ill-fated conversation in the summer house.

And he was developing the horrible thought that she really was quite indifferent to what had transpired between them all those summers ago. Which infuriated him even more. He had spent six years berating himself for his behavior, deliberately avoiding this house because of her, and it all looked to be unnecessary. He felt the veriest fool. And that made him even angrier.

He had never felt so ignored. Robert, Pen, and Harry were all included in the circle of her teasing this morning. Only he was left out. And it was a disconcerting notion that he had only himself to blame. Upon reflection, he *had* been rude to the point of boorishness in his every conversation with Miss Montford, because of his discomfort. No wonder she did not deign to acknowledge his presence. She could only expect another set-down.

He was acting like a veritable coxcomb. His behavior was, in truth, as abominable now as six years ago. While she had been nothing less than unfailingly polite. Ainsley was chagrined at his ragmannered behavior. No other female made him feel like such a callow youth. Why did she?

It was his own guilt, of course. Once he had apologized to her, he would be able to act in a rational manner when in her presence. He had worried and agonized and fretted for so long over this imaginary conversation that it loomed before him like an ominous dark cloud on the horizon. All he had to do was utter those few, well-chosen words and everything would be right again.

But how would he contrive to meet Cecily alone?

2

Cecily spent the remainder of the day awash in last-minute details. If it had not been for Pen, Cecily doubted she would even have had time to dress properly for the evening.

Twisting about, Cecily took one last look in the mirror. There was, she admitted, little that could be done to style her short curls into a more elegant coiffure. The green ribbon and the silk flowers made it look more *recherche*. She nervously smoothed her skirts and made one last attempt to tug her bodice a bit higher. Mama had assured her the dress was nothing exceptional for a young lady who had passed her first Season. But Cecily was still unaccustomed to seeing quite such an expanse of snowy white skin staring back at her from the mirror. She sighed. A truly mature lady would never worry that her neckline was too low.

And with this dress, Ainsley Powell would be forced to notice her—and she could display her supreme indifference to him. With a newly smug smile, Cecily snatched up the wispy shawl that would only provide ornamentation, not cover, and with a swish of her skirts she headed for the stairs.

In the drawing room, Ainsley chatted amiably with Robert's uncle—at least he thought it was his uncle. Or was he the first cousin once removed? He had just nodded for the umpteenth time at the long-winded explanation of the man's current crop-rotation plan when the uncle's eyes widened in an appreciative look.

"By jove, there's a sight for weary eyes."

Ainsley turned to see what had so captured the man's attention and nearly dropped his glass in shock at the sight. He knew it was impolite to stare, but he could not help himself.

If he had been rather surprised by the revelations of that hussar riding outfit this morning, it was nothing compared to the enlightenment he now experienced. Cecily Montford was a damned attractive young lady—in that dress, there was no avoiding it.

She was a stunner. Slim and delightfully curvy, her short stature enhanced rather than detracted from her appeal. A wave of protectiveness rushed over him. He could visualize himself hovering over her in a delightfully sheltering manner.

And there was no doubt whatsoever in his mind that she detested him. Her cool behavior toward him over the last few days indicated that all too clearly. He was entirely in her black books. And more than ever, he did not wish to be. He could not, of course, utter his abject apologies in as public an area as the drawing room. But by complimenting her on her appearance, he could begin to work his way back into her good graces, and smooth the way for the moment when he could get her alone. Carefully wending his way through the crowded room, he contrived to find himself at Cecily's side.

"A good evening, Miss Montford."

Cecily looked up, surprised. This was the first time she could recall Ainsley actually initiating a conversation with her. His eyes held an odd gleam.

"You look quite lovely tonight. One would have no trouble telling you from a hussar general."

It took all of Cecily's self-control not to stare at him in disbelief. He was paying her a compliment. Then her cheeks reddened. Or was he merely pointing out how inappropriate this dress was? She knew this had been the wrong thing to wear, no matter what Mama said. Now she had Ainsley Powell confirming her mistake.

Then Cecily smiled. Was this not exactly what she had been hoping for? The opportunity to show this maddening man that she was a woman now, and had outgrown her childhood? She suddenly recognized that odd gleam in his eyes—male appreciation for an attractive female. The kind of look she had longed to receive from Ainsley.

"Why, thank you, Mr. Powell," she began, fluttering her long lashes as Susannah did. She twirled about, letting the skirt of emerald-green sarsnet bell around her before it fell back against her legs. "Oh, do you like it?"

Oh, he liked it. His gaze was drawn to the heart-shaped emerald that lay at the end of the chain around her neck—nestled suggestively in the hollow between her enticingly displayed charms. He felt his cravat tighten about his neck.

Cecily sensed the direction of his gaze and casually fingered the chain of her necklace.

"It is very nice," he stammered, struggling to draw his eyes away from the alluring sight. Did she know what she was doing, drawing his attention so blatantly?

Cecily grinned inwardly. So far, her plan was succeeding beautifully. She felt delight at her ability to discompose him so thoroughly. "You look very well yourself. That is quite an impressive cravat."

"A creation of Robert's valet, I fear," he said ruefully.

"Ah yes, he does have a way with cravats," Cecily said. She could hardly believe that she was standing here, flirting with Ainsley Powell. She had succeeded at last! He was finally treating her like a grown woman.

The sight of Cecily in her low-cut gown totally unnerved Ainsley and he struggled to keep his eyes affixed to her face. All intelligent conversation fled his brain. "Dinner seems a bit late tonight," he observed weakly.

"Oh, never fear, it will be announced soon. Tonight is the night for the cake, you see."

"The cake?" he asked.

"Robert did not tell you about the cake?"

Ainsley shook his head.

"It is a family tradition," she explained. "There are prizes hidden in the cake—much like plum pudding at Christmas. It is all rather silly, but it has become a tradition at Montford weddings."

"A charming custom," he said. He looked down into her eager young face and was suddenly aware of the years separating them. He must seem rather old and fusty to her. In her eyes, was he merely a companion of her brother's? Did she compare him with the gentlemen she met in London that spring? And was the comparison favorable? He felt a sharp pang of regret at not having been there this spring. But would she have even noticed? "I remember how much I looked forward to finding the prizes in the pudding." He laughed in a self-deprecating manner. "Lord, what an ancient creature that makes me sound."

"I hardly think that at eight-and-twenty you can call yourself ancient, Mr. Powell." Her smile widened. "Seasoned, perhaps. But not ancient. Even to a youngster like myself."

"Then you must desist in calling me Mr. Powell," he insisted. "It makes me feel far too old and avuncular."

"Only if you call me Cecily," she said. "You pronounce 'Miss Montford' in such a way that I *do* feel like a recalcitrant schoolgirl."

"I beg your pardon, *Cecily*," he said with an easy grin.

"Much better, Ainsley," she replied. She laid a gloved hand on his arm. "Now, if you will excuse me, I see my uncle beckoning. Perhaps we can talk again after dinner." With an impish smile she turned her back on him and walked away.

Ainsley stared after her, a wide grin spreading across his face as he watched the gentle sway of her skirts. Baggage, he thought to himself with a chuckle. He still had not redeemed himself, he knew. But thought he was well on his way to accomplishing his goal.

Cecily struggled against an overwhelming urge to turn around and see just what kind of look Ainsley had on his face right now, after she had deliberately walked away from him. She silently uttered up thanks to her Mama for picking out this dress. She still might feel uncomfortable, but the look of blatant admiration on Ainsley's face was worth any amount of discomfort. Tomorrow she would have her maid lower the neckline on every dress she owned.

For once, the assembled company did not linger over dinner. Dish after dish whizzed by in dizzying speed, as the diners hastened over this necessary part of the meal to get to the event they were waiting for—the cutting of the wedding-eve cake. Cecily, like most of the company, could not keep her eyes off the gaily iced confection sitting on the sideboard.

The origination of this custom was lost in the shrouded past of the Montford family. It had been a tradition as long as Cecily's father and uncle could remember. But the prophecy—that was more recent. It went back to her parents' own wedding. For it was at that event that her Uncle Thomas had found the ring in his cake—and was he not married within three months? Amazingly, the prediction had held true for the past twenty-nine years. Granted, there had not been *that* many weddings in the family. Five or six, at the most, could truly be counted. But each recipient of the ring had been married within the year. That was enough for the entire family to declare that the prophecy was infallible. So each and every one of them looked forward to the cutting of the cake, the passing out of the pieces, and the discovery. Who would get the ring this time? Who would be the next to wed?

Everyone was in a fever pitch of excitement by the time the cake was placed in front of Cecily's father. He looked down his long nose at the table in stern imitation of his own father.

"It is a grave responsibility I have here," he intoned with mock severity. "The ordering about of people's lives is a very serious business." He looked about the table, smiling fondly at Cecily. Carefully, he cut the cake. Everyone waited with sanguine expectancy as the pieces were passed around. Good-natured joking went along, as well as some last-minute trading of pieces. Then they all began; the more eager ones dismantling the confection with their forks in search of a trinket, the more decorous members eating casually.

"Found something!" Robert called out.

Cecily and Pen shared smug glances.

Robert triumphantly held his token aloft. "Good luck," he cried, displaying the miniature horseshoe. "Must mean I will do well at the next Newmarket meet."

Cecily took another bite of cake.

"Money!" shouted Uncle Thomas, displaying the penny.

Everyone laughed. His parsimonious nature was well-known.

"Share it about this time," someone called out, to generous laughter.

Cecily smiled. Until she bit down on something hard. Using her napkin as cover, she carefully removed the object from her mouth, barely believing what she found there.

"I have it," she whispered.

"What's that?" her dining partner asked.

"I have the ring," she said in a louder voice.

"Impossible!" Robert hooted. "The prediction has run out of luck at last. Whoever would want to marry you?"

Cecily shot him a quelling look.

"What the—?" Ainsley extricated something from his mouth. "I have one too."

A hushed silence fell over the table. All eyes turned to Ainsley and Cecily.

"Two rings?" Cecily's father was puzzled. "We've never had two rings before."

"Who gets married first?"

"They're to marry each other," Robert suggested with a wicked grin.

Cecily blushed scarlet and focused her eyes on her plate. She was dying to know the expression on Ainsley's face, but she dared not look. Earlier, she had thought she had reached some sort of accommodation with him, but she knew this would be the end. He would no doubt think she had devised this humiliating scene. She would be lucky if he ever spoke to her again.

"No, it means two weddings," Pen said.

Cecily cast her cousin a grateful look.

"A toast then," Lord Lawton announced. He raised his glass to Cecily. "To the next bride." He turned to Ainsley. "And to the next groom."

Cecily toyed with the remaining cake on her plate. When she finally dared a glance at Ainsley, it was as she imagined. He looked extremely uncomfortable—and irritated. As if sensing her perusal, he turned in her direction, the anger in his eyes flaring as he met her gaze.

Her own anger rose at the sight. How could he think that she had arranged this on purpose? The man must have an insufferably high opinion of himself if he thought anyone would attempt to scheme on such a thing. Besides, it was impossible. No one knew where the prizes were located in the cake; Cook always said that by the time the frosting was applied, she was not certain where things were. It was pure chance that she and Ainsley had both gotten rings.

But how had two rings been secreted in the cake?

Ainsley tried to convince himself that the whole situation was sheer coincidence. There was no earthly way anyone could have known he would get the ring. No one could have planned this.

But yet, there had been two rings, when normally there was only one. He would suspect a prank if Cecily had not announced before all and sundry that she had the ring before he had made his own announcement. It was impossible for her to have contrived such a thing.

And the stricken expression on her face told him

she was at least as uncomfortable as he. Which was entirely his fault. If he had already apologized to her, this could have been an amusing incident for both of them, instead of a painful reminder of that awful scene in the summer house.

He had to talk with her. He had to apologize for his abominable behavior, and lay the matter to rest once and for all. They would never be comfortable in each other's presence until that had been taken care of. It must be dealt with as soon as possible. Tonight.

Cecily endured the good-natured teasing of the ladies when they withdrew to the drawing room, but inside she was not at all composed. In fact, she felt sick at the very thought of what had transpired at dinner. After that muddle with the rings, how was she ever going to talk with Ainsley in a natural manner again?

Of course, that problem would most likely never present itself. She doubted he would ever speak to her again—at least not in this century. And Robert . . . strangling would be too good for him. She would have to devise a more torturous form of revenge for his ill-considered remark. Never before had she been so aware of the havoc mischievous brothers could wreak on one's life.

Once the men rejoined the ladies, Cecily took great pains to keep as far from Ainsley as possible. She could only guess at the embarrassment he must feel at having his name paired with hers. If it was only half her own, it was quite enough.

She played the pianoforte while Pen sang, then dragged her cousin off to the far side of the room where they were unlikely to be bothered. Tomorrow, when everyone was involved with the excitement of the wedding, perhaps then she could talk to Ainsley privately. But not now, when everyone would remark and comment upon it. She would be safe enough in the crowded drawing room.

Then Pen deserted her. Cecily glanced around the room with frantic eyes, wondering who she could next embroil in a pointless conversation. But she dallied too long, for she was greeted with the sight of a determined Ainsley Powell bearing down on her. She shrank from the confrontation.

Admitting her cowardice, Cecily turned tail and ran—or at least slipped out onto the terrace. Perhaps in the dark he would not find her.

Her heart racing, she stopped for a moment to allow her eyes to adjust to the dim light. She did not want to trip over some rough stone and end up sprawling. With her luck, Ainsley would find her in just such an undignified position.

As her eyes adjusted to the dark, and her fears quieted, Cecily realized she was not the only person outside on this warm summer night. She heard two voices—male and female—arguing.

Susannah and Harry! How could they be arguing? The wedding was tomorrow. Ignoring the little voice that told her she would be eavesdropping, Cecily cautiously inched closer to the edge of the terrace.

"Susannah, all I said was—"

"That you have no care for my feelings," came the tearful rejoinder.

"I said no such thing. You are the one who is making such a fuss out of such a simple thing. I only offered it as a suggestion."

"You are a beast," Susannah exclaimed. "A domineering, arrogant, heartless beast."

Cecily drew in her breath. It sounded as if Susannah was working herself into one of her passions.

"Susannah!" Harry exclaimed. "You are being ridiculous."

"I?" she said, her voice shrill. "Ridiculous?"

"Yes," he said sternly.

Cecily jumped as a hand clamped down on her shoulder.

"I want to have a—"

"Shh!" she hissed, turning to see Ainsley close behind her. She waved her arm to silence him. "It's Susannah and Harry. Arguing."

"What about?" Ainsley whispered.

Cecily shook her head. "I do not know. But Susannah is working herself into a fine fury. I pity poor Harry."

"But it is the night before their wedding," he said.

"*I* know that. It is excessively foolish."

"We ought to do something."

"Shhh."

"You are the most selfish man on earth, Harry Arbuthnot. I would rather marry a . . . a goat."

"Oh you would, would you?"

"Well, I certainly have no intention of marrying you," Susannah cried.

"Do not be so foolish," Harry snapped.

"It is not foolish to escape from a marriage that would only be a disaster," Susannah cried. "How could I have been blinded to your true nature for so long? I hate you."

Susannah flashed past Cecily and Ainsley and disappeared into the house.

"Damnation," said Harry, stomping up the stairs. He darted a startled glance at Cecily and Ainsley. "What are you doing here?"

"Eavesdropping," Cecily replied. "What is Susannah in a pet about?"

"I merely asked her," said Harry in a defensive tone, "if we could not stop and visit my parents after our wedding trip. She acted as if I had asked her to travel to the Antipodes."

"What did Susannah wish to do?"

"Why, return here, of course," he said. "I have no objections to your family, Cecily, but I thought it was unobjectionable to wish to spend some time with my own as well." He scowled.

"You cannot let Susannah have her own way all the time," Cecily cautioned him. "She is spoiled enough as it is."

"It may not matter. She says she wishes to call the wedding off."

"Nonsense," said Cecily. "Susannah would never give up the opportunity to be the center of attention for an entire day. We shall just have to bring her around to your way of thinking."

"I am past trying to talk sense with that woman," he said sourly and stalked past them toward the house. "If she wishes to call the wedding off, I shall let her."

"Where are you going?" Ainsley asked.

"To get roaring drunk."

Cecily looked at Ainsley in dismay. "We must do something!"

"What can we do? By interfering, we could only make matters worse."

"But the wedding is tomorrow," she protested. "We cannot possibly allow them to call it off. Think of all the work! All my preparations!"

"Perhaps I can talk with Harry," he said reluctantly.

"I'll go to Susannah," Cecily announced. "You see to Harry. Meet me back here in fifteen minutes."

"All right," he agreed, and ambled toward the house.

It took longer than fifteen minutes to draw the story out of a tearful Susannah, and Cecily was afraid that Ainsley would have abandoned the terrace in exasperation before she arrived. But he was there, waiting.

"Well? What did she say?"

Cecily smiled impishly. "She said Harry was the most selfish creature in the world—to which I agreed."

Ainsley frowned. "I am not certain that is making progress."

"She also said—well, never mind. It was all in the same vein."

"So what did you accomplish?" Ainsley asked coolly.

"She was appreciative of my sympathetic nature, warned me never to be cozened by a sweet-talking male, and generally made a fool of herself."

"I may as well tell Harry to head for home," Ainsley said, scowling.

"Oh, no, things are going remarkably well," Cecily explained. "She even asked after Harry."

"She did?"

"Yes, she said he was probably shooting billiards with Robert or drinking in the library and totally ignoring her distress."

"Did you tell her what he said?"

"No, I told her he was flirting with cousin Pen."

"You what?" Ainsley rounded on her.

"Believe me, that got her attention. She sent me back down to keep an eye on him and report back to her."

"Cecily, what could you have been thinking of?" Ainsley demanded. "You have made a total mull of things."

"I have not," she said. "Think of the progress I've made. Susannah has already gone from thinking Harry's a selfish beast into worrying because he's flirting with another lady."

"I fail to see where that is much of an improvement," he commented sourly.

"You have to understand Susannah," Cecily explained to him patiently. "She loves to be the center of attention, but she hates to lose even more. If she thinks she's in danger of losing Harry, she will do anything to hold on to him. Even agree to travel to his parents'."

"You are certain?" He sounded doubtful.

"I hope so," she replied. "If not, a terrible amount of work is going to go for naught."

"I cannot believe she would call off the wedding at the last moment," he said. "It is just not done."

"Tell that to Susannah," Cecily countered.

"Women are so unstable," he muttered. "Changing their mind at a whim—"

"I beg your pardon," said Cecily in heated indignation. "Everyone knows men are far worse. And pigheaded and stubborn to boot."

Ainsley opened his mouth for a rejoinder, but then closed it. In the silvery moonlight he saw the sparkle of anger in her eyes, the fighting way she held her body as she defended her sex. She looked adorable. For a moment, it took a great deal of effort to remember exactly what they were discussing.

Cecily grew acutely conscious of the intent manner with which Ainsley stared at her.

"Is something wrong?" she asked crossly.

"No," he said, startled by the wayward turn of his thoughts. He couldn't possibly be attracted to this chit. It was the pernicious wedding atmosphere that clouded his thinking. And he suddenly recalled that without some effort on their part, there might not be a wedding on the morrow. "What shall we do next?"

"I will go up and feed her jealous fears with tales of Harry's attentiveness to Pen," Cecily replied. "That will drive her back into his arms."

Ainsley shook his head slightly at her logic, but did not argue. Let Cecily be in charge of this mad scheme.

"I will be back soon, I hope." She darted off.

Ainsley watched her go with rising admiration. The chit certainly knew how to manage her sister. *If* her plan worked. He'd best report to Harry and make certain the man had not drunk the entire decanter of brandy. If Cecily succeeded, Harry would not want to feel wretched for his wedding.

He found a morose Harry still in the library, a generous glass of brandy in his hand. Ainsley offered a few words of encouragement, poured himself a brandy, then hastened back to the terrace to await Cecily's return with more eagerness than he wished to admit.

"How is Harry?" she asked at her return.

"Still drinking in the library," he replied. "Or perhaps he is merely sitting, staring at the glass in his hand. He was not moving much when I spoke to him."

"Poor Harry," she said.

"Progress?" he asked.

She nodded. "I reported that both you and Harry were circling around Pen."

"Thanks for dragging me into this," he said dryly.

"It roused her spirit of combat. She would hate Pen to have more admirers than she."

"What will she do?"

"She sent me down here with instructions to lure you away from Pen."

He laughed. "At least you can report your success in that area. But what about Harry? And the wedding?"

"She wants to think about him for a while longer," Cecily said. "I am supposed to flirt heavily with you, but keep my eye on Harry and Pen and report to her shortly."

"Well, do your best," he said, leaning back against the terrace wall with arms folded across his chest. "I'm ready."

"I would not dare flirt with you," she said primly.

"And why not?" he demanded. "Am I not a worthy target?"

"I do not think a flirtation with you would be a very successful venture. I am certain you are far too accustomed to the London ladies to appreciate my feeble efforts."

"I fear you underrate yourself, Miss Montford," he said. "You shall never know unless you make the attempt."

"You do have some manner of a reputation, you know," she said. "Word is that you are quite an accomplished flirt yourself."

"Pure rumor," he replied. He held up his hands defensively. "Have I done one thing to substantiate such talk? I thought I have remained a perfect gentleman."

Cecily rather wished he had not. She was curious to know what it would be like to flirt outrageously with Ainsley Powell—and have her flirtations returned. A slight shiver shook her body at the thought and she suddenly felt uncomfortable in his presence.

"I must go back to Susannah," she said hastily and fled.

Ainsley remained on the terrace, sipping his brandy with studied slowness. Now that his eyes had been opened, Cecily Montford was turning out to be an interesting study. An intriguing baggage, flitting from coy schoolgirl to practiced flirt in an instant. Young and mercurial and full of life. Far from dreading her presence, he looked forward to her next appearance, eager to discover what new facet she would present.

Robert's little sister had grown up. It even appeared that, miraculously, she forgave him for his atrocious behavior all those years ago. Remarkable. It made him feel even shabbier about his cavalier dismissal of her childish infatuation. Somehow, he would have to make amends. He realized with a sudden shock just how much he would like to be in Cecily Montford's good graces.

Ainsley looked up with unfeigned eagerness when he heard her steps again on the flagged terrace.

"Quick!" she cried. "Get Harry!"

"What for?"

She pushed Ainsley toward the house. "Susannah is coming down. I'll fetch Pen. You fill Harry in on what he needs to do."

"What does he need to do?" Ainsley asked in confusion.

"Flirt with her! Get him out here on the terrace." Cecily raced back into the house.

Amused by the absurdity of this charade, Ainsley nevertheless followed her instructions and dragged a reluctant and slightly maudlin Harry out on the terrace. Cecily and Pen awaited them.

Harry, if not foxed, was at least a bit unsteady, and he leaned against the terrace wall with obvious relief. Cecily arranged the remaining players in a grouping about him that made it all look very innocent—should anyone catch a glimpse of the four—but at the same time would serve to fan Susannah's jealousy.

"Talk!" Cecily hissed at her reluctant companions.

"Nice weather we're having, ain't it?" Harry mumbled.

Cecily glanced at Ainsley and rolled her eyes in despair.

"Saw a new hunter last week at Alvorson's," Ainsley offered, coming to her rescue. "Think I might go back next week and make an offer."

"Do you hunt regularly, Mr. Powell?" Pen asked.

Harry, getting into the spirit of things, nodded vigorously. "Regular out-and-outer, he is. Even hunts with the Quorn. Lord, you should have seen the party we got up for Melton last year. Rented a house and all and invited—"

"Harry," said Ainsley in a warning tone.

". . . a lot of company," Harry finished lamely.

Cecily instantly wondered exactly *what* type of company they had invited, but she dare not ask. She eyed Ainsley with a swift appraising glance. Did he dally with the muslin set? That thought set off a strange churning in the pit of her stomach.

A strangled noise from Harry drew her attention back to her companions on the terrace. Susannah was approaching.

Cecily fluttered her lashes at Ainsley. "Do tell us of your travels this spring, Ainsley. I do so wish to travel someday."

"You would like Italy," he said, wondering if she would. "They have great appreciation for beautiful, red-haired women there."

Cecily found herself blushing. She had not expected him to flirt with *her*. She gratefully grabbed the approaching Susannah.

"Do join us," she said, anxiously scanning her sister's face to ascertain her mood. "Ainsley was about to tell us of his travels."

"You picked such a shocking time to abandon London, Ainsley," Susannah chided, pointedly ignoring Harry. "The Season was so bleak without your presence."

"I quite apologize," said Ainsley with a grin. "Had I known the ladies would be so downcast . . . And to think I missed dear Cecily's debut." He smiled at her in a meaningful manner. "I shall endeavour to make up the slight during the Little Season. You will be coming to town then?"

"Perhaps," replied Cecily in a casual tone. "One hates to make plans so far in advance."

She saw the laughter in Ainsley's eyes and it was all she could do to refrain from laughing herself.

She rather liked flirting with Ainsley Powell. He was so wickedly good at it.

"Mama mentioned that we shall be going to town, so if your parents do not wish to, you may come with me," Pen offered. She turned to Susannah. "Shall you be there as well?"

Susannah darted a quick glance at Harry, then lowered her eyes. "I am not certain." Her face was set in a stony smile. "It depends upon the actions of *certain persons*."

"Dash it all, Susannah, this is beyond foolishness." Harry abandoned his indolence, grabbed her arm and dragged her down the terrace steps.

Ainsley looked at Cecily in consternation. "Did we succeed or fail?"

She wrinkled her nose. "I am not certain. At least we managed to get Harry to take some initiative."

"Just so you explain my role in all of this to Susannah," warned Pen. "I should hate to never be able to speak to Harry again without rousing her suspicions."

"I will," Cecily promised. She darted a sly glance at Ainsley. "I shall tell her you were merely flirting with Harry to make Ainsley jealous."

"Capital idea," said Ainsley in a tone that contradicted his words.

"Susannah would understand *that*," Pen said. "I am going back inside. Let me know when you discover if the wedding is still on."

Cecily stood quietly next to Ainsley, straining to hear any sound from the argumentative lovers. But even in the night's stillness, she heard nothing. Perhaps they had wandered farther into the gardens.

She turned to Ainsley. "Shall we follow them?"

"You intend to spy on your sister?" he asked in mock horror.

Cecily sent him a withering glance. "Do you mean

to say that you do not entertain the tiniest spark of curiosity regarding the outcome of our efforts?"

He grinned. "I am dying of curiosity," he confessed. He placed her hand on his arm. "Shall we go for a stroll, Miss Montford? You never know whom we may run across during our perambulations."

"Quite so," she said.

The nearly full moon afforded enough light for them to traverse the pathway in comparative safety. Cecily felt quite smug about taking a turn about the garden in Ainsley's company—even if they were only in the role of co-conspirators. It meant he was treating her as a lady.

He halted suddenly.

"What—?"

"Ssh." He pointed across the garden.

Cecily squinted, barely making out two figures on the far side of the garden. At least she thought it was two. They were wrapped so closely in each other's arms that it was difficult to tell.

Ainsley took Cecily's hand and they hastily retraced their steps back to the terrace.

"I think we can determine the evening was a success," he said, when they were far enough away not to be overheard. "My congratulations to you, my dear. A masterful plan."

Cecily glowed with pride at his words. "You helped," she said charitably, then giggled. "I hope Susannah will be speaking to Pen tomorrow."

Ainsley chuckled. "And if she is not, you will do something to rectify the situation, won't you? I had no idea you were such a managing female."

Cecily was not certain whether he meant it as a compliment or an insult. "Force of habit," she said with a tight smile. "*Someone* has to take charge."

"And you do it admirably," he said, surprised at how firmly he meant it. "I imagine there is nothing you could not accomplish, should you set your mind to it."

"Really?" she asked eagerly, then dampened her enthusiasm. Here she was, sounding like a schoolgirl again.

"I am surprised you did not come back from your first visit to London with a duke, or at least a marquess in tow."

"I was far too busy organizing Susannah's wedding to pay much attention to *that*," she said truthfully.

"Then heaven help the gentlemen in the future. Perhaps I should ride to London and warn them."

Cecily gave him a sidelong glance. There he was, flirting with her again. Well, if he wished to play that game, she would be more than happy to oblige him.

"La, sir," she trilled, wishing she had her fan. He deserved to be thwacked on the arm. "Whatever would I do then? You would deprive me of all my entertainment."

"Baggage."

"Baggage?" she retorted, an indignant look on her face.

"Impudent, flirtatious baggage," he said, laughing. "You will have all the town at your feet."

"Then why are you, sir, still upon yours?" she riposted.

Ainsley tossed back his head and laughed. "Lord, Cecily, you are a quick one. Why, I'm almost tempted to . . ."

"Yes?" she inquired.

He meant to say 'steal a kiss', but fortunately had gathered his wits before he had blurted out those ill-advised words. He had almost forgotten himself. It would never do. "Never mind," he said, pulling her forward to the terrace steps. "We had better get you inside before they think the night fairies spirited you off."

Cecily was rather disappointed to have their *tête-à-tête* end, but she also did not wish to be found out here alone with him either. By anyone. People would make far too much of an innocent situation.

She turned to him outside the door. "Thank you for your help, Ainsley," she said. "I daresay without it, Harry would be in a brandied stupor in the library and Susannah would still be in hysterics."

"It was all your success, Cecily," he said. He leaned down and planted a soft kiss on her brow. "You go inside. I shall follow in a moment."

Her senses in a whirlwind of confusion, Cecily did as he bid.

Ainsley remained on the terrace, leaning against the wall in a negligent pose. Once again, he had allowed an opportunity to apologize slip by. But caught up in their little conspiracy, enjoying their flirtatious banter, he quite forgot there was something he still had to say to her. And by the time he did remember, he had no desire to ruin what had been an entertaining evening. There would be time enough tomorrow to talk to her.

Amazingly, Cecily found that her absence had been little noted in the crowded drawing room. She circulated among her relatives, making sure they all saw her, then fled into the hall to seek the safety of her room. She knew she would not be able to look Ainsley in the face again this night.

He had kissed her. True, it had been more of a brotherly peck, and on her forehead at that, but it had been a kiss. And her reaction to it shocked even her. She wished to know how a more intimate salute from those lips would feel. Rather pleasant, she suspected.

Still, his actions meant little. Just because they had arrived at some tolerable accommodation with each other did not mean there were any stronger emotions at work. It was a wild leap to imagine he entertained anything more than brotherly thoughts about her. After all, had he not called her "baggage"? Hardly a term of affection. What passed between them on the terrace and in the garden was mere flirtatious jesting.

Cecily realized how very little she knew about his life, other than he shared Robert's interests in sporting. Was he full of secret vices? Did he gamble or have a mistress stuck away in some snug cottage in Islington? She had no idea. For all she knew he was dangling after some elegant and charming heiress. Although she rather doubted the latter— that news would likely have reached her ears.

She liked the way he fell in so readily with her plans tonight. It bespoke a similarity of mind. She knew it had been his startlingly handsome blond looks that had so captivated her during that last ignominious visit. What cared a twelve-year-old for a man's habits, or spending practices? But she was now consumed with an overwhelming urge to know more about him—why had he traveled all about the Continent this spring; why he and Harry and Robert were such friends; and why he had not yet been lured into matrimony.

It was pure curiosity, she assured herself. She was in no danger of making a fool of herself over him again.

But then why had the brush of his lips sent such tremors racing through her?

3

Ainsley was still very much on Cecily's mind when she awoke the next morning. Not even the excitement of Susannah's wedding day could push him from her thoughts. And combined with the thrill from that brief, chaste kiss was the dread that on the morrow he would be gone from her life again. Cecily fervently wished the wedding was still a week away, so she would have the opportunity to spend more time in his company.

Ainsley. Even his name sounded different this morning. Instead of conjuring up humiliation and remorse, it offered promise and laughter. Yet she would be lucky if they had the opportunity to say even a few words to each other during the hectic day.

The Little Season in October looked to be years away. And there was no guarantee he would be in town then. What was worse, he might very well have come to an agreement with another lady by that time. Had not Pen said he was considered a rare catch? What chance did she have against the seasoned beauties of town?

And worse, no other lady would ever remind him of those humiliating moments in the summer house. It was foolish to think he would ever eye her with anything other than brotherly affection.

But with Susannah's wedding only hours away, there was little time to dwell on her own problems. Cecily did not even have time to talk with her older sister, to make certain all the unpleasantness from the previous night had been patched over. Before she knew it, it was time to dress, and it was only when the ladies gathered to prepare for the drive to the church that Cecily was able to speak to her sister.

"Nervous?" Cecily asked, squeezing Susannah's hand.

She shook her head. "Thank you Cecily, for your help last night. I do not know what I would have done if you had not intervened. I—"

"It was nothing," Cecily said warmly. "I had a vested interest in the outcome, remember. I only wished to make certain my move to your room would not be jeopardized."

Susannah smiled fondly and Cecily began to realize that she was actually going to miss her sister.

"Come, girls, come," urged Lady Lawton. "Everyone else has left. Now Cecily, straighten your bonnet. And Susannah, do not fidget during the ceremony. All eyes will be upon you and you wish to appear at your best."

Behind her mother's back, Delia pulled a face. Cecily admonished her with a stern look, then grinned in return.

The short ride to the village church was accomplished without mishap. Cecily followed her mother and Delia to the front of the crowded church, smiling gaily at the assembled neighbors and relatives. Taking her seat, she cautiously looked about until she caught Ainsley's eye. He sat on the other side of the aisle, lolling casually in the pew. He gave her an ostentatious wink. She smiled back, then quickly turned away.

Even though she did not look at him again during the ceremony, Cecily sensed a bond between her and Ainsley that crossed the space separating them. They both had a hand in bringing about this wedding today. They had worked together as a team to reunite the quarrelling lovers. It had been a satisfying experience. One they alone shared, like a secret between them.

For Cecily, who always took on so much by herself, it was a revelation to work so closely with another. She never knew when Susannah or her mother would back out of a project and leave her to finish as best she could. Ainsley had stayed by her side the entire time, playing his part to the hilt. Never once did she doubt she could rely on him. With a shock, she realized just how nice it was to have that kind of trust in another.

When the ceremony ended, and the newly wedded couple prepared to walk down the aisle, Cecily darted another glance at Ainsley. He was smiling broadly and, when he caught her glance, his grin widened. He raised his hand in mock salute.

In all the fuss outside the church, where relatives and guests lined up to be transported back to the house for the wedding festivities, Cecily was surprised when Ainsley grabbed her arm and led her to Robert's prize curricle.

"It is only fair that the two people most responsible for the success of this wedding get at the food first," he joked as he helped her up into Robert's pride and joy.

"Indeed," she agreed. Her pleasure that she would not be crushed into a carriage with numerous relatives warred with her nervousness at being alone with him again.

"That is an impressive bonnet," he said, with an admiring glance at the flower-bedecked creation, as they began the short drive back to the house.

"Why, thank you," she said. "I am particularly fond of it myself."

"That shade of green becomes you."

Cecily eyed him warily. "Are you trying to flirt with me again, Ainsley Powell?"

"Why, I am shocked that you would think such a thing, Miss Montford. I was merely extending to you the modest compliments I would extend to any lady of consequence."

"Oh." He certainly deflated her aspirations.

"Of course, I will flirt with you if that is your wish." He grinned widely.

"I think we are doing fine as we are," she said primly, turning back to face the road ahead. If truth were told, flirting with Ainsley Powell made her a trifle breathless. She firmly reminded herself it was only flirting. Had not Pen said he was accomplished at that art? His present attention meant little.

"I understand there is to be dancing later." He kept his tone casual.

"Montford weddings are rather lively," she admitted.

"Then you must promise to save one for me," he said.

Cecily turned her head to look at him, noting as she did so that he had the tiniest of bumps marring the absolute perfection of his nose. Had he broken it at some time past? A childhood accident, or a sporting mishap? She desperately wished to know. "I should be happy to save you a dance, Ainsley." She would reserve him a waltz, she decided. As a treat to herself.

Ainsley glanced down at the tiny green sprite at his side. Cecily's face was thoroughly hidden by that enormous bonnet, which unnerved him. He still had not spoken his apology to her. He tried to gather the courage to utter the words he needed to say, but it was just not the proper setting. Later—after their dance. That would be the perfect time. He would draw her aside and offer her a formal apology.

It was deucedly awkward to have put it off until his last day, but perhaps that was for the best. It would give her something to think about until they met again. Which he hoped would happen very soon. He very much wanted to see more of Cecily Montford.

Upon arriving back at the house, Ainsley quite properly helped her down from the vehicle. And if he allowed his hand to linger on hers a fraction longer than he should, she did not seem discomposed by the attention. It gave him the opportunity to admire her trim figure for a moment.

"Thank you for the swift trip," she said, flashing him a radiant smile.

That look warmed him down to his toes. And at the same time sent a sharp jab to his midsection. Good God, he was not actually smitten with this imp, was he? Cecily Montford? It was out of the question.

As soon as Ainsley escorted her into the house, Cecily excused herself and made one last quick appraisal of the arrangements. All seemed in order. There was enough food for a small village, with every variety of liquid refreshment. By the time the musicians arrived, the party would be at its height.

Satisfied that all was well, Cecily drifted out to the terrace, where her parents and the newly wedded couple were greeting their first guests. Harry grabbed her by the hand.

"Thank you," he whispered before bestowing a smacking kiss on her cheek.

Cecily blushed profusely.

The afternoon passed in a swirl of activity. Cecily noted, with amused despair, that Robert had not waited long to get up a game of cricket on the back lawn. She should be grateful that he had not proposed a carriage race. From the terrace, she watched the men cavorting across the lawn, their heated actions incongruously contrasting with their formal attire. Nearly everyone had removed their coats, the flashing colors of their multihued waistcoats made them look like a covey of exotic birds. Ainsley, she noted, had dispensed with his cravat and, like Robert, had rolled up his sleeves. She laughed at their intensity. Men were so serious about their play.

Returning to the house, she watched while Susannah and Harry sampled the bridal cake, and helped herself to another plate of food. Cecily felt rather adrift now that there was nothing further for her to do.

In fact, she wondered exactly what she would do for the remainder of the summer. After looking forward to this event for the better part of six months, life would seem sadly flat. Susannah would be gone, and Delia was not much company. Perhaps she would visit Pen for a while. Life around her cousin was always lively. The weather near the coast would be nice.

It would not be all that long until the Little Season in the fall. Cecily decided emphatically that she would go to town for it. Her plan might surprise Mama, but no objections would be made. And it would be enormous fun to go with Pen. Aunt Percy would not be obsessed with trying to find a suitor for her niece. And if she was very lucky, Ainsley Powell would be in London as well. That thought cheered her to her toes.

The long shadows of the late-summer twilight were darkening the drive when Cecily and the other guests tossed rose petals with wild abandon as Susannah and Harry ran the gauntlet from the house to their carriage to begin their wedding trip. Strains of music drifted from the house, reminding Cecily that she had yet to have her dance with Ainsley. There was still something to look forward to this evening.

And indeed, she had hardly returned to the house after watching the carriage disappear down the drive when that anticipated event arrived.

"I have come for my dance," Ainsley announced, planting himself before her as she entered the room.

Cecily held out her hand. "With pleasure, Mr. Powell."

The dance, as she had hoped, was a waltz, and

Cecily felt a tiny thrill at the touch of his hand upon her waist.

"Your sister's wedding has been a resounding success," he commented. "You must be pleased."

"It is a great relief to have it over and done," she admitted.

"You will have to start planning for your own soon," he said.

She looked at him in puzzlement.

"The ring," he reminded her. "You are the next to be wed."

"As are you," she reminded him.

"Perhaps I shall allow you to plan my wedding as well."

Cecily focused her gaze on his cravat. "I am certain your bride would entertain some objections to that."

He did not reply and she concentrated on her steps. But somehow, in the complicated pattern of the dance, Ainsley maneuvered them next to the doors, and in an instant he whisked them both out onto the terrace.

"Much better," he said as he circled her about the terrace. "One could barely breathe in all that heat."

"It is pleasant out here," she agreed. It was a glorious summer's evening, warm and still, with a full, round moon peeking over the top of the trees.

The music died and they stood there hesitantly.

"I thank you—" Cecily began.

"Should you care to go for a walk?"

"Yes." Cecily decided instantly, wishing to linger in his presence. She lay her hand on his arm and they descended into the garden, much as they had the previous night. But instead of confining their steps to that enclosed place, Ainsley led her out across the lawn.

"It is a beautiful evening," he commented as they strolled along.

"Indeed," she agreed.

She thought they were engaged in a casual stroll, but as Ainsley directed her steps imperiously in a certain direction, she had a dreadful idea where he was leading her.

"Perhaps we should investigate the pond," she suggested quickly.

"Might slip and fall in," he countered.

"The gardens will look lovely in the moonlight."

"We saw them last night."

"Ainsley!" Her voice rose in protest.

He stopped and gave her a searching look. "I had not thought you craven, Cecily."

She drew herself up indignantly. "I am not!"

"Good." He took her arm again and dragged her in the direction he wished to go. At last he halted in front of the summer house. It was time to lay the past to rest, forever. There could be no thought of a future until that had been achieved.

"Ainsley, how could you?" she wailed. "I thought we had cried friends?"

"That is precisely why we are here," he said. Keeping a firm grip on her hand, he resolutely went up the stairs and pushed open the door.

"It's dark in here," he commented.

"Good enough reason to leave," she said.

"Should have brought a candle or two," he said regretfully. "Are the benches still here?"

"Along the far wall," she admitted.

Gradually his eyes adjusted to the dim light and he drew Cecily to the bench, gently pushing her down on to it. He placed one foot upon it and leaned upon his bent leg.

"Why are you doing this?" she asked, looking up at his dim countenance.

"Because I owe you an apology, Cecily, for what

happened here six years ago," he said simply. "I acted abominably."

"You did?" She stared at him with a look of astonishment. "I am paralyzed with mortification whenever I think on my own behavior."

"That is only because I reacted so poorly," he said ruefully. "Forgive me Cecily. There I was, not quite twenty-two and very full of myself. The thought that I inspired hero worship in the eyes of a twelve-year-old girl did not further that image."

"I made a cake of myself," she insisted.

"But so did I, and I was old enough to know better. I was far too brutal."

"Well," she said, considering, "perhaps you were."

"Rather than laughing outright, I should have gracefully accepted your gift," he said. "I could have mumbled some pleasing phrases about looking forward to the time you were old enough to court properly, or some such thing. It would have saved the both of us endless embarrassment."

Cecily had never stopped to look at the incident from his eyes. She was astounded to think that he held regrets over his behavior. It made her feel all the more in charity with him.

"Will you accept my apology?" he asked gently.

"Only if you will accept mine, for having been so foolish in the first place."

"You were only twelve," he said. "Something I failed to overlook at the time."

"Then I will forgive you for crushing my aspirations so very thoroughly," she said.

Ainsley squeezed her hand, and sat beside her. "I have told you of all my adventures this spring. But I have not heard of yours."

"There is little to tell."

"Your first Season and there is nothing to tell?" He looked at her askance.

"Well, nothing of importance," she confessed. "I was presented at court, received vouchers for Almack's, and visited and shopped and talked and danced until I was quite full of it."

"And how many proposals of marriage did you receive?"

"None, you horrid man."

"I am shocked. Not a one?"

"I did not encourage anyone," she explained. "Really, I was far too busy with Susannah's wedding plans to even contemplate such a thing."

"But that is the whole purpose of the Season," he protested. "I do not think you were going about things properly. I shall have to explain matters to you."

"Oh?" She eyed him with a glint of amusement.

"Yes." He leaned back against the seat and adopted a learned look. "Now, you start with subtle flirting. You pick out a man who has attracted your attention and glance at him, ever so casually, over the top of your fan."

"I can manage that," she said, wishing she had her fan with her at this moment.

"Once you have made certain he notices you, contrive to put yourself near him. For example, if he is standing next to the punch bowl, draw your escort or chaperon over to the table where he can see you."

"And if he ignores me?"

"He will not," Ainsley insisted. "Then you must contrive an introduction."

"But what if he is a stranger to all?"

"There are no strangers at a ball, Cecily. Now, once you have been introduced, you can begin to discuss commonplace matters, such as the weather, or the quality of the music and such."

"Boring drawing-room talk." Cecily made a wry face.

"Exactly." He smiled. "Flatter him. 'Oh, my lord, how clever' and 'you do not say.' And, as a gentleman, the man will then ask you for a dance. You oblige him with a shy smile."

"What if it is a waltz?"

Cecily felt Ainsley's arm curling about her waist, in the manner of the dance they had shared earlier.

"All the better. It more easily allows for conversation."

"And when the dance ends?"

"You can perhaps ask him to bring you a glass of punch. Or, if the weather is beastly hot, he may ask you to take a turn about the terrace."

"Highly improper," replied Cecily, acutely aware of his touch. "And after he escorts me out to the terrace?"

"Then he will perhaps take you in his arms." He did just that.

Cecily found it very difficult to breathe. She was quite certain Ainsley could hear the pounding of her heart. It sounded like a drumbeat in her ears. "And then?"

"If he is a bold gentleman, he may then wish to steal a kiss," he said softly.

"Oh?" she squeaked.

"Yes. Like this."

He brushed her lips with his.

"And am I to allow such a thing?" Cecily whispered when he had drawn back.

"Only if you wish it," he said.

Cecily took a deep breath. "And what if I should wish him to do such a thing again?" she asked.

"You only need to ask."

"Ainsley?"

"Yes?"

"I should very much like you to kiss me again."

He traced along her cheek lightly with his finger,

then drew her to him, kissing her in a much more thorough manner than before.

"Cecily," he whispered at last, planting kisses on her brow and hair. His voice was shaky. "You marvelous, redheaded sprite. What sort of fairy spell are you weaving upon me?"

Cecily snuggled comfortably against his shoulder.

"I very nearly did not come with Robert, because I was so afraid of you," he said, running his fingers up and down her arm in a manner that sent chills up her spine.

"Am I such a fearsome creature?" she asked.

"You certainly frightened me when you were twelve," he said, with a short laugh. "But I think you are far more dangerous to my peace of mind now."

Cecily quite agreed with him on *that*. For she suddenly realized the difference between her childish hero worship, and the very different feelings she was experiencing now. Despite her disclaimers, she had been courted by a few gentlemen during the Season. And none of them engendered the tumultuous sensations she experienced now in the arms of Ainsley Powell.

"I have not shocked you, have I?"

"Shocked me?" she asked.

"I would be willing to wager this is not the first time you have been kissed in the night by a gentleman."

"Perhaps," she said mysteriously. She gathered her courage. "Would it make you feel better if I told you those were by far the nicest kisses I ever received?"

"It might," he said, tightening his arm about her waist. "Why do you suppose that is?"

"Perhaps it is your vast experience," she teased.

"Or your lack of the same," he countered.

"Well, now that you mention it, perhaps you are right. Maybe they were *not* the best kisses."

He jerked Cecily to him in a quite masterful manner, using his lips and tongue to devastating effect. When he at last drew back, they were both breathing hard, and Cecily's face was a picture of dreamy bemusement.

"Are you more certain now?" he gasped.

"Oh yes," she said breathlessly.

"Good," he said. He relaxed his hold on her, drawing her back against him so her head rested comfortably on his shoulder. "Now, tell me what you have been up to for the last six years, Cecily Montford."

They talked about things important and inconsequential: relatives and friends, books and music, horses, boxing, fashion, corn laws, and illegal assemblies. They did not always agree; indeed, they were in violent disagreement on several matters, but through it all was Cecily's dawning awareness that she was growing to know Ainsley as well as she knew anyone, except perhaps herself. And she was not even so certain of that. The thought made her feel rather odd. How could she feel such closeness to a man she had not seen in over six years? She shivered slightly.

"Cold?" Ainsley asked. He began to take off his coat.

"I am fine," she protested.

"You can't be," he argued, "in that thin gown." He carefully tucked his coat around her shoulders, then drew her back against him, so she rested comfortably in his arms again. "Now tell me again how you charmed everyone at the Delford's musicale."

Ainsley had not intended to keep Cecily for such a length of time; indeed, he had every intention of taking her back to the house before her absence was noted. Yet every time he remembered, Cecily would make some new comment and he lost himself in the pleasure of her conversation.

Not until much later did he notice that the shafts of moonlight streaking the room had moved a considerable distance from where they had started.

"I had better devise a way of sneaking you back into the house," he said at last. "Can it be done without rousing the entire household?"

"Easily," she said.

"Somehow, I thought you would know that," he teased. Then he grew serious. "If there is any question about where you have been, direct them to me immediately. I will not have you taking the responsibility for my actions."

"Oh, pooh," she said. "No one will have missed me."

He stood, extending his hand and drawing her to her feet. He clasped the lapels of his coat and drew her against him.

"Promise me?"

She nodded.

"All right then." He dipped his head and brought his lips to hers in one last, long, drawn-out kiss.

When they at last parted at the bottom of the back stairs, Cecily felt sadly deflated. And confused. They had talked a long time, she at least sharing thoughts she had not voiced to anyone before. He had kissed her many times, embracing her in a manner that no other man had. She grinned—that was at least *one* thing he did not know!

But yet, he said nothing about his feelings for her. There had been no heartfelt declaration of esteem. No promises of a future meeting. She certainly was not a ruined woman, but his actions tonight had certainly been far beyond the bounds of propriety. Did his attentions mean anything? Or was he such a shocking flirt that he accepted this as an everyday occurence?

She knew exactly what her feelings were for Ainsley Powell. She was hopelessly, top over tails in love with him. And not because he was handsome and dashing and older and elegant. Because he was the one person she knew who thought about so many things in the same manner she did. He thought the London social Season was a matter for joking, not a life-or-death experience. He had a sense of humor that heavily emphasized the absurd. And he did not take himself, of all people, terribly seriously. Just as she, he had grown up a great deal in the last six years. She knew this was no recurrent case of hero worship, but a serious matter of the heart for her. But for him? All night, his remarks had been so full of laughter and jest that she did not know what he thought of her. He had kissed her quite thoroughly, but had not tried to go beyond that. She wondered exactly what she would have done if he had?

He was scheduled to leave today—would he depart without even saying good-bye? The thought filled her with cold terror. The last time they parted, she had been filled with cold humiliation. This time, if he left, he would leave her with a broken heart.

Ainsley found it very difficult to sleep. The image of a bright-eyed, red-haired scamp kept creeping into his thoughts.

He was rushing into things far too quickly, he knew. How could he have kept her at his side for so many hours tonight? It was thoughtless and foolish. If they had been discovered . . . He owed Cecily much better than an ugly accusation of disgrace. But every time he thought to bring her back, he hesitated, and then became lost in the conversation, or in the contemplation of her face, or in the sweetness of her lips.

It was madness. She was only eighteen. Far too young to yet know her heart. He knew his own quite well, after all these years, and there was no question that it had been pierced to the core at last. But that did not mean she had been similarly affected. She had every right not to be, after their bizarre history. She responded to his kisses with enthusiasm, but he rather thought she would do that with any gentleman she found amiable, in the interests of "learning about life." If nothing else, he was going to give her a stern lecture on the inadvisability of allowing gentlemen to take such liberties. It was not at all proper.

Yet, miraculously, they had not been noticed, had not been caught in such a compromising situation. So she was free from any compulsion to tie herself to him. And he was not so certain that he had the right to ask such a thing of her yet. Best to wait. She would be in town for the Little Season. He could contrive to find himself at the same entertainments. He could court her slowly and properly, under the watchful eyes of her mama and all of society.

But October was months away. What if someone else came before her in that time, and was less reluctant to press his suit? He could lose her. Forever.

That he could not bear. He would have to say something. Mayhaps not anything as formal as a firm offer of marriage. An expression of interest. A warning not to consider another's proposal until he had the opportunity to make his own. The absurdity of that last thought made him smile.

All right then, he would at least speak to Lord Lawton. He knew his daughter, would know if she deserved to have more time to examine the world before she made an irrevocable decision about her life. He would be guided by her father's advice. Lord knows, anyone's advice would help him at this point. Ainsley was so confused he was not prepared to decide anything on his own.

Cecily awoke with a start, uncertain for a moment where she was and why she was so agitated. The room was bright with daylight; she saw the dust motes dancing in the shaft of light between the curtains.

She sat bolt upright. Ainsley. He was planning to leave today. Had he already gone? Hastily, she clambered from the bed and rang for her maid.

"Find out if Mr. Powell has left yet," she ordered while she struggled into her clothes. She did not know what she would do if he had.

The maid came back with the intelligence that Mr. Powell was still very much in residence, and had, in fact, requested that Cecily would meet with him in the library at her convenience.

He wishes to say good-bye, she thought eagerly. She squirmed impatiently while her maid did up the fastenings on her gown. Quickly dragging a brush through her curls, Cecily blessed her short hair. She hastily examined herself in the mirror, then raced out the door.

By the time she reached the top of the stairs, she had slowed her pace to a more sedate gait. But her heart still raced at an enormous speed. She took each step slowly and carefully, gripping the bannister as if she needed it to help her remain upright.

She hesitated outside the library door, trying to compose herself. She must not reveal her feelings. Ainsley would be most kind, this time, but she would be just as humiliated as she had been by his rebuff six years ago. They were *friends*, so she must act like one.

She pushed open the door. He was sitting on the far side of the room, and he jumped up the moment he saw her. Ainsley crossed the space in an instant, taking her by the hand and drawing her into the room.

"I fear I have kept you waiting," she said as he urged her to take a seat. "I know you wished to depart today and I am sorry if I have delayed you."

"I am amazed you are awake already," he said. "It has not been that many hours since you tumbled into bed."

"The day was too lovely to sleep any more," she said, absently tracing the carvings on the chair arm with her finger.

"I feared you might take a chill from being so long in the night air."

"I am not all that fragile," she said. "Besides, your coat kept me nicely warm."

"Good."

He stared at her for a moment with the oddest look. Cecily lowered her eyes.

"I behaved in a highly improper manner last evening," he began.

"It is quite all right," she replied.

"No, it is not. I should know better." He sighed. "I am a great deal older than you, Cecily," he began.

"A veritable ancient, in fact." She smiled at her jest, but her smile faded at the serious expression on his face.

"Ten years is a considerable time," he said. "I look back on myself at eighteen and it seems like another lifetime." He placed his foot on a chair, leaning his arm on his knee. "And I imagine to you, eight-and-twenty looks like doddering on the edge of the grave."

"I rather think you have a few more years left in you," she teased.

He smiled at that. "I do not want to be caught accusing you of being *young*, Cecily, but you are just beginning your life as a lady in society. I am certain you look forward to your second Season with great anticipation.''

"Oh, certainly," she said. "I cannot wait to try out all the new skills you taught me last night on other gentlemen."

That drew a reaction from him, she thought with a smug smile, watching the flash of anger in his face.

"I fear I set you a bad example," he said, his voice sounding stilted. "It was not at all proper."

"Then I fear I must not be completely proper," she said. "For I rather enjoyed myself."

"Cecily, I am a full ten years older than you."

"I believe we have established our respective ages."

"I am set in my ways. I do not care much for balls and social gatherings and such. I fear I am rather dull, in fact."

"Exceedingly," she agreed.

"You've only had one Season—and by your own admission, you were too busy with this blasted wedding to enjoy yourself."

"Quite so."

"You should have at least one where you can enjoy yourself, unencumbered."

"Definitely."

Ainsley looked at her closely. Her face looked the picture of perfect innocence, but he sensed she was roasting him.

He reached into his pocket and drew out an object. It lay there, glittering, in his palm. The ring. From the cake.

"I think the Montford prophecy wields a powerful influence," he began.

Cecily reached up and drew out the chain upon which her own ring hung. "Coincidence?" she asked.

Their eyes met and they both burst out laughing.

"I do not care if it was coincidence, fate, or a wicked trick on the part of the cook," he said, drawing her to her feet and wrapping her in his arms. "Dash it all, Cecily, I wish to marry you. But I do not want to rush you into a decision. I quite understand if you should like to wait, and look about for another who might be more appealing."

She rather liked the pained expression on his face. Almost, she wished to torment him further. Almost. But not quite. For if he felt half the torment she had in the last few minutes, she would not wish that upon anyone.

"I would be honored to accept your suit, Mr. Powell," she said, in a prim little voice. "After all, the prophecy must be obeyed."

"Are you sure?" he blurted.

"Quite sure," she replied with a wide grin.

"Dearest Cecily," he said, then kissed her in a manner that made her quite certain that there was still a bit of life left in him, even if he had eight-and-twenty years.

Brighton Betrothals
by Sandra Heath

A PROLONGED VISIT to the fashionable hothouse surroundings of Brighton was the very last thing Miss Patricia Fairbourne wished to make, for she was studious and shy and would much have preferred to stay quietly at home in the Lake District with her grandfather. But her aunt, Lady Lindsay, insisted that such a visit was vital if her niece was ever to find a suitable husband, and she was supported in this declaration by Patricia's grandfather, who had himself become concerned over his granddaughter's retiring character.

Patricia had resisted all she could, but in the end had been forced to acquiesce, and so, early in August 1807, she set off most unwillingly on the three-hundred-mile journey south to Brighton, where London's *beau monde* flocked to be with the Prince of Wales at his famous Marine Pavilion, and where Lady Lindsay knew there would be numerous eligible and suitable gentlemen who might be enticed by her niece's quiet, blonde prettiness.

As the carriage drove through the evening shadows toward journey's end, Patricia wished with all her heart that this visit could have been avoided. If her interfering aunt had not herself paid an unheralded visit at Windermere Park during the spring, then her niece's peaceful secluded existence would not have been disturbed. But the moment Lady Lindsay had seen how bookish her young relative had become, she had expressed herself deeply dismayed, and she had repeated this opinion so frequently that it was not long before Patricia's grandfather had begun to agree with her. As far as Lady Lindsay was concerned, there were few things less becoming in a young lady than too much education, and since she thought that Patricia was otherwise attractive enough and well-connected enough to do reasonably well in the marriage mart, a firm promise had been extracted that a lengthy visit to Brighton would be made without too much delay.

Patricia's spirits were low as the sea appeared on the horizon ahead. She was almost there now, and the horror of a full social diary stretched before her over the coming weeks. She didn't want to be launched into society; she wanted to be at home with her books and solitary walks on the shores of Lake Windermere. She gazed out as the carriage bowled over the downland above the town, passing the fashionable racecourse and the army encampments where the Prince of Wales enjoyed the pageant of reviewing the troops. Already there were elegant carriages everywhere, and numerous stylish horsemen and women riding their blood horses along the grassy cliff tops. Brighton was a world away from the home she loved so much, and was everything she was not.

She sighed, and lowered her gaze to the strings of her reticule as she toyed restlessly with them. She was twenty-one years old, small and slender, and her long ash-blonde hair was swept up beneath a wide-brimmed straw hat which was trimmed around the crown with flouncy ostrich plumes. She wore lilac to match her eyes, and it was a color that enhanced her pale, enviably clear complexion. Her face was daintily made rather than beautiful, and its expression was withdrawn as the first white villas appeared at the roadside.

She wasn't alone in the carriage, for her maid, Molly Nicholls, was with her. Molly was a rosy-faced country girl with russet curls and hazel eyes, and she wore a green linen mantle over a simple cream muslin dress that had once belonged to her mistress. She remained silent as the carriage drove farther into the town, for she knew full well how Patricia felt about this dreaded visit.

Soon the road had taken them into the heart of Brighton, where their carriage was soon caught up in the crush of traffic on the wide thoroughfare called the Steine, where the Prince of Wales's residence, the Marine Pavilion, presided grandly over the landaus, barouches, curricles, phaetons, gigs, and gleaming thoroughbred horses of the *ton*. It was a very exclusive scene, made more bustling and crowded than usual because it was the eve of the prince's forty-fifth birthday, and the following day would be completely taken up with glittering celebrations. The whole town was to be decorated and illuminated, and already a small battalion of workmen was engaged upon the endless task of hanging thousands of little lanterns in all the trees and from every balcony and railing.

The carriage left the Steine behind, turning several corners until at last it entered a quiet, leafy cul-de-sac that was situated directly behind the Marine Pavilion's grounds. This was Queen Charlotte Row, where Lady Lindsay had taken one of the terraced town houses that overlooked the royal premises. Patricia stared out at the gleaming windows and polished brass door knockers, and her spirits sank a little further. She was here now, her ordeal had begun, and it would be an age before she could escape back to the Lake District again.

Her aunt's house was the last-but-one at the end of the terrace, and as the carriage drew up at the curb, the door of the house opened and a butler emerged. He was a tall, bony man in a powdered bag-wig, dark-blue coat, and light-gray breeches, and his close-set eyes and hooked nose put Patricia irresistibly in mind of a rather stern parrot. He came to open the carriage door and bow to her.

"Miss Fairbourne?" he enquired.

She nodded, and he quickly lowered the iron rungs and assisted her down to the pavement.

He bowed again. "Welcome to Brighton, Miss Fairbourne. I am Armstrong, Lady Lindsay's butler."

"Good evening, Armstrong," she replied, glancing curiously toward the house at the very end of the row. It was unoccupied, its windows firmly shuttered and its wrought-iron gate chained and padlocked. But even as she looked at it, her attention was snatched away by the shouts of a newsboy who had just taken up his position at the entrance to the cul-de-sac.

"Heiress feared abducted! Heiress feared abducted! Foul play suspected!" he shouted, brandishing his news sheets aloft.

It was such a startling headline that Patricia looked quickly at the butler. "Is someone really missing?"

"I fear so, madam. Miss Laurinda Beresford disappeared from her guardian's residence a week ago, and nothing has been seen of her since. She took nothing with her, and seems to have vanished into thin air."

"How dreadful." Patricia gazed toward the newsboy again.

"Everyone is most concerned for Miss Beresford's safety, madam, for she is a very well-liked young lady." Armstrong turned to conduct her into the house.

Followed by Molly, Patricia stepped over the small stone bridge spanning the basement area, and entered a surprisingly spacious entrance hall with ice-green walls and a black-and-white tiled floor. A black-railed staircase rose at the far end between Ionic columns to a balustraded gallery on the floor above, and at the head of it, there were some impressive white double doors which obviously gave into the drawing room. In the entrance hall itself, there were several other doors, and the flight of steps leading up from the kitchens. In the center of the floor there was a circular table upon which stood a silver dish filled with calling cards, and nearby there were two elegant sofas upholstered in gold brocade. There was a beautifully carved white-marble fireplace, with an embroidered screen before the hearth to hide the smoke-blackened bricks, and in the alcove next to the chimney breast stood a tall long-case clock. As Patricia paused to glance around, the clock began to whir, and then its chimes rang out melodiously into the cool silence.

Armstrong bowed to her again. "I will inform her ladyship that you have arrived, Miss Fairbourne," he said. Then he went up the staircase and vanished through the double doors at the top. She heard voices, and a moment later he reappeared. "If you will come this way, madam," he said.

Leaving Molly in the hall, Patricia went up toward him, and was conducted into a sumptuous crimson-and-gold drawing room that stretched from the front of the house to the back, with French windows and balconies overlooking both the street and the garden.

Lady Lindsay was standing by the fireplace, and she nodded at the butler. "Have Miss Fairbourne's maid and luggage taken to her room, and then see to it that a dish of tea is served in here."

"My lady." He bowed and withdrew.

Patricia's aunt was an elegant widow of patrician bearing and, although she was now past the first bloom of youth, she was still very handsome. Her eyes were brown, her complexion a very delicate pink-and-white, and her hair, once dark and glossy, was now streaked with gray. She wore a turquoise silk gown with petal sleeves and a square neckline that was filled with lace. There was a knotted white shawl draped over her slender arms, and the gown's high waistline was adorned with a golden belt and a little fob watch.

For a long moment she surveyed her niece critically from head to toe, and at last nodded approvingly. "I am pleased to see that the clothes I instructed my London dressmaker to make for you have been so successful. You look very well, my dear, very well indeed."

"Thank you, Aunt Lindsay."

"Don't look like a frightened rabbit, child, for I do not intend to eat you. Come and sit down." Lady Lindsay took a seat on a crimson velvet sofa, and then patted the place next to her.

When Patricia had obeyed, her aunt eyed her again. "I know that you do not wish to be here, my dear, but believe me it is the best thing for you. Few gentlemen can abide bookish females, and unless you are rescued soon, you will find yourself on the proverbial shelf. You have looks and a certain charm, and with a little polishing here and there, you will do well, I'm sure."

Patricia lowered her glance. She didn't want to be polished; she was quite happy as she was.

Lady Lindsay's stern gaze didn't waver. "There is little to be gained by avoiding my eyes, Patricia, for I will not go away. You are here to enter society, and that is precisely what you are going to do, whether you like it or not. You may relax and rest awhile this evening, for I will not thrust you in before you've had time to recover from the journey. But tomorrow is another matter entirely."

Patricia was dismayed. Tomorrow? She had hoped to have at least a few days' respite.

Lady Lindsay ignored her niece's unhappy silence. "Tomorrow is the dear Prince of Wales's birthday, my dear, and all sorts of festivities have been arranged. The prince is to review the troops on the downs, and there is to be a fair there as well, with such diversions as wrestling, races, prize-fighting, and all the usual activities. Then tomorrow evening there is to be a celebratory ball at the Castle Inn assembly rooms, followed by a display of fireworks at the Marine Pavilion. I thought that you and I would forego the junketings on the downs, for it will really be a little too much for me, but we will most definitely attend the ball and the fireworks display."

Patricia stared at her in horror. Attend the Prince of Wales's birthday ball? She couldn't possibly!

Lady Lindsay perceived the alarmed expression. "There will be no wriggling out of it, child, for the prince has expressed a personal wish that you attend the ball. When I dined with him at the Pavilion the other evening and mentioned that you would be here on his birthday, he was at some pains to extend an invitation to you."

Patricia was numb. "The prince knows about me?" she asked faintly.

"Yes, my dear, he does. I have the inestimable honor to be numbered among his friends, and he is always very kind and thoughtful toward those he likes."

Patricia knew that the matter was closed. She would be attending the ball and the fireworks display, and that was the end of it, but at least she could be thankful that she was to be spared the festivities on the downs.

Her aunt was evidently also thinking of the activities preceding the ball. "I really could not face going up to watch the review and so on, for the road is such an inordinate crush that one cannot possibly return to the town again before everyone else does. It really is abominable. I thought you would prefer a ride along the cliffs after breakfast. You do ride, don't you, my dear?"

"Yes, Aunt Lindsay."

"Good. Ah, here is our tea."

A footman ushered in a neatly dressed maid who was carrying a tea tray which was placed carefully on the small table before the sofa, and as the tea was poured, Patricia stole a moment to glance around the room.

It was a beautiful chamber, with crystal chandeliers suspended from an elaborately gilded ceiling. Crimson Chinese silk adorned the walls, and there were crimson-and-gold-striped brocade curtains at the French windows, nearly all of which stood open to the warm evening air. The furniture was French, having been brought over from Paris long before the revolution, and there were a number of richly framed portraits.

One portrait in particular caught Patricia's eye, for it was of Lady Lindsay's son and heir, the present Lord Lindsay. Patricia's cousin Edward was an officer in a crack hussar regiment at present stationed in Ireland, and in the portrait he was dressed in his uniform. It was obligatory for all hussar officers to wear side whiskers and a moustache, and it was a fashion that suited his fair good looks very well. He looked very dashing and attractive, and very far removed indeed from the boy who had once stayed at Patricia's home and tormented her by pulling her hair.

As the maid and footman withdrew, Lady Lindsay perceived Patricia's interest in her son's portrait. "Edward has improved considerably from the rather obnoxious little boy you probably remember," she remarked.

Patricia couldn't help smiling a little as she accepted a cup of tea. "I recall that he was much given to pulling my hair," she replied.

"Oh, he was quite loathsome," her aunt admitted frankly, "but I promise you that he is very much the gentleman now, as I trust you will agree when he comes here on leave in a day or so. He does not know it yet, but I have been making discreet enquiries concerning a match for him. The Earl and Countess of Rotherden are here with their daughter, Amelia. She isn't the most beautiful of young ladies, but she is accomplished and charming, and I think she will do very nicely for Edward."

Patricia wondered if Edward would still come home to visit his mother if he knew about the matchmaking going on on his behalf. He looked the sort of young man who would not lack for female admiration, and who would most probably wish to choose his own bride.

Lady Lindsay sipped her tea and gazed at her son's portrait. "When poor dear Miss Beresford first arrived in Brighton this summer I was certain that *she* was the perfect bride for Edward, but even though I implored him to come home on leave, he simply could not manage it. Then Sir Daniel Kershaw swept her off her feet, and that was that. Now the poor dear creature has vanished anyway, and the Lord alone knows what has befallen her."

Patricia lowered her cup. "I heard the newsboy on the corner when I arrived. What do you think has happened to Miss Beresford, Aunt Lindsay?"

"I will tell you all that anyone knows, my dear. Laurinda is the eighteen-year-old ward of Lord Haldane, and she is not only enchantingly beautiful, but also has a vast inheritance that makes her one of the most sought-after heiresses in England. She could have had her pick of suitors, but she set her heart on Sir Daniel Kershaw who, although well-connected enough, is not the grand match she could so easily have made. Anyway, as far as she was concerned, no one else but Sir Daniel would do, but she reckoned without Lord Haldane, who was absolutely furious when he was informed of his ward's choice. He forbade her to have anything more to do with Sir Daniel, and he threatened Sir Daniel himself with a duel if he persisted in the matter. Such a threat was not to be taken lightly, for Lord Haldane is thought to be the most accurate shot in the realm, and is also an excellent swordsman. Anyway, there was quite a to-do, with Laurinda in floods of tears, and Sir Daniel so wrathful that he sailed very close indeed to that duel."

"Lord Haldane sounds a fearsome guardian," Patricia observed, feeling very sorry indeed for the unfortunate Miss Beresford.

"There are those who regard him as the devil incarnate, but I cannot say that he has ever been anything other than courteous and charming toward me," her aunt replied.

"How did Miss Beresford disappear?"

"Well, as I said, Lord Haldane put a very firm stop to any thought of a match with Sir Daniel, who until then had been proceeding as if it were all a *fait accompli*. He purchased the house next door to this one, and commenced refurbishing it in readiness for his new bride. That all came to a halt when Lord Haldane stepped in, and the house was promptly closed up. But it seems that the lovers were secretly planning to defy Lord Haldane by eloping to Gretna Green. Then, on the very night of the planned elopement, Laurinda suddenly vanished from Lord Haldane's residence on the Steine. She was seen at the window of her bedroom at about nine o'clock, while her guardian was dining with the prince at the Pavilion. But when Lord Haldane returned she had vanished. Poor Sir Daniel waited in the mews lane for her to come to him, but she did not keep their appointment."

Patricia stared at her aunt. "And no one has any idea at all what has happened to her?"

Lady Lindsay pursed her lips for a moment. "Well, there is a whisper going around, but it is entirely without foundation, and to repeat it publicly would be to run very foul indeed of Lord Haldane. It is being said that he has plunged in very deep indeed at the gaming tables, and that the duns are closing in on him. It is thought that in order to get himself out of the scrape, he has been endeavoring to marry Laurinda himself, so that her fortune will become his. She, naturally enough, would shrink from such a match, and so he is suspected of having her incarcerated somewhere until she gives in to his wishes."

Patricia's eyes widened. "Would Lord Haldane really do such a monstrous thing?"

"He is a man with a notorious reputation, my dear. His list of conquests is endless, and no one would ever wish to cross him. No doubt the truth will out sooner or later, but until then, Brighton will continue to buzz with rumor and speculation." Lady Lindsay put down her cup and saucer, and rose to her feet with a rustle of turquoise silk. "Now, my dear, I think it is time I conducted you to your room, for I am sure you wish to change out of your traveling togs and rest awhile before we dine *à deux* at nine. We would normally dine earlier than that, but it was impossible to know when exactly you would arrive. Come, Patricia."

Patricia dutifully rose to her feet to follow her aunt from the drawing room.

Her trunks had already been carried up to the pretty yellow-and-white chamber on the floor above, and Molly hurriedly left the unpacking to withdraw as Lady Lindsay showed Patricia in. The open French windows gave on to a covered balcony overlooking the rear gardens, and the light evening breeze moved the gray velvet curtains a little.

Lady Lindsay conducted her niece straight out onto the balcony. "There, my dear, you can see right into the grounds of the Marine Pavilion," she said, pointing.

Patricia glanced down first into the little walled garden directly below, where a fountain splashed into a raised ornamental pool. The garden was about fifty feet long, and ended at the mews lane, where there were coachhouses and stables to serve the whole of Queen Charlotte Row. Beyond the mews lane were the grounds of the royal residence, with beautiful specimen trees, and close-cropped lawns where peacocks strutted and displayed.

A cricket match was in progress, watched by a gathering of elegant ladies and gentlemen, and there was a polite ripple of applause as a batsman struck a splendid six. A rather fat fieldsman in a tall white-beaver hat pursued the ball, and Lady Lindsay immediately pointed toward him.

"That, my dear, is the Prince of Wales," she said.

Patricia was somewhat disappointed in England's future king, for his former good looks had vanished in rather unbecoming obesity. Very tight lacing was required to squeeze his bulk into the close-fitting clothes required on the cricket pitch, and as he paused to remove his hat for a moment, Patricia felt that his curls were suspiciously chestnut and profuse. Surely he was wearing a wig!

Lady Lindsay's attention had moved on to the spectators, and suddenly Patricia heard her give a slight gasp.

"What is it, Aunt Lindsay?"

"Do you see that gentleman over there? The one in the mulberry coat walking toward the cedar tree?"

"Yes."

"That is Sir Daniel Kershaw."

The missing Miss Beresford's forbidden love? Patricia gazed at him. He was of medium height and slender build, with thick brown hair and an even profile. His coat was superbly cut, as were his cream-corduroy breeches, and his tall-crowned beaver hat was tipped back at a stylish angle. He was very good-looking, and Patricia could understand only too well why Laurinda would have fallen in love with him.

Lady Lindsay touched her arm. "Now do you see that other gentleman? The one standing in the shadows beneath the tree?"

Patricia followed her aunt's finger, and after a moment saw the second man quite clearly. He had observed Sir Daniel's approach, but had yet to be observed in turn. He was tall, with broad shoulders and slender hips, and was one of the most devastatingly attractive men she had ever seen. He had removed his tall black hat, and the evening breeze was ruffling through his tousled dark curls. He wore a charcoal coat and tight-fitting white kerseymere breeches, and a gold pin gleamed in the folds of his intricate neckcloth. His matchless face was cold and unsmiling as he watched Sir Daniel walk unknowingly toward him.

She glanced at her aunt. "Who is he?" she asked.

"That is Miss Beresford's guardian, Lord Haldane," Lady Lindsay replied softly.

Patricia stared, for she had not expected him to

be so young. He could not be much more than thirty, and did not look at all the vile tyrant she had pictured.

From the balcony the two women watched with bated breath as it seemed that a confrontation was imminent between Brighton's two most talked-of gentlemen, but then Sir Daniel suddenly realized his foe was there. He came to an abrupt halt, and for a long moment he simply stared at the man beneath the spreading branches of the tree.

Then Sir Daniel turned on his heel and strode away toward the Pavilion. He paused in the doorway before entering, glancing back at Lord Haldane, and then at the empty house where, but for savage fate, he and his beloved Laurinda would have set up home together as man and wife.

The cricket match had come to an end because the shadows were now too long, and as the players and spectators made their way off the lawns, Lord Haldane left the cedar tree to join them. Patricia gazed after him, still surprised to discover that he was so very unlike the monster she had conjured in her thoughts.

Lady Lindsay pursed her lips, watching until everyone had gone into the Pavilion. "Well, now you have seen the two gentlemen in poor dear Laurinda's life—the one the most of an angel I ever knew, and the other the most of a devil."

"But the devil is astonishingly handsome," Patricia murmured a little unguardedly.

Her aunt gave her a stern look. "Robert Haldane is not the sort of gentleman with whom a proper young lady should associate, Patricia. He is notorious not only because of his ward's disappearance, but also because he is a womanizer. He is a past master of the art of seduction, as far too many foolish creatures have found out, and to be seen with him is to court the ruin of one's reputation. Do I make myself clear?"

"Very clear, Aunt Lindsay," Patricia replied.

"Good. I will leave you to rest now. Dinner will be served in an hour's time, and you may join me in the drawing room when you hear the gong."

"Very well, Aunt Lindsay."

Lady Lindsay smiled fondly at her then. "I'm sure you will enjoy Brighton, my dear, for you are certainly pretty enough to attract admirers. I trust that you have observed my instructions concerning books?"

Patricia hoped that telltale color had not rushed into her cheeks as she nodded. "I haven't brought any with me, Aunt Lindsay," she fibbed.

Lady Lindsay smiled again. "Good, for I mean to send you back to your grandfather with betrothal offers ringing in your ears. *À bientôt, ma chère.*"

As the door closed behind her, Patricia looked guiltily at her trunks. She hadn't done as she had been told, but had brought with her a very large volume of Lesage's *Adventures of Gil Blas* in the original Old French. She was enjoying it very much, and meant to steal a few moments here and there to continue reading it. She would have to see to it that her aunt did not have any opportunity to observe her in her disobedience.

Dinner proved to be a very agreeable meal, for Lady Lindsay was a very charming and witty companion, with a thousand and one anecdotes to relate about the *haut ton*. Conversation did not turn again upon Laurinda Beresford's disappearance, but nevertheless it was of the missing heiress that Patricia thought as she retired to her room that night.

It was a very warm and humid night, and she left the French windows open as she lay on her bed trying to sleep. Her long hair was brushed loose, and she had not tied the ribbons at the throat of her nightgown, but still she felt uncomfortably hot.

The light breeze had died away completely now, and the sounds of the night drifted into the room. She heard carriages and hooves on the Steine, and occasional bursts of laughter from the Pavilion where the prince was entertaining guests. On the grounds, the peacocks were restless, and their piercing calls echoed through the darkness. Down in the walled garden beneath the balcony the fountain splashed gently into its pool, a cool sound which began to lull her to sleep. Suddenly she heard a different sound, a stifled cry which was over so swiftly that at first she thought she had imagined it. She sat up in bed, pushing her hair back from her face and listening carefully. The sound wasn't repeated, but she was sure that someone had tried to call for help.

Flinging the bedclothes aside, she got up, her naked feet pattering on the floor as she went to the balcony. Stepping outside into the night, she listened again, but all she could hear were the earlier sounds—the carriages, the laughter from the prince's guests, the peacocks, and the fountain. She continued to listen, still sure that someone was in trouble, but she heard nothing more.

It was cooler out on the balcony, and the moon was up, casting a silver sheen over Brighton. She stretched her arms luxuriously above her head, forgetting that the throat of her nightgown was unfastened and revealed a little more of her breasts than was entirely seemly. Her ash-blonde hair tumbled richly about her shoulders, and she closed her eyes, taking a deep breath of the summer night. It was a sensuous moment and, as she thought, entirely private.

There was a slight sound from the dense shrubbery just inside the royal grounds, and her eyes flew open as she heard it. She gasped as two figures suddenly emerged from the greenery—a young lady and gentlemen who had obviously been keeping a clandestine tryst. The young lady now seemed of a mind to play the coquette, for she denied her sweetheart another kiss and gathered her white taffeta skirts to hurry away toward the Pavilion, giggling as she went. The young gentleman did not hesitate to give chase. And soon both of them had vanished through a brightly illuminated doorway.

Patricia smiled then. So that was what she heard earlier. Far from genuinely calling for help, the young lady had been teasing and flirting.

She was about to go back into her room when a strange sensation washed over her. Someone was staring at her! The feeling was so strong and certain that she did not doubt for a moment. Putting a trembling hand on the balcony rail, she gazed all around, trying to see whoever it was. At last a tall figure moved into full view on the moonlit lawns, and she immediately recognized Lord Haldane. He made no secret of staring directly up at her, and as he sketched her a rather mocking bow, she realized that he had observed her from the moment she'd appeared. He'd seen how she'd stretched her arms up in that almost abandoned way! Embarrassment rushed hotly over her, especially as at that moment she remembered the ribbons of her nightgown.

Her fingers crept to draw the nightgown closer, and a horridly self-conscious blush warmed her cheeks as she backed into the room. Oh, how she hoped he would never find out who she was!

It was just after dawn the following morning when Brighton began to celebrate the Prince of Wales's birthday. Every bell in the town pealed out joyfully, the army fired cannon on the downs, and at sea the navy saluted the day with the thunder of guns. The streets were soon filled with people, and there wasn't a balcony or window that did not boast an abundance of flags and flowers. The Steine was a worse crush than usual as lines of fine carriages drew up so that their occupants could await the prince's first public appearance. His German band was already playing on the front lawns as the sun shone down from a flawless summer sky. All was set for what promised to be a very happy and auspicious occasion.

As decided the day before, Patricia and her aunt set off after breakfast for their ride along the grassy clifftops above the town. Their horses were hired from a fashionable livery stables on the Steine, and Patricia wore the corded sapphire silk habit made for her by the London dressmaker. Her hair was swept up beneath a little black hat that was a feminine imitation of the tall hats the gentleman wore, and she did not bother to lower the net veil, but left it turned back so that she could observe everything as they made their way through the thronged Steine and then up out of the town.

Lady Lindsay wore an eye-catching habit made of crimson wool, and there did not seem to be a single lady or gentleman who did not acknowledge her as she passed. As if that was not enough to remind Patricia that her aunt moved in very lofty circles, the fact was made very clear indeed as they neared the open clifftops and saw a small cavalcade of mounted hussars riding toward them escorting an open royal carriage. The two horsewomen maneuvered their mounts to the side of the road and as the carriage passed, Patricia saw that it contained a richly dressed little girl and her lady companion. The little girl wore a white muslin frock with a pink sash, and there was a flower-trimmed Leghorn bonnet on her fair hair. Her blue eyes danced with delight as she recognized Patricia's aunt. "Lady L! Lady L!" she called as the carriage swept by.

Lady Lindsay smiled and inclined her head respectfully. "Your Royal Highness," she called back.

As the cavalcade drove on down toward the town, Patricia turned in the saddle to watch, and her aunt explained. "That was Princess Charlotte. She is joining her father on his birthday."

"She seems to know you well." Patricia felt daunted.

Lady Lindsay understood her sudden trepidation. "You will carry all this off splendidly, my dear," she said kindly.

"I hope you're right, Aunt Lindsay, for I don't wish to let you down at all, but I'm so afraid of making a *faux pas* that will embarrass you."

"Patricia, I do not for a moment imagine that you will embarrass me. Just be demure, polite, and remember all you've learned about etiquette, and nothing will go wrong."

They rode on, soon leaving the road and striking off across the open clifftops. The horses' hooves drummed satisfyingly on the springy ground, and the sea sparkled brilliantly beneath the bright August sun. The tang of salt was in the air, and gulls wheeled against the heavens, their wings shining very white. There were no clouds to cast shadows on the grass, and the light breeze carried the scent of wild thyme.

It was so invigorating and rewarding to ride so freely that at first neither Patricia nor her aunt noticed the lone horseman coming slowly toward them on a spirited and willful black horse. It was Lady Lindsay who saw him first, and she reined in with dismay. "Oh, dear, it's Robert Haldane. I really don't wish to acknowledge him, not when it's so very possible that he is behind Miss Beresford's disappearance."

Patricia reined in as well. Color had rushed immediately into her cheeks when her aunt identified the approaching rider. All she could think of was her conduct on the balcony the night before. Would he recognize her now? She prayed not, for had she deliberately set out to appear provocative she could not have done much more, except perhaps raise her nightgown hem to reveal her legs!

Lady Lindsay had hesitated just a little too long for them to be able to ride away as if they hadn't seen him, for he had recognized her and began to spur his horse toward them.

Patricia's dismay increased, and she was too embarrassed to look directly at him, but she nevertheless managed to survey him surreptitiously from beneath lowered lashes. As he reined in beside them, she saw that he was as heart-stoppingly handsome as he had appeared from her balcony, and again she found herself thinking that he did not seem at all the unfeeling tyrant her aunt had described.

He was a man of great style, controlling his rather difficult mount with the sort of consummate skill that would always make him the envy of Hyde Park. Everything about him spoke of privilege and breeding, from his air of authority and confidence, to the blue-blooded perfection of his face. He was also a man of fashion, and the cut of his pine-green coat and cream-cord breeches could not be faulted. A gold pin shone on the knot of his pale-green silk neckcloth, and his tall hat was worn so well forward that the upper portion of his face was in shadow. It seemed to Patricia that that shadow was much deeper in his vivid blue eyes, as well it might be given the mystery and concern surrounding Miss Beresford's disappearance.

His horse capered a little, seeming impatient to spring forward again, and it was a moment or so before he had it sufficiently under control to remove his hat and incline his head to Patricia's aunt. "Good morning, Lady Lindsay." His voice was cool and soft, and without the exaggerated drawl that afflicted so many upper-class gentlemen.

Lady Lindsay reluctantly acknowledged him. "Good morning, Lord Haldane."

His glance moved to Patricia, who immediately knew that he recognized her. Mortified color flooded into her cheeks, and she wished the ground would open up and swallow her.

Lady Lindsay had no option but to effect the necessary introduction. "My lord, allow me to present my niece, Miss Fairbourne. Patricia, this is Lord Haldane."

Somehow Patricia managed to murmur a response. "My lord."

Her intense embarrassment seemed to amuse him a little, for the ghost of a smile played briefly upon his lips as he nodded at her. "I am honored to make your acquaintance, Miss Fairbourne."

Patricia lowered her eyes again, keeping her gaze fixed firmly on her horse's mane. Oh, this was dreadful! It was made worse because she knew her aunt had perceived her strange reaction.

Lord Haldane evidently had no intention of allowing her to shrink away from him, for he spoke again. "Have you been in Brighton long, Miss Fairbourne?"

"I only arrived yesterday, my lord," she replied, giving him an accusing look, for it would not have been too much to ask that he confine the conversation to her aunt. He could see that she felt dreadful about her conduct on the balcony, and so it ill became him to single her out for more than the briefest introduction.

"Will you be staying long?" he asked, the smile again playing briefly on his lips.

"For several months."

"Then I am sure we will meet again."

I hope not, she thought, but somehow she managed a polite smile. "Yes, I'm sure we will," she answered.

"Will you be attending the ball tonight?"

"Yes."

"I trust then that you will do me the inestimable honor of reserving a measure for me?"

The wretched color burned on her cheeks. "The honor will be mine, sir," she said, wishing he would go away. Why, oh, why, had she gone out on that balcony with her nightgown ribbons undone and her hair all tangled and loose? Did he think she really was as forward as her behavior then had suggested? What if he mentioned the tale to others? Was she about to find herself with a reputation?

To her unutterable relief he brought the brief meeting to an end. "Lady Lindsay, I hope you will forgive me if I leave you now, but I have important matters to attend to in town. I trust we will meet again at the ball this evening."

Patricia's aunt inclined her head politely. "My lord."

He glanced again at Patricia. "Until this evening, Miss Fairbourne."

She met his eyes briefly, and then looked away again.

The amusement still lingered on his lips as he replaced his tall hat and then urged his restless mount away.

As the hoofbeats drummed ever fainter over the clifftop grass, Lady Lindsay eyed her niece. "And what, pray, was all that about? I know that it is impossible, but I had the distinct feeling that you and he were not unknown to each other."

"We . . . we've never met before, Aunt Lindsay," Patricia replied, trying not to meet the other's steady gaze.

"Look at me, girl. Now then, I will have the truth."

Slowly Patricia related the events of the night, and as she finished she looked imploringly at her aunt. "I didn't know he was there, Aunt Lindsay, and I didn't realize my nightgown ribbons were so undone, truly I didn't!"

"I sincerely trust you didn't. Oh, Patricia, how could you have been so unmindful of propriety?" Lady Lindsay cried. "The scene you have just described could almost have concerned a *belle de nuit!*"

Patricia bit her lip and bowed her head.

"Proper young ladies simply do not go out on balconies in their undress. They do not leave their ribbons unfastened, and they do not stretch in a manner that can only be described as shameless!"

"No, Aunt Lindsay."

Lady Lindsay turned in the saddle to gaze after Lord Haldane. "Well, we must hope that he sets store by being a gentleman, otherwise your name will be bandied all over Brighton before the day is out."

Patricia was close to tears. She had only been in this horrid place for a day, and already she'd committed a sin.

Her aunt drew a long breath. "Well, what's done is done, and now we must cross our fingers. Come, I think it's time we rode back now." Turning her mount, she cantered back the way they'd come.

Gazing miserably after her for a moment, Patricia gathered her reins and followed. She had already been nervous about the ball; now she positively dreaded it.

* * *

Patricia's ballgown was made of several layers of silver gauze over a sleeveless white satin slip, and it was liberally sprinkled with silver spangles that winked and flashed at the slightest movement. The neckline was scooped low, and was quite perfect for the diamond necklace her aunt insisted she borrow for this most auspicious occasion. Her hair was pinned up into an elaborate knot from which fell several thick ringlets, and there were more diamonds in the pretty star ornament Molly had fixed carefully to the knot.

It was a little early to go down, but the room was rather stuffy so Patricia decided to sit by the fountain in the garden. As she emerged from the house, she took a deep breath of the rose-scented air. She could hear the sound of the Prince of Wales's German band playing on the nearby lawns, and now and then the peacocks added their haunting cries to the summer evening. As Patricia went to sit on the stone parapet surrounding the fountain's raised pool, she tried to compose herself for the hours ahead. Please let Lord Haldane be a gentleman, and let her misdemeanor on the balcony soon become history.

The shadows were long now, and soon it would be dark. Already there were bonfires flickering on the downs above the town, and in the streets of Brighton the thousands of lanterns had been lit. The peacocks on the Pavilion grounds weren't the only birds giving voice in the warm August air, for the evening chorus was beginning. A blackbird sang his heart out in the branches of an apple tree, and two magpies uttered their gutteral cries as they hopped along the roof of Lady Lindsay's house. A small flock of sparrows began to squabble, fluttering and shrieking at one another in the climbing roses growing up the high wall separating the garden from that of the empty house next door. Patricia smiled a little as she watched the feathered quarrel progress, and it was then that she noticed the door in the wall.

She was about to look at it more closely when her aunt called from the house. "Patricia? It's time to go, my dear."

Lady Lindsay looked very elegant and eye-catching in a butter-yellow silk tunic dress over a gray silk undergown. There was a yellow satin turban on her head, and she carried a large fan of flouncy white plumes. She approved of her niece's appearance. "You'll do, my dear, in fact you'll do very well indeed."

"Thank you, Aunt Lindsay."

Her aunt pursed her lips. "I trust that all this effort will not prove to be in vain because of Robert Haldane's influence."

"Do you really think he may tell?"

"It is an amusing anecdote." Lady Lindsay sighed. "I really don't know, Patricia. As I say, he has always been the perfect gentleman where I am concerned, but he does have a notorious reputation, and now there's this sad business of Miss Beresford. I have to tell you that I really don't know what to think or expect of him, Patricia, but we must hope for the best."

It wasn't a response that was calculated to fill Patricia with confidence, and as she and her aunt emerged from the house to enter the waiting carriage, she felt so anxious and apprehensive that she could have fled back to her room and locked herself in.

As the carriage pulled away, Lady Lindsay endeavored to bolster her niece's failing courage. "Don't be faint-hearted, my dear, for even if Robert Haldane does spread a scandalous whisper, I am confident we will survive it. After all, his own reputation doesn't stand all that high at the moment, does it?"

"No, Aunt Lindsay."

"Who knows, in the next few hours you may meet your future husband." Lady Lindsay smiled.

Patricia didn't say anything more. She wished this night was over, and she was back in her bed. More than that, she wished the whole of this visit to Brighton was over, and she was at home at Windermere Park, safe again in her customary seclusion and anonymity.

The closer the carriage drew to the Castle Inn on the Steine, the greater the crush of other vehicles. The air was filled with the clatter of hooves and wheels, and the sound of music drifted from the grassy area in the center of the Steine, where several bands were playing. Crowds of onlookers had gathered to watch the *beau monde* arriving for this most exclusive of occasions. Now that it was almost dark, the brilliance of the lanterns could be appreciated to the full. Brighton twinkled with lights and rang with music as it prepared to celebrate the highest point of the royal birthday.

It was some time before Lady Lindsay's coachman could maneuver the carriage to a halt at the curb by the dazzlingly lit assembly rooms, and as Patricia at last alighted, she steeled herself for the next few hours. She was about to enter the presence of royalty, which would have been enough to endure on its own without the added pressure of whether or not Lord Haldane would find it amusing to relate the saucy tale of Lady Lindsay's provocative niece.

As they entered the assembly rooms, the sounds of the night outside gave way to the strains of a minuet emanating from the ballroom. The entire building was lavishly adorned with flowers, and there were large blocks of ice on special stands to keep the air cool, for with such a crush of guests on a summer night it was inevitable that everything would soon become hot and uncomfortable.

A sea of fashionable and elegant people moved beneath the glittering chandeliers. Jewels flashed, plumes and fans wafted, decorations glinted on military uniforms, and everywhere there were fine gentlemen in distinguished black evening velvet. The drone of refined conversation vied with the playing of the orchestra, and as the minuet came to an end, Patricia distinctly heard the rap of the master of ceremonies' staff as he announced the next dance, a Scottish reel.

The Prince of Wales was greeting his guests in person, and stood at the top of the grand staircase that led up to the ballroom. A long queue of people had formed as he spoke to each person who was presented to him.

Patricia had some time in which to study him, and although she had to admit that she was still a little disappointed, there was nevertheless such an air of charm and courtesy about him that one could quite forget the rouge on his cheeks and the false curls on his head. He was very well corseted into his black evening clothes, and his breast sparkled with diamond orders.

As Patricia and her aunt drew nearer and nearer to the top of the staircase, she began to feel less and less confident. What if she gave an awkward curtsey? What if she stumbled over her words? Oh, the possibilities for failure seemed legion, and increasing in number with each heartbeat.

Suddenly it was her turn, and she was sinking into a thankfully creditable curtsey. The prince smiled as her aunt introduced her, and then he raised her gracefully to her feet again, murmuring to her aunt that he trusted he would see Miss Fairbourne later in the evening.

Patricia was in something of a daze as she and Lady Lindsay moved on. Had she acquitted herself well enough? Evidently she had, for her aunt tapped her arm approvingly. "Well done, my dear. His Royal Highness was well pleased with you."

"He was?"

"Oh, yes, for it isn't everyone he wished to speak to again. Don't look so alarmed, my dear, for it isn't very likely that you will actually be required to speak to him again, for he will most likely forget on a night such as this. But he *will* remember you at a later point, of that you may be sure. Now then, let us see if we can find ourselves an empty sofa."

They gazed into the beautiful ballroom, where a throng of guests made everything a quite dreadful press. The Scottish reel was in progress, with much whooping, stamping, and general merriment, and those guests who were not dancing were forced to raise their voices in order to be heard. It was all very noisy and crowded indeed, and it didn't seem possible that a sofa would be found, but Lady Lindsay appeared to have an infallible instinct for such things. She led Patricia to a corner that could almost have been described as quiet, and there, looking positively inviting, was an unoccupied sofa.

As they took their seats Patricia half-expected to feel speculative glances directed her way, for she was sure that Lord Haldane would not be able to resist spreading the tale of her balcony display. But to her relief, she did not appear to be attracting any untoward interest, and of the lord himself there was as yet no sign at all.

Lady Lindsay was very well acquainted with most of the other guests, and for the next hour or more their sofa drew a steady stream of people wishing to speak to her. Among these people there were inevitably a number of gentlemen who invited Patricia to dance, and on the first occasion she was so nervous that she was sure she would forget the steps, but she carried off the polonaise with sufficient aplomb to give herself more confidence when the next occasion arose. Thus she danced a *ländler*, a minuet, several country dances, and a cotillion, and with each measure her confidence increased and she at last began to enjoy herself. There was still no sign of Lord Haldane, and no hint at all that he had been moved to a sly whisper about Lady Lindsay's niece.

Among the gentlemen to whom Patricia was introduced was Sir Daniel Kershaw, Laurinda Beresford's sweetheart. He was doing his best to appear carefree, but his face was pale and drawn, and the shadows beneath his eyes told of sleepless nights since his beloved's shocking disappearance. Patricia found him very civil and agreeable, and she sympathized deeply with his situation, but somehow she simply could not like him. There was something about him from which she instinctively recoiled, although she could not have explained what it was. It was a feeling so strong that when he invited her to dance she found herself pleading tiredness after so many previous measures, and politely expressing a preference for sitting out the rather boisterous country dance the master of ceremonies had just announced.

The ballroom had become increasingly warm as the hours ticked by, and the blocks of ice intended to cool the air were soon standing in pools of water. The line of French windows down one side of the room stood open to the night, but it remained stifling inside. Patricia didn't realize at first that the temperature was affecting her, but as she danced a reel, the ballroom began to spin. Afraid that she was about to pass out, she withdrew hastily from the rather large set without her partner realizing, and made her way a little unsteadily toward the nearest of the open French windows.

The room still revolved around her, and everything began to go dark, but just as she was about to sink to the floor, a strong arm moved around her waist, and she found herself being firmly propelled toward the blessedly cool night air outside.

"You'll soon recover when you sit down for a moment, Miss Fairbourne," said her rescuer, and she recognized Lord Haldane's voice.

She was vaguely aware that it would not be proper to go outside alone with him, but she felt too weak and unwell to say or do anything to resist, and anyway she was very grateful indeed for his help.

There was an almost deserted lantern-hung terrace outside, and he ushered her toward a stone bench set in an alcove. As she sat down, he beckoned to a footman who stood nearby.

"A glass of water, if you please, and be quick about it."

"Sir." The footman hurried away, returning in a moment with a chilled glass which Lord Haldane held gently to Patricia's lips.

"A sip at a time, Miss Fairbourne, and you'll soon begin to feel a little better."

The water was deliciously cold, and gradually the dizziness began to recede.

Lord Haldane sat down next to her. "Have you recovered a little?"

"Yes, thank you."

"It's insufferably hot in there, and I fear you aren't the only lady to have succumbed."

"You're very kind, sir," she said, giving him a weak smile.

He laughed a little dryly. "Kind is not an adjective that is often applied to me, Miss Fairbourne, especially of late."

She didn't know how to respond, for at that moment she remembered the balcony, and was immediately covered with embarrassed confusion.

He looked at her with renewed concern. "Do you feel unwell again?" he asked quickly.

"No, it's just . . ." She bit her lip, not wanting to say anything more.

"Yes?"

Suddenly she had to tell him, if only to be reassured that he wouldn't spread the tale. She made herself meet his gaze. "It's just that I thought about last night."

"Last night? I'm afraid I don't understand."

"When you saw me on the balcony." There, she'd said it. Her cheeks felt as if they were on fire, and she could no longer meet his eyes but had to look away.

He was silent for a moment, but then gave a rather wry smile. "Miss Fairbourne, when I saw you last night I thought you were all that was natural and delightful."

"You . . . you didn't think I was, er, guilty of impropriety?"

"If you were, Miss Fairbourne, then I was guilty of playing the part of Peeping Tom. Please do not feel embarrassed about what happened, for you could not have known you would be observed, and I give you my solemn word that I will not mention it to another soul."

"You must think me very foolish," she murmured, her cheeks still aflame.

"I don't think any such thing, but perhaps I am of a mind to be a little offended."

She searched his face in the light from the lanterns. "Offended?"

"That you should so clearly fear I might be less than a gentleman."

She bit her lip for a moment. "Forgive me, sir, but you must concede that I do not know you."

"And what you've heard of me since arriving here has no doubt filled you with dread," he said dryly.

"I cannot deny that your name has been mentioned," she admitted.

"Oh, I'm sure it has, and with all manner of lurid supposition added for effect. You shouldn't give credence to gossip, Miss Fairbourne, for it is seldom founded on solid fact, but rather upon the quicksands of speculation. I see in your eyes that you are wondering whether I am a monster to end all monsters, or whether I might, on the other hand, be a misunderstood angel."

She couldn't help smiling. "I doubt very much if you are an angel, sir, but then I also find it hard to believe that you are a monster."

"Ah, the gentle art of diplomacy," he said softly, surveying her thoughtfully.

His gaze disquieted her, for it was very direct and penetrating, but at the same time it made her unexpectedly bold. Almost before she knew it, she found herself asking him a very frank question. "Lord Haldane, what has happened to Miss Beresford?"

"I believe that gossip has it correct, Miss Fairbourne, and that my unfortunate ward has been abducted," he replied smoothly.

"By whom?"

He smiled a little. "I have my suspicions on that score, but I do not intend to voice them just yet as I have no proof. No doubt such reticence on my part might seem to suggest a screen, conjured to conceal my own guilt."

"Is it?"

"My, how relentless you are, to be sure," he murmured, not flinching from her gaze. "No, Miss Fairbourne, it is not a screen, for I promise you upon my honor that I am not in any way responsible for what has befallen Laurinda. I do not deny that I refused her permission to marry Kershaw, but my reason for that was well justified, and I would do it again were she still under my roof. I have always acted with her best interests at heart, and I have never taken my responsibilities lightly where she is concerned. I may have a dastardly reputation where the fair sex is generally concerned, and my list of conquests may be lamentably long, but in spite of all that is whispered of me, I am not deep in debt and have never behaved with dishonor. I trust that you believe me, Miss Fairbourne."

She looked deep into his eyes, and believed him implicitly. "Yes, my lord, I believe you."

He took her hand and raised it to his lips. "That is all I ask," he said quietly. Then he stood. "I think maybe that we've lingered out here for long enough. I'm quite sure Lady Lindsay would come close to the vapors were she to discover that you been alone so long in my presence." He held his hand out to her.

As his white-gloved fingers again closed over hers, Patricia was conscious of a tingle of electricity passing through her. He affected her as no one ever had before, and it was a very disturbing sensation. She drew her hand quickly away, almost as if to break the spell that seemed suddenly intent upon coiling around her. She must be on her guard where he was concerned, for her aunt had warned her that he was not at all the sort of gentleman with whom a proper young lady should be acquainted. But, oh, the delicious confusion of feelings that stirred through her now. . . .

*   *   *

Lady Lindsay was too fatigued by the end of the ball to go on to the Pavilion to watch the fireworks display and so, instead, she and Patricia watched from the vantage point of Patricia's balcony. From there they could see everything, and did not have to suffer the inconvenience of other people spoiling their view.

The night sky was brilliant with Chinese fire, girandoles, cascades, gerbes, and rockets, and the distinguished crowd of onlookers gasped anew with each splendor. The Pavilion itself was bright with lights, and the lanterns strung in the trees still glowed prettily, even though it would soon be dawn.

Acrid smoke drifted through the still air, and as some fiery crimson sprays exploded against the sky, there was a following moment or so of unexpected silence. In that silence, Patricia was sure she again heard the cry for help that had lured her out onto the balcony the night before. It was low and muffled, and was almost over before it began. But she was still certain that someone had tried to call for help, but had been silenced by a hand over the mouth. The sound had seemed to come from her left, but there was only the empty house next door, and its deserted garden where the paths and lawns were illuminated anew as more fireworks exploded into the night.

Patricia put an anxious hand on her aunt's arm. "Aunt Lindsay, did you hear someone calling for help a moment ago?"

Lady Lindsay found the question amusing. "My dear, I can't hear anything at all except the fireworks."

"I'm certain someone called out," Patricia insisted, glancing down again into the garden next door.

"You probably heard a rocket, for some of them

do make strange sounds," Lady Lindsay replied, returning her attention to the royal grounds.

Patricia said nothing more, but the fireworks were no longer of any interest to her. She hadn't made a mistake. Someone had definitely been calling for help, just as they'd called out the previous night. It hadn't been the clandestine lovers she'd heard then, she knew that now. But who could it be, and where were they? She couldn't even tell if it was a man, a woman, or a child.

She continued to listen, straining to hear anything beyond the racket of the fireworks. But even when the last gerbe spluttered into silence and the prince's guests began to retreat into the Pavilion, there was no further repetition of the cry.

She looked down at the garden wall between her aunt's property and the one next door. The next morning she would try to open the connecting door and make a very thorough search. If, as she thought, the cry had come from there, then she would find whoever it was.

She carried out her plan directly after breakfast. Her aunt had gone out to visit a sick friend, and there was no one to observe what she did. Wearing a ruff-throated gown made of pink-spotted white muslin, she slipped out into the garden without even Armstrong realizing where she had gone.

She paused in front of the door in the wall, hardly daring to hope that it would meekly open to her touch, but as she raised the latch, to her astonishment that is precisely what it did. The hinges protested a little, and the climbing roses trembled as some of their sprays snapped, but in a moment she could look through into the garden next door.

There were dappled shadows on the grass as the summer sun shone down through the branches of a walnut tree growing against the wall, and as she stepped through, the scent of her aunt's roses gave way to the headier perfumes of lavender and honeysuckle. Stone-flagged paths radiated from a central area where a white marble sundial stood in solitary splendor. A gardener had evidently been at work recently, proving that Sir Daniel had meant everything to look well when he brought his bride back from Gretna Green.

Patricia moved slowly along one of the paths toward the house. The windows and doors at the back were shuttered like those at the front, and in the mews lane, the coachhouses and stables were silent and deserted. There was a terrace by the French windows of the ground-floor dining room, and alongside were some steps leading down to the kitchen yard, a dark place of shadows where the sun did not penetrate. She paused at the top of the steps, and then went hesitantly down.

It was unexpectedly cool in the shadows, and she shivered, wishing she'd thought of putting on a shawl. The kitchen door was padlocked, and judging by the cobwebs had not been opened for some time. Nevertheless, she felt the urge to rattle the handle, and call out.

"Is anyone there? Can anyone hear me?"

She listened carefully, but there was nothing at all, just the stirring of the August breeze across the garden, and the distant cries of seagulls high against the heavens.

Suddenly a sharp voice addressed her angrily from the top of the steps behind. "Who are you? What are you doing here?"

With a startled cry she whirled about, and saw Sir Daniel Kershaw standing there.

As he saw her face, his expression changed. "Miss Fairbourne, is it not?"

"Yes, Sir Daniel. Forgive me, I know I have no

business being here, but I thought I heard someone calling for help."

He stared at her for a moment, and then gave a slight laugh. "Miss Fairbourne, the house is empty."

She went up the steps toward him. "I know it is, Sir Daniel, but I'm sure I heard something."

He glanced up at the seagulls wheeling far above. "Perhaps they are what you heard."

"Perhaps." The dislike she'd felt for him the night before returned now, although still she could not have said what exactly it was that repelled her so.

He smiled then. "Miss Fairbourne, I must ask your forgiveness for having addressed you so harshly a moment ago, but I thought . . . Well, no matter what I thought, suffice it that recent events have aroused a great deal of very unwelcome curiosity about my affairs."

"I assure you that I have not come here to pry, Sir Daniel."

"I realize that, Miss Fairbourne, which is why I trust you will forgive my sharp tone."

"There is nothing to forgive, sir."

He turned, surveying the sunlit garden. "I had such high hopes of bringing my dearest . . ." He broke off, putting a swift hand on Patricia's arm and pointing down to some shrubs halfway along the garden wall. "Did you see that?"

"See what, Sir Daniel?"

"A viper."

Her eyes widened, for if there was one thing she could not abide, it was snakes. "Surely you are mistaken, Sir Daniel, for vipers do not like to be where there are people."

"Nevertheless, I'm certain that that is what I saw."

"Maybe it was a harmless grass snake," she suggested hopefully.

"With those telltale zigzag markings? I fear not."

She shuddered, staring down at the shrubs. Had he really seen a viper?

He saw the look, and quickly drew her hand over his arm. "Allow me to see you safely back to your aunt's property. I see from the open door that you entered through the garden wall."

"Yes, it wasn't locked."

She kept a very wary eye on the shrubs as he escorted her back to the garden door, and she stepped quickly through into her aunt's garden.

Sir Daniel did what he could to reassure her. "I will have the viper attended to as soon as I can, Miss Fairbourne. And I will block the bottom of the door so that nothing can slip through, but you must promise me not to try to come through again until all has been made safe."

"You do not need to request such an undertaking, sir, for I have no intention at all of setting foot through that door again," she replied with feeling, all thought of the mysterious voice vanishing beyond her dread of snakes.

"Perhaps it's as well," he said, drawing her hand to his lips. "Good day to you, Miss Fairbourne."

"Good day, Sir Daniel."

The door closed behind him, and a moment later she heard him place something at the foot of it. Not long after that she heard a light vehicle, sounding like a two-horse curricle, driving smartly away along the mews lane.

That afternoon she decided to go to the beach, and she took Molly with her both for company and as the required chaperone. It was an opportunity to indulge a little in her passion for reading, and she hid the forbidden volume of *Gil Blas* in her largest reticule. Molly was only too pleased to accompany her, for she was fond of crochet work, and was quite prepared to sit with hook and thread for hours. With these objectives in mind, mistress and maid set off eagerly.

Patricia still wore the spotted muslin gown she'd worn that morning, and with it she put a little brown silk spencer and a wide-brimmed straw hat with brown satin ribbons tied loosely around the crown. Molly was very neat in a green linen dress and little cape, and on her head there was a flower-adorned hat that had once been Patricia's.

Steep stone steps led down from the seafront promenade to the rocky incline at the head of the beach. The two young women walked down through the shingle on the upper portion of the beach, and at last reached the hard, shining sand where the waves were in retreat. A number of people strolled here, and there were riders, some of whom urged their horses through the shallows. The fishing boats that went out each morning for the silver mackerel that abounded in these waters had all been drawn up well above the hightide mark, and so had the neat lines of bathing huts that were required by the countless people who came to the spa for the benefit of the cure.

It was a balmy summer afternoon, quite perfect in every way, and Patricia and Molly strolled agreeably to and fro along the shore for some time before at last seeking a place to sit. They found an ideal spot in the lee of one of the fishing boats, where the shingle was even and would be quite comfortable. Knowing that they were safe from observation, they both discarded their hats so that the light sea breeze could stir gently through their hair, and soon both were engrossed in their separate pastimes.

Patricia struggled with some of the Old French

in her book, but she was determined to master it.
Her grandfather had taught her, and when she'd
proved a good pupil, he'd engaged a proper tutor.
She was more educated than most young women,
and even more than some young gentlemen. She
liked to employ her brain upon something more
than the usual trivial things allowed ladies, but from
time to time she found herself glancing up nervously for fear of discovering her aunt bearing
crossly down upon her. It was so unfair that gentlemen frowned upon learning in a woman, but that
was the way of the world, and she would have to
put up with it. In the meantime, however, she
would steal moments like this, albeit with a horridly
guilty conscience!

Molly's attention began to wander after a while,
and she gazed toward the promenade, where a constant flow of elegant carriages drove slowly to and
fro, and where crowds of people perambulated in
the warm August sunshine. A man selling gingerbread walked there too, ringing his handbell and
shouting out the assets of his gingerbread above all
the others in the town. The sticky sweet was a
famed local delicacy, and Molly had very swiftly
developed a great liking for it.

As his bell continued to ring out compellingly,
she put her crochet work down and looked hesitantly at Patricia. "May I have your permission to
buy some gingerbread, Miss Patricia?"

Patricia smiled. "Of course you may."

"Oh, thank you. I promise not to be long." Molly
scrambled to her feet and hurried away up the
beach toward the stone steps.

Patricia returned her attention to the pages of
her book, and was soon lost again in the roving
adventures of Lesage's hero.

She didn't hear the gentleman strolling toward
her, and knew nothing of his presence until he sud-

denly addressed her. "**Good afternoon**, Miss Fairbourne."

Her breath caught as she looked up swiftly into Lord Haldane's quick blue eyes. "G-good afternoon, Lord Haldane."

He glanced down at her book. "Lesage in the original text? I'm filled with admiration."

She closed the book immediately.

He raised a quizzical eyebrow. "Surely you are not ashamed of your accomplishment, Miss Fairbourne? It isn't everyone who can triumph over the intricacies of modern French, let alone the more ancient form."

"Lord Haldane, my aunt would much prefer me to read ladies' journals."

He smiled. "Yes, I fear she would. May I join you for a while?" He indicated the place next to her.

"If-if you wish."

He tossed his tall hat onto the shingle, teased off his gloves, and then sat down beside her. He wore an elegant light-brown coat and white kerseymere breeches, and the breeze toyed with the lace trimming on his cravat as he leaned back against the fishing boat and glanced at her again. "Are you much given to such learned reading, Miss Fairbourne?" he enquired after a moment.

She blushed. "I fear that I am, sir."

"Fear? Do I take it then that you are indeed ashamed of your accomplishment?"

She looked down at the beautifully embossed cover of the book. "No, my lord, I'm not ashamed of it, but young ladies are not supposed to do such things."

He smiled. "I have never subscribed to the view that ladies should be decorative but empty-headed, and I find it most admirable that *anyone*, male or female, should be able to read Lesage in its original form. Believe me, Miss Fairbourne, I'm most impressed."

"I'm afraid I'm something of an oddity," she said.

"I would prefer to say that I find you refreshingly different, different and very charming."

It was an unexpectedly warm compliment, and suddenly she couldn't meet his eyes anymore. She wished he didn't affect her so, but everything about him seemed to set her at sixes and sevens. Was she simply being a gullible goose? Was she falling for his knowing, practiced ways? She would have to do better than this, for it wouldn't do at all to be taken in by the silken approaches of the first experienced gentleman who came her way.

He seemed to read her thoughts a little. "My intentions are not dastardly, I promise you, Miss Fairbourne."

"I would not presume to think they were, sir, for I hardly imagine you would concern yourself with someone like me."

"Someone like you? And what, exactly, does that mean? Miss Fairbourne, you do not appear to have a very high opinion of yourself, and that makes me most curious. You are beautiful, charming, original, and engaging, and I am more than content to concern myself with you."

Hot color flooded into her cheeks. "You are very free with your compliments, sir."

"Only when they seem called for, which at the moment they appear to be. Last night at the ball you looked every inch a young lady of fashion, and you were certainly one of the loveliest ladies present."

"More compliments?"

He smiled. "If the truth is a compliment, yes, more compliments."

She toyed with the book in her lap. "Lord Haldane, I may have looked a lady of fashion, but I am really very green, and the only reason I was at such a grand occasion was because my aunt is acquainted with the prince. I have never been out in society, I am finding it all an ordeal, and I look forward to the end of my stay here so that I can go home again to the Lake District." She didn't know why she was telling him this, after all she hardly knew him, nor did she really know why she had allowed the present situation to arise, for she was well aware that it would have been infinitely more wise to have made an excuse to leave rather than sit alone with him like this.

He smiled a little at her confession. "Miss Fairbourne, I'm sure that if you give Brighton a chance, you will soon enjoy everything."

"Perhaps." To her relief she saw Molly returning, for the maid's presence would resolve the uncomfortable matter of propriety, but almost immediately the relief turned to dismay as the maid saw that her mistress was no longer alone. Instead of coming to join them, Molly chose instead to retreat tactfully to the lee of another fishing boat, where she sat down to enjoy the slice of sticky gingerbread she'd purchased on the promenade. Patricia wished her in perdition for such ill-placed discretion. What Aunt Lindsay would have had to say if she knew about all this could only be imagined. For, not only was her disobedient niece hiding away with a book, but she was also sitting alone with the most notorious and talked-of lord in Brighton!

She shifted a little anxiously as she imagined her aunt's justifiable wrath, and she gave Molly a dark glance which Lord Haldane intercepted.

"Miss Fairbourne, if you wish me to leave, you have only to say so."

She colored, and then look candidly at him. "It isn't that I wish you to leave, my lord, but rather that I know I am breaking the rules by speaking to you like this."

He glanced around, but there was no one except Molly who could see that they were seated by the boat. "Miss Fairbourne, I think we are safe enough from detection, indeed I only found you here myself because I happened to see you and your maid strolling by the shore and came to deliberately seek you out. It was some time before I actually managed to spot you."

"You . . . you came to seek me out?"

"To inquire if you are now fully recovered from your indisposition at the ball."

"Oh. Yes, sir, I'm quite recovered."

"I'm glad to hear it." He smiled disarmingly.

It was a smile that exposed her to the full force of his immense charm, and she had to look away to hide the effect it had upon her.

He misunderstood. "Have you been listening to more gossip about me, Miss Fairbourne?" he asked suddenly.

"No. Why do you ask?"

"Oh, there is something in your manner that makes me wonder. Last night I promised you that I did not have anything to do with my ward's disappearance, and you told me you believed me."

"I do believe you," she replied honestly.

"I'm glad to hear it, for I would hate to think you took Kershaw's part in all this."

She stared at him. "What do you mean?"

"Simply that if anyone's hand lies behind my ward's disappearance, it is his, although I still cannot prove it."

Patricia's lips parted. "You cannot mean that."

"Why not? Miss Fairbourne, Kershaw is the most plausible rogue in creation, and he is most definitely not the gentleman he pretends to be."

She glanced away, remembering her own instinctive reaction to Laurinda's lover.

Lord Haldane suddenly put his hand to her cheek, turning her face toward him again. "What is it?" he asked, searching her face intently. "Is it something about Kershaw?"

"I was just thinking that I don't like him very much. I felt it last night at the ball, and again this morning."

"This morning?"

"Yes."

"Where did you see him?"

"In the garden of the house he's purchased next to my aunt's."

A light passed through his blue eyes. "The house he was presumptuous enough to acquire in anticipation of marrying my ward?"

"Yes."

He looked curiously at her. "What were you doing there?"

She hesitated. "I, er, I thought I heard someone calling for help, and I went through the door in the wall between the two gardens. Everything seemed to be deserted, but then he arrived and saw me. Lord Haldane, I really don't know why I don't like him, for in truth, this morning he was most concerned for my welfare."

"Your welfare? In what way?"

"He saw a viper by some shrubs, and he escorted me back to my aunt's garden and made the door safe so that nothing could slither underneath it. He promised to have the snake attended to without delay, and made me promise not to go into the garden again until all had been made safe."

Lord Haldane's eyes were piercing. "Did you see the viper, Miss Fairbourne?"

"No," she admitted.

"No, I'm sure you didn't, for I do not believe

there was one," he replied, getting up suddenly. Picking up his hat and gloves, he reached down suddenly to put his fingertips to her cheek. "I will leave you to the tender mercies of propriety, Miss Fairbourne, but I promise you that I've found your conversation most stimulating."

Then he had gone, striding swiftly away over the shingle toward the steps leading up to the promenade. She gazed after him, her cheek still tingling from his touch.

More footsteps approached, and she turned to see Molly returning to join her. The maid sat down and glanced after Lord Haldane. "He's a very handsome gentleman, Miss Patricia," she ventured.

"You aren't to utter a single word about any of this, Molly Nicholls."

"No, miss." The maid hurriedly resumed her crochet work.

After a moment Patricia opened her book again, but the words were a blur, for her thoughts were all of what Lord Haldane had said of Sir Daniel Kershaw.

When Patricia and Molly returned to Queen Charlotte Row, they found a traveling carriage at the door. And when they entered, they saw army gloves and a plumed shako lying on the table in the hall. Patricia knew in a moment that her cousin Edward had returned on leave from Ireland, and she hurried up to the drawing room where she heard voices.

Her aunt was still out, but Armstrong was with Edward, telling him that his mother was well, and that his cousin had arrived from the Lake District. Patricia paused in the doorway, looking at the tall military figure by the fireplace. Edward, Lord Lindsay, was the very image of the portrait above the mantelpiece, and he turned with a grin as he saw her.

"Patricia?"

"Hello, Edward."

He came toward her, taking both her hands and drawing them to his lips. "My, you've changed somewhat since last we met," he said approvingly, leading her toward a chair.

"So have you," she replied.

He grinned again. "Yes, and this time *you* will be able to pull *my* hair." He turned his head to show that not only did he have the side-whiskers and mustache that were *de rigueur* for hussar officers, but that he had also grown his hair at the back in order to wear it in a small pigtail.

She laughed. "Don't tempt me, sir, for my revenge is long overdue."

As she sat down, he continued to look approvingly at her. "You've become quite the beauty, coz. Do you have Brighton at your feet?"

"No, but thank you for the compliment."

He waited until the butler had withdrawn, and then looked earnestly at her. "Is my mother matchmaking for me?" he asked without preamble.

"I fear she is. She believes she has found the perfect wife for you in the daughter of the Earl and Countess of Rotherden."

His face fell. "Not horsey Amelia!"

"I believe that is her name."

"Oh, Lord above," he groaned, turning away. "Amelia lacks only hooves and a tail, and I am sure her greatest regret in life is that she wasn't actually born to thoroughbreds of the equine kind."

"You paint a very vivid picture."

"And an accurate one. Oh, how I *wish* my mother would leave me to my own devices." He looked at her. "I supposed she's busy on your behalf as well?"

"She has hopes of finding me a suitable husband before I return to Windermere," Patricia admitted.

At that moment they heard another carriage arrive outside, and Edward stepped out onto the balcony to see that his mother had returned to the house after her lengthy visit to her sick friend. They heard her delighted voice in the hall, and soon she was hurrying into the drawing room to envelop her son in a flurry of gray taffeta.

Patricia withdrew quietly, leaving them to their happy reunion.

To Lady Lindsay's chagrin, she had a dinner engagement that evening that was far too important to cry off, and so Patricia and Edward dined alone together.

They got on well, and weren't at all bored with each other's company. He had much to tell about life in the army, and she was the perfect listener. She related what there was to tell of her quiet existence at Windermere Park, and told him of the previous night's ball. She also told him what she knew of Laurinda Beresford's mysterious disappearance, although she did not mention her conversations with Lord Haldane.

When she retired to her bed that night, the weather had changed. The pleasant freshness of the day had become a sticky closeness that carried the threat of thunder. The sky was cloudy, without moon or stars, and as Patricia lay on her bed she heard the first distant rumblings of an approaching storm. It was impossible to sleep, and as a flash of lightning illuminated the darkness outside, she got up and went out on to the balcony, being certain this time to tie the ribbons of her nightgown and put on a light pink muslin wrap.

The storm was approaching swiftly, and the next flash of lightning was much closer, its brilliance shining on the Marine Pavilion and the royal grounds. A growl of thunder followed almost immediately, and as it died away into silence, Patricia again heard the little voice crying for help.

"Help me, someone, please . . ."

Her breath caught, and her eyes flew toward the empty garden next door, for that was definitely the direction from which the sound had come. This time she had not only heard the words quite clearly, but she had also detected that it was the voice of a young woman. Could it possibly be . . . ? Laurinda Beresford's name flew into her mind.

Whoever it was called out again. "Please help me. Please—" With that, the voice was stifled once more, and then another flash of lightning was followed almost immediately by a shattering clap of thunder that seemed to shake the house to its foundations.

Patricia's heart was pounding as she ignored the storm and continued to stare down into the adjoining garden. Then without further ado she hurried from her room. All thought of vipers and other dangers had fled from her mind, and she was only concerned with going to the aid of the owner of that pathetic little voice.

The storm was almost upon Brighton now. As she stepped out of the house, a gust of wind rustled warmly through the trees, stirring the leaves. The frilled hem of her wrap fluttered against her ankles as she made her way quickly to the door in the wall. But as she reached out to lift the latch, a tall shadow moved swiftly and silently toward her and a strong hand closed over her mouth to prevent her from crying out.

Terror coursed through her as she began to struggle, but her assailant was by far too strong. Then he hissed urgently in her ear. "For God's sake be still, Miss Fairbourne, for I mean you no harm!"

She froze with shock, for the voice belonged to Lord Haldane.

He spoke again. "I will release you if you promise not to cry out. Nod if you agree."

She nodded, and slowly he let her go, but as she turned to look enquiringly at him he put his finger warningly to his lips. "One unnecessary sound now may ruin everything," he whispered.

"Ruin what? What's happening?" Her low questions were almost drowned by the soughing of the wind through the trees.

"I'm here in the hope of rescuing my ward."

She stared, and then her eyes cleared. So the voice *was* Laurinda's!

He nodded. "I am certain that Kershaw has Laurinda imprisoned somewhere beyond this wall. Somehow she has been managing to call out, and so he took steps this morning to frighten you from going in there again. I've persuaded the town constables to come here with me tonight. I've discovered that Kershaw has made preparations to leave Brighton. Bribes to his servants have uncovered his plans, including the fact that he means to halt in the mews lane here in order to collect something from the house. I believe that that something might be my ward, and it is my hope that the constables and I will be able to catch him in the very act." He nodded toward her aunt's coachhouse, and she saw several shadowy figures standing there. "We've tried to gain entry directly into Kershaw's property, but it's all locked, and so I've taken the liberty of trespassing on Lady Lindsay's property instead, in the hope that she will not mind too much."

"I'm sure she won't, sir, especially if you rescue Miss Beresford."

At that moment they both heard the sound of a carriage being driven very slowly along the mews lane.

"Please go back inside, Miss Fairbourne," Lord Haldane said urgently, his face suddenly lit by another flash of lightning.

"Take care," she whispered, knowing in that moment that her feelings for him went far further than she would have dreamed possible in so short a time.

He turned to beckon to the waiting constables, and she stepped back as they pushed the door open, managing only with difficulty because of the logs Sir Daniel had placed on the other side. The sounds they made were drowned by the rushing of the wind and the downpour of rain as the storm at last broke overhead.

Lord Haldane paused before following the constables. He came back to Patricia, taking her hand and raising it palm uppermost to his lips. Then he followed the constables through into the other garden, and closed the door softly behind him. Patricia remained motionless where she was. Her palm burned as if his lips still touched it, and her heart was now pounding so much that she could hear it above the noise of the storm.

She heard the carriage draw to a standstill in the mew lane, and she trembled with cold and anticipation as she wondered what was happening beyond the wall. The rain dripped from her soaked hair, and her flimsy clothes clung to her as she waited. At last she heard some shouts from the other garden, and her breath caught with hope. Was the game up at last for Sir Daniel? Had Lord Haldane rescued his ward? Oh, how she wished she could open the door and see what was happening, but she didn't dare.

As the shouts continued, lights appeared in her aunt's house. A moment later Edward and Armstrong appeared outside with a lantern, and as they saw Patricia standing there in the storm, they hurried anxiously toward her.

Edward turned her to face him. "What's happening? Why in God's name are you out here like this?" he demanded with concern.

Before she could reply, the door in the wall suddenly opened, and Lord Haldane came through carrying the half-swooning figure of a beautiful young woman. She was very tearful and distressed, clinging to him as if she was afraid of being captured again. Her long dark hair was tangled and unpinned, her heart-shaped face was very pale and drawn, and she wore a white silk gown that had once been all that was stylish and fashionable, but was now dirty and torn.

There was another flash of lightning, and Patricia looked through into the other garden in time to see Sir Daniel struggling furiously in the grip of the constables.

Edward stared, and then looked at Lord Haldane, whom he recognized. "Haldane? What on earth is going on?" His glance moved to Laurinda. "Is this . . . ?"

"My missing ward? Yes, Lindsay, it is. Will you and Miss Fairbourne take care of her for me? I must accompany the constables to see that that felon Kershaw is properly charged and locked up."

Edward took Laurinda in his arms. "I trust you mean to explain to the full, Haldane," he said.

"I will, I swear." Lord Haldane put his hand gently to Laurinda's face. "You're safe now, sweetheart, you're with friends." Then he looked at Patricia. "I will come back here as soon as I have attended to everything."

She managed a smile, but already he was turning to go back into the other garden. Then she followed Edward and Armstrong out of the rain and into the comfort and shelter of her aunt's house.

In the morning it was as if the storm had never

been, for the sun rose again in a clear blue sky, and Brighton basked once more in a perfect summer day.

The town awoke to the astonishing news of what had happened during the night in Queen Charlotte Row, and society was astonished to learn that it was Sir Daniel Kershaw who was the villain of the piece, and not Laurinda's guardian. A constant stream of callers came to Lady Lindsay's house, once it was realized that that was where the heiress was, but Laurinda herself knew nothing about it as she slept the sleep of the exhausted.

Patricia sat by the bed, having just taken over from her aunt as they took turns to see that there was someone there should their unexpected guest awaken. Patricia wore a cream jaconet gown with a lavender sash, with amethysts at her throat, and her hair was pinned up into a loose knot. She turned her head toward the open French windows as she heard the latest cries of the newsboy on the corner.

"Missing heiress found! Sir Daniel Kershaw arrested!"

There was a tap at the door, and Edward peeped around it. "How is she, coz?" he asked in a whisper.

"Still asleep," Patricia replied with a smile, for it was clear that Edward had been smitten with love at first sight when he had gazed upon Laurinda's sweet face.

"You will tell me the moment she opens her eyes, won't you?"

"Of course."

He withdrew again, and silence returned to the room. Patricia lowered her eyes, wondering when Lord Haldane would come as promised. He was constantly in her thoughts. She had even dreamed of him when she had snatched some sleep while her aunt sat with Laurinda. She was falling in love with him, and there was nothing she could do to help herself.

Laurinda began to stir in the bed, and her eyes fluttered and opened. They were soft brown eyes, large and a little frightened as she gazed up at the strange bed-hangings.

Patricia quickly put a reassuring hand out. "It's all right, Miss Beresford, you're safe in my Aunt Lindsay's house."

The brown eyes swung nervously toward her, and then cleared a little as memory returned. "I . . . I remember now. Miss Fairbourne, is it not?"

"Yes. Lord Haldane left you with us while he went to—" Patricia broke off, thinking better of mentioning Sir Daniel.

Tears welled from Laurinda's eyes, and her little fingers curled around Patricia's. "I . . . I can hardly believe that it's over. Is Sir Daniel really under arrest?"

"Yes, you may be sure of it."

Laurinda still held her hand. "He took me in completely at first. I thought him all that was noble and wonderful, and I would not hear a single word said against him. I resented it so much when Lord Haldane refused his permission for us to marry, and I would not believe him when he said that Sir Daniel was a wicked rogue and deceiver. I even went so far as to plan to elope, and it wasn't until the actual day of the elopement that I was forced to accept that what Lord Haldane told me was the truth. He had had enquiries made in Bath, where Sir Daniel spent last winter. It seems that not only had he acquired vast gaming debts which had to be met if he was to escape the duns, but also, he had endeavored to seduce several other heiresses in order to acquire the necessary wealthy bride. It broke my heart to know the truth, but I was glad to have been spared from my folly. I was afraid that Lord Haldane meant to call Sir Daniel out for what he'd attempted with me, and I shrank from the scandal such a duel would stir. I just wanted to forget all about Sir Daniel and begin again, so I didn't tell Lord Haldane that we'd arranged to elope. When he went to dine at the Pavilion, I waited for Sir Daniel, who arrived as planned for our flight to Gretna Green. He expected me to be ready and waiting, and was shocked when I told him I knew all about him and wished to end everything. I told him it would be wiser for him to flee Brighton and begin again somewhere well beyond Lord Haldane's reach. But instead of making good his escape as I expected, he seized me and bundled me into his carriage. He took me to the cellars of the house he bought next door to this one, and told me he would imprison me until I agreed to marry him anyway. He was so desperate to avoid the duns and jail that he was prepared to risk Lord Haldane's wrath."

"How did you manage to call out for help?"

"He left me in the charge of an old woman who was hard of hearing. She was very vigilant, but from time to time at night would allow me to stretch my legs in the passage. When she wasn't looking, I managed to reach a little grating high in the wall. She caught me each time, but I managed to convince her I was only trying to breathe in the fresh air outside." Laurinda bit her lip to try to halt the tears. "I . . . I was beginning to think I would be left there forever, for I refused to do Sir Daniel's bidding. Then he said that he was taking me away to his country estate, where he would marry me by force. I was terrified, especially when he actually came for me. But then I saw dear Lord Haldane, and the constables seized Sir Daniel . . ." Laurinda's voice died away on a sob. "I've been such a fool, and I've said such horrid things about Lord Haldane because he wouldn't give his permission for me to marry. I should have known that he loved me and would never withhold permission unless he had ample cause. I only hope he will forgive me."

Patricia squeezed her fingers comfortingly. "I'm sure he forgives you everything, Miss Beresford."

Laurinda was silent for a moment, and then looked shyly at her. "Miss Fairbourne, when I first saw you last night in the garden there was a young gentleman with you. Who was he?"

"My cousin, Edward, Lord Lindsay," Patricia replied, noting that a faint blush had crept into the other's cheeks.

"Are you and he . . . ? I mean, I didn't know that Lady Lindsay had a niece, and I was wondering if you were here in Brighton to be . . ." Laurinda's voice died away in embarrassment.

"Here in Brighton to be betrothed to Edward?" Patricia finished for her, smiling. "No, Miss Beresford, Edward and I are merely cousins." She couldn't help putting an obvious interpretation on Laurinda's interest in Edward, for it followed too closely upon Edward's interest in her. How gratified Aunt Lindsay would be if she knew, for a match between Edward and Laurinda Beresford had been her original wish.

Laurinda's blush had deepened. "You must think me quite dreadful, Miss Fairbourne, for here I am, fresh from the most dreadful scrape with Sir Daniel, and already enquiring about another gentleman."

"I don't think you dreadful at all, Miss Beresford. Besides, you may care to know that Edward is in quite a state of anxiety over you, and that he has crept to the door on a number of occasions to see that you are all right."

The blush lingered. "Has he really?"

"Yes."

At that moment there was another tap at the door, but it was Lady Lindsay not Edward. She was accompanied at last by Lord Haldane, who went immediately to take his ward's hands.

"How are you, sweeting?" he asked gently, sitting on the bed beside her.

Fresh tears filled Laurinda's eyes, and she struggled up to fling her arms around him, hiding her face against the costly mulberry wool of his coat.

Patricia and her aunt withdrew quietly, and left guardian and ward to their privacy.

Patricia was seated by the fountain in the garden. The light breeze lifted the hem of her cream gown and the sun shone on the amethysts in her necklace as she leaned over to dip her fingers in the cool water of the pool. The sounds of summer were all around, and there was a garden party taking place in the grounds of the Marine Pavilion.

Lord Haldane was still in the house, and she wondered if he would speak to her before he left. She wished her heart hadn't betrayed her into falling in love with him, for such a love could surely only lead to pain. She heard the door of the house opened behind her and she turned hopefully, but it was her aunt.

Lady Lindsay came toward her, and then stood with her hands clasped as she surveyed her. "Patricia, I have something to say to you, but before I do, I wish to know what exactly your dealings have been with Lord Haldane."

Patricia lowered her eyes guiltily. "I . . . I have spoken to him once or twice, Aunt Lindsay. I met him on the beach yesterday, and I saw him at the ball. And I saw him last night in the garden, of course."

"Were any of these meetings assignations?"

Patricia looked up swiftly. "No, Aunt Lindsay." What was all this about?

Her aunt studied her in silence for a moment, and then nodded. "I believe you, my dear. I had to ask because Lord Haldane has requested my permission to speak alone with you before he leaves, and I am naturally concerned that such a gentleman should have any private dealings with my niece. You are under my protection now, my dear, and it is my duty to see that you are shielded from, er, unsuitable acquaintances."

"I am sure that Lord Haldane is not unsuitable, Aunt Lindsay," Patricia replied a little boldly.

"Patricia, I concede that he has been much maligned over this business of his ward, and I also concede that I cannot fault his conduct whenever I have spoken to him, but that does not alter the fact that he has a reputation second to none when it comes to matters of the heart. Bearing this in mind, I wish to know if you are prepared to speak to him as he requests."

"Yes, Aunt Lindsay."

"Very well, I will not withhold my permission, but I will observe the meeting from the house, to see that propriety is satisfied."

"Yes, Aunt Lindsay."

Lady Lindsay began to turn away, but then paused again. "Be careful, my dear, for the inexperienced heart is open to so much hurt," she said wisely. Then she retraced her steps to the house.

Patricia's pulse had quickened the moment she'd been told of Lord Haldane's wish to speak to her. But in spite of the eager anticipation that flowed through her now, she was only too aware of the sense in her aunt's warning.

It seemed an age before the door opened again, and he came toward her. Oh, how handsome he was, and how matchless his elegance, from the cut and style of his mulberry coat, to the clinging lines of his gray cord breeches and the superb gleam on his top boots. His eyes seemed as blue as the skies as he took her hand and raised it to his lips.

"Thank you for agreeing to receive me, Miss Fairbourne."

His touch electrified her again, and she had to draw her fingers away. Tell-tale warmth had already entered her cheeks, and she was sure that if she met his eyes he would be able to read the truth about her foolish feelings for him. "You . . . you wished to speak to me, Lord Haldane?" she asked, hoping she sounded more level and collected than she felt.

"I have much to thank you for, Miss Fairbourne."

"Do you? I don't understand . . ."

"To begin with, you were prepared to believe in my innocence when all others were convinced of my guilt."

She smiled shyly. "I'm sure I was not the only one to have faith in you, my lord."

"Possibly, but you were certainly the only one who led me to find my ward. If you hadn't heard Laurinda's cries, and if you hadn't gone through into that garden next door and caused Kershaw to invent his tale of vipers, then she would probably have been spirited away last night and would be his bride by now."

"I'm truly glad that I was of assistance, my lord."

He turned to glance up at the drawing room balcony, where Lady Lindsay stood observing them. Then he smiled a little ruefully at Patricia. "I fear your aunt disapproves of me."

"You have a reputation, sir."

"A well-earned one, I'm ashamed to say," he admitted, "but it is also a reputation which has of now been consigned to the past."

"A leopard who has changed his spots?" She smiled wryly.

"Yes, Miss Fairbourne, I am become just such a leopard, as indeed I must if I am to be permitted to call upon you."

She stared at him. "Call upon me?" she repeated faintly.

"That is my most earnest wish, unless, of course, such interest does not meet with your favor." He held her gaze. "May I call upon you, Miss Fairbourne?"

Her heart had stopped within her. "If that is what you wish, sir," she heard herself say.

"Perhaps a drive together tomorrow afternoon? With your aunt or a maid to see that all is proper, of course."

"A drive would be most agreeable, Lord Haldane."

He took her hand again and drew it to his lips. "Until tomorrow, Miss Fairbourne," he said softly.

As he walked away, she closed her eyes. He wished to call upon her! Lord Haldane wished to call upon Miss Patricia Fairbourne! Please don't let it be a dream, don't let her suddenly awaken and find she had imagined what had just passed. But as she opened her eyes again, she could still see him entering the house.

Over the next month of that suddenly wonderful summer, Lord Haldane paid constant attention to Lady Lindsay's little-known niece. It was the talk of Brighton, overshadowing even the burgeoning romance between Lord Lindsay and Miss Laurinda Beresford.

To Patricia it was clear that Edward and Laurinda were made for each other and that a betrothal would soon ensue, but it did not seem possible that there would be such a happy outcome for her, in spite of all the attention she received from Lord Haldane. She wasn't an heiress. Indeed, she was a virtual nobody, and it seemed out of the question that such an important lord would find her a suitable marriage prospect. She knew she must be practical, and accept that at the end of the summer she would return to the Lake District, and he would go either to London or to his vast estate in Yorkshire. For the moment, however, she reveled in her summer happiness, a happiness she knew she would remember forever.

Lady Lindsay, who was delighted with her son's romance with Laurinda, was much concerned about her niece, who had by now confessed in private to being hopelessly in love with Lord Haldane. Lady Lindsay had at first been anxious that his reputation would reflect poorly upon Patricia, but that did not seem to be the case, for he appeared to be a reformed character. He did not make one wrong move, nor break a single rule; indeed, he seemed all that was perfect. But nevertheless, Lady Lindsay feared that Patricia was right, and that at the end of the summer there would be a parting of the ways. What if his intentions were matrimonial, however? What if there was a chance of two dazzling betrothals? What a coup that would be, what a triumph! Lady Lindsay resolved therefore to tread very carefully, for no matter what Lord Haldane had done in the past, he was nevertheless a magnificent prize, being one of the wealthiest lords in the realm. She was put in mind of her late husband's passion for fishing, a passion that had led him to stand for hours in the icy waters of a Scottish river, playing a large salmon at the end of his line. Lord Haldane was the most splendid salmon imaginable, and she was ambitious for Patricia to hook him. All things were possible, and the landing of such a fish was worth angling for.

It was toward the end of September that the truth about Lord Haldane's intentions became clear. It happened on a warm evening toward sunset, when Patricia and he were strolling along the beach, watched at a discreet distance by the ever-vigilant Lady Lindsay.

Patricia wore a blush-pink lawn gown with an un-buttoned gray silk spencer, and on her head there was a gray straw hat with a flouncy pink gauze tied lightly around the crown, its end fluttering prettily behind her as she walked. Beside her, Lord Haldane wore a charcoal coat and cream corduroy breeches, and the setting sun flashed brilliantly on the diamond pin in his neckcloth.

The sun was sinking toward the horizon in a glory of gold, copper, crimson and orange, and the sea shone as if scattered with melting jewels. The calls of seagulls echoed in the air, and gentle waves splashed upon the glistening sand. It was a spell-binding summer evening, and even before Lord Haldane suddenly halted and turned her to face him, Patricia knew that this moment was different.

He removed his gloves, and then put one hand to her cheek. "Patricia, I must know if my attentions are still as welcome to you as I hope."

"I . . . I find you all that is agreeable, Lord Haldane."

He smiled a little. "I trust we know each other well enough by now for you to call me Robert."

"If that is your wish."

He became a little perplexed. "Patricia, why do I constantly feel as if you are holding back? I don't understand why you always place a barrier between us, as if you are afraid of something. Surely you know by now that my interest in you goes far beyond mere acquaintance. Friendship is not enough, Patricia, for it is full courtship that I have in mind."

She stared at him. "Courtship?" she whispered.

"Yes." He cupped her face in his hands. "I wish to ask for your hand, but there is something you are keeping from me, a part of you that I cannot reach. Please tell me what it is."

Tears filled her eyes. "Oh, Robert, I was afraid to reveal everything, because I did not think you could possibly wish to marry me."

"Why ever not?"

"Because I am not an heiress, and I haven't even come out properly. I wouldn't have attended the prince's ball if it hadn't been for my aunt, and no one here in Brighton would even have heard of me if . . ."

"Do you honestly imagine that any of that makes the slightest difference to me? Patricia, I adore everything about you, even the fact that you can read Old French, and you've seldom been out of my thoughts since that first night when I saw you on the balcony. I thought you the most beautiful and natural of creatures, and I still think the same. Everything you say and do delights me, and being with you is all that matters to me. I couldn't care less that you don't have a fortune, for I have fortune enough for both of us, and I want to love and cherish you for the rest of our lives." His thumbs caressed her. "I've told you that I love you, my darling, but I have yet to hear you confess the same to me."

"I love you, Robert," she whispered. "I love you so much that I hardly dare believe you actually wish to marry me."

"Believe it, my love, for it is true. I want to make you Lady Haldane, and to keep you close forever. Will you marry me?"

Joy coursed through her veins, and more tears stung her eyes as she nodded. "Yes, Robert, I will marry you."

He kissed her then, drawing her tenderly into his

arms and pressing her close. His lips were warm upon hers, and his fingers curled richly in the hair at the nape of her neck. She could feel his heart beating next to hers, and desire stirred so luxuriously through her that she felt weak. He loved her. He loved her as much as she loved him, and suddenly the future stretched happily ahead into infinity.

On the promenade, Lady Lindsay watched with immense satisfaction. "Hooked, and landed," she murmured, twirling her parasol contentedly. Oh, what a magnificent summer this had been, with Edward suitably matched, and now Patricia as well.

A week later there was an announcement in the Brighton newspaper. The world was informed that Lord Lindsay had won the heart and hand of Lord Haldane's ward, Miss Laurinda Beresford, and also that Miss Patricia Fairbourne had snapped up no less a prize than Lord Haldane himself. The two betrothals were celebrated at a grand ball at the Castle assembly rooms, and it was an occasion which was acknowledged to be one of the social highlights of that magnificent summer, second only to the Prince of Wales's birthday.

Midsummer Masquerade

by Sheila Walsh

THE MIST OF DAWN still hung over newly burgeoning trees, and dew silvered the grass as the two horsemen rode through the Stanhope Gate into a deserted Hyde Park.

"That new animal of yours is a nervy brute, Gideon." Major Sawyer gave his friend's rangy black hunter plenty of room as it began to caracole. "Wouldn't fancy riding him in town traffic."

Gideon, sixth Marquess of Grenville, threw him a scathing look as he ran a smoothing hand along the hunter's twitching neck. "When did you ever know me to own a horse I couldn't handle, Ned?" he drawled. "This fellow hasn't an ounce of real malice in him. He just needs to shake the fidgets out of his legs, which is why I have forsaken my bed at such an ungodly hour in order to let him have his head while everyone else is still abed."

"Not quite everyone." The major gestured with his riding crop.

Away in the distance, a third rider came scorching down the tan on a course set to bisect their path.

"Damned dangerous, if you ask me," muttered his companion, watching the smooth rippling action of horse and rider with narrowed eyes.

Ned grinned. "Do I detect a note of peevishness,

Gideon? You **may lay** claim to any number of properties, but the **park is** still a public place, I believe."

The rider's pace was already slowing, and as the horse approached the junction of the two paths, a capricious late-spring breeze set the skirt of a riding habit billowing, and their mistake became obvious. Ned let out a sudden whoop.

"By heaven, Gideon, it's a woman! And no ordinary woman, either! I'd know her anywhere!" Without waiting for the marquess, he rode forward to meet her.

"Caroline! Caroline Maitland, by all that's wonderful!"

"Ned! Oh, well met. What splendid luck!"

They reached across to grasp hands, both talking at once. The marquess, following more slowly, had ample time to observe the young lady mounted on a glossy well-bred bay. It was the dress that had fooled them, of course. The close-fitting jacket of her riding habit was of bronze-green superfine, braided in black. To complete the illusion, a black shako with a tufted plume, sat audaciously on titian hair, cropped as short as any man's. Close observation, however, revealed a decidedly curvaceous figure beneath the military facade. The young lady was not beautiful, but she had a face that would draw one in a crowd.

Ned turned with a broad smile as he approached. "Gideon, do let me introduce Miss Caroline Maitland to you. You may already know of her father, Sir Humphfrey Maitland, one of our most accomplished and widely travelled diplomats. Caroline, this is my good friend, Lord Grenville."

"Miss Maitland."

"My lord."

She extended a neatly gauntleted hand with no hint of shyness, and perhaps it was sheer perversity—a desire to unsettle her—that made him hold on to it far longer than the introduction merited. Such familiarity would have discomforted most genteel ladies of his acquaintance, but not this one.

Her long jade-green eyes held a challenging gleam beneath their wickedly slanting brows as she looked him over every bit as comprehensively as he had scrutinized her, noting the number of capes on his drab riding coat, and dwelling longer than was necessary on the hint of muscle beneath unwrinkled doeskin breeches. She observed the seemingly effortless way he secured the reins with one capable hand, maintaining absolute control of his powerful horse which was eager to be away. Finally, her glance was drawn to the handsome face. It was, she thought, a face made to express hauteur and ennui—all cheekbones and forehead, with heavy ironic eyelids. As his eyes met hers, her own outrageous eyebrows lifted.

"I have heard of you, I believe," she said, with a hint of humor in her voice. "Do they not call you 'the Nonpareil?' "

The marquess felt an irresistible urge to wrap his long fingers around her slim white throat. Just thinking of it caused his grasp to tighten on the rein. The horse attempted to rear, and all of his considerable skill was required to subdue him. Damn the woman. He caught her eye, and met a look of limpid innocence.

"People are often given to saying foolish things, Miss Maitland. I make it a rule never to regard them."

"Very wise, my lord." She turned at once to Ned. "I heard you had sold out. Surely it cannot be true?"

Ned grinned sheepishly. "Two months since. I hung on for a while after we'd trounced Boney, but life became damnably tedious. And you, Caro?

Surely you have not tired of holding court at the Paris Embassy?"

"That is unkind. But I shall not regard it." Miss Maitland's laugh was husky as she wrinkled her nose at him. "And you are quite right. I would be there, still, had Papa not been summoned to London. We arrived late last evening. But I never sleep well after a sea voyage, which is why you find me here so early, exercising my poor Boris, who likes the sea as little as I do."

"And does your father condone your habit of riding alone in public places in such a reckless fashion, Miss Maitland?"

"My father gives me leave to use my discretion, my lord. Hyde Park does not compare with the Bois de Boulogne, of course, when it comes to giving Boris his head. But I am never reckless, and as for being alone"—she managed to smile and sound reproving at the same time—"That would be most improper. Pierre, is never far away." She signalled to a groom waiting at a discreet distance. "You see how patiently he waits. So now, I must leave you. Papa will be expecting me at breakfast. Also"—a provocative note entered her voice—"I am persuaded that your wonderful hunter must be getting hard to hold, my lord."

"Rolled you up, horse, foot, and guns, Gideon," chuckled Ned.

Caroline Maitland swung her horse round. "*À bientot*, Ned. Do visit us soon in Grosvenor Square. You, too, my lord."

They watched her ride away. The sun, choosing that precise moment to breast the tree tops, bathed her elegant straight-backed figure in golden light and turned the ends of her hair to flame.

"What a girl!" Ned said.

For answer, the marquess let go his hold and the hunter went thundering down the tan. "If she were mine," his voice floated back, "I would long since have strangled her."

Sir Humphfrey Maitland looked up briefly from his newspaper as Caroline came into the sunny breakfast room, still wearing her riding habit. She tossed her hat onto a nearby chair, and ran her fingers through her already ruffled hair.

"Good morning, Pa." She kissed the top of his head as she passed, and sat down opposite him. "You don't mind me coming to table reeking of the stables, do you? I am simply ravenous after all that fresh air."

"Devil a bit, m'dear." Sir Humphfrey was a big man with a strongly boned face, a dominant nose, and a shock of pure white hair, and his eyes, as always, warmed at the sight of this daughter who was, in so many ways, like him, and was his pride and joy.

A waiting footman came unobtrusively with tea, and she helped herself to bread and butter.

"You seem to be in high good humour, Caro. Enjoy y'r ride, did you?"

"Very much, thank you."

"Splendid. I feared you might be missing Paris, being obliged to come away with so little warning. I daresay you had any number of agreeable entertainments planned—summer picnics in the Bois and the like . . ."

Her eyebrows quivered. "My dear Pa, if I am not used by now to being uprooted at a moment's notice, I never shall be."

Sir Humphfrey carved himself another thick slice of ham, observing that it was good to be home, if only to get a decent breakfast instead of all that fancy foreign pap. He reached for another of Cook's delicious hot muffins, and piled butter onto it.

"Y'r a good girl," he said. "Never known you to throw a tantrum. Don't know how I'd have managed without you these past few years . . ."

"Oh, what moonshine! You have an extremely efficient secretary who would be only too happy to remind you of your appointments and keep unwelcome callers at bay, and any one of your exquisite flirts could well play the hostess at your soirees."

Sir Humphfrey chuckled and brushed a small shower of crumbs from his immaculate white whiskers.

"True enough. But John Palmer don't have your subtle charm when it comes to turning away egregious bores. And as for my flirts, as you are pleased to call them"—his eyes twinkled—"They may look very fine, but there ain't a one can wheedle secrets out of intriguers, the way you can."

"What a shocking recommendation for a father to bestow upon his daughter! For shame, sirrah! Small wonder that I am two-and-twenty and still unwed, if that is how I appear to the world at large."

Sir Humphfrey chuckled and pushed away his plate. "Not to the world, Caro. Only to me. Can't say I look forward to the day when you will leave me, though it must come. Time you were married. You've had no shortage of offers, to be sure."

"But none that could tempt me, even for a moment," she said lightly.

"Not even the Comte de Brissard?"

Caroline considered the fiery, impetuous young nobleman who had pursued her single-mindedly from Paris to Brussels and back again, and still refused to give up hope. "Not even de Brissard, for all his vast fortune," she agreed; then adding cheerfully, "I fear I shall not be easily suited, so you may have to put up with me for a while longer."

"Well, I ain't complaining." Her father stood up.

"Now, I must be off. The Foreign Secretary is expecting me at ten o'clock."

"You'll never guess who I saw when I was out—Ned Sawyer. He was with a Lord Grenville. Do you know him?"

Something in his daughter's voice made Sir Humphfrey look at her more closely. She seemed absorbed in the contents of her teacup.

"The mad marquess's heir? Met him a couple of times at White's, not long before old George turned up his toes. He's a distant cousin. I knew his father slightly—a Captain Drayton. Met him at the Hamiltons when I was sent to Naples in the late seventies. Killed later at sea, I believe. The son's a trifle high in the instep, but agreeable enough, I thought. Bit of an unknown quantity. What did you make of him?"

Caroline shrugged, but there was suddenly rather more color in her cheeks. "He seemed to think altogether too much of himself for my liking. I remember Lady Jersey mentioning him the last time she was in Paris. He is become quite a figure in Society, it seems. She said they call him 'the Nonpareil.' "

Her father chuckled. "Don't let the manner fool you, my dear. Society may choose to lionize him, but if I'm not much mistaken, under that façade there's a very different man—and one I think I would not like to cross."

Within days, Caroline was besieged by callers, and the drawing room mantel was littered with calling cards and invitations.

"At this rate, I shall scarcely be at home for a single night," she exclaimed to Ned when he called.

"Which is exactly how you like it," he said, giving her a droll look as he disposed his slim figure in the most comfortable chair and stretched out his long legs. "Trust you to arrive just as the Season is in full cry. I hope you mean to give one of your own famous balls while you are here."

"The arrangements are already in hand for the middle of May. Pa is expecting to remain in London for at least three months, and always has so many people he must entertain."

The drawing-room door opened and Gort, who was rather more of a major domo than a butler, and went everywhere with them, announced, "Lady Sophie Winter," and stood aside as a petite vision in cerulean blue stepped past him, uttered a small unladylike shriek, and ran forward to embrace her dear friend. This she did on tiptoe, her golden ringlets brushing Caroline's cheek.

Caroline returned her embrace. "Sophie, how splendid! You must have read my mind. I had meant to call on you before now."

"Well, you wouldn't have found me home. We have been out of town, visiting Arthur's mama, and came back to find your name on everyone's lips!"

"Oh, surely not." Caroline smiled with genuine affection, knowing Sophie's strong tendency to exaggerate. "We've only been in London a few days."

"Some people only need a few hours," murmured Ned, who had risen.

"Quiet, wretched fellow," Caroline exhorted him. "I'm not sure—do you two . . . ?"

"Oh, yes. Ned was at school with my dearest Arthur, and by the greatest good fortune they met up again recently, and instantly renewed their friendship." Sophie beamed at them both. "Don't you think it an extraordinary coincidence, Caro? Almost as if it were meant! With you and I also growing up best of friends, we shall make the perfect foursome. What fun it will be—the best summer ever!"

Ned cocked an eyebrow at Caroline, who was

striving to retain her composure. Finally, they both dissolved into laughter.

Sophie perched on a little gilded rout chair, looking slightly aggrieved. "I don't know why you should find the idea so amusing. I think it's splendid."

"So it is. Quite splendid," Ned agreed. He resumed his seat, thinking that the two young ladies could hardly have been less alike.

Lady Sophie was indeed a lovely creature, with the face of an angel and eyes as vivid as the blue ruching beneath the brim of her most fetching bonnet. But even beauty such as Sophie's might be in danger of being thought a trifle insipid, were it not for the delightful cleft in her chin which denoted an occasional tendency to willfulness—a trait that Ned's friend, Mr. Arthur Winter, her indulgent husband of less than a twelvemonth, still found endearing.

There had never been the least danger of Caroline being thought insipid. From an early age, it had been apparent that she was destined to take after her father, in looks as well as temperament. And as the two girls grew, Sophie, who dearly loved her large happy-go-lucky friend, had been full of ideas for improving her appearance, especially the odd eyebrows and *the nose* which was already threatening to dominate her amiable but plain features. But Caroline had only laughed at these innocent deliberations.

"Dearest Sophie, people will simply have to take me as I am, nose and all. I shall never be a beauty, and I refuse to stoop and play the shrinking violet in an attempt to disguise the fact that I am already five feet seven inches in my stocking feet, and still growing."

From this resolve she refused to be shifted. In the years when Lady Sophie Andrews was having her come-out and being courted by a plethora of eligible suitors, Caroline was enjoying the wonderfully liberating experience of jaunting about the world with her father. And by the time Sophie had fallen in love with and married the rich Mr. Arthur Winter, Caroline was well on the way to acquiring a confidence beyond her years, and had become a popular figure in the social circles of many countries.

Sophie's mama, Lady Lanchester, had thought the whole idea decidedly odd; not at all a suitable kind of life for an impressionable young girl.

"I cannot imagine what Sir Humphfrey is thinking about, exposing the child to so many unhealthy foreign influences," she had said the first time he had taken Caroline to Paris. "Her poor mother would turn in her grave, if she did but know. One can only hope she is properly chaperoned. If that dab of a governess, Brinsdale, is her only companion, I fear the outcome."

"My dear," the earl had said dryly, "I think we may depend upon Humphfrey to do all that is proper. Caroline has always seemed to me a very outgoing child. I daresay she will enjoy the life enormously."

And she did. From time to time, she would sweep into town without warning—as now—each time grown more elegant, in clothes that bespoke Paris in every line. And the hawklike features and odd eyebrows that had made her such a plain child, now gave her a look of distinction that was envied by many a vapid beauty.

And during those brief visits home, Caroline had been brimming over with stories of Paris and Lisbon, Vienna and Brussels, to which Sophie had listened, wide-eyed. Caroline had actually been in Brussels at the time of the great battle of Waterloo. The mere thought of it had made Sophie shudder.

"I do hope that this time you mean to stay," she said.

"For a month or two, at least." Caroline smiled. "My dear, you are looking lovelier than ever. May I take it that married life agrees with you?"

"Oh, yes. It is the greatest fun. One has so much more freedom. I am very fond of Mama, but she was forever telling me what to do. Now, I may do as I please."

"Which largely consists of wrapping Arthur round your finger," murmured Ned.

"That's unfair." But Sophie dimpled. "Well, perhaps, just a little. He takes so much delight in pleasing me. Caro, Mama told me that Lady Jersey told *her* that you no longer had Miss Brinsdale with you, and that you have not replaced her. Is it true?"

"I am indebted to Lady Jersey and your mama for their interest." There was an almost imperceptible edge to Caroline's laugh. "Yes, it is true. There seemed little need to replace dear Brinny. I am no longer an ingenue, and there is always some lady of rank eager to find favor with Pa by including me in her party, should the occasion warrant it, and he is not free to escort me."

Sophie giggled. "I suppose I could now fulfill that role, if you were ever in need of someone."

"I suppose you could," said Caroline. "How droll. I shall remember, should I have need of you."

"Egad, I can't see Sophie chaperoning anyone. Much too flighty." Ned chuckled irreverently.

"Silence, impudent fellow." Sophie put up her chin. "I was thinking of Countess Lieven's soiree tomorrow. But I suppose your father will be attending that, Caro?"

"Yes, indeed. I have strict instructions from Madame de Lieven to make sure he does so . . ."

"Just you wait until Caro gives her own ball, Sophie. I tell you, it is an experience not to be missed." Ned chuckled. "Shall you invite Grenville, Caro? You made quite an impression on him."

"But hardly a favorable one, I think," she said. "I believe strangulation figured quite forcibly in his language at the time."

"Oh, do tell me!" begged Sophia, observing their laughter and hating to be left out. And when Ned had treated her to a graphic account, she cried, "Caroline! How could you tease Grenville so? I'm sure I wouldn't dare!"

"Oh, pooh. Ned exaggerates. And besides, he was being unbearably patronizing."

They were still laughing when several more callers arrived, and as the room began to fill up, the conversation became general. Sophie's Arthur came to collect her. He and Ned conversed for a few moments, and then the rather serious young man bore his wife away.

The following evening, a great number of carriages converged on the Russian Embassy, and by the time Caroline and her father arrived, Madame's reception rooms were already thronged with a dazzling crowd. Lord Grenville, having arrived but a moment earlier, was well placed to observe the affection with which Sir Humphfrey and his daughter were greeted by the vivacious little countess.

They made a handsome couple—Sir Humphfrey in a mulberry coat adorned with orders from several grateful governments, a brocade waistcoat and black knee breeches. And Caroline, a tall graceful figure at his side, in a simple high-waisted gown of straw-colored silk, its brief bodice encrusted with ecru lace studded with tiny gems. Her cropped hair, swirled casually *à la Brutus*, was threaded by a narrow filet of gold, also studded with tiny gems.

Sir Humphfrey bent to whisper something in the Countess's ear, and her eyes twinkled as she tapped him playfully with her fan.

"Your papa is a wicked man, Caro," she said severely. "Take him away and let him try his wiles on one who does not see through him as I do."

As they moved on, the marquess was directly in their path. He was standing a little apart, watching the gossiping throng with a coolly ironic eye, which moved inevitably to encompass Caroline and her father. Caroline returned his gaze with interest. She was not particularly drawn to saturnine men, but even she was forced to acknowledge that he was a handsome devil in his black swallowtail coat, his long legs looking even longer in the slim trousers that had long since been *de rigeur* on the Continent, but had only recently found favor in London. The severity of his dress was relieved by a silver brocade waistcoat, and a diamond pin nestled in the snowy-white perfection of his cravat.

All that and a fortune to boot! she thought. To mammas with daughters to bestow, he must appear as manna from heaven.

"Grenville, isn't it?" her father was saying jovially, thrusting out a hand. "We were talking about you only last week. Isn't that so, m'dear? I believe you and Caro ran into one another in the park."

The marquess bowed with scrupulous politeness to Caroline, a hint of sarcasm in his voice, as he replied, "An apt description, sir. It was, to quote Lord Wellington, the nearest-run thing you ever saw."

Sir Humphrey laughed. "Kicking up the dust, was she?"

"Nothing of the kind," Caroline retorted, her head thrown back. "You were never in the slightest danger, my lord."

It came as something of a shock to Gideon to realize that she was less than half a head shorter than he. He was accustomed to standing head and shoulders above most ladies of his acquaintance, and found her straight frank look somewhat unnerving. From the faint gleam in those jade eyes, he knew that Miss Caroline Maitland was reading his thoughts with disturbing accuracy.

"In fact," she continued blandly, "I would venture to suggest, my lord, that you might be in rather more danger here, with so many eager young misses among Madame de Lieven's guests."

The irony in her voice was unmistakable. Her father rumbled with mirth and said Caro had a point there. But before the marquess could reply, Sir Humphfrey was accosted by a gentleman in puce who bore him off on some urgent and confidential matter.

Left alone, there was a silence, which to him became irksome, though she continued to look serene. Good manners finally obliged him to say, "In your father's absence, pray allow me to escort you into the salon, Miss Maitland."

Her eyebrows quivered, the eyes danced. "You are very kind, my lord."

"You mistake," he said abruptly. "I am seldom kind."

"That's frank, at least," she said amiably. "Much better to be straightforward with the world. I do hate people who dissemble, don't you? And it means I can be equally frank. The fact is, I have long since grown used to being deserted by Pa on the flimsiest of pretexts, and am well able to fend for myself. So, you need not feel obliged to bear me company."

The marquess laughed unwillingly. "You are very like your father, I think."

"That, I cannot deny, my lord," she said equably. "I am told that my mama was the daintiest, prettiest creature you ever saw, and as a child I was used to think it a little perverse of the Almighty to fashion me in my father's likeness. But now I do not repine. I may not be a beauty, but at least I shall never be overlooked."

"True enough, ma'am, though I was referring to personality rather than physical likeness. Beauty, surely, is in the eye of the beholder?" In spite of the irony in his voice, the marquess, somewhat to his surprise, found himself thinking that she underrated her looks. There was a quality about her that was hard to define, a sense of *joie de vivre* that lit up her whole face—as now.

She was very conscious suddenly of his eyes assessing her. At their meeting in the park, she had thought them almost black, but now she saw they were a deep slate gray, thickly lashed. And they were presently regarding her in a way that brought an unaccustomed warmth to her cheeks.

"Now you have me at a stand, my lord," she said, with a light laugh, "for I am not at all sure whether that was cynicism, or something verging perilously close to a compliment."

"I was simply being frank, Miss Maitland," he said blandly, and without thought put a hand beneath her arm. She did not resist, and together they turned and began to walk towards Madame's main salon, unaware of the interest they were arousing until Grenville looked up and caught the adoring glance of Lady Pringle's very pretty daughter, whose come-out he had recently attended. The child blushed, bit her lip and smiled apprehensively, her ringlets all aquiver as she dipped him a curtsy.

"I cannot believe that you could ever have wished to change places with some shy simpering beauty like Amelia Pringle?" he said abruptly.

Caroline looked across the room, feeling for the

blushing girl. "Poor child! It must be very painful to be that young and unsure of oneself. I was never shy, that I recall. Pa had no time for missish quirks. And even in my salad days, I don't *think* I simpered."

"You are hardly an antidote, now, Miss Maitland."

Her eyes danced. "Why, thank you, sir. Now that I *shall* take as a compliment. In fact, I am beginning to feel quite in charity with you." But, for once it seemed, he would not be provoked. After a moment, she continued affably, "Do you have any family?"

For a moment his face wore that closed look again, and she thought he would not answer. But at last he said, "I have a sister. She is turned seventeen, and is presently living in the country with her mama and her governess."

"You make it sound a rather dull existence, my lord."

"Lucy has never thought it so," he said stiffly.

"I'm sorry. You are quite right. It was impertinent of me to pass an opinion. I daresay your sister has lots of friends, and is as merry as a grig. I suppose I was remembering myself at that age, and how eager for life I was. But then, my own situation was somewhat singular. By the time I was seventeen, I was traveling everywhere with Pa, and having the most splendid adventures. My friend's mother, Lady Lanchester, thinks me forward, and maybe I am, but I hope I am not insensitive."

"I did not infer that you were."

"No, of course not." But the moment of affability was clearly at an end, and it was with some relief that she heard her name called. "Ah, there is Sophie, the friend of whom I was speaking, and she has seen us. Do you know Lady Sophie Winter?"

"We are acquainted." His voice betrayed his

opinion of Sophie. "I know her brother rather better."

"Really? George or Peregrine?" Her mouth quirked irrepressibly. "But I hardly need to ask. Peregrine is a dear, but much too bookish."

"And you think that I am not?" he asked dryly.

"Oh, dear. Now, that *was* insensitive!"

"Also grossly inaccurate."

"How interesting," Caroline said, looking more closely at him—a look he returned sardonically.

"My dear!" Sophie whispered when the marquess, having exchanged the obligatory pleasantries, made his bow and left them. "Ned gave me to understand that you and Grenville were at daggers drawn! And here I find you locked in intimate conversation! I vow there wasn't a matchmaking mama in the room who wasn't wishing you back in Paris!"

"Oh, what nonsense, Sophie. How you exaggerate. I hardly know the man."

But Sophie was not the only one to comment. Caroline was teased constantly by her many friends, who were delighted to see her back in London, until she was obliged more than once, to bite back a sharp retort. Occasionally she would lift her eyes to scan the room, and more often than not it seemed, her gaze alighted on the marquess in the company of a dark, sophisticated beauty who was obviously more than a causal acquaintance.

So, Lady Verena was the kind of woman he favoured. Odd. She would not have thought it. The lady was a hardened flirt, according to Pa. Not that it was any of her business. Yet, as she made ready for bed that night, Grenville's face intruded more than once upon her innermost reflections, and she found herself thinking how very much more approachable he was when he smiled.

As April gave way to May, the days grew longer

and warmer, and with the Season in full swing, Caroline enjoyed it all prodigiously—the balls, the routs and the grand promenade each afternoon in Hyde Park, when she was often to be seen driving her phaeton and pair in procession with curricles and gigs and swaying landaulets. It was said that if you went often enough to Hyde Park at five o'clock in the afternoon, sooner or later you would meet everyone worth meeting. Certainly, on fine days, it seemed that the world and his wife were there, strolling across the wide sweeps of grass beneath the trees—the ladies in their fluttering muslins and silks of every hue, the gentlemen seeking out their latest amours, or doing the polite to eagle-eyed mamas in the hope of advancing their cause as prospective husbands for carefully guarded daughters. And there were dandies, peering amiably over their high starched collar points, and bowing to all as they teetered along on ridiculous heels, displaying their yellow pantaloons and tight-waisted coats.

On one such afternoon, Caroline had taken Ned up beside her. The park was busier than usual, and it seemed that every few yards there was a holdup as friends stopped to exchange greetings. She, herself, had been hailed more than once. Her horses were still quite fresh, but her handling of them drew an appreciative exclamation from Ned as she steered a path between a Stanhope gig and a rather cumbersome, open landau.

This maneuver successfully executed, she chanced to look across the grass, and was surprised to see Lord Grenville coming towards them, wearing a beautifully cut morning coat of Bath superfine and pale gray inexpressibles, and clinging to his arm was an exquisite young creature. They seemed to be lost in animated conversation.

"I thought Lord Grenville eschewed very young ladies," she remarked.

"Most emphatically." Ned followed her glance. "'Now that is interesting. I had no notion he was thinking of bringing young Lucy out this year."

"So that is his sister?"

"Half-sister, actually. Taking little thing," Ned conceded. "Not short of spirit. Her Italian blood, I daresay."

"Really. Her mother is Italian?"

"Neapolitan, to be strictly accurate. Gideon's own mother died when he was barely out of short coats. Father was an naval man, which meant that Gideon passed most of his preschool days with only a tutor for company. I believe Captain Drayton met Estella whilst staying with Sir William and Lady Hamilton in Naples, and was instantly enslaved. Estella was some kind of handmaiden to the Queen of Naples, and when the Court fled from Bonaparte in ninety-eight, he whirled her into marriage." Ned grinned. "What is it they say? 'Marry in haste, repent at leisure.' I gather she led him a merry dance. But once the child was on the way, he brought her back to England, and thereafter she was obliged to live closeted in the country, where she soon lost all her fire. The captain was later killed at Trafalgar. Since then she has grown fat and indolent."

"How sad."

"Gideon was away at school by then, of course, but I suspect he had a rather lonely time of it when he went home."

Caroline was fascinated by this insight into Lord Grenville's family background. That probably accounted for much of his reserve, which would be a natural outcome of such a background.

"He's devoted to Lucy, mind. Guards her close. Godmother or some such left her a considerable sum when she reaches her majority."

"If word of that gets about, his lordship could have his work cut out, fending off fortune hunters."

"Not Gideon. I'd back him to see any unwelcome suitor off."

As they drew closer to the marquess and his sister, Caroline reined in, and there was ample time to observe them as she waited for them to draw level.

They made a handsome pair—Lucy, her face uplifted, chattering away animatedly and he listening with a half-smile on his face that showed his pride in her. In her simple dress of sprigged muslin, Lucy was quite the loveliest, most unspoiled creature she had seen in many a long day. Rich dark brown curls tumbled beneath a chip-straw bonnet, nestling against skin as clear and translucent as magnolia petals.

Ned, too, was watching them. "Now I come to think of it, Gideon did speak a while ago of some trouble over a young man—a local sprig. Seems her mama allows the lad to come calling whenever he pleases, and Gideon don't approve. Maybe that's what finally decided him. Reckons Lucy will be safer under his eye. Takes his role of guardian very seriously."

"I do see why he wishes to guard the child. She is very beautiful," Caroline murmured. As they drew level, she leaned forward. "Good afternoon, my lord."

"Miss Maitland." He touched his hat and bowed. "May I present my sister, Lucia?"

"Miss Maitland." The young girl made a demure curtsy, gazing up in undisguised admiration of Caroline, whose gown was of a particularly vibrant shade of pink which ought to have clashed dreadfully with her hair but did not. It was edged at the neck with ruffles of creamy lace, and she wore a cream straw hat with a sweeping brim adorned with a long curling feather, dyed to match exactly the color of her dress. "I am very pleased to meet you."

Lucy had the darkest, most lustrous eyes Caroline had seen outside of Lisbon and, for a tiny moment, envy stabbed her soul. Then she was smiling down at the young girl. "And I, you," she said. "I wonder, would your brother permit me to tool you round the park?" Her eyes lifted to quiz Grenville. "I would take the greatest care of your sister, my lord."

His expression was sardonic. "I'm sure I need have no qualms, having watched your skillful exhibition of driving this afternoon. Your prowess on horseback is more than equalled, it seems, by your handling of the ribbons."

She laughed. "Oh, it is Pa who must take credit for that. He was quite ruthless with me, you know, and made me practice until I could drive through the narrowest gateway without scraping the paint, before he would permit me to set up my own stable."

"Indeed?" The marquess turned to his sister, who was gazing in wide-eyed awe at the perilously high vehicle. "Would you like to take a turn with Miss Maitland, Lucy?"

"Oh, Gideon! May I?"

Ned had already leapt down, and for answer, Lord Grenville lifted his sister up into the swaying seat, watched by a gathering of interested spectators. Lucy gave a squeak of pretended terror, and then gazed around her in wonder.

"It's like being on top of the world!" she exclaimed breathlessly, and laughed with unfeigned joy.

"We will meet you back here in about fifteen minutes, my lord," Caroline said, and gave a sign to her groom standing at the horses' heads to let them go.

"Is this really your very own carriage, Miss Maitland?" Lucy asked, much impressed, as they moved forward and once more joined the stream of carriages. A delicate flush ran up under her skin. "Oh, not that I disbelieve you, of course, but it just seems so incredible. It is not at all the kind of carriage I would expect a lady to drive." She bit her lip. "Oh, dear, that does not sound quite right, either!"

Caroline chuckled. "My dear Lucy—you do not mind if I call you Lucy?"

"Not in the least!"

"Thank you. And if we are to be friends, as I'm sure we *are* going to be, you must call me Caroline—"

"Oh, I could not do that!"

The shock in her voice drew a wry grimace from Caroline, though she bore up nobly as she insisted, "Then I shall be very much offended, for to be called Miss Maitland by such a pretty young thing as you are, makes me feel dreadfully old-maidish."

"Oh, but you are not in the least . . . that is, I would not offend you for the world!"

"Well then, that's settled." Caroline was silent a moment whilst she negotiated her way past a dawdling landaulet, and set the horses to trot on, which caused Lucy to grip the side of the carriage. A gentleman smiled and bowed, and Caroline smiled back. "I'm sure I should know who he is, but I cannot for the life of me . . . however, that is neither here nor there. Now, tell me, would I be right in thinking that you are to make your come-out?"

Lucy uttered a little gasp. "Yes, indeed, but do you mind if we don't talk about it? The mere thought makes me feel quite sick."

"Oh, dear!" Caroline laughed, but kindly. "Then, tell me instead if you are liking London, Lucy."

"Oh, yes! Prodigiously! It is only two days since Gideon brought me, of course, and I have not been about much, yet. But everything seems so grand, the place so full of bustle and noise and color, with all the fashionable ladies and gentlemen, and the carriages . . . and the shouts of the street vendors. It could not be less like Melthorpe Magna."

"That is where you live?"

"Yes. With Mama and my dear Miss Finch, who is my governess. She has come to London with me, of course, but Mama," she explained with surprising cheerfulness, "suffers a great deal from the megrims."

"I see. That must make life a little difficult for you."

"Not really. When I am not at my studies, I have been used to going riding a great deal with Jack."

They were now within sight of the place where Lord Grenville awaited them, but Caroline, wishing to know more, slowed the horses almost to a standstill on the pretext of admiring a small group of children playing near the Serpentine.

"Is Jack your groom?" she asked casually.

Lucy laughed. "No, indeed. He is my dear friend, Jack Smedley." A small crease appeared in her unblemished brow. "In fact, it is my one sadness, that I was not able to tell him I was coming to London. Everything happened so suddenly whilst he was away on some business for his father. I did leave a letter with his mama, to be delivered to him when he should return, but I have had no word."

Caroline sensed Grenville's hand in this. A quiet word with the lad's father, perhaps, pointing out Lucy's youth and inexperience, the need for her to be given time to gain some experience of the world, before forming any strong attachment. Caroline acknowledged a grudging admiration for his lordship's nobility of motive, but wondered if it was entirely wise. These well-intentioned contrivances so often had a way of kicking back at one. But it was not her place to interfere.

"It is a way young gentlemen have," she said lightly, setting the phaeton in motion again. "Set some new prospect before them, and they forget all else."

"Perhaps," Lucy said slowly. "But it isn't like Jack to do such a thing."

In an attempt to divert her thoughts, Caroline exclaimed, "Oh, my dear Lucy, only tell me what you think of that extraordinary creature. If yellow pantaloons and bright green coat were not enough, he must needs compound his felony with that hideous waistcoat and spotted cravat, and the highest shirt points I ever saw!"

"And, oh, his hat!" Lucy went off into a peal of laughter, which Caroline joined.

The awkward moment was over, and they were both in high good humor as they arrived back at the place where the marquess awaited them.

"No need to ask if you have enjoyed yourself," he said, as he lifted Lucy down and bade her thank Miss Maitland for her kindness.

"It has been the most wonderful treat ever!" Lucy enthused. "And I cannot thank you enough, Caroline." She saw her brother's eyebrows lift, and said quickly, "It is quite all right, Gideon. She has said that I may call her by her first name. Is that not so, Caroline?"

"Indeed, it is." Caroline smiled. "We are resolved to be best of friends."

From the rather piercing look he treated her to, she gathered that his lordship wasn't altogether enamored of the idea, but could hardly say so without giving offense.

Soon, Lucy was a regular visitor in Grosvenor Square, often accompanied by Miss Finch. Although, occasionally, Caroline would call at Lord Grenville's house in Portland Place, and take her back to tea. On one such occasion, Lucy was pale with nervous excitement.

"Caroline, it is decided! Lady Verena is presenting her young cousin at one of the Royal Drawing Rooms less than two weeks from now, and it is arranged that she will present me at the same time. And Gideon is to play his part by giving a Presentation Ball for the two of us at Portland Square."

"That is splendid. I could not be more pleased! You will be the belle of the Season."

A footman came in, bearing a large tray which he set down on a nearby table, and in his wake came a pert young maid with a selection of delicious cakes. Caroline dismissed them with a smile, saying that she would manage for herself.

"If only it wasn't Lady Verena. She always makes me feel as if I had a smudge on the end of my nose. Do you think it is being the daughter of a Duke that makes her look so haughty?"

"Perhaps," said Caroline.

"I wish it could be you instead," Lucy said impulsively. "I wouldn't be half so nervous."

Caroline laughed. "Thank you, my dear. But I am quite ineligible, you know. For one thing, I am not a married lady."

"Oh, I see. It's sometimes hard to remember that Lady Verena is married, for I have never seen her with her husband. She seems to prefer being with Gideon."

Caroline almost choked. As it was, she spilled tea in the saucer. Out of the mouths of babes, she thought, as amid much hilarity, they mopped up and rang for another cup. She managed to murmur something about believing that Sir Marcus eschewed the social scene, preferring his club, by which time the footman arrived and she was able to change the subject.

Lucy suddenly found her time much more taken

up with dressmakers and dancing lessons, and all kinds of tiresome chores. But she still managed to visit and was in her element, helping Caroline to sort out the invitations to her ball—"Are you really expecting four hundred people?"

"Well, they may not all come, of course. But Pa knows so many people, and it wouldn't do to slight anyone."

Lucy blushed with pleasure when her opinion was solicited as to how best the ballroom might be decorated for the great event.

"It is a beautiful room," Lucy sighed, her dark eyes wide in admiration of the full-length mirrors along one side, which trapped the sunlight pouring in through the long handsome windows opposite. The chandeliers had been taken down and carefully washed and polished, and these, too, sparkled in the sunlight.

"It will look even better by night," Caroline said. "I thought I might have lots of greenery banked at the far end, near the orchestra . . ."

"And lots of May blossom and roses for the perfume—and, perhaps, lilies?"

"Lovely."

"I cannot wait to see it!"

"The time will soon pass. You will be out by then, and will no doubt be much in demand, but although I say it myself, it will give you a great deal of address to be seen at my ball."

Lucy giggled. "Yes, but Gideon may not wish it."

"Of course he will. In fact, he has already accepted."

It was unusual for Sophie to arrive in Grosvenor Square much before noon, but it was only a little after eleven when Gort announced her on the following morning. Caroline was standing by the window when she was shown in, and turned at once to greet her.

"I hope I am not too early, Caro, but I simply had to come, as time is of the essence."

"Of course you aren't early. You know I am always up by eight at the latest."

Sophie shuddered. "I'm sure I don't know how you find so much energy." And then the news which she was so eager to impart overcame all other considerations. "Caro, do listen, for I have the most diverting idea to put to you."

Caroline was well used to Sophie's diverting ideas, and as her friend's voice ran on, she was drawn back to the window. Farther along Grosvenor Square, three carriages groaned under the weight of an enormous amount of luggage, and a stout gentleman was hopping about, supervising the disposal of the few remaining items still littering the pavement.

The sight brought on a gurgle of laughter, and as Sophie paused for breath, Caroline said, "Oh, my dear, do, pray, come and see the spectacle. Sir Jasper and Lady Tunbridge are setting out to visit their daughter. From the amount of baggage, one would suppose she lived in darkest Africa instead of Cheltenham."

Sophie came reluctantly. "I saw them as I came in. Sir Jasper is forever making a cake of himself. Caro, did you hear what I said just now?"

"Yes, of course I heard. Your grandmama wishes to stage a performance of Shakespeare's *Midsummer Night's Dream* in her garden on Midsummer Eve, to entertain her cronies. I must confess it sounds a deadly dull way to pass an evening, but I daresay they will enjoy it. Though why she should expect you to arrange it, when she must have any number of minions to do her bidding, is beyond me. Ah, they are off at last."

Below, the postillions signalled their readiness. Sir Jasper clambered aboard and the carriages lurched into motion.

"I knew you weren't listening!" Sophie almost stamped her foot, and the willful little chin quivered. "Grandmama's idea was that I should gather some of my friends together in order to perform the play. And I said I would."

She now had her friend's full attention. Caroline turned, her wickedly slanting eyebrows lifted in amused disbelief. "My dear Sophie, whatever prompted you to contemplate such a harebrained scheme?"

"It is not harebrained," Sophie declared, though already she was beginning to sound less certain. "And it isn't just for a few of Grandmama's cronies. She is to hold a full-scale Midsummer masquerade with masks and everything, and I don't know how many people invited! You must remember Grandmama's lovely house at Chiswich. It has lawns stretching down to the river, and will make a perfect setting for the play."

"I grant you the setting could not be bettered, my dear Sophie. But as for the rest . . ."

"Oh, Caro, how can you be so poor spirited? Only think how often we used to play charades on winter evenings—we still do so occasionally at Christmas tide. *That* is always the greatest fun and I cannot see that a play is so very different. Peregrine is to condense it for us. He is very good at that sort of thing. And"—here she paused—"and I thought at once of you, for you would make the most wonderful Titania."

"Me? As Queen of the Fairies?" Caroline's laugh pealed out. "My dear Sophie, now I know you are quizzing me! And who do you envisage as Oberon? He will need to be all of six feet tall if I am not to dwarf him."

"I—we thought of asking Lord Grenville," Sophie said defiantly.

"Oh, really! Now I know you are funning."

"Peregrine says Grenville used to do quite a lot of acting when they were at Oxford together. I'm sure he would be able to talk him into it. And if the two of you agree, we should have no trouble finding others to join us." Sophie sensed that her friend was wavering. "Oh, Caro! Do say you will do it!"

The prospect of the marquess so far forgetting himself as to play the King of the Fairies intrigued Caroline, and although she had no real expectation of his agreeing, the imp of mischief was in her eyes as she said, "Very well. If you are able to persuade his lordship, I will do my part."

She met Grenville two days later at Lady Sefton's musical soiree. It was an informal occasion, and Lucy was with him. She was looking a trifle pale, but very lovely in a simple gown of silver gauze over white satin. Caroline put the pallor down to nerves, for her presentation was only a few days away. She resolved to set her at ease.

"Gideon has been so generous, you wouldn't believe," Lucy confessed with unusual reticence when she complimented the young girl on her appearance. "He said I must throw away all my home-made dresses, and now I have—oh, ever so many new ones, and a pelisse, and a new riding habit, and two new bonnets—and all from the most elegant dressmaker you ever saw! I should have been in a terrible quake if Gideon had not been there with Lady Verena to help me decide."

The man was full of surprises, Caroline thought, much diverted by this new aspect of his lordship as an authority on ladies' apparel. But, Lucy's pleasure in her new clothes seemed less spontaneous than might have been expected, and again there was that underlying tension in her manner. Caroline drew her aside a little.

"My dear, is anything wrong?" she asked, low-voiced.

"Oh, no! That is, yes, there is, but it is nothing I can talk about just now"—she broke off abruptly, her eyes widening as they looked beyond Caroline's shoulder.

"Ah, here you are, Lucy," Lord Grenville said smoothly. "Miss Maitland." He bowed, his eyes unhurriedly assessing her stylish gown of palest green crepe which echoed her eyes. "The music room is filling up, so we had better take our seats. Will you sit with us, Miss Maitland?"

"Thank you," she said, "but I believe Lady Sophie is expecting me to join her."

"Of course." He paused, a faint, almost malicious gleam in his eyes. "You will have much to discuss, I daresay." And as she lifted an enquiring eyebrow, "The play, ma'am. I believe I am to have the pleasure of playing Oberon to your Titania. I look forward to it."

"You do?" He had almost succeeded in discomposing her. But years of experience in diplomatic circles came to her aid, enabling her to look and sound mildly amused, though she suspected that he had seen beyond her blandness. Even so, it was with profound relief that she heard from the music room the sounds of the small chamber group tuning their instruments.

"Hopefully, it will be, in Sophie's words, the greatest fun," she agreed, and smiled encouragingly at Lucy. "But, pray, don't let me detain you."

Caroline made no further attempt that evening to find out what troubled Lucy, but was not surprised to find her on the doorstep well before noon on the following day. Miss Finch, looking a trifle embarrassed, accompanied her. She was a pleasant woman, slight of build, and unremarkable in looks but, Caroline judged, with a great deal of common sense.

"I hope we are not inconveniencing you, Miss Maitland. I did tell Lucy she ought not to be troubling you with her problems."

Caroline smiled to set her at ease. "It is no trouble, Miss Finch. Truth to tell, I had half-expected this visit."

"Then you know . . . I do hold myself to be very much at fault. If I had been more resolute, but it was not easy with Lucy's mama positively encouraging the—"

"Well, I don't see why she should have done otherwise," Lucy cried in throbbing tones. "Or why Gideon is being so absolutely horrid!"

"Forgive me," Caroline interjected, "but I am quite at sea. When I said I expected a visit, it was because I thought you were looking rather down in the suds last evening, Lucy."

"It is Jack," she announced, her lovely mouth trembling with the force of her indignation. "He has come to London especially to see me, and Gideon has shown him the door without even allowing us to meet."

"Oh, dear."

Caroline's mind was working furiously. She knew exactly what must have happened. Grenville, in his determination to protect Lucy from her importunate suitor, had behaved heavy-handedly. How like a man, she thought. But it would not do to feed Lucy's sense of grievance, or show the marquess in a bad light.

"I daresay, you know, that your brother was taken by surprise, and may have received quite the wrong impression concerning Jack's visit," she said with a sympathetic smile.

"Miss Maitland has a point, my love," said Miss

Finch, throwing a grateful glance at Caroline. "After all, his lordship has never met Mr. Smedley, and to have a complete stranger calling upon you without warning, perhaps even speaking about you to his lordship with a degree of familiarity . . ."

"Jack is *not* a complete stranger. He is my very dear friend!" The indignation was still there, but already a little of the fire had gone out of Lucy's voice.

Caroline exchanged a glance with Miss Finch. "Yes, well, if he is a true friend, Mr. Smedley will see for himself that he was perhaps a little precipitate," she said in bracing tones. "Country ways are apt to be much more casual, you know. Perhaps he is not aware that, in London, there are formalities to be observed. Still, if you can practice patience, I'm sure matters will sort themselves out."

"Well . . ."

"Good. That is settled. Now, how would you like to come driving with me this afternoon? I will call for you about four o'clock."

Lord Grenville was not at home when Caroline arrived in Portland Place, but Lucy was waiting for her, looking charming and much more cheerful in lavender muslin beneath a pretty fringed shawl, and with a matching bonnet framing her face.

The park was already busy, the afternoon warm and fragrant with the scent of new-cut grass carried on a breeze that set the young leaves rustling, and tugged at many a skirt as it threatened to turn parasols inside out amid squeals of laughter.

They were on their second turn of the park when Lucy suddenly cried, "Caroline! Oh, please, may we stop for a moment?"

Caroline obligingly reined in the horses, to find a young man hurrying across the grass towards them. She realized at once who he must be, and used the time it took him to reach them to study the young Lothario. Except that there was nothing in the least romantic about Jack Smedley. He was a little older than she had expected, perhaps in his early twenties, and was rather stockily built. His clothes were neat and of good quality, with none of the odd quirks of fashion that beset so many young men.

"Lucy! I had not expected to come upon you so soon." He doffed his hat to them both, and reached up to take the hands she extended to him.

"Jack! Oh, Jack, I am so happy to see you! And looking so very smart!" Lucy turned excitedly. "You must let me introduce my new friend, Miss Caroline Maitland. Caroline, this is Jack Smedley."

"I rather thought that it might be. I am very pleased to meet you, Mr. Smedley," she said, smiling at him and reaching down a hand. His clasp was firm, and he had a pleasant open face, which betrayed rather more of his feelings than he was aware of as his eyes had rested on Lucy. But this was no fortune hunter, and she was certain from her observation of the two of them together, that he had not revealed the extent of his feelings to Lucy.

"Jack, I am so sorry about what happened yesterday! Gideon had no right to treat you so shabbily."

"Well, on reflection I can see he had good reason." Jack grinned wryly. "After all, we had never met, and I might have been anybody. If I had been less nervous, I would have asked to see him rather than you in the first place so that I could introduce myself properly."

Caroline began to wonder whether he was aware of Lord Grenville's reasons for removing Lucy from Melthorpe Magna. There was nothing in his manner to suggest that he might be laboring under a cloud of injustice.

"But you did get the letter I left for you, telling you where I had gone?"

Jack frowned. "No. It was your mama who gave me your direction," he said. "My own parents were very much against my coming to London. They inferred that I should be intruding, but your mama assured me that I would be made welcome."

"And so you are, most heartily, by me," Lucy exclaimed.

Oh, mischievous woman, thought Caroline. What a coil! Aloud she said, "Nevertheless, I believe that in view of what has happened, a little discretion must be observed if Lord Grenville is to be won over."

"I am sure you are right, ma'am."

"Oh, but . . ." Lucy's lip quivered.

"Patience, child," Caroline scolded her, but with a smile. "I imagine you have somewhere to stay, Mr. Smedley."

"Yes, indeed. I have a friend in Mount Street—Jeremy Saville. We were at school together."

"Lady Saville's son. Excellent. I will be in touch very soon."

He touched his hat, and as they drove away, Lucy turned her head several times to watch him before relapsing into a silence pregnant with reproach. Between this and a care for her horses, Caroline was too preoccupied to notice the elegant woman standing close by, who had been watching the whole incident with keen interest.

The first meeting of the players-to-be had been arranged for the following morning at Sophie's house in Curzon Street. Sophie, as she had predicted, had found no difficulty recruiting support for the venture among the young ladies, who, like Sophie, all vowed it would be "the greatest fun." The gentlemen had proved rather more reluctant, but once it was known that "the Nonpareil" was to grace the production, they had come forward—if not eagerly, at least determined not to be found less willing than their idol.

By the time Caroline arrived, Sophie's drawing room echoed to the sound of everyone talking at once as discussion raged as to what each should wear. Arthur was hovering, endeavoring to play the host, and looking as though he had landed by mistake in Bedlam.

"If I were you," Caroline whispered to him, "I should escape and take refuge in White's at the very first opportunity."

Sophie espied her from the other side of the room, and came hurrying forward. "Oh, good," she said, sounding harrassed and looking not a little relieved to see her. "Now, we are only wanting Lord Grenville and we shall be complete. Peregrine assures me he *will* come. Arthur, perhaps if you were to collect all the gentlemen together . . ."

As if to quell her unspoken fear, the door opened to admit his lordship. He stood in the doorway, raising his quizzing glass to survey the chaotic scene. "I must be out of my mind," he drawled.

"If you say so, Gideon," Ned answered with a grin, "who are we to argue."

"Good God, have they roped you in, too? They must be desperate."

"No fear. You won't catch me treading the boards. I'm just a general factotum, don't y'know, gulled by Sophie into fetching and carrying, helping with scene changes and the like."

The marquess raised a quizzical eyebrow. Then, as his glance lighted on Caroline, his expression changed. He answered her pleasant "good morning, my lord," with a curt bow and turned away quite deliberately to speak to Peregrine.

Heigh ho, she thought. What bee has he got

buzzing round in his head now? But this was hardly the time to confront him. Peregrine was waiting to give out the parts he had labored so lovingly to produce, his thin ascetic face alight with the student's fervor for his subject.

"I have managed to condense the play into five main scenes, with several short linking passages," he explained earnestly when some semblance of silence had been achieved, "thus cutting it by about an hour, without, I hope, in any way losing the spirit of the text."

Caroline noted with some amusement that several pairs of eyes were already glazing over. But fortunately, Sophie also had little interest in the finer points of construction.

"Perry, dear, do get on, or we shall never be ready for Midsummer's night," she exclaimed. "The twenty-fourth of June is exactly a month away, which gives us little enough time to rehearse."

"Which is precisely why I have tried to ensure that no part is too long or difficult to learn," he said patiently. "Perhaps you would be so kind as to hand them round, Sophie."

Sophie was immediately surrounded by a sea of eager hands, and there was much laughter as extracts from the Pyramus and Thisbe scene were read aloud.

"Caroline, you won't object to playing the dual role of Titania and Hippolyta?" Perry asked diffidently. "Gideon has already agreed to do the same with Oberon and Theseus. It doesn't involve a great deal of extra learning; they are in fact widely regarded as two sides of the same coin."

"If that is how they are regarded, it would be churlish of me to force you to split them," she said, straight-faced.

He gave her one of his rare smiles and immediately looked years younger. "Teaching my granny to suck eggs, am I?"

"Oh, I'm sure you would never be guilty of anything so pompous," she said affectionately. Sophie's elder brother had always been a favorite with her. George was very much the man about town, but Peregrine had a shy gentle charm that was most endearing. "I don't envy you, having to direct this unruly crowd. I only hope you may not live to regret it."

But he only laughed and said that this was nothing to the mayhem of college productions.

In the event, little was achieved on that first morning beyond establishing who would do what, by which time all of Caroline's worst forebodings seemed likely to be confirmed. But Perry chided her for her pessimism and vowed he had every hope of bringing off a creditable performance. And in all the noise and bustle, no one seemed to notice that she and Grenville had not exchanged one word other than those demanded by the play.

The day being fine and warm, Caroline had chosen to walk to Curzon Street. And now, having made her general farewells, she made her way through to the small parlor to summon her maid, Ellen, who was waiting there with several other servants.

"Caroline!" Sophie caught up with her near the front door. "Arthur tells me you walked here. You must be exhausted after all that excitement—I know I am. Do at least let Arthur drive you home."

Caroline laughed. "My dear, I am not so poor-spirited that I cannot survive a little excitement without flagging. Besides, I enjoy walking."

"A laudable admission, Miss Maitland," Lord Grenville's cool tones interjected. He had come, soft footed, across the hall to stand at Sophie's shoulder. "But, nevertheless, you will permit me to drive you home."

The offer was delivered as a command, and as such, immediately put Caroline's back up. "Thank you," she said stiffly, "but . . ."

"Oh, that would be splendid," Sophie exclaimed.

Vexed almost as much by Sophie's coyness, as by the marquess's manner, Caroline reiterated, "You are very kind, sir, but I wouldn't dream of putting you to the trouble."

"It is no trouble, ma'am. My groom is already bringing my curricle round. And we do have things to discuss, do we not?"

"Do we, my lord?" Of all things, Caroline disliked being addressed as *ma'am*, but by now, irritation was vying with curiosity, and curiosity won. "Oh, as you will," she said, a trifle ungraciously, and bade Ellen make her own way home.

And then, the curricle was at the door, and in spite of her annoyance, Caroline could not but admire its fine sporting lines, the black paintwork as smooth as glass, and the huge wheels picked out in yellow. His excellent matched pair was harnessed in tandem, and as she stepped lightly up to settle herself into the soft leather upholstery, she longed to have her hands on the reins.

Grenville told his groom to await his return, then sprang up beside her, with a lightness unusual in so big a man, picked up the reins, and called, "Let em go, Dan." The high-couraged horses sprang forward, and it took every ounce of his skill with the ribbons to maintain control. Caroline watched him critically, but could find no fault with his lordship's handling of so fresh a pair.

The traffic was fairly light down Curzon Street, but to Caroline's surprise, he made for the bustle of Piccadilly instead of Grosvenor Square. Wild notions of being kidnapped rose momentarily in her

mind, to be dismissed as nonsense. A momen
later, they were entering Green Park, and she ex
claimed, "What is the meaning of this, my lord'
You said you would drive me home."

"And so I will, Miss Maitland. But what I have
to say to you, cannot properly be said in the noise
and distraction of town traffic."

Having delivered himself of this ambiguous state
ment, he seemed in no particular hurry to begin
and Caroline vowed she would not give him the
satisfaction of knowing how angry she was.

In a quiet corner of the park he finally brough
the horses to a standstill and faced her. "Now
madam, perhaps you will have the goodness to tel
me what you mean by meddling in my affairs?"

Shock held her silent for a moment. Then a very
real sense of outrage welled up in her, though she
spoke calmly. "You will have to be more explicit
my lord, for I fear you have quite lost me."

"Then I will be even plainer, ma'am." His voice
was clipped. "I refer to your duplicity in respect
of certain matters concerning my sister—matters o
which you can hardly plead ignorance, since she
seems to have made you her chief confidante."

"Lucy has confided in me, yes. But I still don't
see . . ."

"Oh, come, Miss Maitland, let us not mince
words. You were seen yesterday in Hyde Park with
Lucy, conversing with a young man to whom I had
shown the door not three days since."

Whoever had seen them must have wished to
make mischief, and Caroline could only think of
one such person. Lady Verena had certainly been
in the park yesterday, holding court with a number
of her admirers. She could well have witnessed the
meeting.

"If you mean Mr. Smedley, yes, we did come
upon him in Hyde Park. Though, who could have

considered the meeting to be of sufficient interest
as to come talebearing to you, I'm sure I cannot
think." She saw him frown slightly. But although
he looked at her with narrowed eyes, he made no
comment.

"A very agreeable young man, I thought," she
went on. "And only fancy, by the most extraordinary coincidence, I had mentioned his name to my
father over dinner shortly after Lucy had first spoken about him, and it transpires that Pa knew Mr.
Smedley senior years ago—had excellent covers, he
said. He used to shoot over them often as a young
man . . ."

"A coincidence, indeed." His drawl almost
amounted to a sneer.

She lifted her shoulders in an elegant little shrug
which sent her fine gauze stole slipping from her
shoulders. She gathered it up unhurriedly. "So, you
see, in the circumstances, it would have been ill-
mannered to do other than stop, quite apart from
the fact that Lucy would have been upset to no
purpose. And that, you could not possibly wish for,
with her Presentation next week."

His face immediately set like granite. "We will
leave that aside, if you please. The fact remains,
you took the course you did, knowing it would
incur my disapproval."

"Which, if I may say so, is ill-founded and abys-
mally shortsighted," she countered swiftly.

"Thank you. When I want your opinion, I will
ask for it."

"That is the remark of a blinkered man."

Caroline heard him draw in a sharp breath, and
knew she had gone too far. "Careful, my lord," she
exclaimed with spontaneous concern, as his fingers
tightened on the reins, causing the horses to job at
their bits. He spent some moments bringing them

under control, which did little to improve hi
temper.

"Enough, Miss Maitland. You may be arrogan
enough to consider yourself an authority on every
thing from the handling of horses to the judging o
character, but don't think you can ride roughshoc
over me. I happen to be Lucy's guardian, and yo
will kindly allow me to know what is best for her
instead of working to undermine my authority."

"That is unjust, my lord!" she declared hotly. "I
have gone out of my way to persuade Lucy tha
you have her interests at heart, but that doesn'
mean that I have to agree with you. I can perfectly
understand how Lucy feels. Mr. Smedley is a pleasant, unpretentious young man of good family, whc
has, until you decreed otherwise, been a gooc
friend to . . ."

"And would like to be more," he counterec
swiftly. "Can you deny that?"

"Perhaps not," she conceded, taking a deep
breath, for anger would not serve Lucy's cause.
"But, having seen them together, I can say withou
hesitation that she is not aware of his feelings
towards her. That must surely be to his credit," she
said persuasively.

He gave her a long, slightly cynical look, but the
full force of his anger seemed to be spent.

"And what is to happen when Lucy is out? They
are bound to meet, you know, for he is staying with
the Savilles, and it will look so odd if you refuse to
meet him." Remembering his own childhood, she
added daringly, "I wonder, sir, have you ever considered what a lonely life your sister must have led,
but for Jack's friendship, with only her mama and
Miss Finch for company?" She saw his lips tighten
at her familiar use of the young man's name, but
still he did not speak. "One might even say that

ou owe him a debt of gratitude that she has not grown up shy and awkward," she concluded boldly.

But this was pushing the case too far.

"You plead Mr. Smedley's cause well, Miss Maitland, but my opinion has not altered one iota."

"Then I hope you will not have cause to rue it," he said quietly. "Lucy has a naturally affectionate disposition. But she has spirit, too. Already, thanks to your heavy-handed behavior, all her protective instincts have been aroused. Should you succeed in driving Mr. Smedley away, one of two things might happen—either she will attempt to go with him, or if, as I suspect, he will not let her, she could do something very silly—maybe even fall into far worse company." She saw that this had made him think, and concluded quietly, "So, for all that you dislike me so, I must tell you that I mean to continue as Lucy's friend. She may yet have need of one."

"I have never said that I dislike you."

Caroline stared, for once almost robbed of speech. 'But . . ."

"I frequently find you infuriating, opinionated and much too coming, but that has little to do with iking." He gathered up the ribbons, throwing her a last look that held a glint of self-derisive humor. 'And, God knows why, but in spite of everything, I find myself trusting your word."

Between the imminence of her own ball, the excitement of Lucy's presentation, and the gathering pace of rehearsals for the play, Caroline had little time to reflect on Grenville's extraordinary outburst. When they met to rehearse, there was no indication of any change in his opinion of her; if anything, the conflict between Titania and Oberon over possession of her little page seemed to take on an extra dimension, and there were several com-

ments about how well she and Grenville were por
traying their parts.

But Caroline did find time to send a note to Jacl
Smedley, asking him to call at his earliest conve
nience, if possible quite early in the morning, afte
her father had left the house, so that they coul
talk undisturbed, but before meddlesome person
with prying eyes were abroad.

He came promptly, and in talking to him, he
earlier judgment was confirmed.

"Am I right in thinking that you are in love witl
Lucy?" she asked without preamble, having sat hin
down in the drawing room with a cup of strong
coffee, whilst she prowled about the room.

He blushed, a little in awe of her presence anc
forthright manner. But, for all that, he replied jus
as frankly, "Yes, ma'am, I am. Though I do no
rate my prospects very high."

"Then you deserve not to succeed," she said
coming to sit opposite him. The sunlight slanting i
at the window came to rest on her hair, turning it tc
flame. "Until now, you have behaved with unerring
good sense, and I trust you will continue to do so
But if you are to win Lucy, that may not be
enough—you may also have to be prepared to figh
for her."

"Believe me, ma'am, if she were older—and i.
I were absolutely certain that Lucy returned my
regard—then nothing would prevent me. I hac
hoped that time would take care of things, bu
her brother . . ."

"Wretched man," she said.

"Lucy is very fond of him, and I believe he ha:
her best interests at heart."

"Well, of course he does—or thinks he does—
which makes everything more difficult. However, I
have overcome worse obstacles, so I beg you not tc

espair. Would you care to attend my ball on
riday?"

The suddenness of the question took him by sur-
rise. "You are very kind, ma'am, but I don't
iink—that is . . ."

"Nonsense. The Savilles are coming," Caroline
aid, as though that were reason enough. "I should
aturally expect them to bring their guest. I will
end Lady Saville a note to that effect. And, Mr.
medley, do you think you could refrain from call-
ig me ma'am?"

The warmth of her smile robbed the words of
ny offense, and he found himself smiling back in
rather dazed way and saying, "Certainly, m—that
, Miss Maitland. And, if you are really sure, I
hould be happy to come to your ball, though I fear
am no dancer."

"Oh, that doesn't matter. I'm sure the country
ance will not be beyond you." Her eyes twinkled.
Everyone will be there, and it will increase your
tanding considerably."

In the park, the talk was all of the Maitlands'
orthcoming ball. There were to be guests from
'aris and Vienna. And other embassies would be
epresented, too, so one heard . . . and almost cer-
ainly the Prince Regent would be there—he and
ir Humphfrey were intimates.

Caroline was aware of the conjecture, but only
miled and would not comment when she was
uizzed. But one Parisian she had not expected ar-
ived a few days beforehand. The first she knew of
is arrival was the sight of him riding beside Lady
ersey's carriage.

"Only see whom I have brought to you, my dear
Caroline," Sally Jersey gushed, with one of her
lightly malicious smiles. "The comte heard that

you were to give a ball, and vowed that nothin⟨
would keep him away."

Comte Etienne de Bressac's flamboyant figur⟨
was already dismounting, handing his reins to ⟨
waiting groom and striding towards her, his curlin⟨
dark hair springing into life as he swept off his ha⟨
his brilliant blue eyes, caressing her as he swept he⟨
a bow. Caroline, very much aware of Lord Gren⟨
ville but a few yards away, arranged her feature⟨
into a smile of welcome.

"Monsieur le comte, how . . . pleasant, an⟨
unexpected."

"*Caroleen—*" his voice was a caress. "It is a⟨
Lady Jersey says. My life has been desolate sinc⟨
you left Paris, and then I hear that the Duc d⟨
Berri is to attend your ball, and at once offer m⟨
services as one of his aides."

"Well, I am flattered," she said, and looking up⟨
met Grenville's sardonic glance. "I look forward t⟨
seeing you tomorrow evening."

The last day of May dawned sunny, promising ⟨
hot day to come and yet another long warm eve⟨
ning, which augured well for the ball's success. Al⟨
day long, Grosvenor Square was alive with activit⟨
as tradesmen's carts came and went, and unde⟨
Gort's watchful eye potted palms and ferns were
carried in by perspiring footmen in baize aprons
dodging between the workmen who were laborin⟨
to erect an awning stretching from the house acros⟨
the pavement to the road.

Caroline was never far from the scene, thoug⟨
she had every confidence in Gort to see all wa⟨
done as she wished. And halfway through th⟨
morning, Lucy had walked round with Miss Finch
to watch the preparations.

Lucy had been much in demand since her come⟨
out, which, if nothing else, had mitigated her disap⟨

pointment over Gideon's views about Jack. Their paths had crossed occasionally when attending the same function, but under Gideon's watchful eye, Jack had been stiff and awkward and there had been no opportunity to exchange more than a few oddly formal words.

But with so many young gentlemen sighing after her, even this had affected Lucy rather less than Caroline had feared—a circumstance that Grenville was not slow to comment upon.

"If you are hoping to score points against me, sir, you are quite out," she had said, as they watched his sister dancing the cotillion with a besotted young man at Almack's one evening. "I assure you that it delights me to see Lucy making so many friends. It is, above all things, what she needs to help her put her relationship with Jack Smedley in proportion."

He eyed her quizzically. "But you still believe Lucy favors him above others?"

"I reserve judgment," she said. "For the moment, she seems happy, and that is all I wish for."

"You will no doubt be flattered to know that Lucy's talk at home is all of your ball, which, in her opinion, is destined to outshine every other event of the Season."

Caroline laughed. "That is because she has had a hand in preparing for it. She is so excited, that I only hope she may not be disappointed."

"Oh, I hardly think that is likely," he drawled. "With the Petit Ballet de Paris entertaining us with their pas de deux, and the Grenadier Guards playing during supper—to say nothing of how many policemen it will take to keep the Square from becoming congested . . ."

"Oh, good God, you poor man!" she exclaimed without thinking, and found herself blushing under his quizzical gaze, and laughing to cover her embarassment. "It is too bad of Lucy to subject you to so much idle tattle."

"On the contrary, I found it all most illuminating. She tells me also that your father has persuaded Prinny to put in an appearance. An accolade, indeed," he murmured ironically. "Though what Lucy will make of such a pudding on legs, I can't imagine. It might blight her belief in handsome princes forever."

"For shame, my lord. That is no way to speak of your future king!" But her laughter bubbled up irrepressibly for all that.

She was less amused a little later in the evening, to see Lady Verena's brother, Lord Edward Panton, paying extravagant attention to Lucy. Lord Edward was younger than his sister, but he was still too old for Lucy, both in years and in terms of experience. Ned had once called him 'a bit of a loose fish,' and she guessed the description was not far out. There was no denying, however, that as the second son of the Duke of Byeford, he was a considerable catch. She could only hope that Grenville would not allow his relationship with Lady Verena to affect his judgment.

At two minutes to ten on the evening of the ball, the first carriage rolled into the Square, and from that moment the success of the event was assured. Soon the entrance hall and the fine curving staircase were alive with color and movement, and a hum of excitement and expectancy filled the air.

"You're looking very fine this evening, m'dear," her father had murmured as they stood at the entrance to the ballroom waiting to greet their guests.

"Thank you, Pa." They smiled like conspirators. "We are a handsome pair, I think."

She had dressed with great care, choosing a deceptively simple gown of oyster pink *mousseline-de-soie*, which had a deep neckline and brief sleeves, all edged with tiny crystal beads. The hem of the skirt was adorned with a deep band of the same crystal, which made it sway gently as she moved. Her only jewelry was circlet of fine gold filigree studded with diamonds, which was threaded through her hair, and sparkled each time she turned her head.

And much later, gazing down from one of the balconies of the foyer which overlooked the crowded ballroom, her heart swelled with justifiable pride. All her efforts had come to fruition.

"Very impressive, Miss Maitland," murmured Lord Grenville, putting up his glass to survey the glittering assembly. He could not remember when he had last seen so many priceless jewels in one place, or so many orders adorning the breasts of the gentlemen. "Lucy did not exaggerate, it seems. Few young ladies can hope to have a French royal duke to lead her into the first quadrille, or be privileged to count amongst her guests, the cream of the Govenment Set, as well as almost everyone who is anyone in the Polite World; that these include all six Patronesses of Almack's, is something of an accolade in itself."

"Yes," Caroline said with engaging candor, "but that is Pa's doing, not mine. All I have to do is invite them and keep them entertained. Pa's circle of friends and acquaintances is legion, you know. As for de Berri, he is an accomplished flirt and a great intriguer, but, as the French king's brother, it is a matter of diplomacy to keep on good terms with him."

"Which you do most charmingly."

She wasn't sure whether he was being sardonic or serious. But, already his glance had moved on, and come to rest. "You include Jack Smedley, I see."

"Yes, of course. He came with the Savilles. Lucy ells me she is promised to him for one of the country dances." She inclined her head to look up at him, her eyebrows quirked, her eyes very green. "You will not mind?"

"If you are hoping I might provoke a scene by forbidding her to dance with him, I fear you are in for a disappointment."

Caroline uttered the husky chuckle he was beginning to know so well. "It never entered my mind. What an opinion you must have of me."

"You can have no idea what I think of you," he returned with suave ambiguity, "or what price I shall exact if I am to practice forbearance."

There was a heady excitement in this verbal fencing that made her heartbeat quicken. "You terrify me! Do put me out of my misery."

His own eyes were liquid bright. "I mean to claim the waltz that is about to begin."

"Oh, what a pity. I am already promised to the comte de Bressac."

"That popinjay! Don't tell me you take him seriously?"

"Not as seriously as he would like me to," she said with a laugh. "He proposes at regular intervals, though I often wonder how he would react if I accepted him. He is very rich, of course," she added provocatively.

"Money isn't everything. So *Caroleen*," he drawled her name softly, taking her arm and leading her towards the ballroom floor, "I will spare you the embarrassment of refusing him yet again."

"This is infamous!" she exclaimed, allowing herself to be swept along. "I only hope Etienne may not call you out. He is renowned for his swordplay, and is, I am told, an excellent shot."

"I tremble at the thought." His voice stopped just short of a sneer as the handsome Frenchman approached.

"I am sorry, Etienne," she confessed, half-laugh

ng, as he began to expostulate, "I had quite forgotten his lordship's prior claim. I will keep the next waltz, I promise you."

"Craven," murmured her captor, sweeping her away.

"Not at all. It is called diplomacy."

The music had a lilting, pulsating rhythm, and it was this rather than Grenville's high-handedness, and his closeness, Caroline told herself, that made her blood leap. She was subconsciously aware of the long windows flung open to the warm night air, letting in all the subtle fragrances of summer; of her father waltzing past with Sally Jersey, and Lady Jersey laughing and saying in amused reproof, "Oh, really, Humphrey!"; and of Lucy in the arms of Lord Arthur Panton, being held rather too close as his lordship bent to whisper in her ear. This last vaguely worried Caroline, but everything was as in a dream, the only reality being the closeness of Lord Grenville, his hand burning into her back as he swung her round, his thigh momentarily taut against hers, his breath warm and seductive against her cheek. Above their heads the chandeliers shimmered with myriad lights, dizzily spinning. Caroline had never experienced anything like it before, and she wanted the dance to go on forever.

But nothing lasts forever. The music ended, and she came slowly back to reality to find Grenville looking down at her, a faint half smile in his eyes. She drew away at once, embarrassed and annoyed with herself for allowing the music to affect her so.

"Thank you," he drawled with soft mockery. "That was most enjoyable—and illuminating."

"Yes, I enjoyed it, too," she said brightly, deliberately ignoring the rest. "Thank you, my lord. Now, if you will excuse me, I must find Pa. He will be expecting Prinny very soon."

The marquess bowed. "I wouldn't dream of

keeping you from your duties." He offered his arm
"Pray, allow me to escort you."

To refuse would have been childish, and migh
well have given him quite the wrong impression
Fortunately, her father proved easy to find, an
with the usual pleasantries, Grenville left them.

After supper, when the ballet had been per
formed and the prince had been and gone, the or
chestra struck up again for a country dance. It wa
as this drew to a close that Caroline became awar
of a disturbance at the far end of the room, and o
one or two heads turning towards one of the sma
ante rooms, whence came the sound of raise
voices.

She hurried towards it, passing Lady Verena
who lingered close by, and was in time to hear Luc
declare in throbbing accents, "You have absolutel
no right to tell me how to behave, Jack Smedley!'

"Maybe not, but I care enough to not wish t
see you making yourself cheap—"

"Cheap!" Lucy's voice rose, to the amused en
joyment of those nearby.

"Lucy! Jack! Be silent at once," Caroline ex
claimed, hurrying in. "How could you be so foolis
as to come apart like this? You could hardly hav
excited more interest if you had fallen to quarrellin
in the center of the ballroom."

"I'm sorry," Jack said stiffly. "The fault must b
mine."

"Well, I'm glad you have the grace to admit it!'
Lucy cried.

"Be silent, Lucy!" Caroline could have cried wit
vexation, but she kept her voice calm and quiet. "
will not have my father's guests disturbed by you
childish tantrums. No—" as Lucy opened he
mouth to protest, "I don't wish to know why yo
were haranguing one another. Tomorrow will b
quite soon enough. If you can't control your emo

tions, my dear, I strongly advise you to go up to my room and rest until you can."

Lucy stared at her, and then at Jack, her big dark eyes liquid with unshed tears. Then she rushed from the room.

"I'm sorry, Caroline," Jack said again. "I should have known better. It was seeing her with that creature, Panton . . ."

"Not now, I beg of you," she said shortly. And then, with a wry smile, "I doubt you were heard by any but a very few people, and they will soon find more tempting scandals to take their interest."

As soon as she could do so without arousing comment, Caroline slipped away from the ballroom to go and see if Lucy was all right. She was crossing the hall when Grenville's voice halted her.

"A moment, if you please, Miss Maitland."

From his clipped tones, she knew that he had heard. Oh, what a coil! She turned slowly.

"My sister. Where is she?"

Caroline drew a deep breath, and looked into his eyes. They were as hard and cold as steel. "I was just going to her. She was feeling a little unwell . . ."

"Don't gammon me, Miss Maitland. I know what happened."

"Then you should also know that the least fuss made about it, the better, sir."

"So that your ball is not ruined?" he sneered.

"So that Lucy's reputation may not be damaged in any way," she said pointedly.

He came very close and said softly, "If there *is* talk, I shall know where to lay the blame, ma'am. You have done nothing but meddle in my sister's life from the moment you met her—encouraging that fellow, Smedley. But you will do so no more."

"That is unjust. And in my opinion, it isn't Jack you should be worrying about. If you had been watching Lucy this evening as you should, you would have seen Lord Edward Panton behaving towards her with more familiarity than I would wish to see if she were my sister."

"But Lucy is not your sister. And I will thank you to remember that in future. It may interest you to know that Panton has already asked if he might pay his addresses to Lucy—" he saw her look of disbelief. "Naturally, I told him that she was too young as yet."

"So I should hope! But you wouldn't really contemplate him as a husband for Lucy?" she asked.

"She could do worse. Though, after this night's work, he may well think again."

"I hope you may be right. As for what happened, if you have a grain of sense, my lord, you will feign ignorance of the whole episode, which was trifling, and be especially kind to Lucy. I daresay, she is already suffering agonies of guilt and embarrassment." Caroline's voice softened. "It can be very painful, being seventeen—can you not remember how it was—how the smallest mistakes would assume the most alarming proportions?"

He did not answer, but looked a little less forbidding.

"I am going now to coax Lucy down. If you would but take a turn round the ballroom with her, it would do wonders for her confidence."

Lucy was sitting on Caroline's dressing stool, gazing miserably at her woebegone reflection.

"Dear me, what a sorry sight! I hope you don't mean to stay up here indefinitely, with so many gentlemen still waiting to dance with you."

"I can't face anyone!" Lucy cried tragically.

"Then you are more foolish than I supposed, and I shall waste no more time on you," Caroline said briskly. "Your brother will be disappointed, for he is even now waiting to claim you for the next cotil-

lion." She saw Lucy's lips quiver, and added more
gently, and with mentally crossed fingers, "He will
not reproach you, I promise."

The ball made food for conversation in the days
that followed. Congratulations were heaped upon
Sir Humphfrey and his daughter, and their drawing
room was beseiged by callers wishing to offer their
thanks and congratulations. To Caroline's relief,
the Duc de Berri did not linger in London, and
Etienne de Bressac was obliged to accompany him
back to Paris.

"But I mean to return very soon, *ma chère*," he
promised.

Caroline had a brief visit from Jack Smedley,
who expressed his regret over what had occurred,
and expressed his intention of returning to Melthorpe Magna almost immediately.

"I wish you will not," she said. "Such drastic
measures are not necessary, I assure you."

"Nevertheless," he said quietly, "I am out of
place here. It is now clear to me that Lucy's path
and mine, are not destined to coincide. I have written to tell her so."

Caroline could not help feeling that his leaving
was a mistake, but it was not her place to dissuade
him. And Lucy, when she brought up the subject,
vowed that she cared not one jot. However, in the
days that followed, there seemed to be a new reck-
lessness in Lucy's behavior. She spent less time with
Caroline and more with Lady Verena and her ladyship's young cousin, Alice, with whom she had
shared her come-out. And, less to be desired, with
Lord Edward and his friends.

Caroline herself was much preoccupied with the
play, the performance of which was drawing ever
closer. Sophie had arranged for them all to go to

Chiswich, so that they might see exactly how and where the play was to be enacted.

"Grandmama has invited us for afternoon tea," Sophie said.

"Are we not rather large in numbers for her?"

"Lord, Caro, you know Grandmama. There is nothing she likes more than chivvying her servants into performing miracles."

"I only hope she does not expect the same from us," Lord Grenville murmured. He had been cool towards Caroline since the night of the ball, but she was determined not to let him see that she minded. He drove himself and Ned down, while Caroline travelled with Sophie and Peregrine in an open laundau, and the others made their own way.

Caroline had forgotten how beautiful both house and garden were. The house was Palladian in style, with a wide terrace at the rear, and gardens and lawns falling away in a gentle slope towards the river. And here were gracefully drooping willows and huge horse chestnuts with their spreading parasol leaves. It was a perfect setting for such a play.

Sophie's maternal grandmother, Mrs. Witherinton, was a formidable old lady: large, and with a booming voice, she ruled her family, friends, and servants alike with the authority of a benevolent despot. On the afternoon of their first visit, she questioned Peregrine ruthlessly as to where he intended to set each scene, and how he wished it to be lit.

"I thought we would have the Palace of Theseus here on the left, Grandmama, which leaves the whole of the center and lefthand side to be split into several sections for the woodland scenes, where most of the story takes place. Lanterns can then be lit and extinguished as each scene unfolds."

"My servants will take care of all that, if you've someone to tell 'em what to do," she said. "I want no expense spared, mind—costume, scenery—all is to be of the finest. I've anything up to two hundred people coming. Giles, m'butler is arranging seating for the terrace, and no doubt some will watch from the windows."

"The costumes will need to be good," the marquess muttered, sotto voce. "I doubt they will hear a word we say."

"Don't spoil sport, Gideon," said Ned.

As Midsummer Day approached, all of Caroline's misgivings about Lucy were intensified. Lord Edward had now become her regular escort and although, to all outward appearances she seemed to enjoy his company, Caroline occasionally thought she detected a kind of desperation in her eyes. But Lady Verena blocked all her attempts to be alone with the young girl in public, and Lucy no longer came to Grosvenor Square with Miss Finch, though whether this was at Grenville's insistence or otherwise, she could not tell.

She missed Lucy's youthful chatter more than she would have expected. But she also worried.

"Pa," she asked at breakfast one morning, after attending a soiree at which both Lucy and Lord Edward had been present, "what do you know of the Duke of Byeford's family?"

Sir Humphrey threw her a quizzical glance over his tankard of porter. "Still worrying about that young protégée of yours, are you?"

She shrugged. "Not worrying, exactly. It isn't my place to worry . . ."

"That's never stopped you in the past," he said shrewdly. "No use telling you not to meddle, I suppose?" And meeting her stubborn stare, "Thought not. Well, as for Bleford—rumor is, he's head over ears in debt and mortgaged to the hilt. It's in the blood, of course. The Panton's were ever gamblers."

"So, it would be to Lord Edward's advantage to marry Lucy."

"Depends on how greedy he is." Sir Humphfrey buttered his muffin. "The child don't come into her money until she's of age, of course, but if he were desperate, he could borrow heavily against his wife's inheritance, and hope to come about before the reckoning." He looked up, his eyebrows quivering. "And, aside from that, I'd expect Grenville to give young Lucy a handsome dowry when she marries."

"That's what I thought," Caroline said gloomily. "If only I could talk to her."

But in the end, it was Lucy who came to her.

It was very late, on a night less than a week before the play. Caroline had just returned from dining with friends, and her father was still out. She was already mounting the stair when the doorbell pealed with sudden urgency, and she paused, waiting to see who could possibly be in such a hurry at this time of night.

Gort followed the footman to the door, and as it was opened, a slight, disheveled figure irrupted into the hall. Caroline was down the stairs in a flash, and was just in time to catch her as she collapsed.

"Lucy! What in the world has happened to you?"

At first Lucy was incoherent. Gort sent the footman for the hartshorn and carried the young girl up the stairs and into the small saloon where he laid her down on a sofa.

"Will there be anything else, Miss Caroline?" he murmured.

"Not for now," she said. "But I shall almost certainly need to send a message to Lord Grenville later."

At this, Lucy grew agitated and Caroline waved Gort away. "Hush, now." She soothed the distraught girl. "I shall not do anything you do not wish. But you cannot want your brother to worry unnecessarily."

"He w-will t-try to make me g-go home," Lucy sobbed.

"No one shall make you go anywhere until you are ready to do so," Caroline assured her, as the major domo entered silently, bearing a cup and saucer on a small tray. "Now, see—Gort has brought you a hot drink."

"It is hot milk, with just a little brandy, and some sugar, Miss Caroline."

"Delicious. Thank you, Gort. Sit up a little, Lucy. You will feel much better when you have drunk this down."

As Lucy sipped the milk, the whole story came pouring out—how she had been at a soiree not far away, in Grosvenor Street, with Lady Verena and her brother and all the usual crowd.

"I think Lord Edward had d-drunk rather more than usual," she explained. "All the w-windows were open, and he persuaded me to go outside . . ."

"Oh, Lucy!"

"I kn-know! But it was so very h-hot . . . and we were only a f-few yards from the house . . ."

"Yes, of course. I didn't mean to sound reproving. Do go on," Caroline coaxed her, although she had already guessed the gist of it.

"At first he just w-wanted a k-kiss, but when I tried to pull away, he w-wouldn't let go, and w-when I said I'd scream, he c-called me names, and smo-smothered my mouth and b-began to tear at m-my gown . . ."

"Hush, now." Caroline took the cup from her shaking hands and gathered her close. "You don't need to say any more. Listen, you shall sleep with me tonight, and in the morning, everything will seem much better."

"And Gi-Gideon?"

"You leave Gideon to me."

He came at once, as she had expected—and as Gort showed him into the little saloon, she saw at a glance that he was furious.

"What nonsense is this?" he said, flinging down her note.

"It is not nonsense, my lord, and be so kind as to lower your voice. Lucy is sleeping not all that far away, and I don't want her disturbed. If you will be so good as to sit down, I will explain."

Caroline walked unhurriedly to a fine rosewood sideboard and poured him a glass of brandy. While he sipped it, she gave him a brief, but graphic account of what Lucy had told her. After a certain irritation, he listened intently.

When she fell silent, he said, "And you have no reason to think Lucy could have mistaken Lord Edward's behavior?"

"None whatever, my lord. Her dress was torn, and she was distraught."

"But, what was Lady Verena about, to let such a thing happen?" The words were out before he could stop them. And then he met her eyes. "I daresay you are enjoying this, Miss Maitland. You did warn me, did you not?"

Caroline was indignant. "I did, but it gives me no pleasure to be proved right—to see that poor child's distress!"

He flushed, and had the grace to look ashamed. "Of course not. I'm sorry." He stood up. "You need have no fear. I shall deal with young Lord Edward. And, thank you. You must not underestimate my gratitude. It is well that Lucy had a true friend to turn to. I shall return in the morning with the carriage to take my sister home."

But Lucy refused to leave Grosvenor Square. She

refused even to see her brother, for fear that he would coerce her into going.

"Leave her," Caroline advised, seeing his chagrin, and for once, pitying him. "It is the shock. But I have had the doctor to her and he says that she will soon come round. For now, you have brought the good Miss Finch, who will know exactly how to deal with her."

The word ran round like wildfire. All kinds of rumors abounded.

"My dear!" Sophie was an early caller. "Is it really true?" And when Caroline confirmed it, "How simply frightful for the poor child! I heard that Grenville had given Lord Edward a thorough thrashing—and I'm bound to say he deserves it."

Whatever the truth, Lady Verena and her young brother beat a hasty retreat to the country. But still Lucy would not return home.

"This is very foolish," Caroline said gently. "There is nothing worse than sitting, moping—and the longer you indulge yourself, the harder it becomes to break free. And besides, your brother is beginning to wonder if I am not turning you against him."

"Oh, but that is not true!" Lucy cried. "No one could have been more encouraging."

"My dear, it is no use telling me that."

"I know." Lucy looked ill at ease. "The thing is, Caroline, I believe I should like to go home for a while. Home to Melthorpe Magna, I mean."

"Then tell your brother so. I'm sure he would understand under the circumstances."

"But, wouldn't it look like running away?"

"Not if you are honest with him." Caroline paused for a moment, then said, "It is the play tomorrow, and the masquerade. You were so looking forward to it."

"Oh, I'm not sure . . ."

"You would be wearing a mask, and no one need know you if you don't want them to." Caroline saw that Lucy was weakening, and pressed her case. "It will be a very beautiful evening—and fun! Sophie's grandmama, Mrs Witherinton, is a splendid old lady. She would see you were well looked after—and Ned will be there, and my father." She played her trump card. "In fact, Pa would be delighted to escort his favorite pretty girl, and you would surely feel safe in his company."

Lucy was very fond of Sir Humphfrey. He made her laugh. "I suppose it would be a pity to miss the play," she said.

Caroline, well content, went straightaway to write a letter, and sent it by one of the grooms to Melthorpe Magna. It sketched in the gist of what had happened, and concluded: I'm sure you know how best to help Lucy, and if you do not seize this opportunity, then you do not deserve her.

Midsummer's Eve.

It was a perfect night, the sky emblazoned with stars, and a three-quarter moon hanging low in their midst. In the background, the river burbled gently, and the garden had taken on a magic all its own, of which the scenery for the play seemed to become a part. A great number of lamps hung in the trees, ready to light up each scene.

By half-past nine, the guests had all arrived to add their own color to the proceedings, with their colorful masks and their fancy costumes, and an air of great excitement prevailed. The players were nervous, but once they had donned their costumes, the magic took them over, too, so that, with the opening scene representing the court in Athens, where Theseus and Hippolyta were to be wed, make-believe at once became reality.

Caroline, looking wonderfully Grecian as Hipployta, half-dreaded having to face Grenville as a loving Theseus. With Lucy's refusal to return home, the atmosphere between them had deteriorated to a kind of stiff formality. But somehow, they played their parts with conviction.

There were sighs from the audience when the scene changed to the enchanted wood, where the young lovers strayed into fairyland and were bewitched. Some gasped aloud as the lamps were lit to reveal Caroline in her bower, a breathtaking Queen of the Fairies, in a floating robe of shimmering sea-green gauze, confronted by the towering cloaked majesty of Oberon, her king.

With his very first—"Ill met by moonlight, proud Titania," Grenville's authority set the mood. As they battled for possession of Titania's little page, the tension between them was palpable, but only they were aware that it had little to do with the play.

The audience laughed uproariously when Titania fell in love with Bottom wearing an ass's head, and even more so over the antics of the rustics as they played out the tragedy of Pyramus and Thisbe at the wedding feast.

Caroline wasn't sure when Grenville's mood changed, but when finally, as Oberon, he reached out for her and said, "Come, my queen, take hands with me," she sensed a softening in his manner that had nothing to do with the play, and her heart quickened.

The audience cheered when all was happily resolved, the players took bow after bow, and in the excitement that followed, Caroline slipped away down towards the river to marshal her confused thoughts.

Jack Smedley used those same moments of excitement to thread his way through the crowds towards the slight figure standing a little apart from

Sir Humphfrey, in a simple gown of white muslin sprinkled with silver stars. The mask could not disguise one he knew so well.

"Lucy," he said softly.

She turned at once, sadness turning to joy as she tore off her mask and flung herself into his arms, crying, "Jack! Oh, Jack, how did you know that I was needing you so?"

It was peaceful down by the river, with only the distant sounds of revelry to disturb the stillness. But Caroline's blood still raced and her thoughts would not be still. Had she imagined Grenville's change of mood? How could she for so long have mistaken her feelings? Her hands crept up to cool the flush that mounted into her cheeks.

He arrived so quietly that she heard no sound, his hands seeming to come from nowhere to cover hers, his strong thumbs stroking the pulse that pounded so madly in her wrists.

Her breath caught on a gasp as he quoted softly against her hair, "Come, my queen, take hands with me — Now thou and I are new in amity."

"Are we—or are we simply bewitched by the mood of the play?" she asked breathlessly, that same pulse now beating in her throat.

"No play can act this powerfully upon the senses . . ." His hands came down to clasp her lightly just beneath her bosom, where her heart was thudding unevenly. He turned her, unresisting, to face him. "You feel it, too. Don't trouble to deny it, for your whole body betrays you, my wonderful, tantalizing Caroline!"

His mouth was warm, gently exploring, and then, as she responded in kind, grew fiercely passionate. "I have wanted to do that for *so* long," he said unsteadily, lifting his head at last.

"Have you really?" Caroline stared up into his

face, etched by the moonlight into strong clean lines. A laugh of pure joy bubbled up. "Oh Gideon, what fools we've been!"

Much later, she drew away a little. "Oh dear, I have just remembered. Gideon—about Lucy. I have something to confess . . ."

"Later," he said.

"But . . ."

"Be still, woman!" Grenville gathered her close, murmuring forcefully, "I have waited a long time to make love to you, and nothing, not even my sister's affairs, will stop me now."

"As you will, my lord," she agreed, surrendering with a sigh.